Can This Be Love?

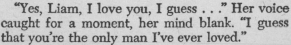

"Yes, Liam, I love you, I guess . . ." Her voice caught for a moment, her mind blank. "I guess that you're the only man I've ever loved."

"Ah, my darling! That you return my love is grand news, but to know that I am the one and only! Do you know how that makes a man feel?"

She had no answer, and he waited for none. His mouth descended on hers. His lips were gentle, incredibly tender, and oh so warm!

She murmured and looped her arms around his neck, her own lips parting. His tongue entered her mouth, not as an invasion, but as an expression of love, of need. Without taking his lips from hers, he untied the sash of the robe and folded it back, and she felt herself opening to him.

He raised his head and his gaze moved slowly down the length of her body. She moaned, and arched slightly, as though he had touched her. It was an incredibly erotic sensation, and she shuddered, biting her lip to keep from crying out.

MIDNIGHT WHISPERS

———◆◆———

Patricia Matthews
and
Clayton Matthews

BANTAM BOOKS
Toronto / New York / London / Sydney

MIDNIGHT WHISPERS
A Bantam Book / October 1981

ISBN 0-553-13389-6

Published simultaneously in the United States and Canada

Bantam Books are published by Bantam Books, Inc. Its trade-mark, consisting of the words "Bantam Books" and the por-trayal of a bantam, is Registered in U.S. Patent and Trademark Office and in other countries. Marca Registrada. Bantam Books, Inc., 666 Fifth Avenue, New York, New York 10103.

PRINTED IN THE UNITED STATES OF AMERICA

9 8 7 6 5 4 3 2

Prologue

The girl came out of the light and warmth of the house into a world of fog.

When the closing door cut away the yellow rectangle of interior light, she was left in a milky darkness that swirled about her with chilling damp. She shivered inside the heavy peacoat.

After waiting a moment to accustom her eyes to the darkness, she began to walk, striding parallel to the front of the house. Off to her right, she could hear the haunting hoot of a safety buoy and the pounding of surf on the rocks below the cliff edge. There was a moon, but the fog obscured it, parting only now and then to let a pale wash of light appear, giving the landscape a ghostly quality that was enhanced by the sound of the surf and the hooting buoy.

The girl walked slowly for a time, head down, apparently deep in thought, and then, as an unfamiliar sound intruded, she halted, turning to face the spot where she knew the cliff's edge to be.

As she did so, the fog parted, and a faint light illuminated the cliff. The girl drew in her breath sharply as two figures appeared limned against the lightened sky, weaving dangerously back and forth on the cliff's edge.

She raised her hand. Her voice, like the cry of a wounded animal, preceded her as she began to run toward the figures. She ran clumsily, like a person mired in dream sand . . .

To "Uncle" Elliott Lefkowitz
with appreciation and affection.

One

———◆———

"Anna?"

"Yes?"

"Where are you?"

"Shannon Airport."

"Are you calling from a public telephone?"

"Yes."

"Very good. You may relax now. How are you, Anna?"

"A little tired, and cold. But I'm fine."

"Good. Now listen carefully, Anna. This is Mr. Midnight. Repeat the name after me."

"Yes . . . Mr. Midnight."

"Listen closely. You are no longer to call yourself Anna Winston. You will forget that name. You are now Angela Williams. You are a professional photographer. You are in Ireland to do a picture story for a travel magazine. Do you understand?"

"Yes, I understand."

"Now, did you get the wig and new makeup, as I instructed you?"

"Yes. It's in my bag."

"Fine. Now, when you leave the phone booth, you will go to the ladies room in the terminal, and you will put on the wig, and you will adjust your makeup accordingly. Do you understand?"

"I understand."

"Then you will take a taxi to the Clare Inn near Dromoland Castle, where a room has been reserved for you. Your luggage is already there. You will trust me. You *do* trust me, don't you?"

"Yes. I trust you."

1

"Good. Because your safety rests with me. You are in grave danger. You will trust me, and I am the only one you *will* trust. You will call me every seven days, using the number you just called. It is in your mind, and you will not forget it. You will call me at midnight, or as close to it as you can manage, no matter where you are on the seventh day. Do you understand?"

"I understand."

"And when you hear the words Mr. Midnight, you will enter into a hypnotic state. Each time you hear the words, you will go deeper into the hypnotic state. Do you understand?"

"Yes. I understand."

"Now, when you leave the phone booth, all memory of this conversation will be erased. You will *be* Angela Williams. Now, be cautious, Angela Williams, and prudent. Call me every seven days. Do you understand?"

"I understand."

"Goodbye and good luck, Angela Williams."

She emerged from the telephone booth as from a womb, born again. Despite the long flight, she did not feel fatigued; on the contrary, she felt quite energetic and filled with a pleasant purpose.

Picking up the small flight bag she had brought with her on the plane, she looked around the nearly empty building until she spotted the sign for the ladies room, then headed briskly toward it.

Once inside, she looked around curiously. The vacant room was strangely different than the public restrooms she remembered. She walked over to the row of large wash basins and placed the bag upon the black sinkboard. Without looking at her image in the long mirror above, she opened the bag and pulled out an auburn wig, styled with short, soft-looking curls.

It was only after she had pulled the wig over her

own hair—tucking in errant strands—that she looked at herself.

For just an instant, her eyes widened, and she had the uneasy feeling that the person looking back at her from the mirror was not anyone she knew. But in a moment the feeling passed, and she went about the task of removing her eye shadow, blusher, and lipstick, leaving a face she did not in any way find remarkable, although an observer might have remarked that even without the help of makeup, she was a beautiful young woman.

Quickly she applied new makeup in shades that complemented the new hair coloring.

Finished, she smiled at herself, testing the effect. As she did so, Angela Williams forgot that she had not arrived wearing this wig and this face.

Throwing away the old cosmetics, she took off her jacket and washed her hands. Then she picked up the jacket and turned it inside out, to reverse the reversible lining—a subdued, heather-brown color.

Removing the tie from her white blouse, she opened the collar and put on the jacket. As she gazed into the mirror to adjust the now open collar, Angela forgot that she had been wearing the jacket any other way.

After a last, lingering look into the mirror, she picked up her purse. Finding her flight bag too large to fit into the opening of the waste bin, she jammed it into a corner and turned toward the door.

Angela Williams had never been in Ireland, and she was looking forward to experiencing it and photographing it for the first time.

Two

Deke Travers rose from the defense table and strolled toward the jury box. The closer he came to the box, the more reluctant he appeared. To a perceptive observer, he would have seemed to have been in the depths of depression.

This insight would not have been far from the truth. Deke was one of the most sought-after defense attorneys in New York, and his many clients, and members of the media, would have scoffed if told that he was painfully shy and had to psych himself up for such a simple court procedure as an address to a jury.

Deke half-turned, looking back at the defense table and his client. To say that Angelo Petri was no better than he should be was an understatement. A rumored button man for the mob, a record lengthier than Deke's arm—pandering, pushing, grand larceny, suspected murder. A sordid history, but one that had no bearing on the charge for which he was being tried in this instance—the murder of a cigar store owner who wouldn't knuckle under for a protection racket. "I swear to God, counselor, I didn't waste the guy! Sure, I laid all kinds of threats on him. But I didn't waste him! Hell, why'd I do that? Dead, he ain't worth a nickel to us!"

Deke was convinced of the man's innocence of this charge. The means by which he reached this conclusion was not admissible evidence, but it satisfied him. He had a strict personal code. He never accepted a client whom he did not believe innocent. He would be willing to concede that he might have been in error on occasion, yet he was positive that the percentage was small. . . .

"Mr. Travers? We are waiting. The court's patience is not endless."

Deke came to with a start. "My apologies to the court, Your Honor." He moved to the jury box, slim hands resting on the railing. He stood straight now, head back, shoulders squared—a man apparently at ease with himself, in control and confident.

There were seven women on the jury panel. Since it is the way of life that most jurors are retired people, four were in their sixties and wanted to mother him. The other three would not have been adverse to taking him into their beds.

Deke was tall, an inch over six feet, too thin, with an underfed look; actually he ate like a horse and was blessed with a metabolism to match. His hair was brown, a touch long, the ends curling. His blue eyes could be as innocent and beguiling as a babe's or could turn arctic cold in an instant. He had a sweet, slow smile that, at its widest stretch, revealed a dimple in his left cheek.

Deke was aware of his looks—but at an unconscious level—and would stoutly maintain that it had nothing to do with his courtroom success.

"Ladies and gentlemen of the jury," he began, his voice low but carrying, "a closing address to the jury is historically for the purpose of summarizing the evidence against the person on trial or, in the case of the defense, the refuting of that evidence. In this instance I will devote very little time to refuting evidence. What is there to refute? All the evidence presented by the state is purely circumstantial in nature. It is true that convictions have been gotten on circumstantial evidence, and often rightly so. In this instance, no.

"I will address myself to the prosecutor's case shortly, but first I would like to touch on another matter, if you will be so kind as to bear with me. Unless a defendant testifies in his own behalf, the record of his past offenses against society is not admissible. The prosecution has tried in every way possible to parade the defendant's past record before you. His Honor, as is fitting, has stricken most of it from the record, admonished you, the jury, to strike it from your minds, and cautioned you that it should have no bearing on your deliberations. That, however, is not so easily done. It is common for all of us to equate a man with his past deeds; to think that if he has committed crimes in the past, perhaps even one of the nature with which he is charged, then he must be guilty in this instance."

Deke paused for a beat, his gaze moving slowly over the twelve faces. He took a deep breath and continued, "I would like to speak on this, with your indulgence. The accused, Angelo Petri, cannot by any means be considered an ideal citizen. In fact, it might not be an exaggeration to state that he has never earned an honest dollar in his life—"

From the defense table came an explosive grunt. It took you long enough, Angelo, Deke thought.

Deke continued. "His police record is extensive, and he has been suspected of a wide range of crime—"

The gavel banged. "The defendant will remain seated!"

Deke turned slowly. Petri was on his feet, halfway across the table, his face a fiery red.

He said in a strangled voice, "But this bird is selling me down the river, judge!"

"Resume your seat, sir! At once!"

Deflated, Angelo Petri sank back down.

"Mr. Travers, the court must admit to some concern. You have the reputation of being an excellent attorney, yet isn't this tack you appear to be embarked upon rather risky?"

Only if I lose, Your Honor, sir, Deke thought.

Aloud, he said, "My intent will soon become clear, Your Honor."

The man on the bench stared at him for a long moment before saying coldly, "Very well, Mr. Travers. But I feel that it is my duty to query the defendant.

"Mr. Petri, I must inquire if you are content with the competence of your counsel. It is your privilege to dismiss him, and seek new representation, if you so desire." The icy gaze swung back to Deke. "And if that becomes necessary, Mr. Travers, you will incur the court's displeasure, sir."

Deke stared back blandly. The man on the bench finally switched his gaze to Petri, and Deke sneaked a look at the young prosecutor. He was clearly dumbfounded by the turn of events.

And well he should be, Deke thought gleefully, since I've stolen his thunder.

"What is the defendant's desire? Do you wish to continue with defense counsel?"

In a choked voice Petri said, "I guess so, judge."

"Very well." The gavel rapped. "You may proceed, Mr. Travers. But with caution."

"Thank you, Your Honor." Deke once again confronted the jury. "To reiterate, my client has been guilty of past crimes. That we have no intention of denying, and you may be sure that the prosecuting attorney fully intends to expound on this subject. Since the defense is not privileged to address you again at length, if I did not speak of this now, it would appear that we are attempting to mislead you.

"But—" Deke slapped his hand down on the railing, and the jurors, each and every one, jumped.

The man on the bench said wearily, "Mr. Travers— must you?"

"My apologies to the court," Deke said, unrepentant. He did not look around, his eyes somehow seeming to hold the collective gaze of all twelve people. "His Honor will tell you, in his charge to you, that in a court of law, a defendant may not be held accountable for his past misdeeds. His record of criminality must not have any weight whatsoever on your deliberations.

"His Honor will also define for you circumstantial evidence. And that brings me up to the crux of the matter before you. The prosecution's case against the defendant is wholly circumstantial. I think that I can safely state that even the prosecution would admit the truth of this.

"With your forbearance, we will now speak to this. Historically police have used certain criteria when determining whether or not to charge an individual with a particular crime. These criteria consist of means, motive, and opportunity. On the surface it would appear that the defendant had sufficient motive. He is in the business of selling protection, a protection racket, in the criminal vernacular, and the victim refused to purchase this protection. Hence, reasons the prosecution, the motive for the victim's demise.

"But is it? Let us examine this more carefully . . ."

Deke's law office was situated on Park Avenue, a prestigious address, indeed, and an expensive one. The building received a new façade every twenty years or so, yet the interior was rarely given attention unless the tenant wished to pay for redecorating out of his own pocket. During his ten-year tenancy, Deke had deliberately not done so. He well understood that a Park Address, even *with* a shabby suite of offices, was a status symbol of its own. His attorney friends in Beverly Hills with their modern offices were utterly baffled by this reasoning, but then they weren't New Yorkers.

The front door to his suite of offices opened into a tiny reception area, which contained a sagging couch, an easy chair, and a coffee table laden with magazines—none less than a year old.

Next to this was his receptionist-secretary's cubicle,

walled in by bulletproof glass—the only decorating he had done. Although the outside door to the office was usually locked, there had been instances in the building of drug-crazed hoodlums barging into offices, brandishing weapons, demanding petty cash.

Aside from Maggie Callahan, Deke employed three law clerks, who mostly did research, and he had a junior partner to handle what corporate law he practiced.

Maggie had been with him since the beginning. She was nudging forty, skinny as a rake, with an angular, bony face and long, flowing auburn hair. She was as efficient as a computer, capable of an incredible amount of work without complaint, yet she was very human, with a pixyish sense of humor and a disrespectful tongue. Deke doubted that he could function without her.

She pushed aside the tiny window and looked out at him. "How did it go, Deke?"

He put his attaché case on the small ledge before her window and propped his chin on it. Grinning, he said, "The jury found for the defense, but I have a feeling that Angelo ain't too happy."

"That piece of dog do! Who cares?" She made a face. "But I'll play straight man. Why ain't our Angelo happy?"

"They arrested him before he could get out of the courtroom. For extortion this time."

Maggie applauded. "Score one for the forces of law and order."

"I have a hunch he'll go up on this one."

"Why? Because you're not defending him?"

"That, and because he's guilty as hell this time. Has he called?"

"Not yet."

"Probably waiting until he's sure I'm back in the office, so he won't waste his dime."

The phone buzzed, and Maggie picked up the receiver. Her eyebrows arched, and she mouthed the words, "It's our boy."

Deke shook his head.

"I'm sorry, Mr. Petri, but Mr. Travers has a full calendar for at least six months and cannot, under any circumstances, take on any new cases . . ."

When she had hung up, Deke said, "You're a wonder, Callahan. Whatever would I do without you?"

"Go bankrupt within a month would be my best guess."

He gathered up the attaché case. "Anything needing attention?"

"Nothing that can't wait. Only this." She slid a copy of the *Wall Street Journal* across to him. It was folded open to a page in the classified section.

"They printed it, did they?" His pulse accelerating, Deke tucked the paper under his arm without reading it. "Did they print it verbatim?"

"Word for word."

Nodding, he turned into his office. His furniture was ancient, and the room was incredibly cluttered. Deke was neat to the point of fastidiousness about his person, but any area in which he worked soon began to look like a pack rat's burrow. A table in one corner sagged under stacks of files, old magazines, and newspapers. Even one of the chairs lined up in front of his desk held a stack of law journals.

Clearing a small space on the desk top, Deke sat down with the *Wall Street Journal* and stared at it, unseeing. In his mind he was reading another paper, an edition of the New York *Post*.

He opened the top file drawer of his desk and after some fumbling, found a file folder tagged April Morgan. It was not too thick, but then it was only six months old.

The first item in the file was a front page from the *Post*: "Heiress Disappears! Kidnapped or Victim of Foul Play?"

April Morgan, 22, only daughter of John Morgan, international business magnate, was reported missing this morning from a sanitarium where she had been confined since her father's tragic death. Police report no leads, and there have been no ransom demands, according to famed criminal attorney, Deke Travers, trustee of the Morgan estate.

One month ago, the heiress' father, John Morgan, and his young wife of one month, were the victims of an accident . . .

Deke's reading eye ceased to register the words, and there was no need to flip through the other documents in the file—more newspaper articles, diminishing in coverage, all reporting no word of the missing heiress; police reports revealing no progress whatsoever; and the report of a prestigious, expensive private investigative firm, equally lacking in optimism.

Finally Deke turned to the *Wall Street Journal*. The ad was succinct, discreet, and purposely vague: "Wanted: an experienced, resourceful man. Purpose of employment: search for a missing person. Renumeration: negotiable but lucrative. Private detectives do not apply."

Included was a telephone number for the line Deke had had installed for just this purpose.

Deke was well aware that there were going to be a lot of crank calls, but he hoped that eventually a gem would emerge. He felt confident that Maggie was capable of weeding out most of the weirdos.

The intercom light blinked. "Yes, Callahan?"

"That special number has been going off like a string of firecrackers, Deke. Ninety-nine percent have been from kinks, but I just took two, one right on the heels of the other. Both sound promising. One Eric Ransom, one Carlos O'Brien."

"I apologize again for dumping this on you, Callahan, but there'll be a bonus in it. Did you tell them that resumés are required?"

"I did. And both said they'd send them right over by messenger. Both asked if the ad meant what it said—lucrative."

"And?"

"I told them that whatever else my employer might be, he was not a tightwad."

He said dryly, "It amazes me how eager you are to spend my money."

"*Your* money? It's Morgan money!"

Deke took a deep breath. "Yes, of course, Callahan. How could I forget?"

* * *

Sitting on the edge of the comfortable bed in her room at the Clare Inn, she opened the heavy manila envelope and dumped the contents out, spreading them one by one on the bed.

She knew, without knowing how she knew, that she had done this before. She did not pursue the thought but proceeded to the business of examining the items one at a time.

Born again!

Now why did that phrase occur to her? With a frown of annoyance, she bent to her task.

First, a passport. Angela Williams. Permanent address: New York, New York, U.S.A. The passport showed the entry stamps of several countries.

A clear but not particularly flattering two-by-two photograph looked up at her. Short auburn hair framed a heart-shaped face, with bright blue eyes shadowed by long, dark lashes; a full mouth, with a sensual curve, caught by the camera in a beginning smile.

She tossed the passport aside.

A temporary driver's permit for Ireland, with another picture.

A letter from *Vacationer's Magazine*, with an embossed letterhead, signed in a flowery script by the editor-in-chief, proclaiming to anyone interested that

Angela Williams was doing a series of photo articles on Ireland. Cooperation appreciated.

A Social Security card and number.

American Express, Diner's Club, Visa cards—all with her signature on the back. A small, elegant case for the lot, with AW in gold.

And lastly, a sheaf of Irish pound notes, neatly bundled by a rubber band, totaling five thousand American dollars.

She went through the items quickly again and found everything in order. Now she turned away from the bed. On a luggage rack against one wall was a leather bag, with wheels and a pulling strap. Beside the bag was a large camera case.

She opened the bag first and began unpacking the clothes, which for one frightening moment, seemed unfamiliar. Everything was obviously expensive and of good quality. By the time she had unpacked, putting everything away neatly, with the deft efficiency of the well traveled, the feeling of strangeness was gone.

Finally she turned her attention to the camera case, which contained two Nikons, rolls of film, and six lenses of various sizes. Her handling of the cameras and lenses was professional, and after a thorough inspection, she nodded to herself, satisfied.

A glance at the bedside clock told her that it was nearing midnight. At the thought of midnight, a small frown creased her face, and she stared blankly into space for a moment.

Then she shook her head sharply and yawned, stretching. It *had* been a long day, and fatigue was now catching up with her.

She undressed quickly, folding her clothes neatly, and went into the bathroom. She started a tub running, and while it filled, she placed a call to the desk, asking that a rental car be out front of the inn for her at eight in the morning.

Then, yawning again, she padded back into the

bathroom, turned off the faucet, tested the water with her toe, and eased down into it, her tense muscles anticipating the caress of the hot water.

And yet, when she was stretched out full-length in the tub, the lapping of the water against her flesh nudged a faint memory in her mind, and a frown flitted like a dark cloud across her features.

Three

———◆◆◆———

Deke thumbed the intercom. "Callahan?"

"Yes, Deke?"

"I've gone over the resumés of both Ransom and O'Brien and also made some phone calls. I had them checked out, and both seem not only authentic, but just about what I had in mind. I assume, by the way, that no other applicants have proved out?"

"All a bunch of flakes."

"No matter, not if this pair work out."

"You sound as if you're thinking of both of them."

"I do, don't I?" He hesitated. "But you know something? It might not be such a bad idea at that. Both seem highly competitive, and a little competitiveness might get better results. In fact, I think I'll see them both together. Can you arrange it?"

"It should be no problem."

"Then take care of setting up the meeting, okay?"

"Will do."

"And, Callahan, buzz Gabe Kemble, will you? I think he should be in on this."

Absently Deke rolled a pencil back and forth across his desk, going over the resumés in his mind, filling in the blanks. Both men had had what could charitably be called checkered careers, but Eric Ransom had led a life that could be a screenplay for a forties Clark Gable movie. At thirty-nine, Ransom had apparently seen it all, done it all. His resumé stated that he had joined the Marines at sixteen, evidently lying about his age. He had received extensive training and earned top marks; since it was between wars, he had apparently become bored and left the corps when his enlistment was up. He had left with the rank of a sergeant, with the possibility of entering officer country; that was a hell of a testimonial right there, considering his scanty education.

Training in weaponry and the ability to handle himself had come in handy in the life he had followed after that. Deke knew that soldier of fortune was a dated term, but it seemed to fit Eric Ransom. He had hunted for lost treasure—the resumé hinted that he had found a few pots of gold—but a taste for the good life soon dissipated any fortunes found; and at other times and places he had hired himself out as a mercenary, fighting in several brush fires in the emerging African countries, probably for whichever side paid the most money. In fact, he had fought in so many countries and on so many different sides that he was persona non grata in many places; the reason, apparently, for his now being in the United States and seeking adventurous, lucrative employment. In addition to his other talents, he also held a pilot's license.

For the past two years Ransom had been on the police force in a medium-sized southern town. He had been discharged from the force about six months ago, not for incompetence—he had evidently been a hell of a cop—but for insubordination. It appeared that Eric Ransom was a rugged individualist and was disinclined to follow orders.

Carlos O'Brien was ten years younger, and his career was less varied. Of Irish and Spanish parentage, he, too, had been a policeman. His first job had been with the police force in Mexico City, where he had served with distinction for three years, and then he had been discharged because he had stepped on some political toes. After that, he had been a claims investigator with a firm that specialized in finding missing persons, most specifically young dropouts.

What struck Deke about the two men was the common chord of their rebel natures. He wanted a man

with daring and imagination. He knew, also, that he
had a sneaking admiration for rebels. He was one
himself, in his quiet way.

Both men were alike in another respect. They were
well-qualified, perhaps over-qualified. But that was
fine. If he could get both of them on the project—but
not necessarily working in tandem, for that could defeat his purpose . . .

The intercom blinked. "Yes, Callahan?"

"Mr. Ransom and Mr. O'Brien have an appointment
with you tomorrow afternoon from three to four
o'clock."

"It may take longer than an hour, Callahan. Do I
have anything urgent after four?"

"Nothing that can't be canceled on short notice."

"And Gabe?"

"Dr. Kemble will also be here. At a quarter to
three. I thought you might need a little time to brief
him."

"Your efficiency dazzles me as always, Callahan."

"I'll make a note of that, to use come raise time."

Gabriel Kemble was ushered into Deke's office
promptly at quarter to three. Gabe probably knew
April Morgan better than anyone living, certainly better than Deke.

Gabe at thirty-one was a much-sought-after psychiatrist. His good looks and low-key manner were as
much responsible for his success as his professional
ability, and that was not to be scoffed at—he was a
top man in his field.

He lounged at ease in the leather chair across from
Deke's desk, long legs stretched out, blond hair falling
over his forehead, pale gray eyes intent on Deke as
he was briefed.

When Deke was finished, the psychiatrist was silent
for a long moment. He took a Monte Cristo cigar
from a leather case and lit it. Finally he spoke
through a haze of blue smoke. "Granted that one or

both of these fellows is what you're looking for, what do you hope to accomplish?" His voice was deep and resonant.

Deke stared. "I just told you—find April Morgan!"

"What if she doesn't want to be found? We've talked of this, and it *is* possible, you know."

"That's one reason I've waited this long, hoping that either the police would find her or she would decide to come back on her own. I feel obligated to find her, Gabe. After all, I am the trustee for the Morgan estate."

"And if you find her and she doesn't wish to come back, what then?"

Deke shrugged. "That will be her decision. Certainly I don't intend to drag her back forcibly. Besides"—his look sharpened—"when we discussed this possibility, you said you didn't believe she went off of her own free will. You said it either had to be by force or a case of amnesia."

"I still believe the odds favor one of those alternatives, yet there is still the possibility that she disappeared of her own volition."

"You shrinks always hedge, don't you?" Deke said, exasperated.

Gabe blew smoke and shrugged noncommittally.

Deke tried to find his face behind the smoke. "Don't you want her found, for God's sake?"

"Of course I want her found, Deke. I'm just not sure this is the best way to go about it. You know what her mental condition was when she left. Being suddenly found and brought back, not to mention the resultant publicity, could cause a trauma from which she might never recover."

"That's not the way it's going to be, Gabe. Give me credit for some intelligence. Anyone I employ to find her will receive explicit instructions not to approach her when and if they find her. They are to inform me first. Then I will go to her, you with me, of course, and we'll approach her without spooking her—"

The intercom blinked. "Yes, Callahan?"

"They're here, Mr. Travers."

"Send them in."

Deke stood up without moving from behind his desk and waited for Maggie to open the door and usher the two men in.

She announced them with a dramatic flourish, then closed the door without bothering with individual introductions.

The taller of the two stepped forward, hand outstretched. "Eric Ransom, Mr. Travers."

Ransom was a big man, not particularly handsome. He had a shock of thick black hair and a deep tan. His brown eyes had a sardonic glint. He moved with the grace of a superbly conditioned athlete, and his grip was firm and just strong enough not to be aggressive.

The second man stepped up, a slight hitch in his stride. He was younger, and alongside Eric Ransom he looked almost frail, yet his eyes held a keen intelligence, and he carried himself well despite the limp. The face under the rather long blond hair was wedge shaped and fine featured, and Deke got the feeling of a strong, driving force, a certain ruthlessness, in the man.

"And I'm Carlos O'Brien." Unlike Ransom's calloused hand, O'Brien's hand was slender and well cared for, yet there was a surprising strength in his grip.

"I know what you're thinking, Mr. Travers," he said. "The limp wasn't mentioned in the resumé, right?"

Deke nodded, smiling slightly. "That question had crossed my mind, yes."

"It only happened recently, the result of an automobile accident. The hip socket was jammed badly, and it's still painful. The doctors assure me that it will go away, but it will take time. However, it doesn't hinder me in any way whatsoever. If you wish, I would be quite willing to undergo physical stress tests."

"I believe that won't be necessary. If you say it doesn't affect your efficiency, I'll accept your word. After all, if either of you gentlemen undertake the assignment, it will be on a contingency basis. If you succeed, you shall be amply rewarded. If not—" As Ransom made a sound of protest, Deke held up his hand. "Oh, there will be an expense account. A generous one, so long as I believe you are showing positive results. Now, why don't you gentlemen be seated, and I'll brief you. I'm sure you're aching with curiosity and wondering if I'm some kind of a nut. In that regard, perhaps the gentleman here can reassure you. May I introduce Dr. Gabriel Kemble? Dr. Kemble is a psychiatrist.

"Am I a nut, Dr. Kemble?"

Gabe took the cigar from his mouth and smiled ever so slightly. "I reserve comment."

Deke laughed and leaned back. "Let's get to it, shall we? Are either or both of you gentlemen familiar with the sudden disappearance of April Morgan?"

Ransom spoke first. "Only vaguely. I was out of the country when it happened."

"Yes, in Canada, I believe." Deke looked at the other man. "How about you, Mr. O'Brien? Are you familiar with her disappearance?"

O'Brien said cryptically, "Somewhat."

"Almost six months back, April Morgan vanished without a trace, and the police, not only in the U.S. but around the world, have come up empty-handed. Your mission, gentlemen, should you undertake it, will be to find April Morgan. It will not be easy, I assure you. After the police came up with nothing, I employed an investigative firm, one I have used many times on criminal cases. Still nothing. So I hired a second. I received their negative report two days before I ran the ad."

Carlos O'Brien cleared his throat. "Is it necessary

that we find her alive and well, Mr. Travers? Or is your goal merely to *find* April Morgan?"

Deke said coldly, "Alive, preferably, but you will be paid should you find her deceased. However, for the present, would it be all right if we operated on the premise that April is still among the living?"

O'Brien shrugged. "Fine with me. I just wanted the ground rules clarified—"

Ransom interrupted. "Don't pay any attention to him, Mr. Travers. You want this girl brought back alive and well, I'm your man."

O'Brien frowned and said curtly, "You're putting words in my mouth, friend. That was not my meaning at all."

As the two men exchanged measuring looks, Deke watched them for a moment. He was pleased at the way things were working out—clearly there was already a spirit of competition between them.

"All right, gentlemen," he said briskly. "I think the thing now is to brief you on the facts, scarce as they are. That is the reason that Dr. Kemble is present. He knows April Morgan better than anyone. Her father made me a trustee of his estate in his will, but I have only spoken to April—oh, perhaps a half-dozen times, and she was in a state of shock at the time. After the accident she was in Dr. Kemble's care for some weeks. Gabe?"

Gabe Kemble pulled reflectively on his cigar for a moment or so before he began. "When April Morgan came under my care, she was suffering from shock and amnesia, caused by her father's sudden death. She also was terrified of human contact . . ."

Four

—◆◆◆—

Gabe Kemble was familiar with patients who were reluctant to go into analysis. But although he had known patients who were terrified of the process itself, he had never encountered an analysand who was terrified of *him*, not necessarily as a psychiatrist, but as a person.

She huddled in the hospital bed, knees drawn up to her chin, hands over her face. He'd caught just a glimpse of blue eyes, darting from side to side. Her long, wheat-blond hair was matted and lifeless, and the nails of her hands had been bitten to the quick. The private nurse had informed Gabe that she spurned any grooming.

He was tempted to turn his back and walk out. He didn't need this. He had a safe, lucrative Park Avenue practice, and for all their quirks, his patients were at least well-groomed and could converse, usually, with reasonable coherence.

Certainly none of them were terrified of him.

Gabe didn't move, telling himself that it was because Deke had asked him to see this young woman as a favor. But Gabe knew that it was more than that. He was bored with his professional life, and had been for some time. He was bored by the spoiled, rich women who paid him, and well, to lay on his couch and drone on about their frustrations. But this woman, this April Morgan, represented a challenge.

There was more to it than that, much more, but that knowledge came with hindsight. He fell in love with April, despite the matted hair, the pallid complexion, the terror crawling across her face—he fell in love with her during that first session. There was about her a bewildering yet bewitching mixture of vulnerability and innocent sexuality that baffled him to the end.

"Hello, April. How are you?"

She cringed at the sound of his voice, and a whimper came from low in her throat.

He sat down in the room's one chair, within easy reach of her hand. In a low, soothing voice he told her a little about himself, receiving no response and expecting none. He used his voice as an instrument, employing words to soothe, much in the same manner as a trainer might talk to a frightened horse.

It worked, to a certain degree. The hands came down, and the muscles in April's face stopped twitching quite so badly. She still would not look directly at him, and he received no vocal response whatsoever, but he was well content when he left the hospital room, pausing at the door to say, "I'll see you tomorrow, April. At the same time."

"Tomorrow?" Deke echoed on the phone that evening. "How about your other patients?"

"I'm taking a couple of weeks off. My practice can stand it, and at the prices I charge, there are any number of psychiatrists willing to take my appointments, hoping to steal my patients, and the patients will probably be happy, too, welcoming a new face and voice."

There was a long silence on the other end. Then, a dry chuckle. "Gets to you, doesn't she? It happened to me as well, Gabe. Before the death of her father, she was just John Morgan's daughter, blending into the background. I'd never even spoken to her. Since his death, I've seen her several times, but in the shape she's in, I doubt she even knows I exist."

"She presents an intriguing problem, Deke. Her health is excellent. I've gone over the test results the doctors here have made, and there isn't a thing wrong with her physically."

"So how are you going about it? Not that I'm prying into your professional secrets, Gabe, but I do have a passing interest in her welfare."

"I'll sort of play it by ear, Deke. I'm going to try and get her to talk to me first. I'll probably try narcosynthesis eventually, using thiopental, the truth serum."

It took three visits before April spoke the first word. On the second visit she seemed less withdrawn and frightened, and during the session Gabe simply talked quietly, discussing anything that came to mind—current plays, films, novels. Having learned from Deke that her one consuming hobby was photography, he brought along a Rollex on the third visit, one that he had recently purchased.

After he had talked for a bit, he held up the camera. "I understand that you're a very good photographer, April. I have never been one for a hobby, going counter to the advice that I give my patients. But I've just about decided to take up photography, and I bought this today. Did I make a good buy?"

He held the camera out to her. April shrank back, but her gaze clung to the camera, and he saw a faint flicker of interest. He urged, "Come on, tell me what you think. I'd really like your opinion."

Hesitantly she took the camera. Cradling it in her lap, her slender hands moved over it with a lover's touch.

"Daddy's dead, isn't he?" Her voice was low, with a husky quality.

Gabe, whose gaze had been fastened in fascination on her hands, jumped slightly and looked into her face. Her features were perfectly composed, but fat tears ran out of her eyes and down her cheeks.

"Yes, April, your father is dead," he said gently. "And your stepmother as well."

"Sheila! I hate her!" April glanced away. "That's terrible of me, isn't it, Dr. Kemble?"

Inordinately pleased that she knew his name, Gabe said, "Not so terrible, April. Many children do not like stepmothers, or stepfathers, either. It happens more often than not. Especially so in your case, since you were full-grown when your father brought her home."

"She married daddy for his money! I tried to tell him, but he just laughed—" Her gaze swung back, a burning intensity in her eyes now. "How long has it been since—"

"Since the accident?" Gabe cleared his throat. "Three weeks, April."

"And I've been here all that time?"

"Yes, April."

"I've been sick, haven't I?" Her fingers began to pluck at the sheet in her lap.

"Yes, but it'll soon be behind you. This, today, is a most hopeful sign. Do you realize that this is the first time you've spoken to anyone?"

Her eyes were growing ever more bright and aware, and her head was held proudly. "What's wrong with me, Dr. Kemble?"

"Well—" He hesitated, rubbing his chin with his fingers.

"I want the truth. Don't lie to me. Don't ever lie to me!"

"If I lie, April, it will be inadvertent." His smile was wry. "But you asked a large question there. This is only the third time I've seen you. Medically speaking, you're in excellent health—"

"But mentally?"

"No, no!" He wagged his head. "You're suffering from traumatic shock, amnesia—"

"Amnesia. Loss of memory, right?"

"Yes," he said cautiously. "But just now you remembered your father's death. What else do you remember?"

Her fingers began to pluck at the sheet again. "I remember daddy being. . . . I remember his teetering on the edge of that bluff up from our beach house. I was rushing toward him, trying to catch him. Then he was gone, and I remember standing on the edge of the cliff, staring down at him on the rocks below, knowing that he was dead. And then"—she got a puzzled look—"the next thing I remember is waking up here, in this room."

"Do you remember anything *before* you saw your father on the cliff?"

Her brows knitted. "Of course. I know that I am April Morgan. I know where I went to school, where we lived here in New York, on Sutton Place." Her voice was chiding and made him feel slightly stupid.

"How about the time immediately before the accident?"

"Well, we went up to our house on the Cape for two weeks. It was a—well, a honeymoon for daddy. I felt awkward going along. I thought I would be the unwanted guest, but daddy insisted that I come. It took us a couple of days to settle in. At dinner on the second day, somebody—I don't remember whether it was daddy or Sheila who suggested it—decided to go for a walk after dinner, along the bluff by the sea. Daddy asked if I wanted to go along, but I had some film that I wanted to develop and—" Her words were coming slower now, uncertain and spaced out. "I remember that I went into the darkroom—" She was becoming agitated. "That's all I remember, doctor!"

"Do you recall seeing or hearing your father and stepmother leave?"

"I don't know, doctor!" Her voice rose. "Please, don't ask me any more! Please don't!"

"All right, April," he said softly. "That's enough for now. You're doing fine, just fine."

He reached out and took her hand. She jumped, her eyes widening, and started to pull away. Then she relaxed, and Gabe saw in her eyes the beginning of trust, and then she looked away from him, as if embarrassed to have shown her feelings.

He released her hand, and she pulled both of her hands back and let them remain quietly in her lap, her gaze still turned away toward the window.

As Gabe watched her, her features smoothed out, all signs of tension disappearing, and he followed the direction of her gaze.

In the utilitarian hospital window, someone had hung a prism, and the late afternoon sun, now hitting the brilliant curve of glass, splashed rainbow light over the floor and walls.

April's gaze was fastened on the bit of glass, and it was apparent that she was close to, if not into, a hypnotic state.

Gabe was elated. Either April had been hypnotized often before, or she was naturally an excellent subject. Whichever, it fitted right in with his plans, for his next step, if he could convince her to try it, was hypnosis.

He leaned forward, speaking quietly. "April?"

Unmoving, she answered in a soft voice. "Yes?"

Gabe raised his voice and touched her hand. Her head jerked slightly, and as if coming awake from a deep sleep, she looked at him in surprise. "Oh, yes, Dr. Kemble, I'm sorry, my mind was wandering. What were you saying?"

He reached forward and again took her hands into his. They were relaxed. "April, there is a technique that I would like to try on you. I think it would be helpful."

He felt her hands go tense, and for a moment she made as if to draw away. "What is it? What do you mean?"

"I'd like to try hypnosis. Sometimes it's very useful in cases like yours."

"You mean, put me in a trance?"

He shook his head. "It's really not a trance, April. The hypnotic state is actually something you have experienced many times on your own."

Her look was dubious. "What do you mean?"

"Well, have you ever been driving a car— You do drive, don't you?" She nodded. "Well, have you ever been driving, say on a freeway, on a familiar route, and suddenly you see your turnoff and realize that you have come miles without being conscious of what you were doing, because you were thinking of something else?"

She nodded thoughtfully, and he could feel her begin to relax slightly.

"And when you're watching a film that you are really involved in and you become aware of what is going on around you, or when you're reading and really caught up in it?"

She gave him a tentative smile. "You mean that's hypnosis?"

"It's the same state. And before you go to sleep at night, when you pass full wakefulness to that state where you are aware of what is going on around you but don't really care?"

She really smiled now. "What you're saying is, I won't be in your power? Like the scenes on the old movies on TV?"

Gabe laughed, pleased to see that the tension had almost entirely left her. "No, you won't be in my power, as you put it. You see, you actually hypnotize yourself. I just help you to do it, and while you're under, you won't do anything that you wouldn't do if you were in a full waking state. There is nothing to be frightened of, and you'll remember everything that you say and do."

She let her breath go with a sigh. "In the movies they always forget."

He gave her hand a gentle squeeze. "You would only forget if I told you to, and I'm not going to do that. So, what do you say?"

She hesitated for a moment and then nodded. "Okay. If you think it will help."

"Good!" He smiled. "Now I want you to make yourself comfortable. Lean back against the pillows and relax."

April did as he requested. She seemed interested and willing to cooperate, and Gabe mentally thanked whoever had hung up the lovely piece of glass.

She was still a little nervous, but determined. "Now what do you do? Make mesmerizing passes in front of my eyes or fascinate me with a sparkling gem? That's what they do on the late show."

"See, you *do* know something about hypnosis. You know about Mesmer."

She smiled slightly. "Yes, that's probably where I got all my wrong ideas. But seriously, what *do* you do?"

Gabe settled himself more comfortably on the edge of the bed. "Well, I usually have my patients fix their eyes on a spot on the ceiling just over their heads. I know it's not very glamorous, but it gets the job done. It makes the eyes tired. Actually fixing the eyes on any bright object, such as a candle flame, is good. So is staring at a moving object like a metronome, where the sound helps also. But in your case, since you seem to like that prism in the window, I thought we'd use that."

She looked at him rather sharply. "I think I've been manipulated."

By God, she was quick! Gabe thought. She might not be able to remember everything, but she was sharp and bright, and he would have to remember that. The only answer he made to her comment was to smile.

"Now, April, I want you to fix your eyes on the prism. That's it. Now relax and listen to my voice. You are growing very relaxed. Very, very relaxed. Take a deep breath. Let it out. As you exhale, you will grow even more relaxed. Every time you breathe, you will grow more and more relaxed. Your eyes are growing very tired. You cannot keep them open."

April's body began to slump slightly as she slid into

deep relaxation, and Gabe marveled at how quickly and with how little preparation she had entered this state.

He kept on talking, his voice steady and monotonous. Her eyes were closed now, and she was breathing deeply and regularly. He knew with the certainty born of long practice that he would be able to send her into a deep state, but he proceeded slowly, sending her from one level into another until she had reached a depth sufficient for his purpose.

"You are very comfortable, and you feel better than you have ever felt. Now, I want you to answer my questions, April. How do you feel?"

April's voice was clear and uninflected, slightly lower in tone than her normal waking voice. "Fine." Her body was now slumped bonelessly, her head hanging low.

"You will not wake up, but you will straighten up, April. You will put your head back on the pillows."

Slowly she straightened, putting her head back, and Gabe had to resist a sudden impulse to push back a strand of hair that had fallen across her cheek. Her face was relaxed, but she looked pale. He decided not to go too far into it today. They could go further tomorrow.

"Fine, April, that's just fine. Now, yesterday you told me you were in the darkroom developing some film when your father left the house. What were the pictures of, April?"

"Coastline scenes."

She looked better today, Gabe thought, and then realized that she had done something different to her hair, and that she had used a touch of lipstick on her lips. A definite sign of improving mental health.

"No pictures of your father or stepmother?"

"No."

"Did you ever take their pictures?"

"I—" Her head rolled upon the pillow; she was becoming agitated. "Not ever of Sheila."

"All right, April. Just relax now. You are very relaxed, and what you tell me, what you remember, will not distress you. You are comfortable. Very comfortable. Now, to go back. . . . You were in your darkroom. Did you know when they left the house?"

"I knew."

Gabe paused for a moment, thinking back to the day before. He was certain she had told him that she hadn't heard them leave. It probably wasn't important, yet it was a puzzling discrepancy. "How did you know?"

"Daddy rapped on the darkroom door. I opened it a crack, and he—and he—"

Gabe prompted, "He what, April?"

She was frowning, as if she found it difficult to remember. Then her face cleared. "He told me that he was leaving and would be back soon."

"That's all he said?"

Again a slight hesitation. "Yes."

"And then he left the house?"

"Yes."

"Your stepmother. Did you see her?"

Her face tightened, and she said sullenly, "No!"

"What is the next thing you remember, April?"

She became agitated again, and Gabe had to stop his questioning to calm her.

When she was quiescent again, he said, "I will reconstruct for you. Yesterday you said you remember nothing from the time in the darkroom until you recall running toward your father as he teetered on the edge of the cliff. Now, try hard, April. There is a time lapse, at an estimate of from thirty minutes to a full hour. You did *something* during that time. Try to remember, April."

She shook her head violently.

"Try, April! Try harder!"

"No, no, no! Nothing!"

Gabe sighed. "All right, April. Relax. You are very relaxed and very, very comfortable." He continued in the same vein until she was once more calm.

"You saw your father about to fall, and you ran toward him. Did you see anyone else?"

"No."

"Your stepmother. She must have been there. Did you see her?"

"No, no! Not Sheila!"

Gabe waited a moment. "April, think hard. Your father and stepmother left the house together. Therefore, it follows that they were walking together along the bluff. You must have seen her as well."

"No, no!"

Her face grew pale, and Gabe considered if he should risk further questioning. But he was able to calm her again, and he decided to go on.

"You were discovered lying on the edge of the cliff, unconscious, April. A jogger found you. He moved you back from the cliff's edge and peered over before going for help. Your father was there, as you said he was, on the rocks. but your stepmother was also there, right on the water's edge.

"When the jogger returned with two policemen, you were still lying where he had left you, still unconscious, and your father's—body was still there. But your stepmother was gone, and the conclusion was finally reached that her body had washed out to sea. Now. I ask you again, April. Did you see Sheila Morgan on that bluff with your father?"

Instead of answering, April turned her face away, her fists clenching.

"All right, April, let me ask you this. Did you see anybody else at the scene of the accident, anybody at all?"

Her head rolled from side to side, and her mouth opened and closed, but no words issued. It struck him that she wanted to answer him, but something held her back.

His shoulders slumped in defeat. "April, I will count backward from five to one. At the count of one, you will awaken. You will feel fine, rested and at peace with yourself, and you will remember everything that was said. Five, four, three, two, one."

At the count of one she opened her eyes, yawned, and stretched like a cat.

"How you feel, April?"

"I feel fine, doctor. That's the way I'm supposed to feel, isn't it?" Her smile was faintly sly. "Isn't that what hypnosis is all about, to make a disturbed patient feel that all's right with the world?"

"That is true, but we are also trying to unlock your memory. Do you recall all that was said here?"

"Insofar as I know, unless you turned a hypnotic lock on something and then threw the key away." Her face became still as she stared at him out of huge eyes.

"Nothing like that, April," he said patiently. "But I am strongly convinced that you know something you aren't telling."

"I thought all this was to get at the truth, that a person couldn't lie under hypnosis?"

"It is to get at the truth, and a hypnotic subject usually doesn't lie, but sometimes it is necessary to dig deeper, much deeper, before the whole truth emerges."

Her smile turned rueful. "So now not only am I a neurotic mess and an amnesiac, but a liar as well. What other bright side to my character do you think you'll uncover, doctor, through your poking around in my psyche?"

He stood up abruptly. "That'll be enough for today, I'll be back tomorrow at the same time."

Her voice stopped him at the door. "So, what's next, doctor?"

"So, what's next, Gabe?"

"That's what April asked me, Deke. My answer was I've scarcely started. I just have to keep digging."

"Drugs? Is that next?"

"Not just yet. I've barely started with hypnosis. Only two sessions so far. I will say this: April Morgan is a wonderful hypnotic subject, one of the best I have ever encountered."

"Okay, Gabe, you're the doctor. No pun intended. But let me ask you this. You think she's lying, even April seems to think she's lying—"

"Not lying, Deke. She's just not telling everything."

"Whatever. The question is, why?"

Gabe hesitated. "I'm not sure, but my guess would be that she's terrified."

"Of what, for God's sake?"

"I don't think that the deaths of John Morgan and his new wife were accidents, Deke. I think they were murdered. What's more, I think that April not only witnessed those murders but got a good look at the killer and even may have recognized him. It's also possible that the murderer realizes that April witnessed it. That could be what brought on her loss of memory. She is *afraid* to remember. . . ."

April had lied by omission. During Gabe Kemble's question and answer session, she had vividly recalled the first meeting with her father's new bride and what had happened immediately afterward. It was a bitter memory, and she could not bring herself to share it with Dr. Kemble or anyone else.

Eight days after marrying Sheila in Mexico, John Morgan had arrived unexpectedly at the Sutton Place apartment, with Sheila in tow. April had known about the marriage but had yet to meet the bride. She had learned of the wedding through a telegram: "Getting hitched today, sugar. Wish me luck. See you soon. Daddy."

The abrupt news had hurt, but the eight-day interval had given April time to absorb the shocking news and come to terms with it. After all, her father had done everything possible for her since her mother died, and it would be selfish of her to begrudge him a little happiness in his declining years. And there was really no reason she should have been surprised by the suddenness of the marriage. How many times had he regaled her with tales of million-dollar deals consummated over a Jack Daniels and water? And due to her father's short acquaintance with Sheila, April concluded that this marriage smacked of a "deal."

April's initial reaction, when John Morgan had breezed into the apartment unannounced, with Sheila on his arm, was one of shock. Her father's wife was about half his age! Her second reaction had been instant and total dislike, a reaction she immediately tried to hide with a too-bright smile. But the expression on her father's face told April that he had caught it.

"Sugar, I'd like you to meet the new Mrs. Morgan. I thought it was about time you two met up."

Sheila, blond, whippet-lean, smiled tightly and held out a hand, thus solving a dilemma for April. She had been wondering if she should embrace her new stepmother, but Sheila had made it clear that such a show of affection was not only not needed but unwanted.

"How do you do, April? John has told me a great deal about you."

"I'm sorry I can't say the same," April responded with a dour glance at her father. She took the proffered hand and found it cool and unresponsive. She rushed on. "But my belated congratulations, Sheila. Welcome to our family."

John Morgan said heartily, "I thought I'd leave Sheila here, so you two can get acquainted."

"Leave her here?"

"Yup. I have to rush off on some important business."

"A short honeymoon, wouldn't you say, April?"

Sheila said tautly. "Almost like being left at the altar."

"I'm right sorry, sweetheart, but it can't be helped. Some things I have to tend to. It can't be put off."

"You might as well get used to it, Sheila," April said. "He's always running off someplace at a moment's notice." She sensed that this was a continuation of a bitter quarrel.

"I knew he was a busy man when I married him, but I don't see any reason why I can't go with him."

"I travel fast and light. No more baggage than necessary."

Sheila's green eyes had an icy glitter. "I come under the heading of baggage, do I?"

He said uncomfortably, "Now you know I didn't mean it that way." He became brisk. "Speaking of which, I'd better get you settled in our bedroom." He looked out into the corridor. "Tom, you can take the bags into the master bedroom. You know where it is."

As the porter started down the short hall, Sheila said, "I need a shower," and followed him.

John Morgan yelled after her, "You want a drink, honey? The sun's well over the yardarm."

Her cool voice drifted back. "No, darling. But don't let that stop you. You probably need one."

Embarrassed, John Morgan looked at April. "She's a little steamed at me for running off. But she'll get over it. Pour you a drink?"

"No, daddy, but you go ahead."

He crossed to the bar in that shambling, disjointed walk she had always found endearing. She tried to find words to somehow comfort him and found herself at a loss. Never in all the years had she witnessed John Morgan in a situation in which he was not in total control. It was one of his strengths and one of the many reasons she loved him so. For the first time in her life she felt a stab of pity for him.

She said, "Your going off like this probably is a little rough on her, daddy. Can't you postpone whatever it is for a few weeks?"

He drank with a toss of his head, shuddering at the jolt of straight bourbon, and spoke without looking at her.

"Can't, sugar. Something has come up, something that I can't afford to put off. Someday you'll understand." He glanced at her now. "What's your opinion of her, April? You're probably thinking I'm an old fool, and I reckon I am, when it comes down to it, getting hitched up at my age."

Tears flooded her eyes, and she went to him quickly. "No, daddy, I don't think that at all. Why shouldn't you get married, if you feel like it?"

He put a big arm around her, and April buried her face against his jacket, inhaling the familiar smells of bourbon and cigars.

He stroked her hair. "Thing is, it was selfish of me, doing it like this, springing Sheila on you out of the blue. It ain't going to be easy for you, or her, either, I reckon. I did want you two to get along."

"We will, daddy, we will," she said, her voice muffled against his jacket. "If you love her, I'll come to love her, too. How can it be any other way?"

But it didn't happen that way. For the first few days that John Morgan was away, Sheila and April circled each other warily, like two strange cats. They were overly civil, speaking only when necessary.

Sheila spent a great deal of time shopping, coming home with boxes and boxes of clothing. The third day this happened, April was in the living room reading. She let the book fall into her lap and eyed the packages with some amusement.

Sheila noted the look and bristled. But she said nothing until she had tipped the porter for carrying her packages up and closed the door after him. Then she whipped around, hands on hips.

"Well? Go ahead, say it!"

"Say what, Sheila?"

"Spit out what's on your mind. Tell me that I'm spending your old man's money like mad while he's away. I'll have you know that he opened charge accounts all over New York for me."

"I'm sure he did, Sheila."

"What else am I supposed to do, what with him running off like this?" Sheila's eyes glittered. "Just because you go around looking dowdy, wearing clothes that look like they came off the rack at Macy's basement ten years ago, doesn't mean that I have to!" She sneered. "What are you trying to do, cast me in the role of the wicked stepmother, while you play poor Cinderella?"

April stood up, the book tumbling to the floor. "I begrudge you nothing, Sheila. And daddy won't, either. He's one of the most generous men alive!"

Sheila glared at her for a moment longer. Then with a muttered obscenity, she stormed off to the master bedroom.

But although Sheila spent most of the day away from the apartment, she always showed up for dinner, served by the housekeeper. They ate in polite silence. But the evening after the flare-up, Sheila hadn't returned by dinner time, and April ate alone. She was just as happy about that, yet as the evening lengthened, she began to worry. Had their quarrel the evening before driven Sheila into leaving John Morgan? April thought this would be a good thing, yet she doubted that her father would think so. He would more than likely place the blame on her if he found his wife gone on his return.

Finally April ventured into the master bedroom for a quick inspection, her ears painfully attuned for Sheila's key in the front door. What she found convinced her that Sheila had not left. Her bags were still there, as well as all the clothes she had purchased. April knew that the woman would not leave those behind.

Feeling guilty for prying, April fled the bedroom and went down the hall to her own room, where she crawled into bed with a book. But now a new worry began to gnaw at her. Had something happened to Sheila? Most New Yorkers turned a deaf ear to all the horror stories about muggings, rapes, and random killings, and April had never been molested, yet she knew that there was more than a grain of truth to the tales. If Sheila was not familiar with New York, she could easily have wandered into a dangerous area of the city.

April had dozed off, the light still on, when a key rattled in the front door, waking her. Her glance jumped to the bedside clock. It was after one in the morning.

Her first feeling was relief that Sheila was all right, and she started to turn off the light so that Sheila wouldn't know that she was still awake. Yet the key continued to rattle in the lock for an inordinate time. April got out of bed, threw her robe on, and padded down the hall in her bare feet. She was halfway across the living room to the front door when it swung open, and Sheila stumbled in.

As April started to turn, to go back toward the hall, Sheila hit the light switch, swinging around at the same time, catching at the door for her balance.

She blinked in the blaze of light, and April, trapped by the other woman's gaze, realized that it was too late to flee.

"Well! Waiting up for me, Cinderella?" Sheila said unpleasantly. "How sweet!"

"No, I heard the key in the lock for so long that I thought you were locked out . . ." April's voice died in mid-sentence. She stared at her stepmother, appalled. The woman was a mess—hair rumpled, lipstick and eyeshadow smeared, clothes disarranged. And she was carrying one shoe, the other nowhere in evidence.

She took two wavering steps forward, and alcohol fumes came at April in waves.

"What are you staring at, Cinderella?"

April's laughter was an involuntary, nervous reflex.

"You look like an accident victim, Sheila. What happened? Were you mugged?"

"Oh, I'd hardly describe it that way," Sheila said airily.

She took several more steps, stopping close to April, who turned her face away from the woman's rank breath.

Then she tensed as she detected another scent—the unmistakable odor of spent sex. Once again, she spoke without thinking. "You've been with a man!"

"Right!" Sheila tried unsuccessfully to snap her fingers. "Right the first time! Give Cinderella the prize, maestro!"

"But you've only been married to daddy for—" April clapped a hand over her mouth.

"So?" Sheila said, never raising her voice. "He goes kiting off without me, right? What am I supposed to do? Damned right I've been with a man, one who appreciates me! And I probably will again. You're thinking of tattling to daddy, right?"

April said distantly, "I hadn't thought that far, no. But I certainly don't approve—"

"You think I give a damn for your approval?" Sheila thrust her face forward. "And you think I care if you tell your daddy? You go right ahead, stepdaughter. I couldn't care less. And you know why?"

April could only shake her head dumbly.

"Because he wouldn't believe you. And even if he did, it wouldn't matter. There's an old Texas saying you may not be familiar with, but I'm sure your daddy is. He's not going to turn me loose, Cinderella, because he's pussy-whipped!"

Five

<hr>

"And that, gentlemen, is pretty much the whole story," Deke said. "Unfortunately, April Morgan vanished on the following day. Dr. Kemble never had the chance to continue with his hypnotic sessions."

Eric Ransom said, "This thought of yours, Dr. Kemble, about the deaths of her parents being murder instead of an accident—do you still believe that?"

Gabe Kemble motioned with his cigar. "I'm inclined to, yes."

"But, as you say, there's no evidence to support it?"

"That is true. There is not."

"Were the police informed of this murder theory?"

"No," Deke said. "In the absence of any proof, I thought it would only confuse the issue."

Carlos O'Brien said, "Then you think it possible that she is running for her life, that a killer is after her?"

"It is a possibility, and it scares the hell out of me."

"A touch melodramatic, wouldn't you say?" O'Brien said dryly.

"Perhaps. But still possible." Deke leaned across his desk. "That is why I wanted not only experienced manhunters, but someone capable of dealing with violence. If April is found, I don't want her alerted. I want her kept under close surveillance, to detect the possibility of any pursuit."

"That may be a tall order, Mr. Travers," Ransom said. "It's been six months since her disappearance. I don't mean the job of actually finding her. If she exists, I can find her, sooner or later. But, if you'll excuse my bluntness, does she still exist? Six months is a

41

long time if somebody is looking for her. She may already be dead. That may even be the reason she disappeared."

Deke thought the man's confidence bordered on the arrogant. He said steadily, "That possibility has occurred to me. But I have a feeling that she is alive, somewhere."

"But if she isn't?" Ransom persisted. "Where does that leave me?"

Gabe stirred. "My God, man, how coldblooded can you be?"

"No, he's right, Gabe." Deke held up his hand, his gaze locked with Ransom's. "If you find that she is dead, and can convince me of that fact, you will still be paid."

Ransom nodded, satisfied, and sat back.

Deke rolled his pencil back and forth across his desk. "How would you feel about working together?"

"Together?" O'Brien said.

"No way!" Ransom said explosively. "He'd only get underfoot, and I'm not splitting any reward money with him."

"No split will be necessary," Deke said. "You both will have an expense account, and the one who finds April first will receive fifty thousand dollars. And it won't be necessary to work together, not in the strict sense. All you will share will be a common goal."

"And what does the loser get? Nothing?"

"That is correct—except your expenses will be paid, and I promise not to question you too closely on that. Don't tell me that, in your diverse careers, you haven't both undertaken projects where you received nothing if you didn't score?"

Carlos O'Brien's cold eyes held a glint of respect. "You're pitting us against each other, aren't you?"

"Right on the button, Mr. O'Brien," Deke admitted cheerfully. "Under the two heads are better, even if not together, theory. So, what is your decision, gentlemen?"

Ransom lit a cigarette and retired behind a smoke screen.

O'Brien said, "I'm willing to give it a try."

"Mr. Ransom?"

"I suppose I'll give it a go, but I'm damned well not happy about it." He grinned, a flash of quick humor. "That fifty thou is a pretty fat carrot, Mr. Travers, as I'm sure you had in mind."

"What I have in mind is finding April Morgan."

O'Brien leaned forward. There was an intensity about him that made Deke think of a strung bow. "About finding her. You say there are, or were, no clues?"

"That is correct. A complete blank." Deke spread his hands.

"What is your guess? Is she in the States or a foreign country?"

Deke hesitated. "A foreign country. But that is only a gut feeling. Plus the fact that a pretty thorough search of the States turned up nothing."

Ransom said, "Does she speak any foreign language? That might narrow it down a bit."

"Not to my knowledge," Deke said.

"Then that would make the British Isles a possibility. Has she ever been there?"

"Ireland once, I understand."

Ransom nodded. "That's a starting point. I gather she didn't have much money?"

It was Gabe who answered. "She had fifty dollars and change in her purse. I went through her purse, hoping to find some hint as to what happened on that bluff. And that is what puzzles me. How could she get out of the country without the money to purchase a plane ticket? And since she didn't use her own passport, she had to use a forged one, and they do not come cheap."

O'Brien said, "Does she have a checking account? And did she cash a check?"

Deke nodded. "She has a small checking account,

and, no, she didn't write a check on it. At the same bank she has a safety deposit box. I got a court order and opened it. Her passport was there, nothing else of any importance."

"Has she ever been employed or had any kind of job training?"

"Neither," Gabe answered. "And that also worries me greatly. How is she managing to survive? On top of having no earning skills, the traumatic shock and loss of memory must have left her close to helpless. She's never really been on her own. Her father, as I understand it, was overly protective."

The fog of the evening before had lifted, and the morning was bright and crisp as Angela Williams got into the rental car in front of the Clare Inn.

The doorman placed her camera bag onto the front seat. Angela nodded a smiling thanks, gave him a bill, and drove away, feeling strange and a bit uncomfortable sitting on the right side, behind the small wheel. She felt even more uncomfortable as she drove the car down the driveway to the narrow country road below the inn.

The girl behind the desk had assured her that she would soon get used to "wrong way" driving, yet Angela found herself tense as she drove down the lefthand side of the narrow road.

The road wound through fields and meadows that were even greener than advertised. Small plots of land were surrounded by low, rough stone walls. The walls showed no evidence of mortar; the stones were simply stacked atop one another, fitting together in a pleasant pattern that charmed the eye. Fat cattle and sheep grazed in some of the fields, and now and then a cottage flashed by.

She was growing more relaxed now, getting somewhat used to the reversed pattern of driving. She felt quite at home here, she discovered. It was a beautiful country, and she had been won over the first night she arrived when a leprechaun of a man named Paddy had shown her to her room; welcoming her with a voice as soft as the Irish mist and as lilting as water over stones.

The day before she had spent in the vicinity of the inn, giving her body time to adjust to the time lag of travel, and dying her hair auburn. The inn itself was pleasant, her room comfortable, and the view superb. Her bedroom windows opened out onto the long slope fronting the inn, vibrantly green and covered with gulls from the nearby lake.

She had awakened to the cawing of the huge, black crows that also frequented the lawn, and she had dressed, then gone to the dining room for breakfast. From the buffet she had filled her plate with scrambled eggs, Irish bacon, and scones. She had cleaned her plate, including a wheat scone that had proved to be a sturdy item of considerable weight.

Then she had taken the walk to Dromoland Castle—about a half mile or so through lush meadows and patches of wood. The day had been a bit overcast, but she had taken some good shots of the castle—both exterior and interior—and wished that she had been booked into the castle proper, instead of the inn.

The castle, rebuilt for the third time in the 1800s, was elegant and looked, Angela thought, much more like a palace than a traditional castle. It was very photogenic, sitting on its low hill, outlined against the sky and surrounded by handsome gardens, trees, and plantings.

Angela had returned to the inn a bit tired but very pleased with herself, and after an early dinner, she had gone directly to bed, where she had slept deeply until her wake-up call this morning.

Now she glanced down at the road map open on the seat beside her. Last night she had marked out today's shooting schedule, making tiny red check marks beside the castles she intended to photograph.

Since the magazine readership was made up primarily of American tourists, most of her picture taking would be of the most interesting and available of the castles that were open to the public. However, there were other castles, *not* open to the public, and some interesting ruins, that she also intended to photograph in the hope that the pics editor would use some of the shots.

By mid-afternoon she had photographed Bunratty Castle, Dunguaire Castle, the Craggaunowen Project, and Knappogue Castle. It had been a very busy schedule, and while her head was filled with images of ancient stone, her stomach rumbled unhappily, reminding her that she had not eaten since her early breakfast.

She began looking for somewhere to stop for a meal, and finally, in Ennis, she found an appealing-looking pub and parked nearby.

The inside of the pub was dim and cozy. The thick, whitewashed walls and low doorways spoke of a long past, and the smell of food made her stomach rumble again.

A little hesitant, not knowing what the rules were here, Angela seated herself and her camera at a small, rough-hewn table in a corner near the multipaned window, where she was able to sit on a comfortably cushioned window seat and face the room.

Angela sat there for a few minutes, letting her eyes adjust to the dimness, wondering whether she was expected to go up to the bar to order. She looked surreptitiously at the half-dozen men and two women scattered around the room and found that they were examining her with frank and seemingly friendly curiosity, for they nodded or smiled as they caught her glance, and she found herself nodding and smiling back.

A rotund man, a white apron tied around his waist, was coming toward her with a pad. "What'll it be, miss?" he asked softly, and suddenly Angela realized that she didn't even know what kinds of food they might serve here.

"A sandwich?" she asked cautiously.

He smiled, seeming to understand her hesitation. "Sure, and we have sandwiches. Ham, turkey, and beef. Or you can have a Cornish pasty, if you like, or apple tart with cream. You can have Guiness, tea, or even coffee, if that's to your liking."

"Oh, tea, please, with milk, and I'll have the Cornish pasty *and* the apple tart."

He nodded, as if he approved of her choice, then went back to the area behind the bar.

In a short while he returned bearing a tray and put down before her a small teapot, a small metal pitcher of hot water, another small pitcher of milk, a lovely, crisp, brown pasty, and a saucer containing a square of apple tart, with a generous dollop of whipped cream.

The food looked fantastic and tasted even better. The pasty, crisp on the outside and filled with meat, was delicious. The tea was hot and strengthening, especially when liberally dosed with milk and the natural brown sugar that seemed so prevalent here. The tart was almost more than Angela wanted, but not quite, and when she had finished up the last bite, carefully scooping up the last of the cream, she felt replete and soothed.

When she glanced up from her food, she found that the rest of the customers had left and she was alone with the man behind the bar.

When he saw that she was finished, he came to her table. "Well, how did it suit you, miss?"

She smiled. "It suited me very, very well."

He bobbed his head. "Glad that it did. You're a stranger hereabouts, aren't you?"

She nodded. "I'm photographing some of the castles for a magazine in the United States."

"Ah, yes," he said, a trifle ruefully. "You Americans are much interested in castles. In fact, most of the castles and keeps in Ireland are owned by Americans. It's a fact!"

Angela didn't know quite what to say, but she didn't have to worry about it because he went on just as if he had received a reply or comment. The Irish, she was discovering, were great talkers.

"But it's not so bad as it might seem. For the Americans have restored the castles and keeps when there were few Irishmen with the money to do it. And of course, most of the Americans were Irish-Americans at that. Of course, there is an exception now and then, like Moher Keep."

"Moher Keep?" she said in surprise. "I don't remember seeing anything about that in the brochure."

The man grinned. "Aye, and you won't, either. The O'Laughlin sees to it that you don't."

"The O'Laughlin?" Angela was curious now. This man certainly knew how to hook a listener.

"Why, Liam O'Laughlin, of course. Sure, and you must have heard of Liam O'Laughlin?"

"Why, yes! He's an actor, a movie actor, an international film star."

"The very same."

Without asking, the man plopped himself down opposite Angela and put his elbows on the table. "I'm Seamus Riley, the owner of this establishment."

"And I'm Angela Williams."

"It's pleased that I am to meet you, Miss Williams." He bobbed his head. "Now, as I was saying, Liam's a County Clare lad, from just outside Ennis. Aye, it's right proud we are of Liam. Many's the time he drops in here for a glass or two in the evening, when he gets tired of being all alone out there on the cliffs. 'Tis said by more knowing men than myself that he's Ireland's answer to the Welshman, Richard Burton. Now, I've never had the pleasure of making Mr. Burton's acquaintance, but I doubt that any man, even Mr. Burton, can match our Liam cup for cup." He grinned, showing square white teeth. "And when Liam's in his cups and gets a bit rowdy, well, Mr. Burton *is* getting on a bit, and he'd sure be no match for the O'Laughlin's fists!"

Angela frowned. "His fists?"

"Aye, when Liam's full of the drink, he gets a bit wild." Seamus Riley shook his head. "He's a strong lad and good with his hands, despite the sissifying influence of them film folk. Yes, Liam can be a real terror when the black mood is on him."

Angela's mind was busy. The pub owner had said "out on the cliffs" and that Liam O'Laughlin dropped by often; that must mean that his home, this Moher Keep, was nearby. . . . Of course! The cliffs of Moher! A must-see tourist spot. A strange place for a man to go for his privacy.

"Isn't he bothered by the tourists?" she asked. "I mean, the cliffs *are* a tourist spot."

Seamus Riley shook his head. "Aye, no. The tourists only go the one place, up the path to Cornelius's Tower. Moher Keep is a distance away from all that."

"But he allows no visitors, not even interviewers or photographers?"

"*Espooially* not interviewers or photographers," the pub owner said with a sly glance at her camera case. "Liam's fond of his privacy and has been known to be a bit rough with those who interfere with it."

He leaned forward conspiratorially. "Why, 'twas only a few months back that one of those boyos from some scandal sheet in your country came sneaking around after Liam up at the cliffs. Liam tossed him straight into the ocean, so I hear. Lucky it was that the poor sod didn't come upon Liam on the high cliffs, or he'd a been a dead one for sure."

Angela was lost in her own thoughts for a moment as a terrifying picture moved across her mind's eye—a towering cliff and a man falling to be crushed on the sea-slick rocks.

"Miss?"

She shook her head, suddenly wishing she had not eaten so much. "I'm sorry?"

"Are you all right, miss? For a moment there, you looked pale as death."

"I'm fine. Thank you for your concern. But I'm not with a news magazine, nor a scandal sheet. I'm doing a piece for a travel magazine."

"For American tourists, is it?"

"Well—yes."

Seamus Riley was shaking his head. "Liam hates tourists almost as much as he hates magazine people. Says they're bloody pests, always chasing after him for his name on a piece of paper. Meself, I never could see the sense in that. Even if our Lord came down and walked among us, I wouldn't be after chasing him for his autograph!"

"I assure you that I am not after Mr. O'Laughlin's autograph," she said in a tart voice. "But I would be interested in pictures of his keep."

"Now that I wouldn't be advising you to try, Miss Williams. Liam says he paid a pretty penny for that pile of stones, just to get away from people. He's even hired a couple of bully boys to keep away sightseers and such. It's all fenced, you see, dogs as fierce as the hounds of hell roaming about. You can't get closer than a mile of the place."

Angela shrugged. "Well, it was a thought. I'm sure there are plenty of castles in Ireland without my bothering with Mr. O'Laughlin's."

"Aye, that there are. We're up to our arses, pardon me, miss, in castles." He laughed wryly. "Any day I'm after expecting some enterprising bucko to start building new ones, all a couple of hundred years old, if you catch my meaning."

Angela paid her bill, tipped the pub owner too much, and left, determined to push all thoughts of Liam O'Laughlin and his inaccessible keep out of her mind.

O'Laughlin wasn't even a particular favorite of

hers. She'd seen all his films, of course, but then she saw most movies released. Film was her profession, she supposed it might even be called her obsession, and she had to confess to a wistful daydream or two about becoming a famous cinematographer. Not that there was much chance of that. That lofty profession was almost exclusively male, and they zealously fended off all newcomers, especially those of the feminine gender.

Angela thought of Liam O'Laughlin as a film personality, not an actor. In all his films he played Liam O'Laughlin. She supposed he was handsome, but he struck her as arrogant, vain, and self-centered, and she had a hunch that his film personality spilled over into real life. What you saw up there on the screen was what you got!

Yet, for all her resolves, her thoughts kept returning to the man and his keep, and Angela realized that it was the challenge he represented that really intrigued her.

The picture taking went well during the next four days. Angela followed her schedule and was content with most of her shots. She was confident that she would have the job done by the end of the two-week deadline.

Yet, the thought of Moher Keep itched at the back of her mind all the while. Browsing through a newsstand on the afternoon of the fourth day, she came across one of the scandal sheets scorned by Seamus Riley. Liam O'Laughlin's picture was on the cover. In the background of the photograph was his third wife. The actor's face wore a dark scowl, and headlines above the photo screamed: "International Flick Star, Liam O'Laughlin, Divorces Third Spouse!"

Acting on impulse, Angela purchased a copy of the scandal sheet and stuffed it furtively into her purse.

In her room at the inn, she read the lurid article. According to the writer, Liam O'Laughlin had accused his latest wife of blatant infidelity. He was quoted as saying that he had caught his wife, former fashion model Kathy Desmond, in bed with an un-named male. She was wearing the diamond he had given her for her birthday only the evening before. The diamond, rumored to have cost a quarter of a million dollars, was, according to the dashing Liam, a token of his love for Kathy. "But my love died the moment I discovered her being unfaithful. I swear by the gods that I will never marry again, and my faith in all womankind is shattered forever!"

Angela made a sound of disgust and crumpled the paper, tossing it into the wastebasket. Why was she reading such garbage?

And yet, early that evening she found herself drawn back to the pub in Ennis. This time the tavern was ringed with cars, and there was a silver-gray Rolls Royce by the front door. Angela got out of her car and picked up her Nikon from the front seat. She hesitated briefly, then returned the camera to the seat, locked the car, and went into the pub.

It was smoky inside, smoke drifting like fog against the lights. The room was packed to the walls, and the sound level was deafening.

But over it all thundered a great, rolling voice. Liam O'Laughlin, it had to be.

Angela stood on tiptoe, craning over the heads to see, just as a man leaped up onto a table. In the murky light there was no mistaking that it was O'Laughlin. He was wearing a black turtleneck and gray trousers, an outfit that showed his tall, wide-shouldered body to good advantage. His hair was thick and black, a lock falling over his eyes as he mo-tioned expansively with the glass in one hand. He stood in profile to Angela, and she had to admit that he was handsome.

And that marvelous voice! How could she have for-gotten that? Even if he had possessed no acting tal-ent, the voice alone would have been enough.

It had the range and resonance of a Richard Burton, yet it struck her that this man had more control of his voice than his Welsh counterpart; he could play it like a musician plays an instrument—to command rapt attention; to sway; to seduce; to mesmerize.

His gesture with the glass failing, he used his voice to bring silence to the room. "Silence, you insensitive clods! Liam O'Laughlin is about to speak to you of life and women. Pearls before swine, as it were."

The room fell silent as a tomb, and Liam grinned crookedly. Angela listened, enthralled, as that rich voice rose, each word rolling off the tongue as though freshly minted:

> "What mighty ills have been done by woman!
> Who was't betrayed the Capital? A woman!
> Who lost Mark Antony the world? A woman!
> Who was the cause of a long ten years' war,
> And laid at last old Troy to ashes? Woman!
> Destructive, damnable, deceitful woman!"

He drank from the glass. "That, you unappreciative dullards, was penned by a playwright in the seventeenth century, Thomas Otway. Now long forgotten, and no doubt deceived by a woman, as has been yours truly." He rolled his eyes heavenward. "How long, sweet Jesus, how long? How much can one mere mortal suffer?"

As the last word thundered out, Liam drained his glass and fell, like a great tree. Those around the table caught and carried him from the pub, and the room rocked with laughter, not mocking laughter but prideful laughter in the antics of a beloved comrade.

Angela followed along as the men carried him outside. Like pallbearers, she thought.

Behind her the room rang again with noise—the clink of glasses, shouts of laughter, and bandied comments. "That Liam! A case, ain't he?" "The drink and women, that'll be the lad's downfall!" "But you know what they say, Tim m'boy. What a way to go!"

Night had fallen outside, and a chill fog crept along the ground. The men bore Liam O'Laughlin to the Rolls, opened the door, and tenderly propped him behind the wheel. He sagged forward, blank face turned toward them. One man found his car keys and put them in the ignition. The car door was closed gently, and they trooped back toward the pub.

"Wait!" Angela said in dismay. She stepped in front of the man who had found Liam's keys. "You can't just leave him like that!"

"Why not, miss?" The man's breath was as rank as a distillery. "That's what we always do."

"But if he comes to and tries to drive away? He's in no condition to drive. He's a menace to others, as well as himself!"

"Can't count the number of times I've seen him like this, and he's always made it home without harm to himself or others."

The man tipped an imaginary cap and stepped around her, following the others inside.

Angela stood in indecision, gnawing at her lower lip, her gaze on the face resting against the wheel. The violence and bitterness she had glimpsed inside were gone now, and he looked at peace.

Then he stirred, lifting his head. He blinked around, his glance sweeping over her without seeming to see her. He fumbled with the ignition, and the motor purred to life. He sat there for a moment without moving, staring straight ahead.

Angela thought of what the man had just told her of O'Laughlin's legendary capacity for alcohol and his ability to function while under its influence. There were men like that, a few, who could consume incredible amounts of alcohol and show little change; some even claimed, true or not, that alcohol sharpened their reflexes. Yet an intuitive feeling told her that Liam O'Laughlin was beyond drunkenness now. Bitterness had obviously eaten at him, and fanciful as it might seem, she sensed something suicidal about him.

He made a move to engage the gears. Sighing, Angela opened the door. "Move over. I'll drive. You're certainly in no condition."

She expected anger, belligerence, but instead he simply said, "All right," and moved over to let her behind the wheel. He was asleep and snoring lightly before she had the Rolls backed around and on the road toward his keep. The Rolls was a pleasure to drive after the small rental car. A fragment of memory whisked in and out of her mind—somewhere she had ridden in a Rolls, had even driven one. She shook her head sharply. Not true; she had never been in a Rolls in her life.

Twice during the last few days, she had driven down the side road as far as the gatehouse to the O'Laughlin estate. The first time she had hoped for a glimpse of the forbidden keep, but the pub owner had been right—from where the road ended one could not see the keep. A high fence—electrified, she was sure—ran right and left, disappearing in the distance. A strictly modern touch, incongruous on this ancient isle.

The second time she had not been sure of the reason for the drive down, and that time the guard at the gate, apparently recognizing the car from her previous visit, left the guardhouse and strode toward her. He was a big, beefy, scowling man, and his hand had hovered close to the gun holstered on his hip. Angela had turned the little car around and scooted away, leaving him shouting and red faced behind her.

Thus it was with trepidation that she approached the gatehouse in the Rolls. Her hope that a different guard would be on duty was dashed when the same beefy man rolled toward the Rolls as she braked. She pressed the button to lower the window, and he flashed a light in her face, passing on to the sleeping figure of Liam O'Laughlin. Apparently he hadn't recognized her.

He grunted, shaking his head. "Bombed again. Poor sod."

Stepping back, he opened the gate and motioned her on with the flashlight. Angela's main thought as she drove down the crush-rock roadway was that the guard must be accustomed to women driving Liam O'Laughlin home.

The thought of other women driving this man home annoyed her, and it was a moment before she recognized the cause. For God's sake, she was jealous! Jealous of a man she had just met—if it could be called that. A man so drunk there was no way he would remember her again. It was irrational, romantic nonsense!

With an angry shake of her head, she drove on.

About a mile and a half from the gatehouse, she rounded a curve in the road, and there it was. Moher Keep. Its sudden appearance so startled her that she slowed to a stop.

It rose tall and black in the luminous mist, a huge tower. She thought she could feel the weight of its age, and she shivered.

From where she had stopped, the keep was about fifty yards distant. There were two windows on the ground floor showing faint light, and over to the right a single bulb glowed over a huge door. But now, suddenly, more windows blazed light, a bright light went on over the massive front door, and two figures emerged, bathed in the headlights of the Rolls. A call from the gatehouse must have alerted the household.

Angela drove on. As she drew up before the door, she could hear the crashing of surf and knew that the keep must be perched on a bluff above the sea.

The two figures were men, both slender and well dressed. They approached the left-hand side of the car, opened the door, and eased Liam out. He groaned, muttering, but did not rouse.

One of the men held Liam propped up, while the other leaned into the car. "I am Thomas, miss, Mr. O'Laughlin's valet."

His accent told Angela that he was British, and the scene so reminded her of similar scenes in movies that she had to restrain a giggle. "I am Angela Williams," she said gravely.

"Miss Williams." Thomas inclined his head. He had a long, narrow, rather serious face, and she estimated him to be about forty years old.

Now he's going to ask me in for tea! she thought.

"Perhaps you would like a cup of tea, miss?"

A chance to see the inside of the keep! "I would love it." She quickly got out of the Rolls.

"Very good, miss," Thomas said. "Afterward, Bert could drive you back to Ennis. Or you may spend the night here, if you wish."

Angela immediately thought of her camera back in the car. What a marvelous opportunity, and she had blown it! She said cautiously, "I would like to stay the night, but do you think he—Mr. O'Laughlin would approve? To be perfectly honest, I'm not an old acquaintance. Nothing like that. We've never even met, not really. I just didn't think that he should be driving, not in his condition."

"If I may be equally candid, madam," he said with a straight face, "this is not uncommon, and our instructions are, in Mr. O'Laughlin's own words, to 'offer any person driving me home sanctuary for the night, but do not promise anything beyond that.' There is always a guest room prepared for just such an occasion."

"Your master's quote includes no mention of supper. I missed mine."

"I will inform the cook to prepare you some food." A glint of humor touched his brown eyes. "The master of Moher Keep would feel dishonored should his reputation for hospitality be besmirched."

"Then I accept. Heaven forbid that Master O'Laughlin's honor should be dirtied!"

The first thing Angela noticed as she surfaced from a luxurious sleep was warmth and sunlight on her face. The next thing was sound—the rhythmic crashing of the surf below. The third thing was not a sensory perception—she was being observed. She could not have given a reason for her knowledge, but she knew, as well as if a presence had been announced by trumpets, that someone stood staring down at her.

"Who is this I see sleeping in my bed?" said Liam O'Laughlin. "If 'tis Sleeping Beauty, I do not feel princely on this evil morn."

Angela opened her eyes slowly to see him lounging against one post of the four-poster, already dressed in a tan turtleneck and doe-colored trousers. Except for the smudges under his green eyes, there were no signs of last night's dissipation. He had even shaved, and his hair was brushed.

"Well? Am I to be provided with a name?"

"I'm Angela Williams. Didn't Thomas tell you?"

"Friendly with Thomas, are you?" He cocked an eyebrow. "Thomas tells me nothing until I have had my breakfast. He knows that I would have him guillotined."

"Then how did you know anyone was here?"

"When I get as snookered as I was last night, I either end up in a hospital bed, or someone drives me home. Ergo, I knew someone was in here. That's the purpose of this room."

She blurted, "Why do you drink so much? It's so—so self-destructive!"

"My dear young lady, I cannot abide a temperance lecture at *any* time," he said, glowering. "But one before I have had my breakfast is abominable!" He turned away, motioning. "Come!"

"Come where?" She sat up, forgetting that, lacking an overnight bag, she had slept in the buff. The sheet slid down, and his gaze fastened on her bared breasts before she could snatch the sheet up again.

"Not bad," he said judiciously, "but I've seen better, size-wise."

Face flaming, she snapped, "My bust size is no concern of yours!"

"True," he said gravely. "Especially at the moment. I never have sex before breakfast."

"Nor at any other time, not with me. I'm sure you're accustomed to women begging to share your bed, but I'm not a movie star groupie."

The green eyes glittered coldly. "My dear young lady, I have made no sexual overtures, nor do I plan to. I was merely offering you breakfast. I employ the best cook in all of Ireland. You have two choices. Either get dressed and have breakfast with me or come as you are. I have breakfasted with nude ladies before. Or you can get dressed and I'll have my chauffeur take you wherever you wish to go. It's of little concern to me, either way."

He turned on his heel and left the room. Angela's anger had already begun to subside, and she realized that she had overreacted. With his reputation as a womanizer vivid in her mind, she had jumped to a rather hasty conclusion.

She laughed shakily. He wasn't going to get rid of her *that* easily! Last night she'd had little opportunity to see much of the keep, and she was determined to see as much of it as he would permit.

She dressed quickly and hurried out of the bedroom. A maid in the corridor guided her to the dining room, leading the way down a stairway that was barely wide enough for the human body. The steps were narrow and wedge shaped because of the tight turns, and Angela could not help but wonder how the women of the past had been able to manage, legs hampered by long skirts and perhaps carrying a candle or lantern.

The walls and stairway were of rough stone. Small,

deep windows, now glassed, permitted framed views of green trees and lawns.

The dining room was large, with a polished wooden table big enough to accommodate twenty or thirty people. Liam wasn't at the table; instead, he was seated in a small breakfast nook set in the far wall. Covered dishes crowded each other on the small, round table, and a platter before him was already heaped with food. Delicious odors rose from the food and made Angela's mouth water.

At the sound of her footsteps Liam glanced up. "You decided to join me, I see." A glint of bawdy humor touched his eyes. "And clothed."

"Disappointed?"

"Not really. In fact, I find you more attractive clothed. Rumpled, but attractively rumpled."

Angela felt color rise to her cheeks and silently berated herself. She said, "Tell me, Mr. O'Laughlin. Do you do *anything* before breakfast?"

"I stopped in to see you, didn't I? But I will confess that is unusual. I woke with a dim memory of a beautiful woman driving me home, and I wanted to assure myself that I hadn't been dreaming. Usually when I wake, I remember nothing. Also, after a night of imbibing, I wake up with a trencherman's appetite, and I find food a most effective antidote for a hangover." He gestured expansively. "Sit. Eat."

She pulled out the chair across from him, started to slide in, then got her first look out the window beside where they sat.

"My God!" she exclaimed.

The window looked on nothing but sky. Then she looked down and saw the cliff plunging dizzily away to the rocks below, the surf foaming around them. For a moment Angela thought she could see the doll-like figure of a man broken in death on the rocks.

Vertigo seized her, and she staggered back. Dimly, she heard his voice. "Angela? What is it?"

Then he had her by the elbow, and it all went away, and everything was normal again.

She mustered a wan smile. "It's all right. That—that view was so unexpected. It shook me a little."

"I *am* sorry. I should have warned you. I'm so used to it. You have a thing about heights?"

"We-ll, yes, I suppose I do."

Liam pulled the chair around until it faced away from the window. Angela sat gingerly and was relieved when she realized that she was far enough back so that she didn't have to see that terrifying drop.

"Food, food in the belly," he said authoritatively. "That's what you need."

She had to laugh. "To listen to you, one would think that food solved all problems."

"Most, my dear Angela, most," he said complacently, then bit into a slice of Irish bacon.

Angela looked at the dishes spread before her and lifted the lid of a large tureen. Scrambled eggs, light and fluffy. Another dish yielded both bacon and link sausage and another, kippered herring. She helped herself to bacon, eggs, and orange juice and took one of the scones, which proved to be much lighter than the ones served at the Clare Inn. Hungrily, she began to eat.

Once during the meal, she started a question, but he waved her to silence. "I have never believed in mixing food with conversation. Eccentric, perhaps, but humor me." His teeth flashed white as he grinned. "And I do have a reputation as an eccentric to maintain. My adoring fans expect it of me."

Almost on cue with the last bite taken, a maid came to serve coffee. Liam made a sound of contentment, took a sip of coffee, and fixed Angela with his glance. "Now, I believe you were about to make a comment? Or ask a question?"

Angela felt a little uncomfortable under his penetrating gaze. She had the impression of a man capable of total, perhaps absolute, concentration. A few minutes ago, it had been his breakfast, now it was her. She had to admit that it was probably a part of his charm and was likely responsible, to a large extent, for his success as a film star.

"I was only going to ask why you won't let interviewers or photographers come here?"

"A man's home is his castle. Surely you know that. And this is my home."

"Yet most movie stars, upon occasion, at least, open their homes to the press."

"I am not 'most' movie stars. I am Liam O'Laughlin!"

Spoken by most men, his words would have been offensively arrogant, but coming from Liam O'Laughlin, it was simply a statement of fact, nothing more.

"Most film people can't live without the limelight," he said. "I accept it as necessary, but I have to have privacy, a hidey-hole, if you like, or I would go stark, raving bonkers. Here, I am my own man. The public and the press have no claim on me."

"I can understand that, but—" She sighed, looking around. "But it is too bad."

"Now why is that?"

"I've been in Ireland for several days, and this is the first keep I've been inside. I'm aching to explore it."

He shrugged. "Not only may you explore it, but I'll give you a guided tour. Then you can go back to your friends in America and tell them you had Liam O'Laughlin as a tour guide." His smile had a sarcastic twist. "They may even ask for your autograph. I haven't asked, but I assume you *are* American?"

She nodded, hesitated for a moment, then blurted, "But I'm a little more than that. I'm also a professional photographer, in Ireland doing a feature on castles."

She had tensed herself for an explosion, but his expression didn't alter. "Pictures I will not allow, but you may explore to your heart's content, and I will make a bargain with you—I am what you Americans would call a castle buff. I am familiar with every castle in Ireland, several that you would never know about. In exchange for your not sneaking a camera in here by the Gods, if you knew how I detested those bloody things!—I will show you castles far more interesting than this small keep."

"Why would you do that?" she asked in surprise.

He frowned, the question clearly taking him by surprise. "To be candid, I'm not sure. I may be simply lonely for female companionship. I've been drunk for two weeks, and it's time I called a halt. In addition, I think I like you."

She said mischievously, "Even if I am an American and a photographer?"

"One of my wives, the second, was American, and I do believe she was the best of a bad lot. As for your being a photographer, we must have an understanding about that. You may never take my picture. You know, certain primitive tribes believe that the camera steals the soul. It could be true."

"I'm surprised that a man in your profession believes such nonsense."

"Nonsense?" His eyes went bleak and cold. "Often, in that blackest of hours just before dawn, I have wondered if that first movie camera so long ago did not indeed steal away my soul."

"Hello?"

"This is Angela."

"Yes, Angela, this is Mr. Midnight. I've been waiting for your call. Tell me, how are you? Is everything all right?"

"Yes. Everything is fine."

"Good. Now, what have you been doing?"

"Taking pictures of Irish castles."

"Will you have the pictures finished in time for your deadline?"

"Yes."

"Good. Now, have you noticed anyone following you, or have you met anyone who has shown an unusual interest in you?"

Angela was silent.

"Angela, do you hear me?"

"Yes, I hear you."

"Then answer the question, please."

"I haven't noticed anyone following me, but I have made a friend."

"A friend? Angela, you will tell me about this friend. You will tell me everything you know."

"It is a man. He's a movie star. His name is Liam O'Laughlin. He is going to show me some castles. He is divorced. He lives in a keep—"

"All right, Angela, that's enough! Do you remember that I warned you to be wary of strangers?"

"Yes. But he isn't a stranger. I feel that I already know him. Because he's a movie star, I suppose."

"Angela, would you be unhappy if I asked you not to see this man, this Liam O'Laughlin, again?"

"Yes, I would be unhappy."

"Did he seek you out, or did you meet by accident?"

"By accident."

"Are you sure of that?"

"Yes, I'm sure."

"Well, then, I suppose your seeing him will do no great harm. In fact, having him with you may protect you. But remember, Angela, you must not get too involved with this man or with any man. You can be friends, but there can be no lasting relationships. Do you understand?"

Again, she was silent.

"Angela, do you *understand?*"

"Yes—I understand."

"It is for your own safety, Angela. It is important for your own welfare. You must trust me in this.

"Now, remember your instructions. You will call me in seven days from today, at close to midnight, and when you hear the name, Mr. Midnight, you will immediately fall into a deep hypnotic state. Do you understand?"

"Yes, I understand."

"Good. Now, when you put down the telephone receiver, you will forget this conversation, and you will feel very, very relaxed and very happy. Hang up now, Angela, and if there is a God, may he protect you from harm!"

Six

———◆→———

Liam O'Laughlin was a changed man after the night he met Angela Williams or, to be more precise, from the moment he stood over her sleeping form in the four-poster bed in his guest room.

Of course, he admitted to himself, he was always a changed man when he met and fell in love with a new woman.

And he *was* in love with her. The question was— would this love endure?

Whatever else he might be, Liam never lied to himself, and he was well aware that he was a difficult man to live with. He knew he drank too much, and he knew that he was subject to fits of depression and moods so dark they were almost psychotic in nature, yet he always treated a woman with tenderness and consideration—until she betrayed him.

He had been told that he expected the impossible in a woman, that the ideal in his mind simply did not exist, yet he was convinced that that was not true, and now he was positive that he had finally found the woman he had been seeking, and found her in Angela Williams.

She was one of the most beautiful women he had ever known, but it wasn't her beauty alone that drew him. She was bright and quick, and there was a freshness about her, an innocence that he had never encountered before.

It never once entered his mind that she might not love him.

Didn't they always?

It had begun when he was nineteen and driving a

taxi in Dublin. The son of a poor farmer, he had left County Clare and headed for Dublin, knowing there had to be more to life than tilling soil as thin as paper and about as productive; shoveling animal dung; and getting drunk with the lads on Saturday night. He was not consumed by any burning ambition; certainly he had no thought of becoming an actor. After success came, he told all interviewers that he had wanted to act for as long as he could remember. "I recall playing dead one day in my cradle. Scared my poor old mum half to death!"

That was expected of him. All actors wanted to perform from the cradle, didn't they?

He went to Dublin to escape the grinding poverty and drudgery of the farm and found that he liked driving a taxi. In those days his nature was sunny— the moods did not come on him until much later—his talk bubbled with laughter, and he could talk wittily on any subject, even if he knew nothing about it.

In later years he recognized that he had been an actor even then—at least an entertainer. The tourists loved his blarney and the brogue, which thickened when an American was in his taxi, and his Irish good looks didn't hurt. Especially with the ladies.

Ah, the ladies! How they loved him.

He could drive them from the airport and have most of them eager to bed him by the end of the trip. At first he was as greedy as a little boy, locked overnight in a candy shop, and about as discriminating, but in time he became more selective.

And by growing selective, he became, almost overnight, a movie star.

One afternoon he picked up a man and a woman at the Dublin Airport and drove them to the Royal Hibernian Hotel. He knew, of course, that they were Americans before they spoke a word. The man was tall, thin, close to sixty-five, and he was furious, waving a huge, fuming cigar like a fire stick. A limousine had been supposed to meet them and had failed to show up.

The woman—sleek, model-chic, not much more than twenty—treated the matter with cool disdain, and her husband with contempt.

Liam smelled a big tip, and he went into his routine—he was charming and witty, and his brogue was as thick as moss. By the time they reached the hotel, the man had relaxed and not only was laughing but entering enthusiastically into Liam's discourse on politics, the world, Americans, and the Irish.

The woman took on a humid look, watching Liam's reflection avidly in the rear-view mirror, constantly moistening her lips, and Liam knew that he had a sexual conquest, if he cared to pursue it.

At the hotel the man tipped him lavishly and said, "I recognize a bullshit blarney line, bucko, and you've got one of the best. I lived here for five years as an Irish citizen, trying to finagle the IRS, but it didn't work out too well. Now don't get me wrong, I don't mind being put on, if it's by the best. Here's my card," he said, fishing one out of his pocket. "Write your name and cab number. I may use you instead of that fucking limo driver!"

Liam was film fan enough to recognize the name—William Thompson. A legend in the business, director of some thirty films, mostly action movies, some shot in Ireland, winner of two Academy Awards. The name, Big Bill, was synonymous with the film industry.

Liam wrote his name, taxi number, and the telephone number of the company on the card, thanked Thompson for his tip, and considered that the end of it.

However, the next afternoon he received a message via radio that Thompson required his services. Liam drove across town, humming happily to himself. The doorman at the Royal Hibernian was expecting him and told him to wait a few minutes. Then young Mrs.

Thompson came tripping down the steps. The doorman handed her in and waved Liam off.

Liam said, "The boss—he's not coming?"

"The boss? You mean Big Bill?" Her laughter trilled. "He hasn't come in years, sweetie." She went through the lip-licking routine. "No, sweetie, I'm the one who called you."

Liam was not particularly shocked by her frankness, a taxi driver heard it all. But he had formed a liking for Thompson, and this woman irritated him. He turned to look back, to tell her to get out. It was a mistake. She giggled, squirming, showing a lot of enticing thigh, and moistened her lips.

He turned back and said stiffly, "Where would you like to go, madam?"

"Oh, my! What's happened to that lovely Irish brogue?"

Sweet Jesus, Liam thought. She's as empty-headed as a loon!

"Why, I want to see the sights of Dublin, what else? A short tour. We have to be back by three, because Big Bill will be back by five, so that won't give us much time."

He chose to ignore the connotations of that remark. Yet he had little choice but to give her the tour. For the first time he wished that he was driving a large vehicle, with a partition between himself and his passenger. But Dublin taxis were small, and he was as aware of her as if she had been naked in the back seat. For the better part of the trip, she rode on the edge of the seat, like a predatory bird on a perch, and once, half turning, Liam almost bumped noses with her.

He kept up a running commentary—half of the time not even knowing what he said. He could not recall ever being so nervous around a female. The feeling was not sexual in nature; he had never been less attracted to a woman.

She must have had brains enough to recognize this because she soon sat back, retreating into a sulky silence. Shortly she said, "That's enough. Let's go back to the hotel."

Liam took the quickest and most direct route back, pulling into the loading zone. She didn't get out when the doorman opened the car door.

Liam faced around and told her the fare. She stared at him, lovely face marred by a frown. "I thought you'd park somewhere and come up with me."

"No need for that, madam. You can just pay me here."

"I'll pay you nothing! You can go whistle for your money, unless you come up with me. What is it with you, anyway?"

She whisked out of the taxi before Liam could respond. He started to charge after her, then subsided. It was worth the loss of the fare to rid himself of her.

Before he could drive away, someone slipped into the back seat. "Don't fret, bucko. I'll take care of the fare. Is that your real name, by the way, Liam O'Laughlin?"

Liam turned his head to stare at Bill Thompson. "It's the name I was born with, aye."

Thompson stroked his mustache with his thumb. "It has a ring to it, we won't have to change it."

Equal parts of anger and bewilderment battered at Liam's brain. "It's daft you must be. It's like you're talking to me through a fog."

"It'll clear up," Thompson said comfortably. He peeled the wrapper from a Havana cigar. "Why don't you drive us to a cozy pub, and we'll discourse over a few Irish whiskies. You *do* drink?"

"Of course I drink, damnit!"

"Good. I never could trust a man who doesn't drink. Find us a pub, Liam, one that never heard of an American tourist. If such a place exists in Dublin."

Liam still hesitated, trying to make up his mind if

the man was loony or if, worse yet, he was seeking a dark alley where he could safely blow his, Liam's, brains out.

"Man, I didn't lay a finger on your wife."

"Don't you think I know that? I led her into thinking I had an appointment until five, then waited for her to come back. If you're wondering how that tells me anything. . . . Dumb Dora never takes a taxi driver to bed in a strange room but always lures them back to our hotel room. She's afraid she'll pick up some strange bug. Can you imagine what it does to a man"—for the first time his face showed bitterness— "to spy on his own wife? She's screwed a taxi driver in about every city in the civilized world, and some not so civilized. She has a thing about hack drivers, does Dora."

Moved, Liam said, "For God's sake, man, why don't you kick her arse out then?"

"Because I need her. She's a lovely piece, and a movie director needs a beautiful broad on his arm. Besides, I usually don't give a rat's ass what she does. This case is different."

"Why am I different?"

"Find us a pub and I'll tell you."

The pub was one Liam frequented, well out of the path of tourists. It was boisterous, but the noisiest group was clustered around the bar, and they found a secluded booth in the back. As a rule Liam didn't drink on duty, but he was consumed by curiosity.

He waited until Thompson had taken a hearty belt of Irish whiskey and lit a long cigar. Then he said, "Now, are you going to tell me what's on your mind?"

Instead of answering directly, Thompson seemingly struck off on a tangent. "What's your education, Liam?"

Again taken off balance by this bewildering man, Liam answered without thinking. "High school, or at least the equivalent to it in the States."

"How's your memory? I mean, remembering what you've read?"

"Better than average, it always seemed to me."

Suddenly he struck the table a blow with the flat of his hand. "Sweet Jesus! Are you ever getting around to it?"

Unruffled, Thompson said, "Ever do any acting?"

"Acting, is it? Never had any desire." A light dawned, and Liam whooped with laughter, a rolling bellow that was to become his trademark, both on- and off-screen. "You mean all this—you want me to *act* in one of your films?"

"Not act, bucko. I want you to star in it."

"Star? *Star?* Me, who's never acted, who's never been before a movie camera? It's me you want to make a star? Man, you're daft!"

"When Bill Thompson says he'll make a star out of a person, it happens. I have never been wrong. I have taken three men and two women from obscurity and made overnight stars of them. I may not be good at picking my women"—his full mouth twisted—"but what I call my star instinct is infallible. I knew the instant I saw you, heard that voice. You have the looks, the voice, the presence, the charisma, but most of all you have that predatory aura that attracts the broads. A look that can be tender but hints at a strong undercurrent of danger."

"And not a wee bit of acting experience."

"Not necessary," Thompson said around his cigar. "I didn't say I'd make an actor out of you. I said a star. They're not always synonymous. Errol Flynn, bless his randy soul, couldn't act for shit, yet he was larger than life up there on the screen. Many movie stars can't act, they're personalities, always playing themselves. That's what I want you to do, bucko, play Liam O'Laughlin. Sure, in the promo bits, we'll mention your being with the Abbey Players, bullshit like that."

"Won't they check and find out?" To his amazement Liam realized that he was almost believing this crazy man.

Thompson grinned, blowing smoke. "Won't matter. If asked, just tell the press boys you were so lousy you were ashamed and changed your name. They'll love it."

"Sweet Jesus," Liam said in a choked voice. "You *are* serious."

"Completely, bucko."

Liam sensed that, in the saner light of morning, he would doubt this conversation had ever taken place. But everything considered, what did he have to lose? "You may be as daft as the village idiot, but by Christ, I almost believe you!"

"If I'm the village idiot, bucko," Thompson said, giving him a yellow-toothed grin, "I'm a successful one. A deal then?" He stuck out his hand.

Liam took it. "A deal."

"One thing I'll tell you now," Thompson said, without relinquishing his grip. "If you had banged Dumb Dora, no dice, no matter what star quality I might see in you. I don't care how many hack drivers she screws, but I'll be goddamned if I'll work with anyone who's cuckolding me. You just remember that, bucko!"

Everything Big Bill Thompson promised came true.

Oh, it wasn't quite that simple, that easy, but what few difficulties there were either Liam overcame by his adaptability and his desire to cooperate, or Bill Thompson brushed aside by sheer force of will. His confidence in his ability to handle any and all phases of movie making would have been insufferable arrogance in anyone else. But how could it be arrogant when there seemed to be nothing Thompson did not know of the business? Not only did he produce and direct the movies, but he even performed cameo roles, and damned near stole a picture with only five minutes on the screen.

The morning after their handshake agreement in the pub, Liam signed a six-month option on his services, to William Thompson, Associates. The money wasn't great, by movie industry standards, but it was ten times more than Liam earned driving a taxi.

It would take six months to get the movie ready to roll, and during that time Thompson turned Liam over to a voice coach. "A great part of your future is linked with that voice of yours. But it needs training and discipline so that you'll know how to use it."

"How about acting lessons?"

"Hell, no! I thought I made that clear. When you step before the camera for the first time, you're a virgin, bucko, *my* virgin! That's the way I want it. *I* take your maidenhead. More virgins have been turned into frigid bitches by men who didn't know what the hell they were doing. When I get you before the camera, I don't want you already deflowered by some bum. Two weeks before we roll, I'll give you a shooting script and a few sessions with a dialogue coach."

The story Thompson was filming was the Sir Walter Scott novel, *Quentin Durward*, more than slightly rewritten, of course, by Thompson himself.

"Scott once wrote that the sight of a ruined castle always made him wish to reconstruct the life and times of what he saw," Thompson said. "I feel the same way."

"But as I recall from my reading of *Quentin Durward*, there weren't that many castles, if any," Liam said.

"Wait'll you read the script, bucko. I've put a few castles in. But what I'm after is the feel of the period, the times, and the people. There's much derring-do in Scott's novel, and a sweep of romantic history. Most of all, it has a happy ending. Too many of the flicks being made by the goddamned snot noses today are full of losers. I'm fed up with it, and I think the movie public is as well."

As the first day of shooting neared, Liam was a nervous wreck, cursing himself for ever agreeing to such insanity. He was certain that the moment he began to speak he would be laughed off the set. Although the story was set in thirteenth-century France, Thompson had elected to shoot it in Ireland. The first scene was to take place on the banks of a flooded river.

When Liam, made up and in costume, prepared to go before the cameras, Thompson had a few words with him, the first real counseling about the movie he had given him.

"Know your lines, bucko?"

"Right now I can say them backward and forward, but I have a sinking feeling I'll forget every word the moment it begins."

Thompson blew smoke and clapped him on the shoulder. "No, you won't. The first few minutes are all action, no dialogue. I purposely set it up that way. You're going to struggle across that flooded river, remember, and there's these two guys on the opposite bank, laughing their heads off at you, while you nearly drown. They won't lift a pinky to help. You're mad as hell when you finally make it, and you're ready to beat the shit out of them. The fact that one is King Louis the Eleventh in disguise has no bearing, since you don't know that yet. Take my word, you're going to be mad enough to carry the scene through."

The ford *was* deep, with a drop-off near the far bank. Not having been warned of this, Liam fell in over his head and came close to drowning, for he had never been a particularly good swimmer.

He came up spluttering and coughing, charging up the bank at the two actors, one portraying the king in his common disguise as a merchant; the other portraying Tristan l'Hermite, marshal of France. Liam berated them soundly for almost letting him drown;

although some of his lines departed from the script, such was his real outrage that the scene worked beautifully.

After Thompson yelled, "Cut!", Liam strode over to him. Dripping, he stormed, "You cigar-chomping sonofabitch, you could have warned me! You had a pit dug in that river, didn't you? Sweet Jesus, I could have drowned!"

Thompson bared his teeth in a grin. "You can't drown an Irishman, didn't you know that? Besides, it made the scene work, didn't it? I figured it would make you mad enough so that if you forgot your lines, it wouldn't matter a damn. It was a perfect take, it goes into the can. Just think, bucko, how you'd feel at the end of the day if we'd gone through about a dozen takes to get it right."

Liam sulked for half a day, but he was soon laughing at himself. Thompson was right—the bastard seemed to always be right.

Things not only went easier after that, but became downright pleasant. Two days later Liam played his first scene with Wendy Frost, who played opposite him as Jaqueline. The script called for them to be in love, and it was easy for Liam, since he did fall in love with Wendy.

At this particular time in life Liam was twenty-three, and Wendy Frost was only nineteen. Yet, at times she seemed much older. At other times she seemed little more than a teasing, fun-loving teenager, an impression heightened by the fact that she was tiny, as fragile-appearing as a golden-haired, blue-eyed doll.

In their first love scene, Liam felt like an awkward dolt, towering high over her, and he took her into his arms very gingerly, and his lips barely touched hers.

"For God's sake, Liam!" Thompson roared. "She's not made of porcelain, she won't break! I've seen more passion in a puppet than you're showing me.

This movie may be set in times of knights gallant and ladies fair, where the boudoir was for sleeping only—at least that's the way Scott wrote it—but I want the love scenes earthy, steamy. Now hold her and kiss her like you mean it. I want a little Tom Jones in this film. A little lust is box office."

Her face turned away from Thompson, Wendy winked and whispered, "Try it, you might like it."

Goaded, Liam crushed her into his arms, his mouth descending on hers so hard that their teeth clicked together.

In the scene Wendy was a barmaid, wearing a barmaid's scanty dress, and he discovered that she was indeed no doll. Her figure was curved and exciting, her breasts full against his chest as her body molded to his.

His reaction was immediate—he got an erection. As he realized what was happening, he tried to pull back, but she tightened her arms around him, and he went with the sway.

"That's better!" Thompson bellowed. "Let's run through it again, and maybe we'll have a take."

As they waited for the signal to roll again, Wendy smiled wickedly. "You see, I said you might like it. One thing—"

Liam, trying to stand so the crew wouldn't be witness to his embarrassing condition, said, "What's that?"

"Maybe, the next time, before we clinch before the cameras, we should take care of"—her glance went down—"*that* in advance, so it won't happen again."

This, in time, they did, and they were married on the set the day the picture was wrapped up. It was Liam's first time in love, and he was enchanted by Wendy, drugged by her abandoned sexuality, and blinded to everything else about her.

The picture opened to generally bad reviews, although a few reviewers had a kind word or two for

Liam's voice and his strong presence on-screen. For the first few weeks after its release, the movie didn't do very well.

"Don't fret it, bucko," Thompson said, waving his cigar. "Bad reviews don't mean shit to Middle America. Wait until the film's in general release. Word of mouth will make it a hit. You're a star, Liam O'Laughlin."

Again, Thompson's prediction came true. But by that time Liam's state of mind was low, and the good news failed to cheer him up. He had taken Wendy on a honeymoon trip to Hilo, and he soon found that she slept with anyone who appealed to her, as readily as she had gone to bed with him.

The first time he caught her at it, she laughed at him. "You're behind the times, Irish. I'm a liberated woman. The time is long past when a woman has to be sexually faithful to one man."

"But you married me!"

"So? If I see some stud I'd like to sleep with, I'll sleep with him. You have the same freedom. Try it, you might like it." She gave him that puckish, oh-so-innocent smile.

Liam was truly baffled, his anger blown away by the enigma she presented. "But *why* did you marry me?"

"Several reasons. I like you, and you're going to be a big star. Big Bill says so, and he's never wrong. Besides, being married has its conveniences."

Liam turned on his heel and walked away.

They had already gone their separate ways by the time they returned to Ireland. Wendy left at once for Hollywood, shrugging when Liam told her he was filing for an immediate divorce.

In Ireland there was a wire waiting for him. It was from Thompson, asking him to come immediately to California. Liam ignored the wire. He brooded over the breakup with Wendy, drinking more than was good for him. Now that his fame was growing, he discovered that most of his old friends were either too much in awe of him or too envious to renew friendships on the old grounds. This depressed him even further.

He was back a week before Thompson finally tracked him down via telephone. "What's with you, bucko? Didn't you get my wire?"

"Yes, I got it."

"Then why didn't you answer? *Quentin Durward* is catching on, just like I said it would, and it's going to make a bundle for everybody. You're what we in movieland call a hot property. I have another project in the works, and I want you out here, to star in it."

"Bill, I've left Wendy, I'm getting a divorce."

"So? What else is new? What does one thing have to do with the other?"

"But we've only been married a few weeks. Sweet Jesus!"

"That's no record. Close but no cigar. What happened? You catch her in the sack with another guy?"

"How'd you know that?"

A windy sigh came over the wire. "Liam, Wendy has calluses on her butt from sleeping around. I think she started at about age ten, maybe younger."

"If you knew that, why didn't you warn me?"

"Would it have done any good?"

Liam was silent.

"Of course not! You had the hots for her, and I knew it would be a waste of breath. Anyway, I knew you'd find out soon enough. Now don't tell me you're all broken up over the tramp and not in the mood to work?"

"Well, I don't feel like standing up and cheering!"

"Good! The film in preparation is a modern yarn, an adventure story, and you're playing a soldier of fortune whose wife has left him for another man. Cynical, disillusioned with women, the character doesn't care whether he lives or dies. Now, wouldn't you call that perfect typecasting?"

Despite himself Liam had to laugh. "You canny bastard! I wouldn't put it past you to have arranged the whole thing with Wendy!"

"If I did," Thompson said cheerfully, "I'd say I should have an Oscar nomination for directing. Now, why don't you get your ass on a big bird and fly out here?"

The soldier-of-fortune picture was a hit right from the first, and Liam's star status was assured.

During the next five years Liam never made less than two pictures a year, three more altogether with Big Bill Thompson. He was in great demand by every studio and every important producer. Along with the fame came the money—he could ask almost any fee he desired. But since he always felt some nudgings of guilt about his sudden, incredible rise to fame and fortune, Liam never went overboard with his demands. First, he would satisfy himself as to the suitability of a film script, often consulting with Thompson, and then he would settle for a reasonable sum of money, with a cut of the net. At the end of the five years, he was a millionaire several times over; and since he still made his home in Ireland, he escaped much of the tax bite.

Yet, he was not happy, and the black moods came on him with frequency.

He had weathered another divorce by that time, which did little to help his state of mind, but much of his unhappiness came from the fact that he was never given a chance to *act*. He was still playing Liam O'Laughlin, just speaking different lines in each new film.

Secretly he began taking acting lessons. After a year, his teacher, a Russian whose English was barely understandable, told him that he was ready to take on almost any role. "Nossing is beyond your range, Lime!"

Liam went to Thompson, who was readying a new picture, with Liam penciled in for the leading role.

"After this film, Bill, I want a part in a serious movie, a role I can get my teeth into."

Thompson rolled the cigar back and forth between his teeth. "I knew this would happen sooner or later. A serious picture, bucko? What do you think you've been doing? I understand you got close to a half mil for your last one. That's not serious enough?"

"Damnit, you know what I mean! I'm not putting down what I've been doing, but they're entertainments."

"A message picture, is that it?" Thompson sneered. "Or maybe Shakespeare?"

Liam flushed. "Maybe, maybe not. I just feel that I'm not exploring my full potential."

"Who gave you that line of shit? No, don't bother." Thompson held up a staying hand. "Some phony-ass acting teacher, I'm sure. Did you ever hear, 'If you want to send a message, use Western Union'? De-Mille, I think, said it."

"Bill, you're not taking me seriously!"

"Oh, I'm taking you seriously, seriously enough to tell you to forget it. Damnation, bucko, you're the most bankable male star around. You try something like you have in mind, somebody will lose a bundle. You've heard the expression, laughingstock?"

Liam said huffily, "Some critics have written that I would do fine in a good acting role."

"How many times do I have to tell you?" Thompson snorted. "Critics do not, repeat, do *not*, sell movies. The people who line up at the box office don't give a tinker's damn for what the critics think."

"Well, I happen to believe you're wrong!"

"Your privilege, bucko." Thompson shrugged. "Just don't try to involve me in it. Now, if you don't mind too much, shall we get on with our 'entertainment'?"

Liam knew it was futile to argue further. Many movie critics were beginning to hint that Big Bill Thompson had lost his touch, that he was behind the times—moviegoers were growing tired of his old-fashioned action movies. Liam had refused to believe this; now he wasn't so sure.

He made the picture with Thompson—another adventure film about a safari hunter, a dying breed of man. The critics dumped on it, aside from a few kind comments about Liam O'Laughlin, but the movie did very well. Liam also did well financially. By that time he was married again, to Kathy Desmond, a well-known fashion model, and he was sure that Kathy was the woman he had been searching for all his life.

In his married bliss and flush with money, he decided, after a cautious probing for outside financing and finding absolutely no interest, to make the movie he wanted, backing it mostly with his own money. He discovered unexpected support from Kathy; she agreed that it was time he was performing in a "serious" picture. If he refused to stretch his talent, he would soon vegetate.

The property he chose was a quiet, introspective novel that had received good reviews but very few sales. Liam liked it because it struck him as a demanding role. The story was concerned basically with two characters—a middle-aged, shy schoolteacher, a recent widower who had never experienced any great love, nor any sort of emotional upheaval in his life, and a young woman of twenty-one, a student of his, a virgin without any experience at love.

There was no dash or fire, no derring-do, in Liam's role, although the script called for him to bloom toward the end of the movie, as their love grew, turning from the drab schoolteacher into a man with a little more color. But it was still a far cry from the Liam O'Laughlin that movie audiences were accustomed to seeing up there on the big screen. When it was learned that Liam was largely backing the movie with his own money, it was not too difficult to arrange the rest of the financing.

The movie was made without a great deal of advance publicity; he thought that the new Liam O'Laughlin should spring on the public unexpectedly. "Like being reborn, my love," Kathy said. "You're going to love being the new Liam O'Laughlin."

At the first preview Liam attended, the audience sat as though stunned through the first few minutes, and then the whispers and the restlessness began. It was clear to Liam that the audience was bored and disappointed. At one very serious moment several people laughed, and before the picture ended, Liam took Kathy by the hand and hauled her from the theater.

For the next few days Liam drank, getting even more smashed every time another bit of bad news drifted in. The critics called the film "O'Laughlin's Folly," and one and all labeled it a candidate for the worst movie of the year.

The decision was made by both the distributors and the exhibitors to quietly bury it. Liam thought briefly of distributing the film himself, but he was told that he would not only be sending good money after bad, but the only places he would be able to get it shown were the art theaters, if there.

He received a wire from Big Bill Thompson: "I never say I told you so. Am working on new project for the old Liam O'Laughlin."

Kathy jeered at him for hiding from the pity and scorn, then tried to console him in bed but turned away in disgust—he was too drunk to perform.

Three days later a TV news flash announced the sudden death of Big Bill Thompson from a heart attack.

The following afternoon Liam came across his wife in bed with another man. He stayed sober long enough to consult an attorney about starting divorce proceedings, then had remained drunk until the morning in Moher Keep, when he stood looking down at the sleeping form of Angela Williams.

Seven

The day was gray and gloomy, threatening rain. Angela straightened up from where she had been squatting while taking a picture of the remains of a castle. Except for a pile of rubble, all that was left of the ancient structure was a turret, looming up like a huge chimney. It was hardly a tourist attraction, and she was probably wasting film, insofar as the pics editor was concerned, but she hadn't been able to resist.

Brown-and-white cattle grazed placidly around the ruins, lifting their heads now and then to gaze at her with incurious eyes. There wasn't another soul in sight and no structures of any kind. For a brief moment Angela experienced a sense of disorientation, almost as if she had been drawn back in time a hundred years or more. She shivered, hugging herself, then turned to make sure that the Rolls was still parked in the lane behind her. The sense of going back in time left her, and she was again in the present, very much back in the present with Liam O'Laughlin waiting in the Rolls for her.

She saw his face in the rolled-down window and waved. Liam waved back, motioning, calling something. The car was too distant for his words to register. Then he pointed north. Looking, Angela saw a slanting sheet of rain moving rapidly in her direction.

She began to run back toward the Rolls, but the rain caught her, and she was soaked by the time she tumbled, laughing, into the car.

"You'll catch your death," Liam scolded.

He took a towel from the car bar and scrubbed her wet hair vigorously.

"But it feels marvelous, Liam, invigorating," she said, voice muffled behind the towel.

When she was reasonably dry, Liam told the chauffeur to drive on, and he poured a brandy for Angela. "Drink it," he said in a grumbling voice. "It should invigorate you."

Angela drank it, welcoming the warmth coursing through her. She noticed that Liam didn't pour anything for himself; she hadn't seen him drink anything but wine since that drunken night when she had met him. She wanted to make some comment about it but sensed that it could be a mistake.

After a moment she was aware that he was staring at her strangely. Unexpectedly, he said, "I've never asked you. . . . How old are you, love?"

She hesitated for just a moment, then gave him a flashing look. "I'm twenty-two."

He turned his face away, but in profile she saw that he was frowning. "I feel a sense of deja vu," he muttered, then laughed harshly. "Just like reliving that double-damned movie!"

"What movie, Liam? I don't understand."

He looked at her with bitter eyes. "I know you haven't seen it, nobody has but myself and a few other unfortunate souls, but surely you've heard of it. O'Laughlin's Folly, the wise-asses called it."

"O'Laughlin's Folly?" she said, still puzzled. "Oh—you mean your last movie!"

"That's what I mean," he said grimly.

She failed to see the connection between her age and the movie—all she knew about it was that it had never been released—but she was fearful of asking Liam questions in his present mood.

She retired into silence, feeling subdued and uneasy. Evidently there was some situation in the film that paralleled the relationship between her and Liam. And again, as she had so often of late, Angela wondered just what that relationship was. At times she was certain that she loved him—for the intensity of feeling she had for him could not be called anything else. And then she would feel that she must get away from him, that there was some kind of danger in caring for him, that she must remain free and uncommitted at all costs.

Also, there was the sex thing. She knew very well his reputation as a womanizer, and she couldn't help but wonder why he hadn't made a single sexual overture to her—unless she wanted to count the repartee in the keep, when he had come into the guest room, but that had been just talk. They had been together constantly, and he had always been solicitous and charming, but outside of some more or less friendly kissing, he had made no attempt to come on to her. Was she *that* unattractive? Or maybe he was gay. So many actors were, she knew; some you would never imagine. Of course, it wasn't that she wanted him to make a move. It just seemed odd that he hadn't. *Could* he be gay? She shot a glance at him from the corner of her eye. His face looked grim and closed. She turned her head toward the window. The possibility that Liam O'Laughlin could be gay was a depressing thought.

The rain was heavier now, the clouds lower, and distant thunder rumbled. For most of the way back to Moher Keep, they rode in silence, Angela worrying over her dark thoughts, and Liam staring moodily out the car window.

Then abruptly Liam turned to her and smiled, and her spirits lightened as she saw that the smile was tender and pensive, not at all forced.

"You know something, Angela Williams? We've been in one another's company for the large part of the day and night for close to a week now, and I know almost nothing about you. Your life before we met, I mean."

She looked away in sudden confusion, and for some unaccountable reason, she was filled with dread.

"Angela? What is it, love? You look strange. If I've invaded forbidden territory—"

"No, it's not that." She drew a deep breath and forced herself to look at him. "What is it you want to know?"

His eyes searched hers for a moment before he said, "Well, I'd like to know everything about you."

"There's not all that much to know," she said, laughing shakily.

"I know you're from America, of course, and that you're a professional photographer. Where exactly in the States are you from?"

"From"—she cleared her throat—"in and around New York. My father was—"

"Was what?"

"He was in banking."

"You said *was*. Is your father deceased?"

"Yes. Both he and my mother were killed in—in an airplane crash six years ago."

"You were left on your own? No brothers or sisters?"

"I was an only child. I lived with an aunt, my father's sister until—until two years ago. She was quite old, and she died, too. To my knowledge I have no living relatives."

"Just an orphan, is it? Poor love." With that tender smile still intact, he touched her cheek with just the tips of his fingers. He appeared thoughtful. "This accident that killed your parents—did the plane crash into the ocean?"

"Yes."

"Ah, then that explains your fright that morning when you looked out my window and saw nothing but the sea."

"I—I suppose so." A dark shadow seemed to flit across her mind, and she turned her face away. "Liam—please, could we not talk about it any more right now?"

"Of course, Angela. I'm sorry if I upset you. I've always been a nosy bastard."

"No, no, it's all right. It's just—" Her voice died away, and she said nothing more, nor did she look at him again. She rode slumped in the corner of the seat.

To Liam, she seemed small and desolate and alone. He longed to hold her in his arms and comfort her, but something about her hinted that she would draw even farther away if he tried.

The earlier rain had been just the front edge of the storm. By the time they reached Moher Keep, it was pouring, the wind almost at gale force, and thunder rumbled menacingly.

As the Rolls drew up before the front door, Liam said to the driver, "Run inside, will you, and fetch a raincoat for Miss Williams? That's a good fellow."

In a moment the chauffeur returned with a raincoat and an umbrella. Liam bundled Angela up in the raincoat and hustled her inside, the chauffeur holding the umbrella over them. As they stepped inside the massive front door, thunder pealed, the sound echoing through the keep like cannon fire.

Angela made a small sound of distress and clung to Liam. He held her very gently.

Finally she pulled back, looking up into his face. "I'm sorry about—in the car. I was rude, and I don't know why."

He touched her cheek with just a fingertip, his face luminous with his smile. "It's all right, love. I had no right to pry." He became brisk. "Now, we have to get you out of those wet clothes. Too bad you don't have a change of clothes here. Maybe we should do something about that—" He broke off. "In the room where you slept before, there's a robe. It's much too enormous for that delicate body of yours, but it'll have to do. Take off your wet things, soak in a hot bath, and then come on down to the study. I'll have a roaring fire and a drink ready for you. Perhaps even some supper?" He looked at her searchingly. "All right with you? I know we planned to dine out, but it's a bloody beastly night, fit for nary man nor beast."

She nodded mutely.

He gave her a playful swat on the bottom. "All right then, along with you now."

Liam stood staring after her as she trudged up the narrow staircase. He was bemused, wondering what he was letting himself in for. Before this, he'd had no cause to question his love for her—and he still didn't question *that*—but she hadn't turned strange on him before.

But then, he amended quickly, that was bad phrasing. She hadn't turned strange on him until he questioned her about the past. Perhaps something terrible had happened that she didn't wish to recall. Even if there was something in her past she was ashamed of, there was nothing wrong in that. God knows there were several things in his own past he wasn't all that proud of!

Angela felt shy when she came downstairs. The robe fitted her like a tent and dragged on the floor. But at least the hot bath had left her warm and comfortable, and her depression had lifted. The reason for being depressed eluded her; it had come on her suddenly when Liam asked about her past.

She came into the study almost timidly. A fire was roaring in the room, and Liam was sitting on a thick rug before the hearth, leaning back against the couch, long legs stretched out before him, squinting through a glass of wine at the leaping flames. A gust of wind rattled the window by the fireplace, rain gusting against it.

The noise startled her, and she made a small sound.

Liam glanced around, his features lighting up with a smile. He came to his feet and strode toward her.

"Love, you look like a lost bunny in that robe of mine. Are you under there?"

He folded her into his arms, not holding her tightly,

but she could feel the hard contours of his body, and his male smell filled her nostrils.

"I'm under here," she said, voice muffled against his chest.

"Aye, that you are," he said in an odd voice. He disengaged himself from her and led her around the couch. "Sit, sit here by me. Did you ever taste mead?"

"I had some the first week I was in Ireland, at Bunratty Castle."

He made a face. "The tourist bit, is it?" Handing her a mug of the mead, he said, "I shouldn't scoff. I understand they do a credible job there, recreating the days of old. And God knows, we Irish shouldn't sneer at the tourists. It's undoubtedly the best industry we have."

He dropped down beside her, his long legs stretched out again. They were not close enough for their bodies to touch, but Angela felt his presence so intensely that it dazzled her senses. Quickly she sipped at the sweetish mead. It set up a glow inside her.

At a sound from the doorway, Liam turned. "Ah, there you are, Mary. Set the tray between us on the floor here." To Angela he said, "We're going to eat on the floor before the fire."

The buxom, rosy-cheeked serving girl approached hesitantly, keeping a discreet distance from Liam, and placed the laden tray awkwardly on the floor between them.

"Thanks, Mary. Will you please turn out the lights when you leave?" He winked at Angela. "We'll dine by firelight, whilst the storm rages outside."

It was snug and pleasant with only the flames illuminating the cozy room. The rain drummed against the window, and now and then thunder boomed.

The food was simple but good—lamb with potatoes and peas, accompanied by thick, dark bread. Liam continued to pour mead for Angela. He contented himself with the sherry, drinking sparingly.

Finally Angela was replete. Liam got up to move the tray away, then sat beside her again. He lit a thin black cigar.

"I've never seen you smoke before," she said in surprise.

"A cigar now and then, that's it. A small habit I picked up from the man who made me famous, you might say." He slanted a grin at her. "Except for the drink, I'm a temperate man, love."

Impulsively she said, "I haven't seen you drinking since that first night."

His face went dark, and Angela held her breath, fearing she had said too much.

"I've no reason to drink now," he said somberly. Then his face lit up with that tender, musing smile, and he turned to her. "You see, you're a good influence on me, Angela."

His eyes were intense, staring into hers, and she felt that he was probing into her very soul. A feeling of dizziness swept over her, and it took an effort of will to tear her gaze away. In some confusion she stared into the flames. Something was happening to her, she wasn't sure what. She was uncomfortably warm, which struck her as rather strange, since the fire had dwindled down. Maybe it was all the mead she had drunk.

She stirred, murmuring something, words that not even she understood, except it seemed in protest of something. Words she couldn't recall hearing echoed in her mind: *Don't get involved, Angela. It's dangerous for you.*

"Angela?"

She started violently, sure that the word came from inside her head, yet the sound of her name still hung in the air.

Dazedly she turned her head and found herself lost once again in the depths of his eyes, which were very close to hers, too close. She felt his warm breath on her face.

"Sorry, love. I guess I startled you. Dozing? Dreaming, perhaps?"

She forced a small laugh. "I must have been."

"I've had dreams, too, this past week. Of you. Silly, I suppose, but there it is. Dreams like those I had as a lad, having"—he smiled slightly—"the impossible dream, dreaming of something unattainable. Yet, that isn't true, is it? For here you are, next to me. You know, of course, that I love you. You *must* know, by this time. Sweet Jesus, I haven't tried to hide it!"

Don't get involved, Angela! She shook her head sharply and said in a barely audible voice, "Yes, I know."

"And you?"

"Yes, Liam, I love you, I guess—" Her voice caught for a moment, her mind blank. "I guess that you're the only man I've ever loved."

"Ah, my darling! That you return my love is grand news, but to know that I am the one and only! Do you know how that makes a man feel?"

She had no answer, and he waited for none. His mouth descended on hers. His lips were gentle and incredibly tender.

She murmured and looped her arms around his neck, her own lips parting. His tongue entered her mouth, not as an invasion, but as an expression of love, of need. Without taking his lips from hers, Liam untied the sash of the robe and folded it back, and Angela felt herself opening to him.

He raised his head, and his gaze moved slowly down the length of her body. As his glance found her Venus mound and lingered there, she moaned and arched slightly, as though he had touched her. It was an incredibly erotic sensation, and she shuddered, biting her lip to keep from crying out.

He combed his fingers through the thatch of blond hair, his touch light. "Ah, you're blond. I thought—"

"What?"

"Never mind, love. It's an old line, probably one I spoke in one of my films."

He kissed her nipples, first one, then the other, and his tongue touched lightly, bringing her almost unbearable pleasure. For a few minutes he caressed her exposed flesh with hands and mouth, and Angela's body leaped everywhere he touched.

Finally, in a thick voice, she said, "Liam, please—"

"Yes, love. Now, love?"

"Yes," she whispered.

He stood back from her, undressing with deft fingers. She closed her eyes, not sure as to the reason.

He said gently, "Angela? Won't you look at me? I think fair is fair, after all."

She opened her eyes slowly. At the sight of his tall figure outlined in the light from the fire, her breath left her in a rush.

Then he was with her again, kneeling on the rug. He tenderly spread her thighs, and she opened to him. He entered her, but only partway, for she flinched and cried out.

He withdrew. "Love, are you a virgin?"

Her thoughts were scattered like confetti. "I—I don't know."

"You don't *know*? How is that possible?"

With a female instinct older than time, Angela reached down between them, blindly finding his erect organ and guiding it into her again. This served her purpose, for it distracted him.

"Ah-h!" His hips drove forward, and he thrust into the liquid heat of her.

Again, she experienced a small stab of pain, lesser this time, but sweet pleasure replaced it almost immediately, blotting out any discomfort.

Her legs rose and clamped around his narrow hips. Liam pinned her shoulders to the floor with his hands and moved in and out of her with an ever-quickening rhythm.

Angela's body was a riot of sensations now. Blazing

heat spread out from her center, and every nerve sparked with a sweet, incandescent fire. As their bodies moved in unison, she lost all sense of identity and became one with him. There was room for nothing else in her mind but this man, this sweet, marvelous man, who was giving her such delight.

She felt a gathering inside her, both a blossoming and a contraction. Her body began to shudder, and as her ecstasy soared to almost unbearable heights, she reached up, cupped both hands around his face, and drew his mouth down to hers. Suddenly she cried out deep in her throat and bit down hard on his lower lip.

Almost at once Liam groaned, and she felt his penis throbbing inside her, in orgasm. She put her arms around him, holding him to her with a savage intensity. As a final shiver of ecstasy shook her, she let her arms loosen and fall away. She felt curiously disoriented and very peaceful, as if all anxiety had been drained from her.

Angela murmured an endearment as Liam slowly disengaged himself. She raised her head just enough to see him step to the fire and feed it until it was blazing. Once again, she saw his body outlined by the flames, and she realized that she wanted him again. Amazing! Then the warmth of the renewed fire reached her, and the lingering heat of her passion made her drowsy.

"Love?"

She opened her eyes with a start. "Yes, my darling?"

"Angela, I want to ask you something—"

In an intuitive leap she was sure she knew what he was going to ask, and she was not ready to make that decision. Her glance flew to the ancient clock over the mantelpiece, and she sat up.

"Good heavens, look how late it is! I must go."

"Go? Go where?" He frowned. "I thought you'd spend the night here, with me?"

She was shaking her head. "No, no, not tonight!"

She softened and smiled tentatively. "This has all happened so fast, Liam. Can't we take it one step at a time?"

"That's not my way. I'm a creature of impulse."

She touched his lips with a finger. "Then perhaps it's time you learned to proceed more slowly, considering all that's happened to you—oh!" she said in dismay. "I am sorry, Liam!"

"No, it's all right." He laughed ruefully. "And you're probably correct about proceeding more slowly, but somehow I feel that this time I'm not wrong in pushing. But I'll do as you ask and wait. One thing, however."

"What's that?"

"If you're not spending the night, the least you can do is to postpone your departure for a little while longer."

She took note of his renewed vigor with some surprise, drawing back slightly. Then she relaxed, smiling softly, and reached out for his erect penis. "I don't think a few minutes more will matter."

Since coming to Ireland, Angela had driven cautiously and was still unaccustomed to driving on the left side of the road; when she did drive, she was careful to concentrate all her attention on the act.

Tonight, however, her emotional state was such that her thoughts were directed inward, instead of to her driving. Fortunately the highway was mostly deserted, only an occasional car flashing by.

She was torn two ways. The last two hours spent with Liam were the most delightful in her experience, at least that she could recall. She loved him desperately, and yet that demon inside her head kept battering at her, the voice getting stronger and stronger: *Don't get involved, Angela. Don't get involved!*

It sounded so loud that it seemed to be inside the car, and she sent an exasperated glance at the seat beside her on the right. "Why can't I get involved with Liam? I love him!"

The words were out before she realized that the seat was empty. Angry at herself, she pounded on the empty seat with her fist.

When she glanced up again through the windshield, she was blinded by the glare of headlights of an oncoming vehicle. For a few seconds she was disoriented, sure that she had wandered over onto the right-hand side of the narrow road. Then she realized that the vehicle was on *her* side of the road. Somewhat adjusted to the glare now, she glimpsed the high, boxlike shape behind the headlights and knew that it was a truck coming toward her.

The road she was traveling on was a very narrow, two-lane country road, with box hedges crowding in on either side. From her daylight travel along these roads, Angela knew that behind some of the hedges were ancient stone fences, and even the hedges themselves presented hazard enough, since they were thick and matted together.

The truck kept coming. Angela pounded the heel of her hand on the horn, the sound blaring in the night air. The truck didn't slow, and it was now less than a hundred yards away.

She gave the wheel a hard yank to the right and sent the small car veering over to the right-hand side, praying there were no vehicles coming in that lane. There were no cars, but she had no time to breathe a sigh of relief, for the truck bulling toward her also switched lanes and was hurtling straight at her again.

Left with no time to think of alternatives, Angela gave the wheel another twist to the right and plowed nose-first into the thick hedge. The car began to slow immediately, and she tromped on the accelerator, trying to get out of the way of the truck. The hedge was too thick, however, and the car jolted to a jarring stop. But she had managed to get just far enough into the hedge to escape the truck, which passed within inches of her rear bumper, the motor roaring like an enraged beast.

Angela glanced around just in time to get a glimpse of part of the logo on the side of the truck: "——Truck Rentals."

Then the vehicle was gone, its roar receding in the night, and all was quiet. Her car engine was dead, and the only sound disturbing the silent night was the sound of metal crackling. Angela sagged as a wave of dizziness passed over her. She fought against it, and slowly her head cleared. She had been thrown forward when the car came to a crashing halt, but the seat belt had saved her from serious injury. Her chest hurt from the pressure of the belt. Cautiously she took a deep breath, and since there was no sharp pain, she concluded that no ribs had been fractured.

She turned the key to restart the motor. It started, but there was an awful clatter somewhere in the front, and when she put the car in reverse and tried to back out of the hedge, the car didn't budge. The motor stalled again, and this time it refused to start.

Angela unbuckled the seat belt and pressed down on the door handle. The door was blocked by the hedge, and she had to push with all her strength to open it enough to allow her to edge out. She scratched her hands and face as she forced her way the few feet to the roadway.

Once there, she looked in both directions. There were no cars in sight, and apparently the sounds of the crash had attracted no attention. Now, what should she do?

She tried to remember exactly where she was. She had traveled this same road almost every day since meeting Liam, but she had been so engrossed, after leaving him tonight, that she had taken little notice of what she had passed. It seemed to Angela that she had driven through a small village a short way back. There was sure to be a telephone available so she could call him.

Now why had she thought of calling him first? Why not the police? Even as the thought formed, she knew that she had no intention of calling the police. That could open up a Pandora's box of questions, and that must be avoided—for what reason she didn't know.

Determinedly, she struck out the way she had come. After walking for a half mile, she wondered idly why no cars had come along. Yet it *was* late, and this road was never crowded with traffic. She passed a darkened farm cottage now and then, but she decided against banging on a door at this hour.

She trudged on. After more than a half hour of walking, she was becoming tired and was seriously contemplating rousing some farm household after all. Then she rounded a small curve in the road and saw a few dim lights ahead.

It was a very small village—a dozen buildings altogether, including a gas station, a pub, and two stores. All were closed and dark, but at the gas station there was an outside public phone.

Angela fumbled for a coin in her purse and inserted it, praying that the phone would not be out of order. She dialed, and in a moment Liam's number was ringing.

It rang and rang, and she was despairing of it ever being answered, when the receiver was picked up on the other end and a frigid voice said, "Yes?"

In the rush of relief it was a moment before Angela could find her voice. "Please, I must speak to Liam."

"Madam, Mr. O'Laughlin is abed."

"Thomas? It *is* Thomas, isn't it? This is Angela Williams."

"Oh, Miss Williams." The voice thawed slightly.

"I know it's late, Thomas, but I need to speak to Liam. There's been an accident."

"Are you all right, Miss Williams?"

"Yes, at least I think so. But would you get Liam for me, please?"

"Of course. Right away."

Fighting back a wave of nausea, Angela leaned her forehead against the coolness of the glass, the earpiece tight against her ear.

In an amazingly short time, Liam's concerned voice said, "Thomas said you had an accident, Angela. Are you injured, love?"

"No, no." She managed a shaky laugh. "But my car won't run. Could you come get me?"

"Was another car involved?"

"There was no collision, no. A truck ran me off the road."

"Where are you?"

She told him as best she could. Before she was finished, he cut her off. "I know where you are, love. Stay right there, and I'll be with you in a few minutes."

She was leaning against the phone booth when the Rolls came purring up the road. Liam jumped out of the car and strode toward her, taking her into his arms. To her chagrin Angela found herself weeping softly.

Mouth buried in her hair, he made soothing noises. She stepped back, rubbing the tears from her eyes. "Sorry, I didn't mean to cry on your shoulder."

He grinned crookedly. "That's what it's there for. Besides, even if you aren't injured, you're probably suffering from delayed shock. Where is your car?"

"Up the road about two miles."

"What happened?"

She explained.

"A rental truck, but you didn't get the name or the license number?"

She gestured vaguely. "No, it all happened so quickly."

"We could call the police, I suppose, but I doubt it'd do much good."

"I'd rather not, Liam. There'll be questions and—"

"I understand. If it was rented, the driver was

probably an American, used to driving on the right side of the road. Likely they would never find him. Come along, we'll take you to the keep. I'll call the rental company in the morning and report it." He grinned. "It looks like you'll have to spend the night with me, after all."

She shook her head. "I'd rather not, Liam, not tonight. I must be back at the Clare Inn by midnight. I have a phone call to make."

"At midnight?" He stared at her, started to add something, then shrugged and helped her into the Rolls. Starting it, he turned the car toward the Clare Inn.

Angela put her head back against the headrest and closed her eyes. The soft murmur of the motor was a lulling sound, and Angela was almost asleep when Liam spoke again.

"There's something I want to ask you, love. This strikes me as a good time to bring it up. When your defenses are down"—he chuckled softly—"in a manner of speaking. Sneaky of me, perhaps."

"What's that, Liam?"

"I'm asking you to marry me, Angela."

Eight

"*Will* you defend me, Mr. Travers?"

Deke took his time about answering, his gaze on the pencil he was rolling back and forth across the small table in the jail conference room. Rita Spence, the woman across the table, had been arrested and charged with deliberately killing her husband in their bedroom at two o'clock in the morning. According to the story she had just told Deke, she had mistaken him for a prowler and had shot him with a pistol taken from the bedside table.

Deke looked across the table at her. She was a pretty woman in her early thirties, a brunette with a heart-shaped face and a voluptuous figure. Right now, she looked harried, the pretty face marred by a worried frown.

"The trouble with your story, Mrs. Spence, is that it's been used numerous times before, to cover for deliberate murder, so I can well understand why they're going for murder one. There is a possibility that I might bargain, get them to drop murder one, if you'll plead guilty to manslaughter. That saves the state time and money, can get you out of here on bail, and will get you a lighter sentence."

She was shaking her head vehemently. "No, no! I would still go to jail, and people would still believe that I killed Don on purpose!"

"But you didn't?"

"No, I swear!" she wailed. "There had been rumors of a prowler in the neighborhood, and Don insisted that I keep one of his guns in the bedroom. In a way he was as much to blame as I. Don was a gun nut. He had a whole room just for his gun collection. It cost a fortune. He had this macho image, you see. He said that a man should have the right to own guns, to protect himself and his loved ones. I was always nervous enough with guns in the house, but one in the bedroom, and loaded, put me into a state. When Don blundered in, waking me out of a sound sleep, I panicked and—" Her gaze dropped away. "I wasn't expecting him home that night, you see."

"Why, Mrs. Spence? Was he out of town on business?"

She shook her head and spoke in a barely audible voice. "No, he was seeing another woman. He hadn't made a secret of it, and it wasn't unusual for him to stay away all night."

Deke sighed. "And the police know this, of course?"

"Yes."

"That makes it even more damaging for you. In their thinking, you shot your husband out of jealousy, and now you're covering up."

"But that wasn't the way it was, I swear! I didn't love Don any more, and I was thinking of leaving him."

"This had been going on for some time?"

"Yes." Her mouth twisted bitterly. "I'm sure it started not too long after we were married. I'm so stupid, it just took me awhile to catch on."

"And you, Mrs. Spence. Is there another man in your life?"

Her eyes widened. "Oh, no, nothing like that!"

"You're sure now? If there is and you're trying to hide it and it comes out in the trial, it'll be just that much worse for you."

"There is no man. I think my experience with Don has turned me off men, at least for the time being."

"Mrs. Spence," Deke said patiently, "it will go better for you if you downplay that kind of talk. If what you say is true, your bitterness over your husband is understandable, but it will only place you in a bad light if it comes out in court. I'm not telling you to lie, just don't volunteer. From this moment on, speak only in answer to a direct question."

She leaned forward eagerly. "Then you will take my case?"

"I'm not quite ready to commit myself fully, but it's possible."

Disappointment shadowed her face. "You're thinking of the money, aren't you? There's very little, and I know your fees are high. Don made good money, but he spent it almost as fast as he earned it. About all he left me is the house, and that's heavily mortgaged. It may take years to pay you, but I'll manage it somehow."

"Mrs. Spence, I'm not an altruist, but money is not always the motivating factor in my accepting a defense. If I defend you, we'll manage the financial arrangements, without you being in debt to me for the rest of your life."

She blinked in bewilderment. "But you're one of the top defense lawyers in the country! How can you undertake a case without considering money?"

"To be successful a defense attorney requires a certain amount of fame. Or notoriety, my detractors would call it," he said, smiling. "I have not gained my notoriety by defending only the wealthy. Unless they have a sensational aspect, the crimes of the rich are mundane more often than not. I will be candid with you, Mrs. Spence. There are a number of factors in your predicament that intrigue me, and if I decide to defend you, I will hope to accrue future benefits from media publicity. So, you see, financial concerns aside, I will benefit."

Rita Spence was frowning, her hands twisting nervously in her lap. "You keep saying 'if'!"

"First, I must satisfy myself that you are telling me the truth, that you are innocent, as you claim. Now, please don't take offense." He held up a staying hand. "Regardless of what my many critics maintain, I never undertake a defense until I thoroughly convince myself that my client is innocent."

"But I've told you the truth, I swear," she said bewilderedly. "What else can I do to convince you?"

"I have my own method, rather unorthodox, true, but it has never failed me. First, you must give me your trust, and your written permission to proceed. Allow me a few minutes to explain fully, and then you consider carefully before you decide. . . ."

"Mr. Midnight, this is Angela."

"Yes, Angela. I've been expecting your call. Is everything all right?"

She hesitated.

"I said, is everything all right, Angela?"

"Yes. Everything is all right."

"Are there any problems?"

She hesitated again.

"Angela, can you hear me? Are there any problems?"

"I'm not—"

"All right, Angela. Relax now. You are feeling very relaxed. Very calm. You will tell me what is bothering you, and you will be very calm about it. Now tell me. What is wrong?"

"There's not—there's not anything *wrong*."

"Are you all right personally? Are you well?"

"Yes, I am well."

"Is everything going all right? Your pictures and so forth?"

"Yes. Everything is going very well."

"And your friend, this O'Laughlin, are you still seeing him?"

"His—his name is Liam, Liam O'Laughlin."

"Are you still seeing him, Angela?"

"I am still seeing him. I—I am going to marry him."

"Oh, my God! Angela, repeat what you just said."

"I am going to marry him."

"Angela, listen carefully, very, very carefully. You cannot marry him. Do you understand? *You cannot marry him!* You must tell him so."

"I—I *am* going to marry him."

"No! Angela, listen. All right, here's what we will do. Relax, Angela. You are becoming very, very relaxed, but you will remain standing, and you will not drop the telephone receiver. Do you understand?"

"I understand."

"Good! Now, you are sinking deeper and deeper into the hypnotic state. With every word I say, you will go deeper into the hypnotic state. Now, you are very, very deep. You hear nothing but my voice. Now. . . . You are no longer Angela Williams. You will forget everything that has happened to you in Ireland. You are now someone else. You are now Robin Mayfield, and you will depart for England at *once*. Do you understand?"

"Yes. I understand."

"Good! Now, let me tell you something about yourself, Robin Mayfield, and explain what you are going to do next."

The intercom buzzed.

"Yes, Callahan?"

"Carlos O'Brien is on two, Deke. He's calling from Shannon Airport."

"Thanks, Callahan. By the way, I think you'd better tape this." Deke pressed the button for line two and said, "Yes, O'Brien?"

"As the saying goes, Mr. Travers, I have bad news and good news."

Deke leaned forward. "I'm in no mood for comic routines. Did you find April?"

"Well, yes, I think so. That's the good news."

"Then she *is* in Ireland?"

"Was, would be the word. If the woman I found is April Morgan, and I'm sure she is."

Deke's hand gripped the receiver until his knuckles shone white. "What do you mean, was? Has something happened to her?"

"Well, she's disappeared again. That's all I know at this time."

"That's the bad news, I take it. How did she get away so quickly, and why didn't you alert me the instant you found her? Those were my instructions."

"I didn't have time to be absolutely sure the woman is April Morgan. She was registered at the Clare Inn as Angela Williams. Except for different-colored hair, which could be a wig, and a few other minor details, she fits the description perfectly. But I wanted to be sure she was the right woman before I called you."

"All right, what happened?" Deke sighed. "How did you lose her?"

"I've been following her for three days. That wasn't hard to do, she's been in the company of this movie star, Liam O'Laughlin, most of the time. I've gotten friendly with one of the bellmen at the Clare. I bribed him to sneak me a glass with her fingerprints on it. So, last night I followed her to this O'Laughlin's castle. I decided she wasn't going anywhere, so I knocked off for the evening. I turned the glass over to a fingerprint expert. I just talked to him, by the way, before I made this call."

"And what did he say?"

"It's April Morgan, all right. The prints on the glass check with the set that you gave me. So now we know that Angela Williams is April Morgan, but she's vanished again." The voice sounded disgruntled. "She seems to be quite good at that."

"How do you know that for sure?"

"I went back to the Clare Inn this morning. She's been driving this rental car. I was a little worried when I didn't see it parked before the inn, so I had a word with my bellman. He told me that she had had an accident in the rental—"

"An accident!" Deke sat up in alarm. "When was this? Maybe she's injured, in a hospital somewhere."

"No, that was my first thought, but my bellman told me that O'Laughlin drove her back to the inn around midnight last night and there wasn't a scratch on her."

"Then if she returned to the hotel, how did you lose her?"

"You didn't let me finish," O'Brien said sharply. "The bellman thought she was in her room, since he'd seen her come in. I sent him to check. He came back and told me she was gone. She had left her luggage behind, but she is definitely gone. She checked out, paid her bill, and then simply vanished. Since then, I've been checking around. No luck. I staked out the O'Laughlin place, until he drove out in his Rolls. He drove to the Clare Inn. In a short while he came out in a rage. My bellman told me that O'Laughlin was supposed to pick the Morgan woman up at the inn, so apparently she took off without leaving any word for him. I followed O'Laughlin to a pub in Ennis, where he is busy getting smashed right now. As a last resort I came here, to Shannon, thinking she may have taken a plane out. But nobody answering to that description has taken a flight out of here. I don't know where to go from here, so I called you."

Deke was silent for a moment, then said slowly, "She must be in Ireland somewhere."

"Somehow, I have a feeling that she isn't. I don't know yet how she managed to get out of the country, but I'll damned sure find out!"

"Have you checked for a private flight?"

"Not yet. But that's next on my agenda."

"Okay, keep looking. But this time, if you get so much as a hint of where she is, call me. At once! And if you notice anyone else other than you and Ransom showing any interest in her, or if she seems threatened in any way, I want you to look out for her. I want her back *alive!* Understood?"

"Understood, boss man," O'Brien said.

"Where is Eric Ransom? Any word from him?"

"Who knows where that turkey is? Probably looking for our girl in Paris. He's a player, likes to loll around the hot spots. Spending your money. My advice to you would be to dump him."

"I'll decide that, O'Brien. You're not doing all that well yourself."

"Touché, boss man. Over and out."

Deke hung up the phone and glared at it balefully. Carlos O'Brien was too flippant by far, a smart ass. If he didn't show some results soon, it might not be a bad idea to dump *him*.

He punched a button. "Callahan, get me Gabe Kemble, will you?"

When Gabe's deep voice came on the line, Deke said, "They found her, Gabe. In Ireland."

Gabe said eagerly, "Is she okay?"

"She was, up until this morning. She's done the vanishing act again."

As he drove away from the Clare Inn, Liam O'Laughlin was too depressed to be really angry with Angela. It had happened to him again, a woman had failed him. The thought was uppermost in his mind as he drove faster and faster.

When he had dropped Angela off at the Clare shortly before midnight, she said softly, "I'll be waiting for you, darling Liam. Eight o'clock tomorrow morning."

"I don't know why we have to wait that long," he grumbled.

Her smile was tender. "A woman has to have a little time to prepare herself for such a big step as marriage. Besides"—she looked off, frowning—"I have to make this telephone call."

"Not to ask someone's permission, is it?" His voice was suspicious.

"No, no. I need to ask no one's permission to marry the man I love." She touched his cheek. "I'm over twenty-one."

"Well, all right," he said, somewhat mollified. "But I don't know why I can't let you run in, make your call, then take you back home with me. Look at all the time we'll be wasting."

"Darling, we'll be together for the rest of our lives. Liam." She looked at him almost pleadingly. "You *are* sure? It will last?"

"I know you're thinking of my other wives. I don't blame you, love. But this is different, this is for always. I knew that from the very start. All those others—sad mistakes, every one. As we say in the industry, this one will be a take. Print it!"

Her gaze still on his face, she nodded slowly. "Just so long as you're sure."

"I'm sure. I've never been so certain of anything in my whole life, love."

She leaned over to kiss him on the mouth, then was out of the Rolls in a flash and through the door of the Clare. Liam watched until she was out of sight—it was his last look at her.

Now she was gone. He knew, deep in his gut, that she was gone not only from the Clare Inn, but from Ireland and from him. It could be that the someone she had had to call was a lover from out of her past, and the result of the phone conversation had been that she was returning to this lover. It could be that whatever the mystery was about her past had caught up with her. For whatever reason, she had decided that she did not want one Liam O'Laughlin.

Now, speeding toward Ennis, Liam laughed. It was a sound utterly without humor, the sound of the bitterness within him, a bitterness that he had thought was gone forever with the appearance of Angela in his life.

Well, he had been wrong. Sweet Lord, how wrong could one man be, and for so many times!

He scarcely slowed the Rolls as he entered the outskirts of Ennis, slewing it around on the graveled parking lot alongside the pub. He sat for a moment, the motor still purring softly, as he contemplated the ancient pub. Why was he *here*, of all the pubs in Ennis, here where he had first met Angela, even if he had not known it at the time, besotted as he'd been. Still, it was his favorite pub, and if he couldn't drink here, where could he go?

With a snarl of self-contempt, he got out of the Rolls and went into the pub. It was shortly before the noon rush hour, and the dim pub was almost empty. Liam made his way to a booth in the back. Normally when he was drinking, he sought out company. With a few drinks in him, he liked to perform to an appreciative audience. But this day he was in no mood to socialize.

Seamus Riley hurried over, his round face blooming with a wide grin. "Well, if it isn't the O'Laughlin! We haven't seen you in a while, lad!"

"I went off the track there for a bit," Liam growled. "You'll be seeing me regularly now."

"It's a little early for the boys to be in yet," the pub keeper said.

"That's fine with me, I crave solitude. Be a good bloke and fetch me over a bottle of Irish. And when the boys do come in, pass the word. I'm in a foul mood, no fit company for man nor beast."

This statement received a surprised look. "No company today?"

"You've always had good ears, Seamus Riley. What's wrong with them today?"

Looking hurt, Seamus went away. Liam was sorry for wounding his feelings, but when Seamus came back with a glass and the bottle, Liam didn't bother to apologize.

He drank slowly, pacing it out. When the noon rush hour began, Liam rejected any friendly over-

tures, of which there were few, since he saw that
Seamus, busy as he was, had a private word with every new arrival. The level in the bottle lowered
slowly.

Always before, when Liam embarked on a pro-
longed drinking bout, he was able to clear his mind of
thoughts about whatever had brought it on and
concentrate on the booze—until he reached a certain
stage of drunkenness. Then he could let the black
thoughts creep in, the liquor blunting them.

This facility failed him this time. Thoughts of Angela kept popping into his mind. The way she smiled
shyly at times, and the other times when her whole
face lit up with the brilliance of her happiness. The
way her hand would creep out like a timid mouse and
touch his face or hand in a fleeting gesture of affection. The way her flesh glowed with a pink, almost
translucent flush in the firelight before and after he
had made love to her. The way her body moved tentatively at first under his and then became bold and
demanding in her mounting passion . . .

Liam swore aloud and slammed the glass down
onto the table. He peered blearily around the pub.
The noon rush had waned long since, and the afternoon crowd was coming in. Blurred faces turned to
him in astonishment at the sounds he made; on some
faces he saw a touch of fear. The O'Laughlin was
well-known for his violent rages when he was on the
drink.

"Seamus!" he bellowed. "Don't you ever serve a
man a bite? A man gets hungry when he drinks!"

Seamus, behind the bar, bobbed his head and sent
a waitress over to Liam's table. He ordered the rare
beef sandwiches and a pot of tea. In a moment the
barmaid returned with the pot of tea. Liam poured a
cup and drank. The tea was scalding, but such was
his condition that he scarcely noticed.

By the time he'd drunk the second cup, it had

taken the edge from his drunkenness, and his perceptions were sharpened. He noted with surprise that the day was done, and it was dark. He ate part of one sandwich, dumped the rest back onto his plate, and grimaced with distaste. He beckoned the barmaid over and ordered another bottle. When it came, he resumed drinking.

Angela was mostly gone from his thoughts now, merely hovering like an unhappy ghost just on the periphery of his mind.

To hell with her! Another woman had wronged him. So what else was new?

Another drink should exorcise her completely. He drank it down, then stood up. It was the first time he had stood in hours. Apparently the liquor had numbed his bladder, as well as his brain.

He took a step and almost fell. He righted himself with a hand on the booth. Slowly he straightened, struck a pose, and bellowed, "Attention, you clods! Liam O'Laughlin is about to enlighten you with a rare bit of wisdom!"

They gathered around, eyes bright with anticipation. A hush descended as the rich voice soared.

"If all the harm that women have done
Were put into a bundle and rolled into one,
Earth would not hold it,
The sky would not enfold it,
It could not be lighted nor warmed by the sun."

There was a brief pause, until they were sure he was finished, then the applause broke. Glasses were hoisted in toasts, and voices called for more.

"More?" He glared at them. "What more is there? That tells it all, and more!"

Suddenly his stomach heaved, and Liam feared he would vomit all over those close to him. That would be the final indignity.

He swallowed convulsively, forcing back the bile, and began shoving his way through the crowd. They parted for him, like the Red Sea, and he staggered out of the pub. He was, he thought, a Moses without his staff.

The ribald connotation of the phrase forced a chuckle through his gritted teeth. He was drunk, good sweet Lord, he was drunk! Going without liquor for all this time, and then pouring it down his gullet like water, had undone him. Waves of dizziness assailed him as he stumbled in a weaving path to the Rolls. Finally he got the door open and slumped behind the wheel.

He fought back fiercely against unconsciousness. Be damned if he would pass out here and be the object of ridicule!

Gradually he gained a semblance of control over himself and started the car. He drove slowly and carefully out of the parking lot and along the streets of Ennis. But once beyond the city limits, his control began to slide away, and he found it difficult to concentrate on driving. It was early in the evening, and there were a good many cars on the road. Several times he let the Rolls wander over onto the right side of the road and jerked awake just in time to avoid an oncoming car.

When he turned onto the road leading toward the keep, the traffic was almost nonexistent as usual. Except for a few scattered farmhouses, the only thing to draw traffic was the keep at the end of the road.

Suddenly anxious to get home, Liam speeded up, his foot coming down hard on the accelerator. The road was arrow-straight for miles, and he sent the Rolls zooming along. Then he dimly remembered a sharp curve and began to slow, tromping hard on the brakes. The car slowed for just an instant and then sprang free again, as would a wild animal suddenly freed from its leash.

The sharp curve was outlined starkly in the glare of

the headlights. Liam tried desperately to wrench the Rolls around the curve. It was simply going too fast. Perhaps if he had been sober . . .

The Rolls slammed grill-first into the stone wall, and Liam died before his last thought was completed.

Nine

Robin Mayfield hummed to herself as she moved about her room in the Inn on the Park, unpacking the bags, which had been waiting in her room when she arrived.

She was impressed by the hotel. It was very luxurious, but then she was accustomed to luxury. As the only child of well-to-do parents, she had always been given the best of everything; and when her parents had died in the plane crash a year ago, Robin had inherited a considerable sum of money.

As she thought of her parents, she frowned slightly, but it was not sorrow that caused the expression. She frowned because she had so little feeling about her parents' death, and it seemed to her that she should feel more; but then, everything about the death of her parents was vague, dreamlike—the funeral, the reading of the will by that nice young man. . . . What was his name? . . .

She shook her head, as if trying to clear it. Well, whatever his name was, he had advised her to take a trip abroad, to get away from unhappy memories, to see some of the places she was interested in as a student of archaeology.

Robin took the last item of clothing out of the bags and placed the empty suitcases in the closet, then gazed around the comfortable room. So here she was, in London; and the young man's advice must have been good because she felt fine now, clearheaded and relaxed, anxious to sample the English life and to see some of the places she had long dreamed of.

She moved to the big windows and stood looking

out. Down below, the street teemed with those square, black, boxlike taxis unique to London, and she could see Big Ben in the distance. Across the way was an apartment building. The floor she was on was higher than the building. On the top floor of the apartment building was a penthouse, surrounded with small trees and green shrubs. Bright flowers bloomed in long planters.

As she watched, a young man came out of the penthouse with a watering can in his hand. Ahead of him bounded a dog, a huge, hulking brute. The dog capered about the roof while the young man watered the flowers.

Suddenly he glanced up, and their eyes met briefly. On an impulse Robin waved gaily at him. Smiling, he waved back. Unaccountably, this small exchange further lifted her spirits. It seemed to bode well for her stay here.

She turned back into the room, then hesitated at the sight of the stack of books lying upon the table by the window. Sighing happily, she sat down and lifted one, then another. Finally she settled on a tome titled *Mysterious Britain*, and soon she was engrossed in the details of an older time.

Evening shadows were gathering when Robin finally glanced up with a start. It was late, and she was starving. She walked over to the phone to call room service, then hesitated, her hand on the receiver.

Her first evening in London, her first *time* in London, and she was thinking of eating in her room!

No, she would find a place to eat outside the hotel. She changed into a tweed suit and walking shoes, then rode the elevator down to the lobby. The hotel was alive with people. A family of Arabs crossed the lobby. The husband and wife wore flowing white robes; behind them, like a flock of chicks following in the wake of a mother hen, were a half-dozen children of varying ages, all in Western clothing.

Piano music came from the tea room at one end of

the lobby, and Robin hesitated for a moment, then went on outside. She had heard that it rained a lot in England, but today the weather was clear and dry, unseasonably warm for October.

The Inn on the Park was situated on a wedge of land, shaped like a slice of pie. Approaching the narrow end and the traffic circle, Robin could see across the busy street. To her left was the serene greenery of Hyde Park. On her right was the Hilton Hotel, with square, black taxis loading and unloading; a number of sleek Rolls Royces were parked in front. She frowned at one black Rolls, and something tickled her memory. She shook her head sharply and concentrated on navigating the traffic circle safely—no mean feat, since cars spun around it as if they were on a merry-go-round.

She made it across without getting struck and started up Park Lane, strolling along without any destination in mind, just drinking it all in. She passed a restaurant advertising the best hamburgers in London. Halfway up the block, she stopped and turned back. She hadn't had a hamburger in—how long? However long it had been, she couldn't remember.

She had two, and they were reasonably good hamburgers. As she started on the second, Robin laughed quietly to herself. Here she was in London, a cosmopolitan city with literally dozens of gourmet restaurants to choose from, and where was she? In a hamburger place, surrounded by half a hundred or more noisy Americans!

It was still early when she returned to her hotel, but she was tired, and she intended to get an early start in the morning. She took a bath, got into her nightgown, and slipped into bed. The last thing she did before going to sleep was to call room service and order an early breakfast and place a wake-up call for seven-thirty.

Her sleep was sound, except for a troubling dream, from which she woke with a small yelp of fright. But already the details of the dream, nightmare, whatever it was, had blurred in her mind.

The jangle of the bedside telephone woke her in the morning, and she thanked the voice cheerfully informing her that it was seven-thirty. She barely had time to slip into a robe before a rap on the door announced breakfast.

She had ordered a substantial breakfast—scrambled eggs, bacon, croissants, jam, and a pot of coffee. Lifting the heavy silver lid from the plate, she was pleased to see that the bacon strips were the wide, thick slices she had so grown to like in Ireland . . .

Robin froze, frowning into space. Why had that thought popped into her head? She had never been to Ireland.

With an exclamation of annoyance, she set the lid aside and sat down. Spreading a napkin across her lap, she began to eat. There was a morning newspaper, folded once, on the tray, but Robin didn't open it until she had finished the bacon and eggs and the first cup of coffee.

Then she poured a fresh cup, spread butter and jam on the last croissant, and unfolded the newspaper. As she ate the flaky roll, she let her gaze move idly over the front-page news stories. The energy crunch was getting worse. Gold had climbed to over six hundred dollars an ounce. The dollar had slipped again. Irish actor Liam O'Laughlin was dead in a tragic auto accident.

She opened to the second page and began reading . . .

Liam O'Laughlin? She knew the name, of course. Everyone in the civilized world did. But why did the name make her feel so strange?

She turned another page but couldn't concentrate on the print. Images of a face danced across the page—the face of the man on the front page. But *that* face was wearing a promo smile, the counterfeit currency of famous people. The face she now saw was by turns grave, intent, smiling, and intimate. Robin closed her eyes to shut the face out, yet it was still there.

Robin felt as though her sanity were slipping away. A flood of images battered at her mind, and a familiar voice spoke, growing stronger, then receding, but always coming back clearer than the time before, like waves pounding a beach as a storm grew. Words formed, echoing. *Angela . . . love . . . marry, marry in the morning!*

The images of Liam O'Laughlin and his words of endearment tumbled through her memory like the colored flakes of a kaleidoscope. Then the pieces fell into place, like a film run backward in a projector, and Angela-Robin knew.

And in that same instant, as pain and confusion ripped her mind, something closed down. She sat unmoving, hands relaxed in her lap, eyes staring at the newspaper in front of her.

A knock sounded, and a voice called, "Maid!" Angela-Robin did not respond.

She sat on as the sun wheeled high overhead, and shadows began to collect in the room.

The telephone rang. She showed no reaction. It rang on and on. Finally she stirred, making a vague gesture, and a whimper came from her.

The phone stopped—then began to ring again almost immediately.

Slowly, moving with the jerky movements of a marionette, she got up and crossed to the bed. She picked up the receiver, put it to her ear, and sank down onto the unmade bed.

"Robin? Is that you, Robin?"

Angela-Robin did not respond.

"Robin? This is Mr. Midnight. I know it isn't our usual time to talk, but I was worried about you. I'm here, Robin, in London. I thought I should be close, in case you needed me—Robin?"

She said nothing.

"Robin, I know it's you! I checked with the desk, and you're registered. Damnit, answer me!"

Her lips moved, making a croaking sound.

"What, what did you say?"

"Li-am. Li-am—I—I—"

"You don't know anybody by that name, Robin! Robin, listen to me . . ."

Her hand holding the phone dropped listlessly into her lap. Ignoring the tinny squawk of the voice on the line, she sat unmoving, staring straight ahead.

An hour later she still had not moved, not even to hang up the receiver, when a sharp knock sounded on the door. She evinced no awareness of it and did not even turn her head when a key clicked in the lock and the door swung open.

The light was dazzling white, blindingly white, and the voices, as they came and went, had a hollow sound, as though traveling down a long tunnel.

"She's a very sick girl—"

"—very puzzling case."

"A complete withdrawal from reality. Observe how she lies in the fetal position much of the time. There is a strong possibility that she may be catatonic—"

"Bullshit, doctor! That's bullshit!"

"There is no need to be offensive, sir. You asked for a medical opinion, sir, and I gave you one. Further opinion is that the psychological damage is severe, perhaps irreparable—"

"I refuse to accept that, doctor. I'll take over from here."

One voice was naggingly familiar, the others not familiar at all.

Then there was a long sensation of movement, after which the light bleeding through to her eyes was more pleasing, muted, and not all white. The only voices she heard now were female.

And then the voice on the phone . . .

"Dear, there is this nice man who wishes to talk to

you." A hand took hers and closed it around something cold and hard. "Oh, damn! All right, if you won't hold it, I'll hold it for you."

The receiver was pushed against her ear, and a voice came into her head. It was painful, and she moaned, trying to pull her head away.

"Now, dear, we mustn't be difficult. This is for your own good." Another hand clamped around the back of her skull and held her head still.

"April, this is Mr. Midnight. Can you hear me?"

The voice exerted an inexorable pull, and her consciousness began to surface toward it.

"April, you hear me, I know you do. I'm terribly sorry for all that has happened to you. Much of it was my fault, and I hope some day that you will forgive me. It was all for your benefit, I swear. You've been hurt terribly, I know. But you must put it behind you. You are still in danger. April, do you understand?"

"Yes." The word of response was wrenched from her, and at the same time she became more aware of her surroundings. A kindly face framed in gray-black hair beamed maternally from above her, and a soft voice said, "There, there, dear. It's all right now."

"April? This is Mr. Midnight. Relax and listen to my voice. You will forget all that has happened. You are relaxed and very, very comfortable, and you will erase from your memory all that has happened. Relax, make your mind a blank. Your mind is a white slate, from which everything has been erased. You will now go deeper and deeper into the hypnotic state. Do you see the slate?"

"—yes."

"Good! Now, on that slate write these letters, R-O-B-I-N M-A-Y—"

"No!" she moaned, sitting upright. "April, I'm April!"

"Oh, dear, sweet God! Have I really done— Listen! You *must* listen to me. This is Mr. Midnight. Relax now, relax. You must sleep now, sleep deeply, and without dreams. Sleep now, my dear, sleep . . ."

But it wasn't that easy, and she did dream, at least it *seemed* a dream.

They were at their house at Cape Cod. They were seated around the dinner table—April, her father, and Sheila.

Sheila and John Morgan were quarreling, and April, cringing with embarrassment, was wishing again that her father hadn't persuaded her to come here with them.

"Lord Godalmighty, I've eaten better victuals in a hobo jungle," her father roared, thumping the table with his fist.

John Morgan, sixty, with a leonine mane of silver-blond hair and blazing blue eyes, looked more like an oil field worker than the "International wheeler-dealer" *Time Magazine* had once called him. But then he had started as an oil field roustabout, so why shouldn't he look like one?

"You'd know more about hobo jungles than I would," Sheila said in icy anger, her green eyes glittering like cut glass in her fury.

April hated Sheila, and it was more than stepmother hate. She did not begrudge her father a woman, or a wife, but there was something evil lurking beyond Sheila's cold eyes.

April couldn't understand what her father saw in her, but then Sheila was an actress by profession—although not greatly successful at it. Perhaps she had played a different role until after the marriage vows were said.

Her father pushed the charred steak around on his plate with a fork. "I didn't expect a gourmet cook, but I didn't expect steak like shoe leather, either."

"I didn't say I could cook. If you expected the little woman in the apron, humming happily in a kitchen, you married the wrong woman, John. I should think that a man with your money could afford household help."

"In the city, yes, but this is a delayed honeymoon, sweet," John Morgan said, good-humoredly now. "This hardly seemed the place to bring help along."

"I don't see why not." Sheila glared at April. "You brought *her* along."

"Now by Lord, that's enough!" Again his big fist thumped the table. "April is my daughter!"

One fact about Sheila April had learned was that even in the grip of Sheila's frequent, icy rages, she rarely raised her voice. Now she did. She leaned across the table and shouted in John Morgan's face, "I know that very well! You never let me forget it! And whose bright idea was it to bring her along?"

April had had enough. Giving a choked cry, she jumped to her feet and started out of the room.

Her father's voice halted her. "Don't mind us, sugar. I reckon most husbands and wives squabble, even on their honeymoons." In one of those quicksilver changes of moods, his voice changed, equable now, with a hint of bawdy laughter in it. "That always makes it great fun to make up. When you get hitched yourself, you'll find that out. Sugar, it's a nice evening. Sheila and me, we thought we'd take a little hike along the shoreline. Whyn't you come with us?"

"No, daddy. I want to develop some pictures." She tried to keep her voice even. "You can go without me."

"Whatever you say, sugar."

April hurried on into her darkroom, locking herself in. Then she briefly gave way to tears. She reached a decision. She was going back to New York in the morning and leave the newlyweds alone. Much as she disliked Sheila, her stepmother was right. A honeymoon was no place for a stepdaughter!

April had not seen her father for six months prior to the day he showed up with a new wife, and that was the reason she had allowed him to talk her into coming here with them. It had been a mistake from the start, and she had known it. She would rectify that the first thing in the morning, and she had a strong feeling that John Morgan would be relieved.

Wiping the tears from her eyes, April turned on the red light. In a few minutes she had the pictures in the developing pan, the pictures she had taken of Sheila and her father yesterday, their first day here. As the images of Sheila began to emerge in the developing fluid, anger rose in April. She dug her hands into the pan and took the pictures out, ripping them into ribbons. She wanted no pictures of Sheila Morgan!

She tensed as a light rapping of knuckles sounded on the door. "April, open the door for a jiffy, will you?" her father said in a low voice.

She turned off the red light and opened the door a crack, her gaze going past his shoulder.

John Morgan grinned sheepishly. "Naw, sugar. She's already gone on. I'll have to catch up. I just wanted a word with you first. You're going back to the city in the morning, I reckon?"

She nodded mutely.

"I figured as much, and it's probably for the best. Big mistake, my bringing you up here. It's just that I hadn't seen my little girl in so dadblamed long."

She stared into his worn face for a long moment. Her anger at Sheila renewed itself, and she considered telling him about Sheila's unfaithfulness. But she knew that her stepmother was right—it would be a waste of breath and would only hurt him more.

She said hastily, "I'm going back home tomorrow, daddy, yes."

He nodded glumly. "Yep, that's the best all around. April"—he glanced around furtively and lowered his voice—"listen close to me now. If something should happen to your old daddy, there's something I want you to know."

"Daddy!" Her hand flew out to his face. "Don't talk like that!"

He grinned abashedly, turned her hand over, and kissed the palm. "Certain things we all have to face in this old world, sugar. I ain't getting any younger, you know."

"You'll live forever!"

"I've always had it in mind to, but the Almighty may have a different idea." ·

"Is that all you meant, getting old?"

"Sure was. Now what else could I be thinking of?" His gaze searched her face. When she made no reply, he tightened his grip painfully on her hand. "Now you listen to me and don't forget what I'm telling you . . ."

Somewhere in the back rooms of her mind, a door slammed shut, and April opened her eyes to find herself trembling, as if the fluttering of her heart were shaking her whole body.

Breathing deeply, she lay there until her heart slowed and then went over the scene again in her mind. It played the same as it had before; she could remember every detail until that last moment when her father leaned forward to whisper his last words; and try as she might, April could remember no more, even though she had the strong feeling that it was very important she do so.

"Robin, this is Mr. Midnight. How are you feeling?"

"Am I Robin?"

"Yes. You are Robin. Robin Mayfield. Repeat that name."

"Robin Mayfield."

"Now, Robin, how are you? Are you feeling better?"

"I—I don't know. I don't feel *bad*."

"Good. That's a step in the right direction. Did you sleep well?"

"I—I had a dream. It frightened me."

"Do you remember the dream?"

"Yes. But maybe it wasn't a dream. Maybe it was something that happened to me once. I—I'm confused."

"It's all right, Robin. It's all right. The confusion will go away, I promise you. Now, you said that the dream frightened you. Why?"

"Because I couldn't remember. There was something I was supposed to remember. It was important. My father—"

"All right, Robin. Relax now. Sink deeper into the hypnotic state. You are very relaxed. Now, Robin, tell me your dream, or your memory. Tell me slowly, and from the beginning, everything you can remember about it."

During the days, Robin felt that she existed in a delicate, precarious state. The thought foremost in her mind was that she was Robin Mayfield, an archaeology student, an orphan, but with many close friends who cared about her. For some reason it was important that she hang onto this thought, and she did so, returning to it as a source of comfort during the day, a refuge from—what was it a refuge from? Well, that didn't matter, really. Robin Mayfield was safe. She was cared for. She had been ill, but she was getting better and soon would return to her interrupted tour of England.

She ate quite a good lunch, which pleased the day nurse; and although she felt fragile, she was in no pain. Had there been pain? She was sure there had. Pain of some kind, but it was gone now, and she was getting better.

But that night she dreamed again, a really frightening dream this time, a dark dream that rolled in, chilling as the mist inside her mind. It was night, very late, and she was walking along a sea cliff, searching for her father. She could not remember when she had left the house, or why, but she felt driven by an urgency she could not explain. She *had* to find her father.

The night was black, the sky only slightly lighter than the sea below, which could only be seen when the incoming tide slammed breakers against the base of the cliff. The sound of the breakers seemed charged with anger, an elemental roar that touched chords of foreboding in her mind.

The fog was coming in, sliding thick tendrils over the edge of the cliff, easing clammy fingers inside her jacket. Where *was* her father?

She wondered if she should return to the house. She hesitated at a spot where the cliff veered out sharply into a point. The fog was too thick now to see the point itself, but April remembered it from previous visits.

Suddenly she became frighteningly aware that she was not alone. There was someone out there on the point, hidden by the fog. Over the boom of the breakers she heard the sounds of a scuffle, a muffled cry.

She turned toward the sound, and at that moment the fog parted.

Dimly she could make out the forms of two people locked in a struggle on the edge of the cliff; and as she peered at them, her heart hammering furiously, the half-moon slid for a moment out from behind a cloud bank. The moon was free for only an instant, but it was long enough for her to see that the struggling pair were her father and stepmother, teetering precariously on the edge of the sheer drop, locked in a terrible and violent embrace.

The fog closed in again, just as a scream escaped from her throat, tearing at the walls of her throat like a small, fierce beast.

She rushed toward them, but as she moved, so did they; in a slow-motion dance choreographed by horror, they fell together, out of sight, out into the void, the only sound Sheila's scream. They were gone.

She fainted then, in the dream, smothered by a fear

too great to face, and in her bed she tossed and cried out, leaping awake. Her heart was pounding, and her head ached with a throbbing insistence.

She rolled toward the edge of the bed. She must get some water, some aspirin, but before her feet touched the floor, the telephone rang, the harsh sound of its jangle irritating her already aching head.

She picked it up automatically.

"Robin, this is Mr. Midnight. Are you all right?"

"Mr. Midnight! Oh, Mr. Midnight!"

"You sound distraught, Robin."

"I had a dream."

"A bad dream? Did you have a bad dream, Robin?"

"Oh, yes. Oh, it was awful!"

"Don't cry, Robin. Tell me the dream. And as you tell me, the fear and pain will go away. They will leave you. Tell me the dream, and then it will be gone, and when the dream is gone, you will be Robin Mayfield, and you will feel fine. You are in England to do something you have longed to do for as long as you can remember, Robin, exploring archaeological ruins. Henceforth, when your phone rings and you hear the words Mr. Midnight, you will answer as Robin Mayfield. Do you understand, Robin?"

"I understand."

Three weeks later, Robin Mayfield emerged from the sanitarium. Relaxed and smiling, she turned her face up to the bright afternoon sunlight and took a deep, steadying breath.

A black taxi pulled in at the curb. Robin got in, settled back against the cushions, and said, "The Inn on the Park, please, driver."

Ten

Robin had no desire to join a tour group and be herded around like sheep in a flock, so she rented a car and drove to the city of Bath, eager to visit the famous Aquae Sulis. What she had read about the town and the Romans' ancient baths fascinated her.

The baths had been built by the Emperor Claudius around AD 43, construction beginning shortly after the Romans invaded and conquered Britain. The temple itself had been dedicated to the Roman goddess Minerva and the Celtic deity Sul, who was supposed to preside over the great hot springs. Aquae Sulis, when completed, drew enormous crowds, and soon became famous throughout Europe.

Aquae Sulis' popularity lasted for four hundred years. Two factors caused the baths to decline—the rising of the sea level and the fall of the Roman empire. Rome could no longer defend Britain, and it was invaded by the Picts, Saxons, Scots, and Irish. The baths fell into disuse, and Robin had read an ancient Anglo-Saxon poem that told sadly of what the town of Bath looked like in the eighth century—a ghostly ruin, the masonry crumpling away into the dark pools, weed-grown and bird-haunted.

The hot springs were in use again in the Middle Ages, yet the Roman baths remained buried under centuries of debris, forgotten. In the eighteenth century the gilded bronze head of Mercury was uncovered by a workman, but it wasn't until 1878 that another workman discovered the Roman reservoir, and then excavation began. Work continued sporadically, and the great complex of baths was uncovered.

From her reading Robin knew that excavation and renovating were still being carried on today, and she was looking forward to her visit with great anticipation.

It was a weekday, and the height of the tourist season was past. Still, a great many people swarmed the narrow streets of the ancient city, and there was a line of people waiting to get into the baths.

Robin felt a pull of disappointment; it somehow seemed a sacrilege that tourists with cameras slung over their shoulders should be invading a place almost holy in its antiquity.

But when she finally bought her ticket and walked inside the first room, having waited until a tour group had gone on ahead, it wasn't long until she fell under the spell of the place. She managed to stay by herself most of the time. She ignored, as best she could, the Victorian pillars and statues added by the English in later times, and she concentrated on the Roman remains. She wandered happily through the great complex of roofless baths. She lingered long around the main bath, touching the worn paving, the lead lining. She could easily imagine how it had been in Roman times, with steam rising from the water heated by hypocausts under the floors, and the sun slanting in. It would have been a place of civilized, social pleasure, filled with the sound of water, the cries of hawkers selling perfumes and honey cakes, and the conversation of important men discussing matters of state or hunting or somebody's wife.

After a time Robin wandered on, through the other rooms and corridors of the baths, lingering again in the rooms with mounted artifacts—temple pediments, Roman tombstones, sculptures of Roman gods and goddesses. She became immersed in the past and almost forgot the present. In her daze she was occasionally startled when she brushed against a gaily attired tourist. Muttering embarrassed apologies, she would hurry on.

Slowly something began to nudge at her mind, something that caused a faint shiver of apprehension. She surfaced to the present and looked around, trying to figure out what was bothering her. Glancing suddenly to her right, out into the open area around the main bath, she saw a slight, slender man staring at her. As their glances met, the man turned abruptly aside and stepped out of sight behind a pillar; he walked with a slight limp.

Robin realized then what had been nagging at her. She had seen the same man watching her at least twice before. She had thought nothing of it at the time and probably would not now, except for the limp.

Why was he watching her? Was he planning to put a move on her? It was the only reason she could think of. She was obviously by herself, and as protection against the chill in the air today, she was attired in a beige sweater that fit rather snugly, accentuating her breasts.

The only way to handle it was to ignore him. She wasn't through here yet, and she certainly had no intention of allowing his furtive surveillance to frighten her away.

She turned away abruptly and strode into another chamber, a large, roofed room just off the outdoor bath. The light was poor in here, and steam rising lazily from several pools gave the chamber a spooky appearance. There were only a few people inside. Clearly the chamber had been hewn out of solid rock. Grottoes went back into the stone walls. A narrow bridge arched over a stream of water.

Robin crossed over and ventured back toward the rear. The rock floor was slippery with moisture, and she had to watch her footing. She moved along cautiously, peering into the nooks and crannies in the walls. Lights were situated in the floor at intervals, illuminating the grottoes. There was one dark area where the spotlight was apparently not functioning. Robin edged cautiously back into the crevice, trying to make out what lay back in the darkness. After a moment's hesitation she ventured farther. Suddenly she froze at the sound of soft footsteps behind her.

Belatedly, it occurred to her just how foolish she had been. Knowing that the man had been watching her, she had ventured into this cul-de-sac. She tensed, holding her breath as the footsteps came closer. Then she whirled blindly and bolted. She careened into a man. He grunted sharply, then wrapped his arms around her. Robin, head still down, hit out at him with her fists.

"What the devil!" said a male voice, with an unmistakable British accent. "Are you bloody mad, woman?"

Robin became still, then slowly raised her head. A pair of amused brown eyes stared down into hers. The face was handsome, with an aquiline nose and a charming smile.

This wasn't the man who had been watching her!

Suddenly aware that he was still holding her, Robin said in a low, furious voice, "Let go of me!"

"That depends," he said. "If I let you go, will you promise to settle down? That right hand of yours packs a wallop, especially for such a pretty bird."

Robin drew a deep breath. "I'm sorry. Yes, I'll settle down."

He let go of her and stepped warily back, but he was still blocking her path. "Now what was that all about? Perhaps I frightened you. I assure you that I had no such intention."

"You did frighten me, yes." She peered past his shoulder into the nearly empty outer chamber. "There's been a man watching me."

"A masher? Where is the blighter?" He turned to gaze around.

For the first time Robin noticed that he was dressed rather nattily for such surroundings. He wore an exquisitely tailored blue blazer, soft gray slacks, and a white-on-white shirt, with a blue-dotted tie. She answered absently, "I don't see him now, but I thought you were him."

He looked at her again, grinned crookedly, his gaze lingering on her breasts. "It's easy enough to understand why he might be watching you. You're a very pretty lady, you know that? I'm Roger, by the way, Roger Blaine."

"Robin Mayfield," she said automatically.

He laughed. "A pretty bird with the name of a pretty bird! Now, that has to be a good omen. The robin has always been my favorite among the winged birds." He became serious. "Look, how about joining me for a spot of tea? It's the least I can do after frightening you like that. Maybe we'll spot your masher, and I'll send him kiting off, you may be sure."

Robin hesitated briefly. She glanced at her watch and realized that she had been wandering for three hours. She was hungry. "I think that would be nice."

Roger took her arm and led her out of the chamber and up the stairs toward the main entrance.

"Wait." She held back. "Where are we going? I haven't finished here. I haven't seen everything yet."

"My dear, we must go outside for our tea. You can get nothing decent inside. How long have you been here, by the bye?"

"About three hours."

"Three bloody hours! And you haven't seen everything?"

"I'm not a tourist, you know," she said with some indignation. "Just rush in and out, so I can get back home and tell people I've been to the Roman baths."

"Well, you're obviously American," he said amusedly. "If not a tourist, why are you here?"

"I'm an archaeologist. Well, a student anyway," she amended quickly. "I'm here to study the historic sites. Stonehenge, Avebury Ring, and the rest."

"You need a guide, you know." They were outside now, and Robin resigned herself to following his lead.

"I don't want a guide. I'm not interested in listening to a tour guide's practiced spiel."

"I wasn't thinking of that kind of guide. I was thinking more of someone like myself. This *is* my turf, as you Americans say, and I know it like the back of my hand."

She looked at him in astonishment. "You're a professional guide?"

"No, no, nothing like that. But I am familiar with all the sites you mentioned."

He seemed evasive, and Robin didn't press it. He had her curiosity aroused now, but she decided to bide her time. He led her to a tea shop on Grand Parade, overlooking the River Avon and the Pulteney Bridge.

They were escorted to a table near the window. It was an enchanting view—the bridge, delicate and pale, hanging over the weir.

She turned her attention to Roger Blaine, who was ordering tea and sandwiches for them. His face was alive, and he used his hands extravagantly as he talked. He had a commanding presence and a touch of the sardonic in his manner. There was something about him that eluded Robin. Then it came to her. He seemed, by word and gesture, to stress his masculinity a touch too much—projecting what she thought of as a macho image.

She puzzled over it. He was certainly masculine enough, although she sensed a strong sensitivity behind the image. So why did he come on so strong?

Now he turned to her, brown eyes sparkling, mobile mouth set in a slanting grin. "Why the serious look, little Robin bird? Thinking about your masher?"

She started. "No. In fact, I had forgotten all about him." In truth she had; it had been in her mind as they left the Baths to watch and see if the limping man followed them. But so intrigued was she by this man that she had completely forgotten.

Involuntarily her glance darted out the window. Of

course, the foot traffic was so thick that she wouldn't
have been able to see the limping man even if he had
followed them and now had the tea room under observation, but surely seeing her with Roger would be
enough to discourage him! Robin gave a mental
shrug, dismissing the limping man from her thoughts.

She took a sip of the hot, aromatic tea and looked
across the small table at Roger. "You said you're not a
professional guide, so what are you?"

He looked directly at her and said a touch defiantly, "I'm a fashion designer, and a bloody good one,
I might add."

Robin knew then why he flaunted his masculinity.
In a profession well noted for homosexuality, Roger
was afraid he would be thought gay! It amused Robin
slightly, and she sipped tea to hide a smile. She
would never have thought him gay and would have
wagered that few women would. Roger Blaine gave
off an aura of maleness as powerful as the most blatant stud.

"What is a fashion designer doing at the Baths?"

"I have a theory." He leaned back, gesturing with
both hands in that graceful way of his. In time she
was to learn that he couldn't talk without using his
hands, and yet, his gestures gave him an added elo-
quence.

"The business of fashion designing tends to be
ingrown. Designers are like cruising sharks, feeding
off each other's ideas. The more trendy, the more far-
out, the better. Or so most of my colleagues seem to
think. I disagree. When I'm ready to design a new line,
I root around in the old places, basing my designs on
clothes worn in earlier periods. The reason I'm here
today is that I'm thinking of using the early Romans
as models."

"I know little of fashions," she said, "but it strikes
me as a good idea."

"Of course it's a good idea." He was smiling. "It's
always worked for me before. Last year's line was

based on the Elizabethan period. Now, you won't give away my secret, will you? The profession is full of copycats. It's said that imitation is the best form of flattery, but that kind of flattery I can do without."

Robin was chewing on a bite of her sandwich. Swallowing, she said, "That still doesn't explain why you came poking into that grotto after me, scaring me half to death."

He grinned again. "I don't spend *all* my time working. I'm also a confirmed bird watcher, the unfeathered variety. I spotted you poking around in there, and I wondered what the bloody hell? I hope I'm forgiven for spooking you. I should have said something first."

"You're forgiven, Roger."

"In that case," he said cheerfully, "how about my invitation to serve as your guide?"

"That would be nice, I think. But I'm going to other sites, sites not of Roman origin."

"No problem. I still haven't made up my mind yet. I may benefit from other sites as well and change my whole concept completely." His grin flashed. "To my knowledge, no one has used the Druid influence yet!"

The trouble was, what Roger showed her during the next week was not what she had come to England to see. He knew London as well as he claimed to know the historic sites outside of the city, and he insisted on showing her, as he put it, *his* London. "Not what the tourist sees."

Specifically he showed her London at night. Under Roger's guidance she saw London at its worst and its best. Roger seemed to have entry into every night spot in London.

Almost every night they attended the theater, for which he managed to get the best seats. They ate in fine restaurants that served excellent food, and in hidden-away places where the food was just as marvelous. He took her to the casinos. Robin had never gambled, and he taught her how. In gambling he seemed as extravagant as in everything else, losing what seemed to Robin to be frightening sums, yet the losses never seemed to bother him. He apparently took as much delight in losing as he did in winning.

Robin had to admit that she was dazzled by it all, and when she registered a weak protest—"Roger, I didn't come here for the night life!"—he waved his hands at her, laughing. "Robin bird, haven't you heard that ancient adage, all work and no play? We'll get around to your bloody ruins. But first, we play. I haven't enjoyed myself so much in years. And you know why?" His smile turned tender, and he caressed her cheek with his knuckles. "You're lovely and marvelous, and I do believe I'm a little dotty over you!"

What else could she do but go along with him? She had to admit that she was also enjoying herself immensely. With this impetuous, charming, slightly mad man she could forget everything. There was no past, no future—everything was now, this minute! She refused to think about where it might be leading. Every time she wondered if she might be falling in love with Roger Blaine, an inexplicable apprehension seized her, and she turned to him, letting his laughter sweep over her.

Even so, the reason why she was here nagged at her, and she probably would have insisted that they make the expeditions he kept promising, if he hadn't made love to her.

They had been to the theater, a zany musical comedy; and her ribs ached from laughing. They ate a large dinner in Soho and then cabbed back to the Inn on the Park.

Roger said, "We need a nightcap."

The bar in the foyer on the second floor was just closing when they reached it, the barman pulling the grill across the entryway. Roger's waving a ten-pound note under his nose did not stop him from closing.

Robin said hesitantly, "We could go up to my room and order drinks from room service."

Roger looked at her, a smile tugging at the corners of his mouth. "You certain you want to risk that?"

"Risk what?"

"Well," he said, "I do have a reputation, you know. The London grapevine has passed the word that it's not safe for a woman to be alone with Roger Blaine."

"I'm not worried, if you're not."

"Then what are we waiting for?"

He took her arm and marched her to the elevators. Going up to her floor, Robin did begin to worry—a little. During the past, hectic few days, she had been so caught up in the dizzying pace he set that she had given little thought to Roger as a sexual partner. Although she had always been aware of him as a male, he had made no sexual overtures. Now that she thought of it, he hadn't even kissed her, nothing more than a goodnight peck on the cheek.

Although they were alone in the elevator, he had not let go of her hand, and she was intensely aware of his nearness. A warm sexual feeling swept over her, and her senses came so vividly alive that she could feel the strong beat of his pulse in his hand. She knew then that she wanted him and that she would not resist any advances he might make. She still balked at thinking of love in connection with Roger Blaine, and did not now, yet his physical appeal was powerful. And how long had it been since a man had made love to her?

The elevator door sighed open, and Roger's voice jarred her out of her reverie. "Robin? Dear one, what a brown study!"

"Sorry." She smiled. "Just thinking."

Inside the room—which suddenly seemed crowded with Roger's male presence—she went directly to the phone and called room service.

Roger was looking around the room with apprecia-

tion. "This is quite a room." His look was quizzical.
"And here I thought you were just a poor student."

She flushed. "I never said that, not exactly. I *am* a
student, but I was left some money when my parents
were killed."

"Recently?"

She frowned. "Yes, not too long ago."

"Ah, I am sorry." His eyes locked with hers, and
Robin felt herself growing warm again.

When the drinks arrived, Roger sprawled in the
leather chair by the table. He sighed and took a
hearty drink. "It's been a hectic few days, hasn't it?"

"It has, and I have to get back to—"

He held up a staying hand. "I know, back to
your—what do you archaeological types call
them?—digs? You will soon, my solemn oath on it."

She said quickly, "I don't want you to think that I
haven't enjoyed myself, because I have."

His gaze was intent. "Had fun, did you?"

"I did."

Carefully he put the glass down on the table, stood
up, and crossed to her. Just as carefully he took her
glass and placed it against his with a clinking sound.
This deliberate conjunction of glasses struck Robin
as symbolic. His every movement seemed performed
in slow motion, in sharp contrast to the racing of
her heart, the hot flow of blood through her body.

Roger took her hands and drew her up, and his
mouth found hers. The kiss was at first tender, tentative, and then became fierce and demanding as her
arms went around him. Locked together, they moved
in a slow dance toward the bed, until the backs of her
knees struck the mattress.

With his lips still on hers, Roger began to undress
her. She helped him, terribly conscious of his mouth
upon hers and the feel of his hands on her body. Her
skin felt hot, and a sensuous lethargy began to steal
through her limbs.

Then his lips were gone from hers, and he was

kneeling in front of her as he peeled her panty hose down and off. His head dipped, and Robin moaned, shuddering. Fingers tangled in his hair, and she stood swaying, eyes closed.

When he stood up, she felt bereft, and she cried out again. Gently he pushed her down onto the bed, manipulating her like a mannequin. He stretched her out on the bed and stood back, shedding his own clothing with dispatch.

And then the long, hard warmth of him was next to her, drawing her into his arms, until she could feel his entire body against her from her face to her toes. Gratefully she pressed into the warmth, relaxing into his kiss, drawing a strange mixture of comfort and excitement from his eager lips and gently probing tongue; and then, just for an instant, a terrible sadness gripped her, and she felt tears start in her eyes as the memory of another face flickered, almost subliminally, in her mind and then vanished as Roger's warm, exploring fingers touched her nipples, sending a message down the nerve pathways to her groin. She felt herself shudder with desire.

She moaned slightly, and the sound seemed to excite him. Bending his head, he teased her nipples with his tongue until she began to toss her head rapidly from side to side, wanting to beg him to put an end to this almost painful ecstasy; and then he was above her, his face nuzzling the side of her neck, his hand low between their bodies, guiding his organ into her. She reached down to help, feeling mindless except for the throbbing of her body, nothing existing for the moment except the two of them, two bodies, now connected as he drove into her and gave a sigh that was almost a cry.

Robin felt herself contract around him, as if to hold that part of him there, but he was moving, moving in a wonderful, smooth, powerful rhythm, moving inside her, against her. She could hear his breathing, loud and excited against her ear, and his excitement fired hers. She moved under him, raising her hips, moving them from side to side, matching her movements to his to maximize her pleasure and his.

And then that wonderful, awful pressure that built and built with each stroke until, in a gut-contracting spasm, her body clenched, and she shuddered from head to toe as Roger, driving into her now with wild abandon, raised his head from beside hers and pounded out his own release. Robin could feel him throb inside her, and in the relaxing of her own passion, she felt a great tenderness for him. She drew his body against hers, hugging him close, murmuring his name, enjoying the feel of his hot, sweaty body, now heavy upon her.

Roger kissed her shoulder and raised his head. "Still fun, Robin bird?"

"Oh, yes! Yes!"

They lay that way for a long time, until their pounding blood had quieted. Robin began to feel uncomfortable beneath the weight of his body, and she made a small movement. Roger moved off, to lay by her side.

She slept. When she woke, Roger was looking down at her, an expression of tenderness on his face. "Did I make you happy?"

She nodded. "Yes, Roger, you did. Couldn't you tell?"

"Well," he drawled, "you ain't seen nothing yet." He stretched contentedly. "I have a great evening planned for tomorrow night—" As she started to protest, he motioned with his hands. "Now wait. I know what I promised, and we'll do it. I have the day free after tomorrow, and we'll visit Stonehenge and the Avebury Ring. Stonehenge"—he made a face—"was something at one time, but now they've got it roped off, and you can't get very close. The bloody tourists were wearing the ground away, can you imagine?"

"I don't care, I want to see it."

"And you shall, Robin, I promise. But first, we play

again tomorrow night. There's a new club just opened, casino and all. I hear the floor show is bloody marvelous."

"That sounds great, if on the next day—" She looked at him severely.

"I promised you, didn't I?" He feigned indignation. She frowned suddenly. "How late will we be?"

"Oh, we'll make a night of it," he said cheerfully. "Come dragging in at dawn. By then I figure you'll be worn out and I"—he leered—"can have my way with you."

She was shaking her head. "I can't, Roger. Not tomorrow night. I have to be back here before midnight."

"But it won't be really swinging until then," he said in dismay.

"I'm sorry, there's no help for it. I *must* be back in my room by midnight."

"Why?" He looked at her, amused. "Are you Cinderella in disguise? If you don't meet the prince here by midnight, you'll turn into the scrub lady? I'd prefer you pass up any rendezvous with Prince Charming and return to scrub lady."

"It's nothing like that, silly! I have to make a telephone call at midnight. It's important that I do."

"At midnight? Good heavens, that sounds mysterious!" His eyebrows climbed. "Aren't I to be made privy to your secret? No, no!" He made pushing motions with his hands. "Forget I asked that, my darling. It's none of my affair, and I have no right to pry."

"Mr. Midnight."

"This is Robin."

"Robin! Where have you been? I was worried. You're a half hour late! What happened? Are you all right?"

"The traffic held us up. I am fine."

"Us? Who were you with, Robin?"

"A man. Roger Blaine."

"Tell me how you met this man, this Roger Blaine, Robin, and who he is."

"I met him at Bath. He's British, a fashion designer."

"Did you meet him by accident?"

"He—he picked me up."

"Picked you up? You mean he had been following you?"

"No. Yes. I mean, he saw me there, in the baths, and wanted to meet me."

"An Englishman. A fashion designer. Did he explain what he was doing at the baths?"

"He said that he often goes to the ancient sites for inspiration for his collections."

"Yes. Well. Have you been seeing him often?"

"Every night since then."

"*Every* night? Then you must like him."

"Yes, I like him."

"Has he—? Have you been to bed with him, Robin?"

"I— yes."

"Damnit! Ignore that, Robin. I shouldn't have asked you that. Sometimes I go too far. Now, listen very carefully, Robin. You are very relaxed, and you are sinking deeper and deeper into the hypnotic state. Do you understand?"

"I understand."

"Good. Now, Robin, I am going to tell you something that you must remember. Whenever you are troubled, whenever you feel—confused, just remember that someone loves you very much. Someone cares. Do you understand that?"

"Yes. I understand that."

"And later, when this is all over, you will remember that and all that I have done for you. Do you understand?"

"Yes. I understand."

"I wonder if you do. Now, how deep are you, Robin?"

"I am at five."

"That's very deep. Good. Now, you must leave England at once. It is very important that you do. You are no longer Robin Mayfield, you are—"

"No! No!"

"Robin! Listen to me! Relax now, take a deep breath, you are—"

"No! No!"

"Robin! This is Mr. Midnight. You will listen to me, and you will do as I—"

Robin slammed the receiver down. Snatching up a sweater from the bed, she ran for the door. In her haste it took her several moments to fumble the door open.

As she shut the door and started down the corridor, the phone began to ring inside the room. It had an angry, insistent sound.

Robin clapped her hands over her ears and ran as one pursued toward the elevators.

Eleven

——◆◆◆——

When Roger Blaine saw the movie, *The Man Who Loved Women,* he found it very easy to identify with the protagonist, for he certainly loved women—all women.

Yet, he did not believe himself to be afflicted with satyriasis or see himself as a victim of a Don Juan complex. It was just that he liked women and enjoyed their company much better than he did the company of men.

The sexual relationship wasn't always his goal. He could enjoy their company without that, if necessary. Of course, he liked the sexual part and had made of himself a superb lover, but it was as much to please women as himself.

What it came down to, he supposed, was that at his stage of the game, he didn't need to prove his masculinity. In the beginning, because of his choice of career, he had worked on projecting a macho image, but he had long ago outgrown such youthful insecurities, and it was partly for this reason he had not come on too strong with Robin Mayfield, feeling content to let matters take their natural course.

He had to admit that he liked Robin better than any bird he had known for a while, which surprised him somewhat, since he was not overly fond of Americans. Proving, he supposed, that the exception proves the rule. Learning that Robin was an active and passionate lover was a pleasant bonus.

Concern for the future was a trait Roger did not possess, so he spared little thought as to what the future of their relationship might be. He was a day-at-a-time fellow, and he was very pleased to discover that Robin made no demands for a commitment, either before or after he made love to her.

There was a certain mystery about her that intrigued him. It struck him that her past was a closed book, and Robin would resist the attempt of any man to open it.

Tonight, for instance, was a good example. She refused to disclose the nature of the mysterious telephone call she had to make, and she had been upset when their arrival back at the hotel was delayed by a half hour.

But mysterious or not, Roger was still surprised when the doorbell of his ground floor flat rang, waking him out of a sound sleep at two o'clock in the morning, and he found Robin on his doorstep. Her cheeks were wet with tears, and her eyes were unnaturally wide.

"My God, Robin, what's wrong?"

Taking her arm, he drew her inside. Something made him step to the door and look both ways along the street. The street was deserted.

So what did I expect, he wondered, some mobster in a trench coat, hand in his pocket, dogging her footsteps?

He closed the door, locking it carefully, and turned again to Robin. She stood as he had left her, hands dangling at her sides, staring straight ahead.

"What is it, darling? What's happened? The telephone call you had to make—is that it? Bad news?"

She shook her head wordlessly.

"Now tell me! Something has happened to upset you, that's bloody plain!" He took her by the shoulders and shook her. "Tell me! Speak to me, Robin!"

She shook her head again, hair whipping back and forth across her drawn face. "Please, Roger. I can't talk about it." Her voice emerged as a whimper, but she seemed to be coming out of shock. "I'm not even sure what happened. I just know that I couldn't stay in that hotel room another second. Can I spend the night here, with you?"

Roger was so exasperated he wanted to shake her again. But he made his voice tender. "Of course you may stay here, little bird. I'd be most happy to have you share my bed."

She nodded, as if reassured. "We'll still go to Avebury tomorrow, won't we?"

"We will. Today now, actually. And since it is so late, you'd better get some sleep, Robin bird. I only have one bedroom, but I can use the couch tonight."

"No!" She seized his arm and hugged it to her. "I don't want to be alone."

In bed, with the lights out, Roger was at a loss. He sensed that her emotional state was delicate, that she was balanced on a thin edge, and he feared that she might run screaming from the flat if he so much as touched her.

Robin solved the dilemma for him. She moved next to him, clinging fiercely. Mouth against his throat, she whispered, "Hold me, Roger! Make love to me!"

He started out being tender, but there seemed to be a savage need in Robin this night. His mind told him that it was probably forgetfulness she was seeking, not Roger Blaine.

It didn't matter all that much. He was soon caught up in the fierceness of her passion and found himself lost in it, until only his physical sensations were real to him.

When it was over, Robin lay still beside him. Her even breathing told him that she was asleep. The faint glow from the night light revealed that her face was at peace now, and yet when he touched her gently, he found her eyes wet with tears. My God, he thought, what terrible thing has brought her to this state?

He felt an incredible tenderness, a great need to protect and shield her. It was an emotion he had never before experienced with any woman.

He lay watching her face, wondering exactly what was happening to him. It was some time before he went to sleep.

Roger didn't wake her, and it was close to noon when Robin finally opened her eyes. She blinked around with a momentary look of fright. Then her gaze settled on Roger, sitting in a chair beside the bed, sipping a cup of coffee.

"What time is it?"

He looked at his watch. "Ten minutes until twelve."

"Twelve!" she sat up in dismay. "Why did you let me sleep so long?"

"You needed the rest. It was after three when you went to sleep."

"But we were going to Avebury and Stonehenge today!" She squinted at him in suspicion. "You let me sleep, hoping you wouldn't have to take me!"

"Not true, Robin bird. There's plenty of time, the whole afternoon." He stood up. "Why don't you take a quick shower and get dressed? I'll prepare us a bite of breakfast."

It was after one when they finally left London, speeding down the four lane highway in Roger's Jaguar. There had been no mention of last night, and although he ached to ask her again what had happened, he refrained. He was just happy to see that she apparently had recovered from the emotional upset. At least on the surface she seemed composed, and he was glad to leave it that way.

Robin's first impression of Avebury was that it was like something from a book—a fairy tale, not quite believable.

The old, old village, complete with half-timbered houses, thatchroofed and quaint, sat within the site of the huge ring of stones. Robin found the effect a little eerie and could not help but wonder if the ancient site had, over the many years of the village's existence, affected the inhabitants in any way.

She shivered slightly, and Roger put his arm around her.

"What is it, Robin bird?"

"I don't know. It feels strange here. It looks so charming, so quaint, but I felt— I'm just being silly, I guess. Overimaginative."

He nodded and pulled her close. "It's the bloody stones. They affect some people that way, although I cannot say that I've felt it myself. Around four thousand years old, they are; about the same age as Stonehenge. Maybe it's trying to think back that far that gives a person vertigo, so to speak. They say that people with psychic ability are affected the most. Are you a psychic, my little Robin?"

Robin, feeling a little embarrassed by her fancies, shook her head. "Not that I know of. Just too much imagination, I suspect." She shook herself, as if to throw off her negative feelings. "Now, you've been here before. Tell me about it. I want the grand tour."

Roger took his arm from around her shoulder and linked her arm with his. "Very well, you will get Professor Blaine's special cram course on the Avebury Ring. The great stone circle of Avebury," he said pompously, "is evidence of a tremendous physical effort, on the same level as the construction of the Pyramids, if on a smaller scale. It is believed that the Neolithic peoples were motivated to build this, as well as the sanctuary and the enclosure on Windmill Hill, by religious cult concepts.

"Avebury Circle itself encompasses an area of approximately twenty-eight acres. Inside the great outer circle are two smaller circles, called the northern and southern inner circles. The main circle is surrounded by an outer bank, ranging from fourteen to eighteen feet high, built up with chalk excavated from the inside ditch.

"The difference between the top of the bank and the bottom of the ditch was never less than fifty feet. As you must realize, the construction of such an earthwork was an enormous task. At the present time the great ditch is silted up to at least half its former depth. When the archaeologist St. George Gray excavated here between 1908 and 1922, cutting across the ditch, he discovered that the bottom of the ditch was, on the average, about thirty feet below the present ground surface—"

"Wait, wait!" Robin said, laughing. "When you get into the role of tour guide, you take it seriously, don't you?"

He waved his hands. "I try to oblige, my lady. I thought you wanted to know everything about Avebury."

"I do, I do, only not all at once! But you're sweet." She tucked her arm in his again. "I appreciate it."

Roger laughed, and they slowed down to a stroll. Robin took a few pictures of the great stones with the small camera she had brought along. She stopped by one stone that reared up like the tooth of some ancient monster of unimaginable size. She ran the tips of her fingers over the rough texture of the stone. The feel of it caused a tingle to run up her arm, as if the stone had a message for her, and her alone.

She said musingly, "Don't you have any feeling for any of this, Roger?"

"Not particularly." He shrugged. "It's impressive, bloody impressive, but no messages, I'm afraid."

"But these stones, so huge, so heavy. Think of the work it took for primitive people to quarry them and put them in place, with almost no tools."

"If you think these stones are something, wait until you see the ones at Stonehenge. There are no indigenous stones of any size within a hundred miles of Salisbury Plain, but there are a number of theories as to how the stones were brought there. One says they were hauled from as far away as Wales and had to be brought by water—"

"Stonehenge!" Robin glanced at her watch. "It's after three! If we're to get to Stonehenge, we'd better leave now!"

"Agreed. If you're through here, Robin bird."

"If not, I can always return another day. I must see Stonehenge today. I've been waiting too long as it is."

They stopped on the way to Stonehenge for tea and sandwiches. Fortunately, the distance between the sites was not great. Still, it was growing late by the time they arrived at the location.

As Roger drove the Jaguar down the road and turned off onto the parking lot, Robin was dismayed to see a high wire fence extending for what seemed an endless distance; the stones themselves were roped off and patrolled by guards.

Noting her look, Roger said, "Too bad you weren't here a few years back. Before they closed it off, you could walk among the stones, even touch them, but no more. They were being worn away. Four thousand years hadn't been able to destroy them, but millions of tourists were wearing them away, bit by bit, touch by touch."

The wind was blowing across the Salisbury Plain when Robin and Roger got out of the car in the parking lot across the highway from the stones. Robin was surprised that the stones could be seen in their entirety from the road, through the wire fencing.

Roger bought their tickets from a bunkerlike booth, below the level of the road, and Robin looked through the windows of gift stalls with their books, paperweights, and other memorabilia of the famous site.

A refreshment wagon was parked nearby, and families, clutching ice cream bars and cans of soda pop, sat about the area, resting before or after their tour of the stones.

Robin found the scene incongruous, and it should have been a turnoff; but the brief glimpse she had gotten of the stones had already touched her in a way that she could not explain, and she knew that nothing that modern man had done, not the fences, not the parking stalls, not the souvenirs nor the ice cream bars, could detract from the power and dignity of the place.

They went through the tunnel that passed under the roadway, and they emerged on the other side, only a short distance from the stones. There were not a lot of people present, a scant dozen or so, and a few guards.

Roger and Robin walked toward the stones, and Robin found herself holding her breath.

The air was fairly clear, but the light was just beginning to fade; fat, battleship clouds scudded briskly overhead, blown by the same wind that touched cold fingers to Robin's cheek and plucked at her jacket.

Slowly they walked along the designated route, set off by rope guidelines. Robin let her breath go with a sigh. They could not be more than fifteen feet or so from the stones. The stones reminded her of a jumble of huge building blocks left by a giant child on an empty plain. Most of the visitors were quiet, and Robin could well understand why. These huge bluestones and sarsens stood like a ring of petrified giants out of the past, and the power of their four thousand years was in them and around them.

The wind blew steadily, and Robin shivered and edged close to Roger. "There are voices on the wind here," she whispered, half expecting him to laugh at her, but he only smiled gently and reached with his left hand to clasp her hand where it clutched his arm.

Robin shivered again, but not from the cold. If she had been asked at that instant to explain what she felt, she doubted that she would have been capable of a rational explanation. She only knew that she felt a power here, a tremendous power, but a power that did not frighten—it was too great, too old, too calm, and too sure.

Around and around she walked, looking at the circle from every angle and then photographing the stones with her little Olympus XA; and all the time, she felt that she was soaking in strength. Roger did not hurry her.

After she had viewed the stones from every angle, she looked at Roger. A fragment of a poem had come into her mind, and she began to recite it:

> "Then ignorance, with fabulous discourse
> Robbing fair art and cunning of their right,
> Tells how those stones were made by the devil's force,
> From Africk brought to Ireland in a night;
> And thence to Britannie, by magick course,
> From giant's hands redeem'd by Merlin's sleight."

Beside her, Roger said, "The poem, 'Stonehenge,' by Samuel Denyel."

She stared at him, unable to disguise her surprise. "Why, yes."

"You see, there's more to me than women and clothes."

Robin smiled, touched that he had known the poem. "I always thought there was," she said softly.

Roger glanced up at the sky. "It's getting on a bit. Are you ready to leave?"

Robin shook her head. "Once more around, please."

Slowly they began making another circuit of the stones. On the west side, they came abreast of a guided tour group. The guide, a tall woman in a gray walking suit, was saying: "The stone at the foot of the trilithon is called the Altar Stone, because of its position. Although some people have attempted to attribute the building of Stonehenge to the Druids, this is unlikely, as the stones predate the Druids by a considerable period of time. The Druids may have used the site, however, at a later date . . ."

Robin sighed. "It's too bad. The idea of the Druids building this place is so romantic!"

Roger looked at her in mock horror. "Next you'll be

telling me that Merlin built the bloody thing, and here I thought you scientific types dealt only in facts!"

She shrugged. "We usually do, although actual facts are a bit harder to come by. Still, that doesn't mean that I don't have an imagination, that I'm not intrigued by the romantic or a touch of mystery."

"You're something, Robin bird," he said amusedly. "Perhaps I should show you Old Sarum."

Robin frowned. "Old Sarum? I don't recall reading anything about such a place."

"It's not all that well-known and not nearly as publicized as Stonehenge, for example."

"What's the mystery about it?"

"It is situated on a hill outside of the town of Salisbury. It was originally a castle within a walled city and was the original location of Salisbury. Sometime in either the twelfth or thirteenth century, the facts are few, the population deserted Old Sarum. Some stories have it that the city was deserted overnight. At any rate, the people moved away and established the town of Salisbury on the plain. Some even call Salisbury New Sarum to this day."

Robin was intrigued. "I'd love to see it!"

"You shall, Robin, my love." He took her arm. "Let's finish here first."

"But it *is* getting late now. How far is this Old Sarum?"

"A fair drive, but it's better seen at night. There's a full moon tonight, and if we sneak in there after dark, after it's closed to the public, we'll have it all to ourselves."

"Closed to the public? Is it guarded?"

"Not exactly, not to the extent that Stonehenge is. Tickets are required by day, and there is a fence, but it will be no trouble to get in. It will, as Americans are fond of saying, be a piece of cake."

Robin was dubious. "I don't know, it sounds. . . . Why can't we go tomorrow?"

"Where's your sense of adventure? You speak of feeling a sense of the eerie here, of Merlin's touch. At night Old Sarum is even more so. Ghosts of the people once inhabiting the walled city seem to walk around, and under a full moon, why, there's no telling what we'll see! In fact, I'll tell you a little secret." He leaned close to whisper in her ear. "Without you along, I'd be afraid to venture there."

It was long after dark when they finally made it to Old Sarum. Roger had insisted on their having dinner and a couple of drinks first, and Robin capitulated. He did have a slightly mad side, this Roger Blaine. Yet she knew that a lady of his would never suffer from boredom.

The entrance to Old Sarum was a winding dirt lane off the main road, up a rutted hill and onto a small, unpaved parking lot, which was empty of cars. There *was* a full moon, but it was occasionally hidden by scudding clouds. From the parking lot, Robin could see wisps of fog drifting across the plain spread out below the hill on which sat the ruins of Old Sarum.

There was a small building at the edge of the parking area, and a light burned over a ticket window, but it was empty. Just beyond the ticket booth was a wire gate, barring access to a wooden bridge.

"See?" Roger flapped his hand. "Not a bloody soul around."

"How about that?" Robin pointed to a heavy padlock and chain on the gate.

"Watch." From his pocket Roger took a small, thin piece of metal, which glinted wickedly as the moonlight struck it. He fiddled with the lock for a few minutes. Then metal clanked dully, and Roger stepped back, opening the gate with a flourish. "Just call me Raffles, the gentleman burglar, m'lady."

Robin went past him with a sidelong glance, her thoughts uneasy. He seemed so adept at picking locks, and too glib by far about it. Was lock-picking a talent that a clothes designer would possess? Was Roger Blaine something more than he pretended? Her thoughts flashed back to that day at the baths and their meeting. Had Roger arranged for it to happen that way?

She was past him now, her heels clicking hollowly on the wooden bridge. She stopped, her breath catching as she looked over the side. She had wondered why there wasn't a fence around the entire hill. Now she saw at least one explanation. The bridge spanned a wide ditch, a dry moat of some width and depth. The sides were quite steep, and from all indications the ditch circled the castle mound completely.

"That's right, Robin," Roger said in her ear. "That's why it isn't necessary to fence the mound. That and the fact that Old Sarum doesn't arouse that much interest in the tourist community." He took her elbow. "Come along."

From the other side of the bridge, a rather steep slope led up to the ruined castle. Halfway, Robin held back, looking down toward the parking lot. A car had just entered the lot, driving slowly, and without lights. Strange!

She tugged at Roger's sleeve. "A car just came into the lot, with no lights on."

He followed her pointing finger, then shrugged lightly. "Likely just a pair of lovers searching for a little privacy. Whoever it is, it's nothing for us to worry about."

Robin still felt a strange unease. "I—I have a bad feeling about it."

"Afraid it might be your Bath masher? Come along, Robin bird." He laughed. "If you have bad vibes now, wait until you get inside!" He clamped a hand around her wrist.

Robin went along reluctantly, looking back over her shoulder. The moon had come out, glinting off the windows of the car down below.

Roger gave her hand another tug, and she went

along silently. The moment they topped the small rise and she saw the courtyard of the castle and the crumpled walls and rooms surrounding it in the glow of moonlight, she forgot about the car below. The silence was strange; the only sound was the wind, a strong wind sweeping up from the plain below. It seemed to sing, and for a moment Robin imagined she could hear a babble of voices riding on the wind. So strong was the impression that she tilted her head, listening hard. The voices, if such they were, had the sounds of an incantation of evil. An involuntary shiver passed over her.

Robin gave her head a shake, chiding herself. And the sound became the wind again, nothing more.

Roger touched her elbow. "Over there, to our left is what is left of the original bakehouse. The grassy circle in the center was the inner bailey of the castle. The ruins over on the right are the remains of Bishop Roger's Palace." His laughter was low. "No relation, that I know of. The building rising straight ahead, the most complete left standing, is the postern tower. Let's go up there first."

They began walking along the graveled walk bordering the grass. "The view from up there is spectacular. You can see the remains of Old Sarum town, as well as the ruins of the cathedral."

Their feet crunching on the gravel was the only sound to be heard. Even the sighing wind was momentarily still. Roger guided Robin up the steep slope, then up worn steps to the battlement and to the lip of the mound from where they could look down onto the moon-bathed plain below.

Roger pointed out the site of the ancient town, keeping up a running commentary. Suddenly Robin was certain that she heard something from the courtyard behind and below them. She twisted her head around, but the old stone blockhouse obstructed her view. Sneaking a quick glance at Roger, she saw that he was gazing off toward the lights of nearby Salisbury, saying something about the city, his hands in motion.

She took three quick steps to her right, to a spot where she could peer back at the courtyard, her glance taking it in with one sweep. She saw nothing—

Wait, just to the left, over by the chapel ruin! Had it been a movement, a shadow? Robin stared intently. If there had been anything, it was gone now. Probably a dog, or maybe a night-prowling tomcat.

"Robin? Where—? Oh, there you are!" Roger crossed to her. "Be careful around here, my love. It's not all that safe at night. Many of the chamber roofs have fallen in, and you could tumble right in. They should be railed off, really, but again because it's not terribly popular—" He chuckled. "There're even some privy pits, quite deep. The bloody plumbing was quite primitive, you know. But I know where the dangers are located, so don't let go of my hand. Let's go along the bank here, over to the palace. From the edge of the embankment there, you get the best view of all."

They started walking, picking their way carefully. There was a path of sorts, but it was strewn with stones large enough to trip over.

To their right yawned a black hole. With a firm grip on her elbow, Roger guided her to it, just as the moon hid behind a cloud. It would have been impossible to see all the way to the bottom of the hole even if the moon had been shining; the hole was too deep. Robin felt a lurch of vertigo. Determined not to let Roger know, she gritted her teeth and didn't move back.

Abruptly she heard a whisper of sound behind them, like the shuffle of footsteps. She turned her head and saw a dark figure, face hidden by shadow, rushing right at them, hands outstretched. It was clear that the onrusher intended to push them into the pit! Into Robin's mind flashed the thought of the close to ten thousand dollars in traveler's checks in her purse.

She screamed, and Roger whirled. The attacker was almost upon them. With a shout Roger shoved Robin aside, then grappled with the onrushing man. The shove knocked Robin off her feet, and she landed with a hard thump on the stony ground.

Looking up, she saw the two men locked together, struggling fiercely on the edge of the pit. An image lanced into her mind of two other figures locked in a life-and-death struggle on the edge of a cliff, and she gasped.

Then she was on her feet, caught in the grip of such terror that every instinct told her to flee for her life. Yet she realized that, for the moment at least, it was not her life so much in peril as Roger's. His assailant was several inches taller, broader, and clearly the stronger of the pair. He was gradually forcing Roger closer and closer to the brink of the pit. Even as she watched, she saw Roger lose his footing and almost fall into the pit. In a desperate lunge he managed to scramble back and tried to dodge around his attacker, but the bigger man was too quick. He snaked out a long arm, pulled Roger to him, and then began to force him toward the pit.

For another moment Robin trembled on the edge of indecision—flee for her life or rush to Roger's aid?

Then a muffled cry was wrung from Roger. Without thinking, Robin rushed at the figures and attacked Roger's assailant from behind, kicking at the backs of his legs with her sharp-toed boots and beating on his back with her fists. She received no reaction and redoubled her efforts. In her frustrated anger she closed her eyes.

Then her wrists were seized in a cruel grip. Her eyes flew open. The first thing she saw was that Roger was gone and that she was in the grasp of the attacker.

She stared straight into his face, determined to

recognize him if he let her live and she ever saw him again. The moon was out from behind clouds, washing his face in cold light.

Robin blinked. Something was wrong, off kilter. His face was blank, featureless. Then she knew—a stocking was stretched tight over his face, rendering him unrecognizable. She couldn't even see his eyes.

There was no time for further thought. She was sent flying through the air. She tensed herself for impact with the ground, but it did not come. With a lurch of dismay she realized that she was falling into the pit!

She struck then, but not on hard ground—on something soft and yielding, something that absorbed most of the impact. The knowledge hit her like a blow—she had landed on Roger! She almost screamed, but some instinct warned her to be silent. Roger made no sound, nor did he move.

Robin stared up at the opening of the pit. She could see the black, menacing silhouette of the man above limned in the moonlight.

Pebbles rained down from above, one hitting her on the cheek. She closed her eyes again, and just in time, as a flashlight beam struck her in the face. She forced herself to lie perfectly still, not even daring to breathe.

She heard a muttered obscenity and assumed that their attacker was furious because there was no ready access to her and Roger; after all, the man's purpose had to be robbery, and he hadn't yet accomplished that. *Was* there a way down into the pit?

She listened intently, straining her ears until they ached. After what seemed an eternity, she heard footsteps going away. Robin opened her eyes cautiously. The moon was behind a cloud again, and she could see very little. It was totally dark around her, and the square opening of the pit was only a lighter darkness.

"Roger?" she called softly.

There was no answer.

She rolled off him, feeling the knees of her panty hose tear on the rough stones. Kneeling, she felt for his face. He was lying on his back, but his head was twisted at an odd angle. Her fingers found his half-open mouth. It was a moment before the fact registered that there was no stir of breath against her fingers.

"Roger?"

Both of her hands found his face now, and his head rolled loosely on his shoulders.

Dear God, he was dead! His neck had been broken by the fall!

Panic struck Robin like a hammer blow. Surging to her feet, she attempted to run but careened off one wall of the pit. She was trapped down here with a dead man. Oh, dear God! Roger! Roger, whom she had held, warm and alive in her arms was now only dead flesh; and up above, quite possibly, lurked the man who had thrown them down here.

Her stomach contracted into a knot, and she felt as if she might vomit. Her teeth began to chatter, and she clutched herself with her arms, as if the pressure could hold her trembling body and mind together.

How was she going to get out? It must be at least fifteen feet to the top of the pit.

With a terrible effort, she tried to concentrate on that one thought alone—getting out. First, she must get out.

Slowly she began to grope her way along the wall but stopped after a few feet, afraid that she would come upon Roger's body. If she should stumble over the body in the dark . . .

Oh, Roger!

Hot tears scalded her eyes. The memory of him holding her, loving her, murmuring her name: *Robin*.

Suddenly a fear that had nothing to do with her present situation froze her mind. Robin? Her name wasn't Robin, it was—

She shook her head. She must not think of that

now. If she did. . . . She must *not* think of this now. Now, she must think only of getting out of the pit, but this mental command went unheeded. Like a fast, jerky series of slides, images began flipping in and out of her mind—a cliff, lonely and dark; a man, her father, falling; a young woman with a cold face, her father's wife; a man talking to her earnestly and softly, telling her she was—

She clapped her hands over her eyes and swayed from side to side, but her hands could not block out the tumble of visions in her head—a hospital room bathed in a wash of rainbow light; and a voice talking, a telephone; a voice talking, telling her she was someone else, that she was Angela. Yes, Angela Williams. She was in another country, Ireland. Yes, Ireland. There was a tall man with drama in his deep, laughing voice. Oh, dear God! Liam! Liam O'Laughlin . . .

She gasped and pressed her hands to the rough, cold stone wall. She felt as if she were shattering, breaking up into tiny bits and pieces, as brittle and translucent as glass.

She sobbed, feeling torn beyond all bearing; and as she did so, a name came into her mind, spoken by a voice she knew and loved—had once known and loved? *April!*

Like a wave of heat after freezing cold, the voice and name warmed her. April! She was April Morgan, and the voice, she knew, was that of her father.

Her tears began to lessen. April Morgan! She was someone. She had a name. It was something to hang onto, and she clasped the thought to her. There were other thoughts, just beyond her awareness, but she knew that she must not pursue them now. Now, she must cling only to the name that gave her identity and some measure of strength. Now she must concentrate on getting out of this place. She must think only of that.

Straightening, she forced herself away from the

wall of the pit. The moon was still behind the clouds, and she could see nothing. Since neither she nor Roger smoked, neither of them carried a cigarette lighter or matches. She turned her thoughts away from Roger and began to make her way around the sides of the pit, feeling along the walls with her hands and placing her feet gingerly.

One wall, two. . . . Her foot hit something on the ground, and she felt herself cringe, but it was something hard, like a piece of wood. She stooped and carefully felt along the ground until she found it. It *was* a piece of wood. Her hands followed its contours, and after a few minutes of blind groping, she realized that it was a rough ladder!

She breathed a small sound of relief and began trying to hoist the ladder upright against the wall, praying under her breath that it would be long enough to extend to the top, or near enough so that she could scramble out. It was heavy and quite awkward to handle, but at last she had it leaning upright, braced firmly on the ground. It came to within about two feet of the top.

She started up. The ladder was old, the rungs loose, and she tested each one before putting her full weight upon it. She had been in such frantic haste to escape this dreadful pit that all other considerations had gone from her mind, but halfway up, escape within her grasp, April's mind began to function again.

What was she going to do about Roger? Seek help to get his body out of the pit? The police, perhaps? At the very thought of the police, she began to tremble again.

The main thing she had to do was get away from here—not only from the pit and Old Sarum, but England as well. She started up the ladder again. Three rungs from the top, she halted as another thought struck her.

Once out of the pit, how was she going to get away

from the site? Granting the hope that their attacker was long gone, Old Sarum was relatively isolated. It was a long walk to where she could expect to find help. And she didn't want help—she wanted transportation.

There was only one thing to do. It took a supreme effort of willpower for April to force herself back down the ladder; and it took even more willpower to kneel beside Roger's body and fumble her way through his pockets.

As if in league with the evil powers plaguing her this night, the moon was out full now, and she could see Roger's open, staring eyes inches from hers. It seemed to April that he stared at her accusingly.

She clamped her own eyes shut and turned her head aside. She doggedly continued going through his pockets until she found what she wanted—his car keys.

Clutching them tightly in her clammy hand, she whispered, "I'm sorry, Roger. Forgive me."

She climbed up the ladder again. When she was near the top, April poked her head cautiously up above ground and swept the area with her glance. Nothing moved, and she heard nothing but the night birds and the sigh of the wind. But the courtyard below was filled with menacing shadows, which could easily conceal the man in the stocking mask.

She took a deep breath and used her hands to lever herself up the two feet between the top of the ladder and the edge of the pit. When she finally stood fully erect, she looked around again and listened intently. It appeared safe enough.

Over to her left were stone steps going down into the courtyard, but she avoided those and made her way along the embankment. This way she was less vulnerable to a sudden attack. Finally she reached a spot from where she could see the parking lot. A sigh of great relief escaped her. Roger's car was the only one in the lot; the one she had seen pull in without lights was gone. The logical assumption was that it belonged to the attacker.

She began to hurry now, scrambling down the embankment and running through the cut and across the wooden bridge. When she had crossed the bridge and headed toward the parking lot, April thought she heard following footsteps on the bridge. Still in full flight, she risked a quick glance back over her shoulder. There was no one in sight.

She ran on and out of breath and trembling, reached the Jaguar. Quickly she unlocked the car and slipped inside. It took her a few precious minutes to start the unfamiliar automobile. Then she whipped it around and down the narrow, unpaved road to the highway at the foot of the hill.

Turning right, she accelerated, glancing up occasionally into the rear-view mirror to see if she was being followed. Even after she was convinced in her mind that there was no trailing car, she was still tense and apprehensive. Too much had happened this past hour. And Roger, poor Roger lying back there . . .

April began to tremble again. Roger's death was a horror she knew she would never forget. Worst of all, she felt somehow to blame, although it had to be an incident of random, senseless violence.

The thought was no consolation, and the trembling increased to the point where she had to pull off the road for a few minutes to get herself under control.

It was twenty minutes short of midnight when April entered her room in her hotel. She had been lucky enough to find a place to park Roger's Jaguar on a side street a block away, and she had settled her bill before coming upstairs.

Now she began packing quickly, throwing her things into suitcases without concern for neatness.

At one minute to midnight, the telephone rang, an ugly, shocking sound that caused her to freeze. As it continued to ring, she found herself moving to answer it, like an automaton.

Halfway to the nightstand, she skidded to a stop. "No!"

Whirling about, she snatched up her purse and the smallest bag from the bed, the one with her necessities, and ran from the room, leaving the larger bags behind.

Behind her the phone continued to ring.

At Heathrow, she found that the earliest flight leaving was a plane to Frankfurt, departing in twenty minutes. April bought a one-way ticket, using the Robin Mayfield passport, since that was the only one in her possession.

As she started toward the boarding area, she passed a bank of telephones, and the thought of Roger dead entered her mind. How long would he lie there undiscovered?

She continued on toward the boarding area, but her steps became slower and slower. Finally she sighed and turned back to the telephones, dug a coin out of her purse, and found the number to call for the police.

A woman's voice answered, inquiring how she might be of assistance.

Talking in a low, hurried voice, April said, "There is a dead man in Old Sarum. In one of the pits. Roger Blaine. He was murdered."

The voice on the telephone became more alert. "Miss? May I have your name, please?"

Behind her, April heard her flight being announced. Without another word she hung up the phone and sped down the corridor.

Twelve

—◆◆◆—

"Yes, sir, this is the night manager. How may I help you, sir?"

"There is a Robin Mayfield registered at the Inn on the Park. Has she checked out?"

"I shall be happy to check for you, sir. Will you hold for a moment? Or shall I call you back?"

"I believe it's best that I call you back. Fifteen minutes?"

"Very good, sir."

"Sir, Miss Mayfield did indeed check out. According to our records, she checked out shortly before midnight."

"Did she leave a forwarding address?"

"I'm sorry, sir, she did not."

"She left no word at the desk as to where she might be going?"

"No, sir, she did not. But I did speak to the doorman. He informed me that he handed Miss Mayfield into a taxi, and he overheard her instruct the driver to take her to Heathrow."

"That strikes me as rather strange that you should go to the trouble of checking with the doorman."

"Well, yes, I agree, sir. It is rather unusual. But immediately following your first call, I was informed by a hotel employee that the door to Miss Mayfield's room stood open. I made a quick check of the room. Two bags, half-packed, were open on the bed, and several items of clothing were in the closet."

"By any chance did you see any travel folders left behind that might indicate her destination?"

"No, nothing like that, sir. Sir, may I inquire as to your interest in Miss Mayfield? I may have been a touch rash confiding as much as I have, since I have not been made privy to your name."

"It is of no importance. I'm merely a friend, very much concerned for her welfare."

"Shall I inform the police of her disappearance?"

"No, no. I think that would be premature. We don't know that she's actually disappeared, do we? She did check out, after all."

"That is true, sir. About her belongings. If you will provide me with an address, I shall see to it that she receives them."

"No need of that. Robin Mayfield is a wealthy woman. She'll hardly miss a few items of clothing."

Deke lived on Central Park South, in a small penthouse apartment on the top floor of an old building, with a deck crowded with potted plants of every description. The apartment was small by penthouse standards—a living room, one bedroom, tiny kitchen with a bar top for dining, and a small den Deke used for a home office, with an old-fashioned roll-top desk; but since he was a bachelor, the living space was sufficient for his needs.

The rent on the apartment was exorbitant, due to the cost of New York apartments in general, and the prestigious address in particular; he could have lived in a more luxurious, modern apartment for the same rent. Yet he held the same view toward it as he did his office—it had a feel of permanence about it. There was nothing in the apartment much younger than himself, with the exception of the plants. He wasn't an antique nut, he just liked things well-worn and comfortable.

On this particular evening, Deke was sitting in his easy chair, the unread evening newspaper slipping from his fingers as he reviewed his most important case again in his mind.

"If Ransom or O'Brien don't find her soon," he said, half-aloud, "and if the mystery of her father's and stepmother's deaths isn't cleared up soon, I'm going to have to consider other measures. But the hell of it is, *what* other measures? The whole thing is like a series of puzzles, puzzles within puzzles, and sometimes I'm afraid of what I'll find when that last puzzle is revealed.

"Maybe the decision to employ that pair was a blunder. Just goes to show what panic will do to a man's reasoning powers. Maybe the best thing to do is let her run free. No, goddamnit, I can't do that! If this thing isn't cleared up, she'll be running for the rest of her life. I can't have that. I *won't* have that!"

He broke off, staring off into space. He had been telling himself that his relationship with April Morgan was that of an attorney toward the daughter of a valued friend and client. Now he wasn't so sure.

With a snort of self-derision he recalled thinking only a short time ago that Gabe Kemble was in love with her.

"Now the shoe's on the other foot," he said aloud. "How does it feel, Deke, old boy?"

Was he in love with April? He had to conclude that it was entirely possible. How many times had he heard the aphorism: Never become emotionally involved with a client. As if the April Morgan problem weren't complicated enough already!

A ringing phone shattered his mood. With a start he glanced at his watch. He had let time slip past.

He picked up the phone. It was the answering service for his office. "Mr. Travers? I apologize for bothering you at home, but this does seem rather urgent, and the call is coming from London. A Mr. Eric Ransom."

Deke sat up alertly. "Yes, put him through, please."

Eric Ransom's deep voice came over the line. "Mr. Travers?"

Deke said tartly, "Who else would it be, Ransom?"

After a moment's hesitation Ransom said, "You don't sound very pleased to hear from me, Travers."

"You don't expect me to shout with joy, do you? Do you realize this is the first time you've called me in two weeks?"

"I've been busy, too busy to bother with reports."

"I haven't heard recently from O'Brien, either. Not since Ireland. You happen to know where he is?"

"The Gimp?" The sneer in Ransom's voice was undisguised. "I don't know where he is, but I'm in London."

"In London? April is in London?"

"She *was* here. She flew out last night."

"You and O'Brien are two of a kind," Deke said in disgust. "I've only heard from him once, from Ireland, and *he* was calling to tell me that he had found her and lost her again."

"Oh, but there's a difference," Ransom said smugly. "I know where she went from here. She took a flight to Frankfurt."

"Frankfurt?" Deke leaned forward. "You sure about that?"

"I'm sure, sure enough that I'm calling from Heathrow, with a ticket to Frankfurt in my pocket. I'm climbing on a jet to Frankfurt thirty minutes from now."

Deke made a quick decision. "No. No, you're not, Ransom. I want you to drop it, as of this minute. This whole thing was a mistake, a stupid move on my part. As soon as I hear from O'Brien, I'll be telling him the same thing."

There was a brief silence, then Ransom exploded. "You want me to drop it! Where the hell do you/get off telling me that, after all the time and effort, not to mention money, that I've put into this thing!"

"Your expenses will be paid, I told you that at the start."

"Expenses! Shit! That's peanuts. No way! You promised fifty thousand to the man who found this girl, and now that I'm about to collect, you're calling it off! Not only do I intend to collect the money, I want to see this thing through. I've got a curious itch about this whole thing, and I have to scratch it."

"But it's not going right. It's gotten out of hand. First, O'Brien finds April, and she runs. Now you find her, and she runs."

"Big difference. The Gimp found her and probably let her know it, in his clumsy way. With me, she did the disappearing act *before* she was aware of me."

"You don't know that."

"Oh, yes, I do. That's the way I operate. When I find her, I'll have her nailed for you before she knows it."

"No. I can't risk it. I want you to drop it. Now!"

"Listen to me, Travers. We have no written contract, true, but we do have an oral agreement made before witnesses. Look it up, Mister Attorney. An oral contract is binding. No, I find April Morgan for you, you owe me fifty thousand."

"Ransom, you'll not get a dime from me!"

"When I find April Morgan, and I will, depend on it, we'll see about that!"

Before Deke could respond, the receiver was banged down on the other end. Deke hung up slowly, feeling frustrated and bitterly angry. Had he set something in motion that he couldn't stop? In the beginning he had thought it a workable plan to hire a capable man or two to find April and set up a guard over her. Now it had backfired. A chilling thought struck him. Did Eric Ransom plan to kidnap April and hold her for ransom?

The irony of the man's name hit him forcibly, and he laughed without humor.

"Deke? Dr. Kemble is on three."

"Gabe? How are you?"

"Deke, I have some bad news. At least I think it's bad news, it's certainly puzzling."

Deke sighed, rubbing a hand down across his face. "This seems to be my day. Is it about April?"

"Indirectly."

"Now what does that mean?"

"Well, you know, since her disappearance, I review her file every so often. I keep going back to it, hoping to find a clue to what happened."

Deke tensed and leaned forward. "And you found something?"

"Not in the file itself. You see, Deke, they're missing."

"April's file? But how could that be? You sure you haven't simply misplaced it?"

"That was my first thought, naturally. But my secretary and I have searched every inch of my office, and she swears that she replaced April's file the last time I looked at it."

Deke was frowning, thinking furiously. "Her file is the only one missing?"

"Yes."

"No doubt of that?"

"No doubt whatsoever."

"Then it can mean only one thing. Someone got into your office somehow and stole her file. They were looking for her file specifically."

"What do you think it means?"

"God alone knows. Nothing good, you may be sure. Have you any idea how long it's been gone?"

"It could have been any time within the past two weeks. It was just over two weeks ago that I pulled it."

"Things are getting out of hand, Gabe." Deke sighed. "I've had news of April again. I was going to call you, but I've been busy trying to make some arrangements." Succinctly he told Gabe the substance of Eric Ransom's telephone call.

"So April is in Frankfurt now?"

"It seems likely."

"What do you plan to do?"

"What I should have done when I learned that she was in Ireland. I'm flying to Frankfurt, hoping to find her before Ransom does. The whole thing's backfired, Gabe. I know, you warned me that I might be making a mistake. But I thought that pair might find her and keep an eye on her, while in the meantime I could learn more about what happened at Cape Cod that night." His voice turned bitter. "I don't know any more now than I did, and April is in even more danger."

"I'm going along, Deke."

"There's no need for you to do that. It's not that much your problem, and you have a practice to consider."

"It *is* my problem, and April is more important than my practice."

Deke sat up, suddenly alert to the passion in Gabe Kemble's voice. He had known that Gabe had been attracted to April during those all too brief psychiatric sessions with her, but the full extent of the psychiatrist's emotional involvement hadn't been apparent to him until now. It was on the tip of his tongue to demand that Gabe stay out of it, when Gabe spoke again.

"Besides, when you find her, you're going to need me. God knows what mental state she will be in. Bad, probably, now that she feels she's on the run."

"I imagine she always thought that, Gabe." Deke's mind wasn't on what he was saying. He was wondering what to do. He couldn't stop Gabe from going to Frankfurt. He cursed himself for telling the psychiatrist as much as he had. He sighed and said, "All right, Gabe. If you insist on going, I can't very well stop you. But we'll have to wait until after tomorrow. I'm involved in a court case. That's why I've been so busy. I've been trying my damnedest to get a postponement, but the judge is adamant. He refuses to grant one, and it'll take another day to wrap the case up—"

"No, Deke," Gabe said firmly. "I'm not waiting. I'm leaving on the first flight to Frankfurt that I can get. You can fiddle around here all you want. Not me."

"Damnit, I'm as worried about April as you are, but I can't get away today. It's just not possible! I would be disbarred if I just took off. The judge is pissed off at me. He won't even allow another attorney to replace me. One more day can't make all that much difference!" Even as he said it, Deke wondered how true that was.

"I don't have to wait for you. You said yourself that April may be in grave danger."

"Gabe, I can't stop you from going on ahead, but I do wish you'd wait for me."

"Sorry. I'll see you in Frankfurt. I'll let you know where I'll be staying."

A floating body was found lodged against the pilings under the Fifty-ninth Street Bridge on the East River by two teen-agers. They first thought of obeying the admonition of their parents—"Don't get involved!"—but the possibility for excitement was too tempting. They hailed a police cruiser and directed the uniformed officers to the body.

Both were seasoned officers, but the sight of the drowned man—later determined to have been in the water for at least a month—was enough to make them queasy. Fortunately, all they had to do was pull the body up onto the bank and follow the routine—radio for homicide investigators, wait for them to arrive, make a verbal report, and then leave.

Thus, by the usual routine, the bloated, stinking corpse was passed along the various channels and shortly ended up on the autopsy table under the scalpel of an assistant medical examiner. There were no identification papers on the corpse—even the clothing labels had been removed.

Cause of death was much easier to determine. Death was by gunshot wound in the heart, the .32

caliber bullet still lodged in the left ventricle. It was determined that there was not enough water in the lungs to be the cause of death—prior to the bullet wound.

Identification of the dead man was a slower, more tedious process.

Lieutenant Harker was the homicide man in the charge of the investigation—at least the dead man's file ended up on his desk. He went through the normal routine, halfheartedly, since it seemed likely to him the dead man in the end would become a permanent John Doe. The fingerprints were routinely sent to the FBI in Washington.

Two days later he received a telephone call from the bureau. As he hung up the phone, he said, "I'll be damned!"

The detective at the desk next to his glanced up. "What's up, Ray?"

Lieutenant Harker leaned back. "Remember that floater the two kids found in the East River a few days ago?"

The other man looked vague. "I remember something about it, yeah."

"Well, I would have bet we'd never put a name to him. Turns out I'm wrong."

"So? Who was he?" The other detective grinned. "The long-missing Judge Crater?"

"According to the infallible FB of I, the floater was some guy by the name of Carlos O'Brien."

Thirteen

On the jet to Frankfurt April was tired beyond belief
and emotionally drained. Her thoughts were a disoriented tumble. Memories of Liam and Roger, fragment-
ed and cloudy, moved in and out of her mind. Both
dead; and she feared, without any concrete evidence,
dead because of her.

Abruptly the memory of that night by the fire in
Liam's keep came to her. The memory was stark and
clear, with no misty edges. A melancholy smile
shadowed her face as she recalled not knowing
whether or not she had been a virgin. Why on earth
had she been so uncertain about that?

Apparently the faceless Mr. Midnight, thoroughly
indoctrinating her on all other aspects of each new
identity, had failed to fabricate a sexual history for
her.

Dear God, the real April Morgan had lost her vir-
ginity a few weeks short of her eighteenth birthday!

She and her father had been living in Houston at
the time, and April was in her first year at Baylor
University. Baylor had been her choice; John Morgan
had wanted her to attend a "fancier" college, but
April, in a rare act of rebellion, had refused.

"Daddy, you've been sheltering me too much.
You've kept me in private schools all my life. I think
it's time I got out from under the umbrella and
learned what the real world is like."

"You're right, of course, sugar. You go right ahead.
But remember, if you don't like it, don't be bashful.
Just let me know."

And it was true that after a few weeks April did

177

have doubts about her decision, yet those very doubts proved her right. For much too long John Morgan had stood between her and what he called "the shit-kickers out there." Her problem didn't come from her studies—April had a fine mind and always did well in class. The problem had its roots in the past, in the time after her mother's death, when April was only five years old. There were no female relatives on either side to offer her mothering, and since April spent a great deal of time traveling with her father from place to place, she had little opportunity to make any friends. She suspected that she might not have anyway, for she was already showing signs of being pretty much of a loner. So at Baylor she found herself having difficulty making friends, particularly girl friends.

As far as the boys went, it was not that there weren't plenty of them around; and she did not lack for attention, but she found that she didn't know how to "play the game," as it were. She found small talk difficult, and the teasing, flirtatious mannerisms that seemed to come so naturally to the other girls were not at all natural to her. April supposed the boys thought her standoffish, but since she found none of them terribly attractive, or particularly interesting, she didn't really care.

And then she met Martin Halloway. Martin was a B.M.O.C.—a big man on campus—a wide receiver on the Baylor football team and a good, solid student besides. He was tall and good looking, with a rather sweet smile and a thick head of curly black hair.

However, all of these assets would not have made an impression on April, if he had come on like the other boys, the Billy Bobs and the Bobby Joes, who thought that the way to a girl's heart was through a slap on the fanny and a sweaty wrestle in the back seat of a car.

Instead, Martin had approached her like a gentleman, like one person approaching another, instead of a bull in rut.

They met, in fact, in the college library, over a book on English history, and April, impressed with his sensitivity and serious mien, was attracted to him immediately.

They started seeing one another, and the friendship expanded rapidly into a romance. They had several dates, and not once during the entire time, did Martin attempt a pass. In fact, he was so gentlemanly, so unfailingly proper in his behavior toward her, that April began to wonder if there was something wrong with her. Wasn't she desirable? Didn't he like her? Was he *gay*?

So when the time came—and it did come—that he finally made his move, she had no thought of resisting him. Her body, she realized, had been ready for this for some time. It was only her mind that had held her back, and now he had disarmed this mental guardian. Almost gratefully, she fell into his arms and into his bed, finding in herself depths of passion that she had not known existed, reveling in the thought and pleasure of "being a real woman" at last. It was heady stuff, very romantic.

April gave no real thought to the future, even their future. She was only a freshman, after all, and Martin a sophomore. They both had to finish school before they could think of anything permanent. In fact, the idea of a permanent relationship never entered her mind.

However, evidently it had entered Martin's, because one evening, after they had finished making love in his room, he asked her why she had never introduced him to her father.

She glanced at him in some surprise. "I didn't know you wanted to meet him. And besides, he's gone so much."

He stroked her hair with his hand. "Well, I thought

it might be nice for him to meet his future son-in-law," he said softly.

"Son-in-law?" she repeated, startled. "What are you talking about?"

"You and me, naturally."

She moved slightly away from him. "You've never mentioned this before."

He shrugged. "I thought you knew. We're so close. I thought it was understood."

"We still have to finish school," she said slowly.

He shrugged again. "We don't *have* to wait until then. Lots of people get married while they're still in college, and in our case. . . . Well, I mean it's not as if we would have money problems."

April felt a small click in her mind, a warning. "You mean because of daddy? Because he's rich?"

For once Martin, usually so sensitive to her moods, did not seem to gauge her unease, but pressed eagerly ahead. "Well, he *does* have it. I mean, we can't just ignore that fact, can we? And it will make things a lot easier for us. We could get married now, instead of having to wait. Wouldn't that be great?"

He squeezed her hand, and April felt an ache in her throat. "Yes, of course. Great."

When she left Martin's room, April went home to her own room and fell across the bed. She was remembering things, small hints that hadn't meant anything at the time, but which now fell into place. She was pretty sure that this was what Martin had had in mind all along; that he had arranged to meet her, to court her, not because of undying love or passion, but because of John Morgan's money.

That evening after dinner, she went to visit her father. She told him about Martin and about what she felt and feared.

She had always felt that one of the best things about her relationship with her father was the fact that he always listened to her seriously. Even as a child, he had treated her confidences with respect, and she had therefore always been able to tell him anything. She did so now.

"Ah-h, so that's it! I'm sorry, sugar." He took her hand and pulled her against his shoulder. "I knew this would happen sooner or later, and I broke my hump trying to think of some way to prepare you for it. But there is just no way, you have to experience it for yourself."

"I wish I could give all the money away!"

"Don't say that, April, don't ever say that!" he said sharply. "The fellow who said he's been poor and he's been rich and it's better to be rich knew what he was talking about. *I* know from personal experience. This business about poverty being ennobling and the poor inheriting the earth is just so much wind."

She pulled back to look up into his face. "But, Daddy, how am I ever going to know whether a man loves me, or the money? Not that I love Martin or anything like that. I wouldn't marry him on a bet."

"I know, sugar. It's always going to be a problem for you. You're a beautiful girl, but even if you were ugly as sin, the boys would still be haring after you. In fact, if you were ugly, it'd likely be easier for you. Then you'd *know* they were after the money and could act accordingly." He cupped her chin, tilting her face up. "You're going to have to live with it, learn how to handle it. You're levelheaded, thank the good Lord for that much!"

She gazed into his face trustingly. "I'm lucky I have you. You can always advise me."

"No!" he said harshly. "You're going to have to make your own evaluation of the man, each time you get involved." His voice became gentler. "I won't always be around. And even if I was, it wouldn't work. You may think right this minute that you'd follow my advice. But if there's one truth in this old world, it's that a boy or girl in love, or thinking they're in love, almost never follows their folks' advice. Most times it works the other way. Let a girl's daddy turn thumbs down on some old boy, and that drives her right to the altar with him!"

April automatically checked into one of Frankfurt's best hotels, the Frankfurter Hof.

It was only after she was in her room that she wondered if it would not have been wiser to have chosen a less conspicuous place.

Since the experience at Old Sarum, much of her memory had come back, and hourly, she was remembering more. She knew who she really was now, and she was concerned about her passport, which bore the name of Robin Mayfield.

She had heard that it was possible to purchase forged papers, but she didn't have the least idea of how to go about doing so. She had, luckily, plenty of money—how and why she had it she did not know—so funds were not an immediate problem, yet she felt very uneasy traveling under the Robin Mayfield name. She must find a way to get a new passport.

More and more agitated, April sank into a chair and pressed her hands to her temples, trying to will herself calm.

Pictures and random thoughts kept intruding into her mind, unsought. Her father, his young wife, the scene on the cliff. Ireland, Liam, Roger—and through it all, soothing and insistent, talking, coaxing, the voice on the telephone.

April shook her head angrily. Who did that voice belong to? What was he trying to do to her? The voice said that he was a friend, that she should trust him, but how could she do that now?

And that silly name, Mr. Midnight! A name out of a comic strip or a children's book. Mr. Midnight. *Who was he?*

She shivered and clutched her arms with her hands. If he called her, if she heard that voice again, would she be able to resist him? Or would she lose herself again, become Betty, or Sarah, or God knows who else?

She drove herself out of the chair, shaking her head. Yes, she was remembering a great deal, too much perhaps, yet there were some things that were still obscured by a kind of mental curtain, such as her father's last words on that awful night. He had said something to her before he had gone out, but try as she might, she could not recall what it was.

She shook her head again, as if to clear it of the worrisome thoughts that clung to her mind. Perhaps she should order tea. She was probably hungry; in fact, she *was* hungry. Maybe she would feel better when she had some food in her stomach. Reaching for the telephone, she tried not to think about the instrument in her hand as she dialed room service.

During her first two days in Frankfurt, April never left the hotel. She took all her meals in her room and spent the time trying to fill in the gaps in her memory.

But on the second day, she began to feel confined and decided that she had better go out for at least a short while. In the room was a brochure describing an all-day boat tour of the Rhine River. April read through the literature and came to a decision—tomorrow she would play the tourist and try, for a few hours, to forget all that had happened. That afternoon she went down to the tourist office in the lobby and made arrangements for the tour.

The next morning she joined a dozen other tourists on a tour bus, which picked her up at the hotel. Most of the passengers were American, with a few other nationalities sprinkled among them. The driver was a dour, middle-aged man who spoke little English.

The tour guide was another matter. Slender, slight, with sunglasses and long blond hair, he walked with a slight limp. But he spoke excellent English, had a charming smile, and was glib and ingratiating.

"Welcome aboard, ladies and gentlemen. My name is Rudi Ernst. I am a student in Frankfurt, working part of the time as a tour guide to improve my command of the English language. And"—the charming smile flashed—"to pay my way through the university."

For some strange reason, being in the relatively small confines of the bus, April felt sheltered, free from any threat. She relaxed, dozing part of the way, for she had slept poorly since regaining control of her true identity. She scarcely listened to the guide's practiced prattle.

The first stop was the town of Wiesbaden. The guide said, "We shall stop here in Wiesbaden for a half hour, ladies and gentlemen. Those of you who wish to shop will find prices more reasonable here than in Frankfurt. I would advise you to purchase your souvenirs and gifts here."

April remained on the bus, shaking her head as the guide looked at her questioningly. She had no desire for a souvenir, and she had no one for whom to buy a gift.

During the half hour that the bus waited in Wiesbaden, she dozed in her seat, luxuriating in the feeling of security that the bus afforded her.

All too soon, it seemed, the others returned, clutching packages, laughing, complaining about the unequal exchange between the dollar and the mark.

After leaving Wiesbaden, the bus began to travel along the Rhine, and April became engrossed in the scenery. There was much to see—fields of dried corn stalks; small, picturesque villages; quaint churches with wispy, elegant spires reaching toward the clear and very blue sky. And then vineyards and more vineyards as they entered what the guide called the Rhinegau, the wine-growing district. It was almost time for the harvest, he told them, and the vineyards were therefore closed to visitors.

April relaxed against the back of her comfortable seat, enjoying the tour. The bus stopped again in a charmingly quaint town that the guide informed them was Rüdesheim. "We will be here for an hour," he told them, "and then we will board the boat for the tour on the Rhine. You will use your luncheon tickets here, and then after lunch, you must gather at that white tower on the river's edge." He pointed it out. "Now follow me, and I will take you to the restaurant."

The restaurant proved to be delightful. April and the other passengers were seated at a long wooden table. They could see into an inner courtyard, where a German trio was playing polkas, while a baritone in lederhosen and a feathered hat sang lustily to an accompaniment of accordion, organ, and drums.

The rest of the tourists chatted and laughed, while April sat quietly, drinking a glass of Liebtraumilch.

The menu offered three choices of luncheon for the tourists: bratwurst and sauerkraut, sauerbraten and German potato salad, and fried chicken. Since April didn't care much for German food, she opted for the chicken, which turned out to be surprisingly good.

The people around her were laughing and talking, but April felt removed from them. She finished her meal quickly and excused herself. She wanted to see something of this town, with its typically German architecture and narrow, cobbled streets.

The village was full of shops, and April, despite herself, was drawn into them, to find walls of cuckoo clocks, racks of horn-handled knives, shelves of trolls, elves, and gnomes, and rows of small toy hedgehogs, called Mikis, in all manner of costumes.

April could not help smiling. The small figures, with their bristly hair and pert, sassy faces, were delightful, and finally she bought one for herself: a small musician, holding a musical score in one hand

and a baton in the other. He would be her good luck piece.

Captivated by the town, she had no idea of how much time had elapsed until she looked at her watch and realized that she had only a few minutes to get down to the boat.

Hurrying, almost running through the crowded streets, she was struck suddenly by the feeling that someone was following her.

Panting, April forced herself to slow down, to gain control of her feelings. It was only her imagination, of course. No one knew she was here. How could anyone be following her?

Still, the feeling persisted. She picked up her pace again. It was past the time that the guide had told them to meet at the tower.

She reached the appointed spot out of breath, with her heart racing. There were only a few of the members of the tour there, and it was at least a half hour before all of the others returned from the shops, with their inevitable purchases.

By the time they boarded the boat, April's heartbeat had calmed, and she no longer felt that she was in danger.

"Silly, just plain silly!" she scolded herself; but, considering all that had happened to her in the past few weeks, perhaps it was understandable that she was nervous and on edge.

The steamer was clean and white, with colored pennants flying from guide wires. The sound of a German band blared over the loudspeakers. She found a chair on the lower deck, a little out of the sun, for she had a tendency to sunburn.

It was a picture-book day—perfect for seeing the Rhine and its scenery. Clouds, high and plumply white, ornamented the extremely blue sky, and as the boat pulled away from the dock, April began to relax again.

As they steamed into the main body of the river,

the band music was replaced by the voice of Rudi Ernst, informing them that they were now heading upriver and advising them to look at the right bank, where fields of grapes, in beautiful, ordered rows, lay like patchwork on the unbelievably steep hillsides.

In the fields April could see people working, clinging to the almost perpendicular fields like tenacious bugs. She found it incredible that anyone could work on so precipitous a slope.

And then there were the castles, looking like every fairytale ever illustrated, castles of austere splendor, of hulking strength, of timeless beauty, all of them perched on the rocky heights, looking down on the river.

And then the towns. April shook her head; they were almost too picturesque to be real. Assmannshausen, where they picked up additional passengers, made her wish that she had time to disembark and wander through its marvelous streets and wooded walks, which she could see from the boat. She sighed pensively. It was all so lovely that it was difficult for the moment to remember all the dreadful things that had been happening to her.

And then they were passing Lorelei rock, from where, according to legend, a siren was supposed to have lured men to their deaths. April found it disappointing. She had always pictured rocks rising from the river, statuelike, dramatic; but instead, there were only sheer cliffs rising high on the right, dark gray and blank. Then they were past the great walls of stone and arriving at Sankt Goarshausen, where they disembarked to return to the bus for the trip back to Frankfurt.

It had been a lovely trip, and April was very glad she had come. She had traveled through some of the most beautiful scenery she had ever seen and had thoroughly enjoyed it. There was a feeling of history and of great age here. From what she could remember, the history, in the main, had been dark and bloody; yet the river, the beautiful cliffs and hills, and castles had a sense of purpose and peace.

Rudi Ernst's voice cut through her thoughts: "Ladies and gentlemen, here in Sankt Goarshausen, we will again board our bus for the return trip. After boarding, we will drive up onto the top of Lorelei rock, onto the bluff, where we will stop for approximately twenty minutes so that you may admire the view. It is a wonderful view, and I'm sure you will enjoy it. Those of you who wish to take pictures will find it an excellent site for that purpose."

Within a few minutes the boat nosed into the wharf, and the tour group filed off the water craft.

"You will notice," Rudi Ernst said, "that the tour group comprises only a small portion of the passenger list. Many of the people living along the river regularly use the boat for transportation, although many more use the trains that run along both sides of the river."

April smiled to herself. So romance was not completely dead in the human heart. Not as long as some people chose the leisurely but beautiful river route, as opposed to the trains, which she had seen speeding along the river banks like rockets.

The bus began climbing, and eventually the land flattened out. They passed a number of vineyards before they turned off onto a narrow, paved road, which ended on a parking lot alongside a graceful white hotel. On the lawn was a statue of the Lorelei siren—graceful, otherworldly, and white as a swan against the green of the lawn.

After leaving the bus, the guide cautioned them to return in twenty minutes, and the group dispersed into its individual components. The land the hotel was on jutted out in a sort of semicircle, falling away in the sheer cliff that was the Lorelei. April chose to go around to the south side of the hotel, following a faint path, whereas the bulk of the bus passengers noisily went to the other side, which was nearer.

The path wound for a few yards through a growth of shrubbery and trees and then opened out upon a breathtaking vista. From where April stood, the cliff plunged almost straight down, but it was slightly uneven, with enough bumps and shelves along it to support a few hardy plants.

She could see across the Rhine and for miles to the south along the river. There was quite a bit of river traffic, and she stood with one hand supporting herself against a small tree, staring out and down. Along the sloping hillside to her left were the inevitable vineyards clinging to the slopes.

As she stood, bemused, April heard soft footsteps behind her but didn't look around, assuming that it was one of the bus passengers. The footsteps came closer and were now almost upon her. Some sixth sense alerted her of danger, and she started to turn.

As she did so, a hand seized her arm in a viselike grip, and another hand clamped over her mouth. She was staring directly into the coldly smiling face of Rudi Ernst. The first thought to enter her mind was that he was going to rape her. But in broad daylight and with a large number of people within hearing distance?

Then she noticed something that sent a chill of terror racing down her spine. He was forcing her slowly but inexorably toward the edge of the cliff! There was a narrow railing along the cliff edge, but it was flimsy, and the space beneath it was large enough to allow a person to fall under it.

April began to struggle, but Ernst had a wiry strength for such a slight man. She tried to bite his hand so she could free her mouth to scream, fighting fiercely all the while. Inch by inch he propelled her nearer the edge. Already she could feel the ground sloping away under her. Then one foot was slipping on loose earth, then the other, and she fell.

She landed on her stomach on the very edge, her feet and legs dangling over. The fall knocked the wind from her lungs, and she had no breath left to scream. She dug her fingers into the soft earth, but she could find little to hold onto.

Rudi Ernst slammed his booted foot down on her hand. The pain was excruciating. Then he placed his foot against her head and pushed, and she slid over the edge. She hung for just a moment, not yet in free fall, and saw him turn and limp away.

Then she fell, clawing at everything she could find that might stop her descent. Her hands closed around a frail bush rooted between a crack between two rocks. It broke her fall for several seconds.

The image of her attacker limping away was imprinted in her mind forever, and she remembered seeing the man watching her at Bath, the man with the slight limp, and she knew that it was the same man. And Roger, Roger had not been the intended victim at Old Sarum! He had just been an obstacle to be eliminated so the killer could get to her!

And the truck in Ireland that had almost collided head-on with her—it had been done purposely! Someone had been trying to kill her. The sudden knowledge was numbing.

She had no time to puzzle over it, for the bush suddenly pulled out by the roots, and she was falling again. A despairing scream ripped from her throat, and she knew that she was going to die.

Just as total despair closed over her, she struck hard against something that stopped her fall. She had time to ascertain that it was a shelf of rock protruding out from the cliff about fifty feet down, and then she began to slide again, for the shelf was only about two feet wide, and already her feet and legs were slipping off. Frantically she scrabbled for a handhold and finally managed to lodge her fingers in a crack in the rock.

Her hold was almost jarred loose when her full weight came down on her fingers, but she managed to retain her grip. She rested for just a moment, then slowly, painfully, began to climb.

Inch by inch she drew herself up. Her arms began to tremble from the effort, and she knew that she couldn't hold on much longer. Then she had one knee on the ledge and then the other. She pulled her body up and turned lengthwise. There was just enough room for her.

Trembling, April closed her eyes and waited for the panic to subside and for her breath to come back.

After a time she opened her eyes. She was lying on her left cheek, and she found that she was staring almost straight down at the broad river far below. The sight terrified her, and for a moment she almost passed out. Quickly but cautiously, she turned her head the other way. What she saw there—a wall of rock inches from her eyes—was of little comfort.

She shifted slightly so that she could look up. The cliff bulged outward just above her, and she couldn't see beyond the bulge.

April forced herself to be calm and considered her options one by one. She seemed fairly safe so long as she remained exactly where she was, yet when night came on, and it wasn't far off, she would eventually doze, and one wrong roll in her sleep, and she would take the long fall to her death. Already the sun had disappeared behind the mountain, and the air was becoming chill. It would be cold here this time of the year. She shivered and felt herself slip an inch, toward the edge. Hurriedly she squirmed back until she was touching the rock face of the ledge.

Had anyone heard her scream as she fell? Although it seemed an eternity, it had only been ten minutes or so. She strained her ears but could hear no commotion above. Faintly now, she heard the sound of a bus motor starting. Clearly no one knew of her fall, except the man who had pushed her. She opened her mouth and screamed as loudly as she could. She screamed until her throat was raw and hoarse. The sound was loud here, echoing against the mountain, but it was soon evident that she couldn't be heard.

Boats plied the river far below. Could she attract the attention of someone on the river? The possibility seemed remote. It was highly unlikely that she could be seen by the naked eye, even if she waved something. Even if she was seen, more than likely whoever saw her would simply conclude that she was waving in a friendly fashion. Only someone spotting her with a pair of binoculars might divine her predicament, and the chances of that happening were infinitesimal. Aside from all that, it would be dark soon.

She could die here and never be missed. If any of the tour group—and she hadn't gone to the trouble to speak to a single one—noticed that she was missing and asked the guide about her, they probably would be told that she had left the tour earlier. When she didn't show up at the hotel within a day or so, they would notify the police and empty her room, and that would be the end of it. Who would miss Robin Mayfield? She didn't even *exist*, except on paper!

The only thing left was to climb up the cliff face. Was that at all possible?

She drew herself up into a cramped, crouching position and craned her neck upward so that she could see around the jut of rock above her. At a rough estimate she had fallen probably fifty feet. Not all that far by measurable distance, yet fifty feet up a cliff almost vertical was a different matter.

And yet, the more April studied it, the less forbidding it seemed. There were ledges, bumps, and dips, and here and there a shrub or a stunted tree had somehow found a place to grow in the rocks.

It would be very dangerous; if she slipped, it would mean her death. She couldn't hope to be lucky enough to find something to stop her fall again. But suddenly she knew she was going to make the attempt.

Aside from the fact that it seemed the only alternative, something else propelled her. A deep anger had been growing in her since she had realized that someone was trying to kill her. And this same someone had murdered Roger Blaine and even possibly, Liam O'Laughlin. The further fact that she hadn't the slightest inkling as to the reason behind it made her that much angrier.

Grimly determined now, she swept the cliff with her glance, searching for the best place to start. She had to make her move before darkness fell; it would be doubly dangerous then.

Water drainage had eroded a small, sloping trench along the cliff face to her right, ending at the shelf on which she lay. It was narrow, about a foot in width, and quite shallow, yet about six feet up was a small tree growing on another ledge. If she could work her way to the point where she could grasp that tree . . .

April knew that if she thought about it too long, her courage might fail, so she started. Lying on her right side, she began squirming up the narrow trench, fingers digging into the hard earth. Once she slipped and slid all the way back down to the narrow shelf and only saved herself from tumbling off at the last second.

Trembling, she rested for a few minutes, then began clawing her way up the trench again. This time she made it all the way to the second ledge. Her nails were torn and bleeding. She ignored the pain, gritting her teeth in grim determination, and studied her next move.

She could see no more rock ledges, but the slope of the hillside from here to the top was gentler, with scattered shrubs here and there. Also, she noticed that there was a thin layer of soil over much of the solid rock.

After she had rested for a few minutes, she straightened up, keeping her body flattened against the cliff. She placed a foot on the roots of the slanting tree and tested it. It seemed firm enough. The question was—would it support her full weight?

"There is only one way to find out, girl," she said aloud. The sound of her own voice startled her. Looking about, she saw that the sun was gone now and twilight was creeping in.

Gingerly she placed both feet on the short tree trunk and slowly levered herself upright. How fortunate that she had worn boots today!

The tree bent under her weight, but it held. She dug her torn fingers into the earth and slowly, painfully, pulled herself up the cliff bit by bit.

Her progress was very slow, indeed. More than once she slipped, each time managing to stop her slide just in time. The knees of her pants were soon ripped open, and her kneecaps were scraped and bloody. She had gone beyond the threshold of pain in her torn fingers; they were numb.

She doggedly continued to claw her way up the cliff.

Before she was more than halfway, darkness fell, and she was so exhausted that she had to rest frequently. Once, during a rest period, she turned her head and looked down at the river. It was lovely, with the string of lights along the shore. Two passenger boats plowed along, and from one, faint strains of music reached her ears. Quick tears burned her eyes. Angrily she blinked them back.

The night was black, and the only way she could gauge her progress was by the faint light at the top of the cliff. It seemed to be as far away as ever.

Realizing that trying to judge her progress was only discouraging her, April kept her head down and did not look up again.

After an interminable time, her head suddenly struck something cold and hard. She looked up. In a daze of disbelief April saw that she had rammed her head into a steel pole supporting a section of guard rail.

Carefully she reached up, gripped the pole as best she could with her torn hands, and hauled herself up. In a few moments she was sprawled safely on the flat ground beyond the guard rail. Tears filled her eyes again, and this time she let them flow unchecked.

But in a few minutes her anger flared up, and she forgot her weariness in her desire to see that Rudi Ernst paid for what he had done.

April got to her feet and limped toward the parking lot. Both the gift shop and the fast food stand were closed and dark. There were lights on in the hotel, but she hesitated to go there in her disheveled condition. She knew she looked a sight and they might not admit her.

She saw a row of pay telephones near the gift shop, and she hobbled toward them. She skidded to a stop, despairing. Her purse! It had been in her hand when she had fallen, and of course it was gone. She hadn't remembered it until that moment. Fortunately her traveler's checks and her passport had been left behind at the hotel in Frankfurt. But that did her no good now.

Then she recalled putting a coin purse into her jacket pocket before leaving the hotel so she wouldn't have to delve into her purse for small change.

She rammed her hand into the jacket pocket and breathed a sigh of relief. Thank God, it was still there—a small miracle in itself.

Opening it, she limped on toward the telephones. On the shelf she arranged a small circle of German coins, inserted one, and dialed the operator. Dear God, let her speak enough English to understand me!

When a woman's voice answered in German, April said, "Operator, do you understand English?"

Fourteen

April had not been in the Frankfurt office of Detective Franz Lenz fifteen minutes before she realized that it had been a grave mistake to report the attack to the police.

At first, when she had finally made her way up the cliff to safety, it had seemed the sensible thing to do. It was only after thinking the thing through that she realized the difficult situation she had placed herself in. Also, the detective was not exactly the most helpful or sympathetic listener she had ever confided in.

Franz Lenz was a middle-aged man, going to fat, with thinning brown hair combed sideways in a laughable attempt to hide his bald spot. His full mouth had a skeptical twist, his muddy brown eyes were cynical, and April could see that he did not believe a word she had told him.

Earlier, he had sent a man to her hotel to pick up her passport, and now, as they talked, he continually glanced down at her passport photo. "Now, shall we have your story again, Fräulein Mayfield?" His English was fair, but he spoke it in a way that made it obvious that it was, to him, a foreign language.

She sighed. "I've already told it to you twice."

"It is good police procedure to have a story repeated several times." He smiled coldly. "In that way we detect any discrepancies, nein?"

"But I—" She gestured at herself, at her torn and filthy clothes and at the blood caked on her hands and knees. "Can't I at least go to the hotel and clean myself up, then come back here?"

"All in good time, fräulein. Please. Once more."

She told the story again. Those muddy eyes never left her face, and she could feel the weight of his mounting skepticism.

"The tour guides are employees of the German government, fräulein," he said heavily. "They are screened carefully and are of the highest quality. Yet you ask me to believe that this guide pushed you off the cliff at Lorelei?"

"It happened just the way I told it. Why don't you check with the guide, this Rudi Ernst, and see what he has to say?"

"Fräulein, the hour is late." He looked from his watch to her face, as though accusing her of causing him loss of sleep. "A call has been made to the tour company, I assure you. There is no way we can contact the guide or his superiors until tomorrow."

"Then why don't we wait *until* tomorrow? That will allow me a good night's rest, and I can return then." She knew, even as she spoke, that she had no intention of talking to this man ever again, not if she could help it. His smile turned wolfish, almost as though he were reading her thoughts.

"The tour stopped for lunch? You had wine with your meal, nein?"

She blinked, puzzled. "Of course."

He made a steeple of his plump hands, peering at her over it. His smile was knowing. "And it is customary for such tour groups to visit one of our fine vineyards and sample its product, nein?"

"No, that was to be done on the way back to Frankfurt, I was told." It suddenly dawned on her what he was getting at. "If you think I was unsteady from too much wine, you're wrong! I did not fall, I was pushed! Can't you understand that?"

"And by the tour guide, an employee of our government?"

"Yes! I don't care who he works for, he did it!"

"Why, fräulein?"

"I don't know why!" She pounded a fist on the desk

and winced as pain shot up her arm. "I was hoping that you could find that out."

"He did not try to steal your purse, you admitted that. Yet this man you had never seen before today pushed you off Lorelei?"

"As hard as that may be to believe, that is precisely what happened." She remembered her thoughts as she was falling—that the limping guide must be the same man she had seen watching her in Bath. But she had no intention of telling this man of that. If he wired London for information on her . . .

The detective's muddy eyes were speculative, and once again she had the fancy that he was reading her mind. He said, "Have there been any other attempts on your life, fräulein?"

"None that I know of," she said too quickly.

"You stated that you flew in from London. You were there for how long?"

"Two weeks."

"Anything unusual happen there?"

She said steadily, "No, nothing."

He leaned back, seeming to relax some of his hostility. "You must admit, Fräulein Mayfield, that yours is a strange story. Strange, indeed!"

"I can't help that, it happened just the way I told it."

"We shall see, we shall see. It is late, as you were so kind as to point out." He leaned forward. "You may return to your hotel now. You have no plans to leave?"

"No, none," she lied, looking straight into his eyes.

"I will pursue this matter tomorrow, and I shall be in touch with you when I have some results."

"Thank you, officer." She stood up, started to leave, then hesitated. "I have no money for a taxi. Would you be kind enough to provide transportation in one of your police cars?"

"I am afraid that is not possible," he said flatly. "Our budget does not provide for such contingencies.

There is a streetcar stop right outside the door. The car will take you to within a block of the Frankfurter Hof."

She started away again and got as far as the door before his voice stopped her. "Fräulein?"

She turned back. He was holding her passport up between two fingers. "It is the law that you should have your passport on your person at all times."

She moved to take it. "If I'd had it in my purse, it would be lost, at the bottom of the Rhine right now."

He wouldn't even allow her that small victory. "That could well be, but you still disregarded the law. We in Germany, fräulein, are careful to obey the law at all times."

If, as many said, Frankfurt was the armpit of Germany, the area immediately around the train station, would have to be considered the pisshole of Frankfurt. Kaiserstrasse, the street across from the station, was a section of sex shops, sex shows, cheap bars, pimps, and prostitutes. April had been told that the area seethed with the criminal element of Frankfurt.

It was after midnight when April got out of a taxi before the station. She had left the hotel with all her money, approximately ten thousand in cash and traveler's checks, her passport, and only the clothes on her back. She had no intention of returning to the hotel.

Only the greatest sense of urgency would have brought her to this area. Even the taxi driver seemed concerned.

"You want—here?"

She was already outside the taxi, paying the fare. "Yes, this is where I wish to go." She paid him and added a generous tip.

The driver stared at the money in his hand, then up into her face. "Bad people here."

"I'll be all right. I have business here," she said firmly.

He drove away, shaking his head dolefully.

April was far from as confident as she sounded. Late as it was, there were still a great many people on the street, which was lit by glaring neon. Some were not of the neighborhood—the men ducking in and out of the sex shops. Others, male and female, did belong here, and they eyed her curiously. Some of the men, as gaudily dressed as the varied colors of the brazen neon, paused to give her a bold appraisal. She had never knowingly seen a pimp, but some instinct warned her that they were assessing her as a prospect for their stable.

She couldn't stand here like this any longer. Two doors up was a bar. She started toward it, and one man, with a ferret face and eyes that crawled over her like exploring hands, barred her way and spoke a few words in German. The words were foreign, but his meaning was unmistakably clear.

April stepped around him. Clutching her purse in both hands and vividly aware of the money pinned in her bra—a fortune to the predators on this street—she ducked into the bar.

The interior was like a cave, with the rancid scent of an animal's lair. A naked woman with heavy thighs and pendulous breasts danced tiredly on a small, round stage. Men perched on stools around the stage, glasses in one hand, money in the other.

A small bar in the corner was empty. As she slid onto a stool, the bartender came down to her. "A brandy, please." He frowned uncomprehendingly. April slowly mouthed, "Brandy," and this time he nodded and smiled.

When he returned with the brandy in a bell glass, she said, without any real hope, "Do you speak *any* English?"

He looked blank, asking a question in German.

She shook her head, dug some marks out of her purse, and paid him. The bartender went down to the other end and with bored disinterest resumed watching the naked woman.

April took a sip of the brandy. Now what was she going to do? In planning her moves, the language problem hadn't occurred to her. Just being in a place like this was bad enough, but not being able to communicate her need made it that much worse.

She glanced over at the stage, wondering if any of the men intent on the woman spoke English. Frustration welled up in her until she wanted to scream. Time, time was so precious. When that detective found that she was no longer at the hotel, he would almost certainly put out a general alarm for her.

She had only a day, two at the very most.

April took one more drink of the brandy, then got up and left the bar.

The next bar she came to was just that, a bar. But again, the bartender didn't speak a word of English. Several of the customers were American servicemen from the Army base outside of Frankfurt, but she doubted that they would be able to help her.

She had been on the bar stool only long enough to learn that the bartender spoke no English, when a soldier, in the last stages of drunkenness, made his way down to her.

"Heard you speaking English to the barkeep, sugar. You American?"

"I am," she said, drawing into herself.

"And alone, I reckon?" He had a thick southern drawl.

"That should be obvious." Knowing he was about to put a move on her, April gathered up her purse and prepared to leave without touching the brandy she had ordered.

He placed a hand on her arm. "Then how's about I buy you a drink, sugar?"

"I'm not even drinking the one I ordered."

She stood up, but he still had his hand on her arm, and he tightened his grip. He leered unpleasantly.

"Oh, I get it! You're hooking, a drink won't cut it for you. Okay, how much? At least you're home folks, not like those German broads working the street."

"I'm here on business." She tried to wrench her arm from his grasp. "Let me go!"

"Oh, I know you're in business, sugar, so name your price."

April felt that she was about to burst open with accumulated frustration and rage. Without any forethought she swung her heavy purse. It caught the soldier full in the face. He grunted, reeling back, blood spurting from his nose.

April was already gone, striding from the bar.

Another bar, and yet another.

She was on the verge of giving up, and had to force herself to try one more time. There were only three customers in this bar. The man behind the bar was black. She had already turned to leave when she noted that fact and turned back, hope flaring. She knew that black servicemen often opted for remaining behind in Europe after their service time was completed. Was it possible that he was an American?

He was heavy shouldered, muscular, balding, brown as a walnut. His eyes narrowed as he saw her come in, but he said nothing, didn't move from where he leaned on one end of the bar as she slid onto a stool.

A man in a rumpled business suit turned as April sat down. His bleary eyes widened, and he immediately moved to take the empty stool next to her. "Well, hi, baby! You're just what I've been looking for!" His clammy hand clamped around her wrist.

A large, brown hand snaked across the bar to fasten onto the white hand and bent a finger back. The man in the business suit yowled in pain. "Hey, what the hell!"

"I'm going to break your finger, stud, if you don't back off and leave the lady alone," the black bartender said evenly.

"I was only—"

"I know what you were only." He increased the pressure on the finger, and the man yowled again. "You're getting my dander up. Now shag ass out of here."

He lifted his hand, and the man slid off the stool, almost falling in his haste, and scurried from the bar.

The black man looked at April and said mildly, "Of course you can't blame the guy too much. As the saying goes, what's a lady like you doing in a place like this?"

"Thank you," April said, trying to still the trembling in her voice. "I came in here—" She cleared her throat. "I need help. You're an American, aren't you?"

"I was. Right now, you might say I'm a man without a country." He gazed at her in speculation. "You need help, so you saw I was American and black to boot, so you figured I was a touch. Right, momma?"

"Nothing like that. This is the third—no, fourth—place I've been in."

"You're really cruising, aren't you?" he said, amused. "You must be in some kind of a bind. So, lay it on me."

She drew a deep breath and took the plunge. "I need a passport, a forged passport."

His eyes narrowed. "Who sent you to Caleb?"

"Caleb?"

"Me." He jabbed his chest with a thumb. "Caleb Jones."

"No one sent me to you, Caleb. I knew of no place to go except down here. As I said, yours is the fourth place I've been to."

"The innocence of little children," he mused. He added roughly, "It's not very bright. You have any idea, lady, the things that can happen to you here? And neither is it very bright to go around asking every hustler for a forged passport."

"But I haven't done that. You're the first."

He said musingly, "Saying I could help you,

momma, it's going to cost, usually what the traffic will bear."

"I expected that."

His gaze took in the obviously expensive cut of her clothes. "Yeah, I should have figured that. But since that's not my usual line of work, I probably can manage it without too much bread."

"Then you'll help me?"

"I'll see what I can do, but it'll be through a third party. He'll never know you and vice versa. What name do you want on it?"

"I hadn't thought that far. So many names—" She laughed, recalling the names given to her the past few months by the voice on the telephone.

"Something funny?"

"It's too complicated to explain, and you'd probably think I was crazy—if you don't already." She thought hard for a moment. All at once the true incongruity of the whole scene struck home to her, and she laughed again. "How about Lisa? How does that sound?"

"As in Mona Lisa?" he asked gravely.

"I hardly think I fit that image, but why not? Lisa—Lisa Smith?"

Caleb shook his head. "Not Smith. I don't know what you're running from, lady, and I don't want to know. But Smith would be like waving a red flag to any smart dude. And Jones, forget that one as well."

"All right. Lisa Starr. That exotic enough?"

"No worse than Rip Torn." He was smiling now, for the first time. "I like your style, momma. Two more things you have to do—no, three. First, you have to trust me."

"I trust you, Caleb." Suddenly sobered, the banter at least lightening her mood, April said, "I have no choice, do I?"

"Then you have to give me a thousand dollars, American, now. I think I can get it done for that price, but the guy I know always wants his money up front. He doesn't work on spec."

"All right. Where is the ladies room?"

He pointed to a battered door at the back of the room. Caleb's expression was amused as she slid from the stool and headed in that direction.

"Watch out for the roaches," he called after her as she opened the door.

Roaches were the least of it, she thought, trying to close her nose against the overpowering odors of vomit, urine, and cheap perfume.

Closing herself into one of the flimsy stalls, she unpinned the handkerchief from the inside of her bra and took out a thousand dollars. Looking at the money, she hesitated. It was a risk, but one that she must take.

After giving Caleb the thousand dollars, she would have very little cash left. Tomorrow she would have to go from bank to bank in Frankfurt and cash in the eight thousand left to her in traveler's checks. She hoped the police detective would not miss her until she had time to cash all the checks.

Back in the barroom, she slid the bills across the bartop. Caleb took the money without counting it and put it into his pocket. Again, she wondered if she was being foolish, trusting this stranger.

"Second thoughts?"

"Not really." She smiled palely. "Besides, I have little choice, as I said."

"The second thing I need is a picture."

"How about the one in my own passport?" She was already taking it from her purse, then she stopped. "No, I'll need that tomorrow for identification."

"Up the block four doors is an all-night arcade. There's one of those do-it-yourself photo booths. That'll do fine. Go get it done and bring it back to me."

"When can I pick up the new passport?"

"I come on duty at six tomorrow afternoon. I'll have it for you then."

"That soon?"

"For a thousand bucks my man works fast."

She stood up from the stool, then hesitated. "Is there a hotel around here you'd recommend for tonight? I don't want to go back to mine."

"Around here? Momma, the hotels around here are hotbeds for the hookers. You don't want a hotel, anyway. Look, I know a woman who takes in guests. It's comfortable, not too expensive, and she serves a good breakfast. Best of all, she's a friend of mine, she's not nosy, and she can keep her mouth shut. If I tell her to, she's never seen you. Shall I give her a call?"

"Would you, Caleb?" She looked at him in gratitude. "I can never thank you enough. Why are you doing this?"

"Why? Momma, I don't know your troubles, and I don't want to know. But you're on the run. You're scared to death. I've been on the run, and I've been scared. I know what it's like."

Fifteen

Gabe Kemble left Frankfurt's Intercontinental Hotel with one idea fixed firmly in his mind—find April Morgan.

He had arrived in Germany late the day before, and after sending a cablegram to Deke Travers, telling him where he was staying, he had spent a restless and sleepless night asking himself why he had come. It was a question for which he could find no satisfactory answer.

His logical mind told him that he had little chance of locating April. He had no picture of her—those newspaper clippings had been stolen with her file—and he was not familiar with the city. Also, he didn't know the language.

Yet, he had felt compelled to come. He could no longer just sit back and wait for further developments. He must be doing *something* to find and to help April. Why he must do this, he did not know, or did not *want* to know, he wasn't sure which.

So, he wasn't a trained investigator, but he was intelligent, resourceful, and fifteen years of psychiatric training and experience should certainly give him some insight into the patterns of human behavior.

He got up early, still feeling tired from jet lag, and found under his door Deke's answering cable. Deke would be arriving sometime late in the afternoon.

After a hearty breakfast catered by room service, Gabe pulled out the large map of Frankfurt and began to mark it off into sections. Since he had no clue as to April's whereabouts, it seemed to him that his best bet would be to canvass all hotels in the city, from the most expensive to the smallest fleabag. After all, April had to be living somewhere—*if* she was in the city.

It was early afternoon by the time Gabe came to the Frankfurter Hof, one of the older and better hotels in the city.

Feeling hungry, footsore, and somewhat discouraged, he had lunch in the elegant dining room, and then, refreshed, he approached the desk clerk, a tall, fair-skinned man with a cold, pinch-nosed face, and shuttered eyes.

Mentally gearing himself for another struggle with the language, Gabe asked the man if he spoke English. To Gabe's delight, the clerk haughtily nodded, evidently unwilling to give away any samples.

"Excellent," Gabe said pleasantly, determined to be polite in the face of the man's evident unfriendliness. "I am looking for a friend who is supposed to be staying here. Robin Mayfield. Has she arrived yet?"

As Gabe spoke the name, the clerk stiffened slightly, and something flickered behind his gray eyes. Gabe felt his pulse quicken.

"Will you repeat the name, please?" the clerk asked in harsh, heavily accented English.

"Robin Mayfield. Has she arrived yet?"

The clerk's disdainful gaze raked Gabe up and down before he said, "One minute, please. I will check."

To Gabe's surprise the man didn't look in his registration book, but went instead through an inner door behind the counter.

Gabe stood for a few minutes in indecision. Had he gone to fetch April? That made little sense, he could have buzzed her room or had her paged. All the while hope was building in him. She must be here, there was little doubt but that the desk clerk had recognized the name. At the same time a feeling of uneasiness swept over him.

There were no seats in the lobby, so he could only stand by the desk, his impatience mounting.

After a long wait, the desk clerk returned, but instead of approaching Gabe, he went down to the other end of the long desk and conferred with the woman at the checkout section. After a moment's fidgeting, Gabe strode down to him.

"Pardon me?"

The man looked at him as though he'd never seen him before. "Yes? How may I help you?"

"I was inquiring about Robin Mayfield, remember? Is she staying here?"

"If you will be patient, sir, the answer will be forthcoming."

"But wait for what, damnit?"

The clerk dismissed him by turning a shoulder and resuming his low-voiced conversation with the checkout girl.

Utterly baffled and growing angry, Gabe forced patience on himself. He walked over to a pillar before the bank of elevators and stood with his arms crossed, glowering at the man behind the desk.

More time passed, and Gabe was girding himself to confront the clerk once more, when a heavy-set man in a rumpled suit strode across the lobby to the desk clerk. They conversed in low voices for a moment. The clerk's gaze settled on Gabe, and he nodded his head in that direction.

The heavy-set man came toward Gabe, walking with a rolling gait. Gabe straightened up from the pillar, more mystified than ever.

The man said in harsh English, "You are inquiring about Robin Mayfield?"

"Yes, I am. Where is she?"

"You are American?"

"Yes."

"Name, please."

"My name is Gabe Kemble. Dr. Kemble. Now, this

has gone far enough. Who are you, and what interest do you have in Apr—Robin Mayfield?"

"I am Franz Lenz, of the Frankfurt police."

"Police? What do the police have to do with this?"

"You will come with me, please."

Lenz took Gabe's arm. He shook it off angrily. "No! I demand to know what this is all about!"

"All in good time." Lenz took a firmer grip this time. "Come with me, please. You do not wish to make a scene, nein?"

It was mid-afternoon by the time Deke Travers arrived at the Intercontinental Hotel in Frankfurt. He was surprised to find that Gabe was out and had left no message for him. On inquiry he learned that Gabe had received his wire, so he knew of his, Deke's, approximate arrival time.

He was in his room unpacking when the telephone rang.

"Deke, this is Gabe—"

Deke broke in. "Did you find April?"

"Well—yes and no."

Deke's hand tightened on the receiver. "That sounds like a replay of Ransom and O'Brien! Explain, will you?"

"It's an involved story. I think you should get down here."

"Down where?"

A sigh came over the line. "The police station."

"Police station! What the hell? All right, which one and where?"

Gabe gave him directions, and Deke left the hotel room without even freshening up. He got into a taxi outside the hotel.

At the police station he was directed to a room where Gabe awaited him with another man.

Gabe came to greet him with outstretched hand. "For once I'm glad you're an attorney, Deke. The way things are going, I may need one. Gabe, this is Detective Franz Lenz. Detective Lenz, Deke Travers."

"What is this all about?" Deke demanded. "What have the police to do with April?"

"Fräulein Mayfield came to me two days ago, claiming that a tour guide had pushed her over the cliff at Lorelei," the detective said. "I investigated her story, but when I called the hotel to report to her, Fräulein Mayfield had disappeared. Now, I learn that more people are seeking her." His scowl was directed at Deke. "And you, Herr Travers, what is your interest in this woman?"

"I am the trustee of her estate." Succinctly Deke explained about the deaths of John and Sheila Morgan and April's subsequent disappearance. He omitted mentioning Eric Ransom and Carlos O'Brien.

"A psychiatrist and an attorney," Detective Lenz said heavily. "A strange combination, nein?"

"Not so strange," Gabe said. "We're both concerned."

Deke said, "And with good reason, it seems. What's this about her being pushed off a cliff?"

"Fräulein Mayfield came to me with a rather strange story, accusing a government employee of trying to murder her. I was most skeptical of her story. But my investigation disclosed a disturbing circumstance. It seems that the tour guide was *not* an employee of the German government at all, but an imposter.

"The guide assigned to the tour was attacked in his apartment the night before and tied up. Then this imposter presented himself to the bus driver shortly before the tour was to depart and told the driver that the regular guide was ill and that he was a replacement. Since the time was short, the driver accepted the imposter without verifying with his superiors." Lenz went on to repeat "Fräulein Mayfield's" story.

Deke said tersely, "Have you found this imposter?"

"Nein. We have been unable to discover his identity."

"Are you pursuing the investigation?"

"Nein." The detective spread his hands. "To our actual knowledge, no crime has been committed. We have only the woman's story for that, and since she has disappeared—"

"But certainly you're looking for this imposter!" Gabe said hotly.

"We are. The routine is being followed, but I have little hope for success."

"But April! If she's disappeared, something may have happened to her! It's your job to look for her!" Gabe was working himself up into a temper.

Deke put his hand on the psychiatrist's shoulder. "The officer is doing his best, Gabe. April isn't their problem any longer."

"Damnit, it's their job to find out what happened to her!"

"They'll do what they can, I'm sure." He tightened his grip, his fingers digging in. "We'd better go now and let the detective get on with his duties. Thank you very much, Detective Lenz."

Deke was tight with apprehension. Would the man just let them walk out like this?

To his relief Detective Lenz shrugged. "It is nothing more than my duty." His smile was false. "We attempt to cooperate with the Americans."

Deke, not letting go of Gabe's arm, eased him toward the door. Just as he opened it, the detective said, "Herr Travers?"

Deke looked back over his shoulder. "Yes?"

"Will you remain in Frankfurt?"

"Yes, for a few days at least."

Outside the police station, Gabe was seething. He pulled away from Deke's grip. "Why didn't you push that guy into looking for April?"

"Gabe, if the police find her, they might really hassle her."

"Why?" Gabe glared at him, his voice rising. "Why would the police hassle her?"

Deke noticed people staring at them. He took Gabe's arm again. "Let's walk and talk."

Deke took a few moments to get his thoughts in order. He said slowly, "Did it ever occur to you that there is a possibility, just a possibility, mind you, that April may have been responsible for her parents' deaths?"

Gabe skidded to a stop. "You think that *April* killed her own father?"

"I don't necessarily think that, but it's a possibility, you must admit," Deke said defensively.

"I'll admit no such thing! April is incapable of murder."

"You don't know that, Gabe. That's an emotional reaction."

"No, it isn't. I had her in analysis, remember?"

"For what—three sessions? Come on, Gabe, that's not enough to really know."

"It is for me," Gabe said doggedly. "All this time you've been thinking that April pushed her father over that cliff?"

"Damnit, do you think I *want* to think that?" Deke's voice was agonized. "But it has to be considered. It would explain so many things, the reason she blocks out the memory of what actually happened. Don't misunderstand me. I don't think for a minute that she killed him deliberately. But April hated Sheila, she's admitted that freely. Suppose, just suppose, she was fighting with Sheila, and John tried to get in between, and both inadvertently tumbled off the cliff to their deaths. You must admit that is a possibility." As Gabe started to shake his head, Deke said harshly, "All right! But if *I* think that way, you must admit to the possibility that the police might think along the same lines."

Some of the anger faded from Gabe's face. "Okay, I'll grant you that is a possibility." They resumed walking, and after a minute, Gabe said, "But without the aid of the authorities, how are we going to ever find her?"

"We look for her ourselves. At least I intend to do so. I've arranged to take some time away from the office, and I will search until I find her. If April has left Frankfurt, and we have every reason to assume that she has, she had to get a forged passport here. We have to find the person who sold it to her and learn what name she's using now."

"You're not going to use Ransom and O'Brien any more?"

"No. That was the worst mistake I ever made."

After another short silence, Gabe said, "Who could be trying to kill her, Deke? Pass the reason for a moment, but who?"

"From the story April told Lenz," Deke said grimly, "the guy who pushed her off Lorelei has to be Carlos O'Brien. The phony guide limped, remember? Since April has never seen him, nor even knows of him, she wouldn't be on her guard."

Again Gabe stopped. "But why? What earthly reason could O'Brien have? He was hired to *find* her, not kill her!" Then his gaze fastened on Deke's face, his eyes widening. "Wait, I remember something. During that interview, one of those two asked if you'd pay the fifty thousand for April dead, and you as much as admitted that you would! Damn you, Deke! You signed her death warrant!" He seized Deke by the arm and shook him.

Deke didn't resist, and he let himself be shaken until some of Gabe's anger had been worked off.

Finally, with a sound of disgust, Gabe let go of Deke, turned on his heel, and strode off. Deke called after him, "I hope you're feeling better in the morning, Gabe. With or without you, I'm going looking for whoever sold her a forged passport!"

*   *   *

Deke had known it wouldn't be easy, but he had hoped for a little luck. For the most of two days it seemed that luck wasn't on their side. He knew several criminal attorneys in Frankfurt, and he went to them, nagging at them for names, for contacts in the Frankfurt underworld who might, for a price, help them.

They canvassed the city from early morning until far into the night, talking to the dregs of Frankfurt.

At one point Gabe said in disgust, "Deke, I can't believe that April would contact any of these people. They're scum! How would she know *how* to contact them?"

"Who else would she contact? If you want something illegal, you go to criminals. It's that simple. I would guess that she went at it hit or miss."

"If she did it at all."

"April is not stupid, Gabe. She knows that she couldn't stay here, not as April Morgan, not as Robin Mayfield, nor leave Germany as either one."

"That's another thing I don't understand. All those names! In Ireland, Angela Williams, in England, Robin Mayfield."

"She's running, Gabe. She knows enough to use assumed names."

"Where did she get the money? She stayed at the most expensive hotels, and she had no money, Deke, we both know that!"

"When we find her, all that will, hopefully, be answered."

"I guess you're right about one thing. She managed to buy forged passports before, so she knows how to go about it by now. Unless—unless somebody is supplying her with new identities."

Deke looked at the psychiatrist sharply. "But who? Gabe, she doesn't know anyone. She's a loner, she always depended on her father for everything."

"Damnit, I don't know, Deke! Sometimes I think this April Morgan, the one we're trying to find, is a totally different April from the one I hypnotized in that sanitarium!" Gabe shrugged helplessly. "But that's crazy, isn't it? It sounds like something out of a multiple personality case, like *Three Faces of Eve,* something like that."

"Who knows whether it's crazy, Gabe? All I know is I feel like I'm on a merry-go-round, trying to grab the brass ring, always just out of reach, a brass ring that I can't even see!"

The merry-go-round stopped on the evening of the second day.

They had exhausted all the sources given them by Deke's attorney friends and were now doggedly going from bar to bar, without too much hope.

"We might as well start with the bars in the Kaiser-strasse," Deke said. "That's the most logical spot."

They were already familiar with the street, since most of the underworld types they had talked with frequented the area.

"I hate to think that April came here," Gabe said, as they got out of a cab. "It must have been embarrassing."

"People can force themselves to do many things, when fear drives them."

Two hours later they had canvassed most of the bars without success. Not having a picture of April made it worse. Deke spoke enough German to make himself understood, but they had been greeted with blank looks and a hostile attitude all the way.

Entering another bar, Deke said, "I think I'm about ready for a drink. How about you? We've earned it."

"For the first time in my life," Gabe said despondently, "I can see the attraction of getting bombed as a way of forgetting all problems."

The bartender, Deke noticed, was black. He came down the bar to them. "Gentlemen," he said, his brown face without expression, "what's your pleasure?"

"Chivas Regal on the rocks for me. Gabe?"

"A glass of white wine, please."

When the bartender placed their drinks before them, Deke took a swallow of his, then held up his hand to stay the bartender. "You're American, right?"

"Right."

"Well, look—" Deke took a deep breath. "We're looking for someone, another American. A young woman, going by the name of Robin Mayfield. Or maybe April Morgan." As he talked Deke never took his gaze from the other's eyes. He felt a prickle of elation as he noted a slight widening of the bartender's eyes at the mention of Robin Mayfield.

"You fuzz?"

"No." Deke smiled tightly. "And I have a strong hunch that you know we're not the police. There's an intangible something about cops that a man like you would recognize immediately."

The brown face tightened. "A man like me?"

"Yes, and no offense. Look—" Deke leaned across the bar. "I'm Deke Travers, an attorney in New York. And this is Gabe Kemble, Doctor Gabe Kemble. And you?"

"Caleb Jones."

"Fine, Caleb. I am the trustee of April Morgan's estate. Or Robin Mayfield, as you may know her. Dr. Kemble has treated her."

Caleb said tonelessly, "As I may know her? What's with you two dudes? I'm a bartender. I serve drinks. That's it."

Deke ignored the interruption. "April is running. Someone is trying to kill her. If you're as perceptive as I think you are, you could tell that she was frightened. Now, she was in Frankfurt, we know that much. We also know that an attempt was made on her life here, and it came goddamned close to succeeding. We're almost sure that she has left Frankfurt. To do that, she had to buy a passport." Deke paused to take a sip of scotch. "And you know what I think, Caleb?"

"No, man. What do you think?"

"She came to you, and you helped her. Therefore, it follows that you know the name she's using on the forged passport."

"I know one thing, man, you *talk* like a lawyer." Caleb was quiet for a moment, his gaze moving from Deke to Gabe. "Say I saw this chick, just supposing, mind you. And say I knew she was running. How do I know that you two dudes aren't the ones she's running from?"

"If she came to you for help, Caleb," Deke said quietly, "and you helped her, I think it was because you knew that she truly needed help. And to know that, you didn't just accept her word. So, if we tell you we're trying to help, not harm her, you'll have to look beyond what we say and make up your own mind."

Caleb shook his head admiringly, smiling slightly for the first time. "You're something, man, you know that?" He turned to Gabe. "How about you, doctor? I'm supposed to take you on faith, trust, and so forth?"

Gabe's face suddenly twisted. "For God's sake, man, if you've seen April, if you know anything about her at all, tell us! Her life may hinge on our finding her before it's too late!"

"Hey, now," Caleb said softly. "You're one strung-out dude." He turned his back and picked up a bourbon bottle from the back bar and poured a generous amount over an ice cube. He sloshed the cube around in the glass for several moments, staring down into the liquor. Then tossing back his head, he threw the drink down his throat.

Without turning, he said, "When the man hired me, he said I'd be out on my black ass if I so much as sniffed a cork while behind this bar. Ain't you two ashamed of laying this on me?"

He faced around, gaze locking with Deke's. "Lawyer, huh? *Her* lawyer?"

Deke nodded silently.

"All right! If I'm wrong, I'll. . . . But then if you guys are giving me the straight scam, and I keep mum—" He nodded abruptly. "Okay, I saw the chick. She came here, scared out of her shoes. Robin Mayfield, she said. But then she said a strange thing. She said she'd had many names, and that I'd think she was crazy if she told me why. So I arranged a passport for her. She took a flight out of Frankfurt within the hour. Wait—" He held up his hands, palms out. "Don't ask me where she went, I don't know that. Stupid chick started to tell me, and I stopped her. That information I didn't need."

"The name, Caleb," Deke said softly. "It would be nice if we knew where she went, but with the name on the passport, we can find her. It may take some time, but we'll find her."

Caleb's face was like dark stone. "Let me see some identification, gents."

Deke reared back, startled. "Well, sure—" He took out his card case and opened it on the bar. "Gabe?"

Gabe followed suit, and Caleb studied the contents of both card cases. Finally he nodded. "Okay, at least this jibes with what you've told me. Of course, you could have worked it all out beforehand, but that seems a little elaborate."

"Caleb, we're legitimate, believe me. One thing strikes me as curious, though. Why didn't you ask me for identification *before* you admitted that you had helped April?"

"Because"— Caleb moved his face to within inches of Deke's—"if you mother fuckers are jiving me and I learn that this girl is harmed because of my flapping mouth, I'll be looking you up!"

What is it about April, Deke wondered, that attracts men immediately?

He said, "I'll accept that, Caleb. The name, please?"

"The name on the passport is Lisa Starr."

Sixteen

The word for Salzburg was picturesque. Riding in a taxi from the airport, April saw the mountains hulking up in the night, the ancient castles and cathedrals along the river and in the city. The night was cold, and the air was pure.

But most of this April noticed with only a part of her mind. She was still wound tightly in a cocoon of fear, and even the flight from Frankfurt had failed to break her free of it. She felt like a wounded animal being stalked, and she badly wanted to crawl into a hole, where she could safely lick her wounds and overcome her terror.

The taxi driver spoke passable English. When April asked for a good hotel with a maximum of privacy, he said, "The Goldener Hirsch, lady. It is old world and is very, *very* old. It has been a hotel for six hundred years."

April did not wish to shop for a hotel, so she told the driver to head straight for the Goldener Hirsch, and when she found there was a vacancy, she took it.

"The airline misplaced my luggage, they promised it would be along shortly," she said in explanation for her lack of baggage.

She held her breath when the courtly man behind the desk asked, in stilted English, for her passport. Then she sighed, angry at herself. There was no reason in the world that he should give it more than a passing glance.

"Thank you, Fräulein Starr, and welcome to the Goldener Hirsch," he said, closing the passport with a snap and beckoning to a bellman.

She was escorted to a small, ancient elevator and taken up to the third floor. There was a feeling of great age about the hotel, with its thick, white walls and arched doorways, yet it had a quiet charm, and the old-world courtliness of the man at the desk and the bellman put April at her ease.

And when the bellman opened a door with a huge brass key and motioned her in, an immediate feeling of security embraced her. It wasn't merely a room, she had a small suite. There was a long entryway, a sitting room, a large bedroom, and the usual roomy bath, with the enormous tub.

There were no closets, but beautifully carved and ornamented clothes chests stood in the entryway and the bedroom. All of the doorways and windows were arched, the windows showing the thickness of the plastered walls.

The couch and chair in the small sitting room, the curtains, and the spread upon the king-size bed were made of a cheerful fabric, printed in the peasant fashion, adding the final touch to rooms that could have come from Hansel's and Gretel's cottage.

When the bellman had shown her the rooms and she had tipped him, April locked and bolted the door, then moved over to the narrow window. She opened one side outward. Strains of music and the sounds of laughter and conversation drifted up to her. Outside the window was a well, going all the way down to the ground floor.

She was safe here. And with that thought some of her fear left, and she was overcome with weariness. It seemed as though she had not enjoyed a sound, restful sleep for days. She undressed quickly and ran a hot bath, remaining awake with an effort until she was finished.

She was asleep within seconds after falling into bed, but her dreams were uneasy, and on awakening, she remembered disturbing fragments. She was tired, listless, drained of all emotion. Even though her fear had receded, she knew that it would return again if she ventured outside the hotel. She ordered breakfast sent up to the room but ate little of it, contenting herself with several cups of coffee.

April spent the day in the hotel room, refusing maid service, unbolting the door only for room service. She washed out a few things. Since she had left everything in the hotel in Frankfurt, all she had was what she had on. Soon, she would have to purchase a new wardrobe. But not now, not now!

She watched television disinterestedly, understanding little of what she saw. But by evening she was angry with herself, remembering how she had cowered in the hotel room in Frankfurt. She realized that if she catered to fear now, she would be afraid for the rest of her life.

So, as darkness fell she got dressed. It took some time because she stopped several times. Each time, she sank into lethargy in the chair in the sitting room, staring unseeingly at the television screen. Each time, she finally managed to force herself out of the chair and go on dressing.

Finally she was fully dressed and could logically delay no longer. Literally gritting her teeth, April opened the door and stepped out into the hall. She was seized by a feeling of vertigo. Dizzy, she leaned against the wall for a moment.

It could be from hunger, it could be a delayed reaction to all that had happened, yet she knew it was neither. Inside the room, behind locked doors, she felt secure; outside she was vulnerable. Even the empty corridor felt vaguely threatening. She heard the whine of the elevator coming up and tensed herself, her gaze riveted on the elevator door, but it stopped on the floor below.

She pushed herself away from the wall and pressed the button. Thankfully, the elevator was empty.

Downstairs, as she started for the dining room in the rear, she had to pass by a small bar beyond the lobby. It was empty of customers, only a plump bartender leaning on one elbow behind the tiny bar.

She went in, ordered a scotch and soda, and sat down at a corner table where she could see the lobby. As she drank, several people passed back and forth, but no one came in, nor even spared her a glance. She finished the drink and ordered another. April seldom drank more than one drink, but the bite and warmth of the liquor were relaxing her, and with each sip, her fears gradually lessened.

By the time she went into the small dining room, it was late, and she was immediately shown to a table. April ordered a substantial meal, rich Austrian food, and ate heartily.

Hunger appeased, she lingered long over coffee. The atmosphere in the café was relaxed and charming, the waiters friendly and eager to please, and she no longer felt threatened.

She decided that she would not hide in her rooms. Tomorrow, she would see the town of Salzburg—but no guided tours. She shivered, remembering.

The next morning she left the hotel and strolled along the cobbled streets, lined with shops old and new. With its quaint shops; many cathedrals; the ancient fortress, Castle Hohensalzburg, brooding on the town from the heights; and the colorful native costumes, Salzburg had the look of a storybook village. Yet there was an ageless reality about it that impressed April. The citizens wore their native costumes because they wished to, because they were comfortable in them—not to provide an Austrian Disneyland for the tourists.

After a two-hour walk, she grew weary and took one of the horse carts for a leisurely tour of the inner city. At no time did she feel she was being watched or followed. Had she given them—whoever *they* were—the slip at last? She fervently hoped so!

When she got off the cart, April strolled through

the Kapitalplatz on the south side of the cathedral.
She paused, staring up at the massive bulk of the
fortress on the hill. She was strangely drawn to it and
finally walked up the slope to the funicular railway
that ran up to the castle.

The view from the cliff was spectacular. From the
far side she could see for miles in the clear air, across
a spreading valley, with colorful houses, green fields,
and a winding river, to the distant, snow-capped
mountains.

On the city side, the town of Salzburg could be
seen in its entirety. The fortress itself was over nine
hundred years old, yet it had been well kept and
looked as it had for centuries.

She rested for a while in the main courtyard, underneath a three-hundred-and-fifty-year-old lime tree.

In the end she took the guided tour through the
great castle, viewing the State Apartments, the Gold-
en Chamber, the Court Room, the Keep, the Torture
Chamber, and the "Salzburg Steer," an organ built in
1502.

Into April's thoughts intruded the memory of her
supposed purpose in visiting the Avebury Ring and
Stonehenge in England—she was supposed to be an
archaeological student. Wryly she recalled that she
had never before had the slightest interest in the subject, and yet now she was fascinated by this place
and knew that she could spend days exploring it.

Then she remembered Roger Blaine, lying dead at
the bottom of the pit at Old Sarum. She closed her
mind to all thoughts of Roger and hurried to catch up
with the tour.

It was late afternoon when a tired April returned to
the Goldener Hirsch, laden with packages. She had
spent the last hour shopping for new clothes. She was
tired, yes, but she was also contented. It had been an
interesting day, and little thought of danger had disturbed her.

A taxi was drawn up before the hotel. The bellman

was busy with several pieces of luggage, and a tall, broad-shouldered man wearing cowboy boots was lifting a woman from the taxi and putting her into a wheelchair as April came up.

She stood back out of the way while he wheeled the chair across the narrow sidewalk toward the door. The bellman had already gone inside. The tall man struggled to hold the door open and push the chair inside at the same time.

April put down her packages and hastened to help, holding the door open. He flashed her a grateful smile and rolled the wheelchair inside. April noticed that the woman was slender, with dark hair streaked attractively with white. April judged the pair to be in their late thirties.

April followed them inside, the bellman taking her bundles. The man in the cowboy boots was at the desk, and he faced around as she came in. "My thanks, ma'am. Sometimes I take on more than I can handle."

There was a Texas twang to his deep voice, and April looked at him more closely. His face was ruggedly handsome. His rather large nose had been broken some time in the past and reset crookedly. His thick hair had a reddish tint, and his face was deeply tanned and weathered, lines radiating outward from his dark eyes. There was a certain world-weary, cynical look about his features, yet they had a strength that was reassuring, and his whole appearance was such as to be attractive to women, April was sure.

She started, flushing as she realized that he was speaking, and a glint in his eyes told her that he was fully aware that her scrutiny was more than casual.

"I beg your pardon?"

"I was introducing myself, ma'am. I'm Walker Longley, and this is my sister, Susan."

"How do you do? I'm—" For a panicky moment April had to search her memory for the name she was using; it was the first time she had spoken it aloud. "I'm Lisa Starr."

"I'm right please to meet you, Miss Starr."

He put out his hand, and April hesitantly took it. Hers was lost in his big hand. He didn't let go of it, turning her toward the wheelchair. "Sis, this is Lisa Starr. Ain't it nice to meet a fellow American so far from home?"

The woman in the chair had a sweet voice and an even sweeter smile. "It is indeed, Walk. Are you staying here long, Lisa? In Salzburg, I mean?"

The question startled April for a moment. "I haven't really given it much consideration." She remembered the nice day she'd had and how taken she was with Salzburg, and she added, "But I believe I may."

"Good! Since my brother and I intend to stay for a while, perhaps we can see more of you."

She held out a slender hand, and April took it, surprised at the woman's strength. She remembered reading somewhere that people losing the use of their legs often compensated by developing strong arms and hands.

Walker Longley smiled, his teeth startlingly white against his deep tan. "Sis was in a car accident back home and had her legs banged up pretty good. The docs back there don't seem too hopeful, so we just packed up and hiked ourselves to a clinic in Switzerland. She's been under treatment there for some months, and things are looking up. But they wanted to stop treatment for a spell, so we decided that we'd sashay about and see something of Europe while we're over here."

"They are optimistic, then?"

"Oh, yeah. They say she'll be up and about in time."

April smiled. "I'm glad."

The man at the desk called Walker's name. He

winked at her. "I reckon we have to get settled in, little lady. See you soon now."

April nodded and crossed the lobby, bemused. She experienced a little anticipatory thrill at the prospect of seeing the big man again. In fact, they both seemed to be very nice people, and she thought it would be good to cultivate friends. Thinking back, she recalled that she had not made friends in any of the other cities, except for Liam and Roger—and that was another matter entirely.

After a leisurely bath and a change of clothing, April was refreshed and hungry. Downstairs, she started past the small bar, saw that it was deserted again, and went in. Just before she reached the bar, a voice hailed her from one corner. "Miss Starr? How nice to see you again so soon!" Walker Longley stood, uncoiling his long body.

God, April thought, he's so big! She felt a trifle intimidated, yet there was something about his sheer size and the battered face that was reassuring.

"Mr. Longley." She glanced around. "Where is your sister?"

"Sis is feeling poorly. She's been through hell these past months. She needs a rest, more than anything."

He pronounced *thing* with a broad A, and April suddenly found herself near to tears. His size, his open, breezy manner, the physical strength that he projected, as well as his voice and manner of speaking reminded her of her father.

Moving toward her, he squinted in concern. "What's wrong, little lady? Your face suddenly got all clouded up, and I surely hate to see that happen to a face as pretty as yours."

April shook her head, angry at herself. "It's nothing. As my father used to say"—she smiled palely—"a shadow just moved across my grave."

"Hey now, that's what my old daddy used to say!"

He beamed. "Your daddy a Texas boy, by any chance?"

"He was. Before he—"

"Passed on, has he? Aw, hell, I'm sorry." He cupped her elbow in his big hand. "You were about to order a belt, right? I insist that you join me."

April hesitated briefly, then found herself nodding. "All right, I think I'd like that, Mr. Longley."

He steered her toward his corner table, motioning to the bartender with a jerk of his head. "One thing, though. No more of this 'mister' business. I'm up there, Lord knows, but that makes me feel old, old!"

April had to laugh. "Okay, Walker. But you have to call me Lisa."

"Now that's a deal, little lady."

He made a production out of pulling out her chair and settling her in it. "Hope you're not one of these militant feminists, who scolds a man for holding doors open and such like. I'm old-fashioned, I reckon."

"I don't mind, I rather like it."

"Good, good!" He folded his big frame into the small chair with difficulty, then focused his dark eyes intently on her face. "Now you have to satisfy my curiosity, honey. What's this Lisa Starr? That sounds like something right out of Hollywood land. That your real name? I know, I'm being nosy, it's a failing of mine."

April hesitated just a beat too long before she lied, "That's my real name, hard as it might be to believe."

His weathered face showed nothing. He spread his hands. "You tell me, I believe it."

The bartender came over with their drinks. Walker raised his glass, a lopsided grin on his face. "Here's to a Texas lady."

"No, no," she said swiftly. "My father was a Texan. I was born on the East Coast."

"Same difference. You've got Texas blood, that's the important thing." He drank deeply. "Your father was an oil man, was he?"

Her breath caught. "Why, yes, he was. How did you know that?"

"Hellfire, honey, any old boy from Texas has to be hooked up with oil some way." His brows knitted. "Funny, though, I thought I knew most of the oil boys. Don't recall any Starrs."

"That was years back. My father was a roustabout in the Texas oil fields in the early days. For the last number of years he was into many things." She gave a rueful laugh. "To tell the truth, I was never too sure what he was into. Business always bores me."

"Spoken like the daughter of a true tycoon."

To change the subject, April said, "What do *you* do, Walker?"

He shrugged and gave her that lopsided grin. "Little of this, little of that."

She was disconcerted. Somehow, she had gotten the impression that Walker Longley and his sister were wealthy people. Then she said lightly, "Does that pay well?"

He gave a bellow of laughter, throwing back his head. "Oh, I like your sense of humor, honey!" He grew serious, pushing his glass back and forth, studying the wet rings on the table. "It's not quite like that. I quit going to school after I graduated from Newcastle High, and I went to work as a rigger with my daddy in the oil fields. He was a wildcatter, my daddy, and he had brought in so many nonproducers that some called him Dryhole Longley. Always behind his back, of course. My daddy was feisty and loved nothing better than a good scuffle."

He took a drink. "We went from field to field. Then he struck it, and I mean big! Happens sooner or later to most wildcatters, if they've got the guts to stick with it. Trouble is, daddy never lived long enough to enjoy it." His face darkened with melancholy. "But then I reckon I shouldn't say that. He didn't live to enjoy the spending, but I think he got all the boot he needed out of knowing that he'd finally struck it, after more'n twenty-five years of being laughed at.

"But he left me with quite a bundle, money that I could play around with, and that's pretty much what I've done. I reckon you could call me an investor. I invested daddy's money and did all right. Oh, it has its ups and downs, because I like to invest in things with risk. Where's the boot, otherwise? Right now, I'd have to say we're riding one of the ups, me and sis." His grin flickered. "If we weren't, we couldn't afford that Swiss clinic, the expensive doc, and this place here."

He beckoned the bartender for another round of drinks.

When the drinks came, Walker Longley launched into a lengthy, funny, rather salty anecdote about his father and an oil field in Texas. April listened, breaking into frequent gales of laughter. Walker was a practiced storyteller and was capable, she was sure, of embroidering any tale to make it more entertaining.

He thumped his glass down. "Now, little lady, you're going to have to let me buy you supper. And tomorrow, we'll see some of the sights, you and me. Sis says she's not up to it yet. Between you and me"—he leaned forward confidentially—"she doesn't want to be a burden. She hates for me to have to shove that chair of hers around, she purely does."

He was moving a little fast for April, and she felt like slowing him down a little. Then she thought, why not? Why not go with the flow and enjoy herself? She'd had little cause for enjoyment of late.

He was saying, "I hear tell there's a gambling joint up on top of that mountain. You like to gamble, honey? Shoot craps, things like that?"

She remembered Roger and the casinos he had taken her to in London, remembered all too vividly, and she started to shake her head.

His gaze grew intent on her face. "There you go,

Lisa, getting that clouded-up look again! What'd I say, what'd I say?"

"Nothing, Walker," she said hastily. "I guess I'm just not too crazy about gambling. It seems—well, such a waste of money."

"Not the way I do it, honey. You watch old Walk with those cubes, and you will agree. Course, poker now, that's really my game. That's where you separate the men from the boys." His face took on a reminiscent look, then he shook his head sharply. "But I reckon I'd better not get into a poker game with these foreigners. Shitfire, these people all have strange faces. When I set down to cards, I like to play with some old boys that I know. I can read 'em like an open book."

"Will you be coming home soon, Deke?"

"I don't know, Callahan," Deke said, sighing.

"You've got calls stacked up here. Some sound pretty important."

"I've made up my mind, Callahan. I'm not giving up here until we find April." He added gloomily, "Or until we find out what's happened to her. I haven't filled you in on that yet. Somebody is trying to kill her."

"Kill her?" There was an anxious note in his secretary's voice. "Who could be doing that—and why?"

"I haven't an answer for either question. But I have a strong suspicion about the first."

"Whom do you suspect?"

Without answering directly, he said, "Have you heard anything from either Ransom or O'Brien?"

"They haven't called, no." Maggie's voice was thin. "Deke, surely you don't suspect *them*?"

"From some things we've learned, it seems likely that Carlos O'Brien tried to kill April in Frankfurt."

"Oh, no! But why, why would he do that?"

"That's one of the mysteries. The only reason I can think of is that they hope to collect the fifty thousand on her, dead, since I was damned fool enough to promise to pay it even if they found her dead."

"But that's callous, ruthless! They aren't—I mean, they didn't strike me as being like that."

"I didn't think so, either," he said morosely. "But it could be we're both wrong, whatever consolation that might be. Eric Ransom even threatened to kidnap her, if and when he found her."

"Deke—no, I can't believe that." There was the sound of a sob in her voice.

Deke held the receiver away from his ear for a moment and stared at it, completely mystified. Was Maggie Callahan crying? Why? Surely it couldn't be for April! Although she hadn't put it to him in so many words, he had always known that she didn't entirely approve of his spending so much of his time, and money, trying to find April. She'd said to him, early on, "Deke, I think it's wrong for you to spend all that money, the firm's money. *Your* money. Since I've been handling the checks, I've found out it is your money, not Morgan money. What if you do find her and she doesn't want to be found? It could be that she would take it into her head not to repay all that money, and there's nothing you could do, not a damned thing, since she didn't authorize it."

He put the receiver to his ear again. "Callahan?" There was no answer, and he couldn't even hear her breathing. For a moment he thought that she had hung up, but the line was still open.

He waited impatiently. Then he heard a cough over the wire. "Callahan? What the hell is going on?"

"I'm—sorry, Mr. Travers. But I—"

He laughed uncertainly. "Hey, what's this mister shit? I don't think you've called me that since about the first week you went to work for me!"

"Mr. Travers," she said, her voice oddly formal. "I have something that I must tell you, before I change my mind. You're not going to like me very much after you've heard."

"For Christ's sake, Callahan, will you get to it!"

"Eric Ransom is my—well, we're lovers."

The news was so unexpected that Deke was stunned into momentary silence.

"Mr. Travers?" she said tremulously.

"Yes, Callahan, I'm here," he said slowly. "Eric Ransom is your lover. If I read that bit of news correctly, this means that you steered him into this situation. Am I correct in that?"

"Yes, Mr. Travers. It was one of those things. I met him several months ago. He's the most exciting man I've ever known, always off to glamorous, faroff places, doing exotic things, the kind of man you only see in the movies. When you placed the ad for someone to look for April Morgan, Eric was at loose ends. I thought your proposition would be ideal for him, and when I mentioned it, he jumped at the chance. I thought"—her voice sounded clogged with tears again—"you'd both benefit—Mr. Travers?"

"Yes, Callahan, I'm still here, still trying to sort this all out. The other one, Carlos O'Brien. How did he come into it?"

"From what Eric told me, they'd been on a job together down in South America, and they figured they'd try another one together."

"That was quite an act they put on, when I hired them and afterward, pretending to be—well, friendly enemies, at least."

"From what Eric told me, they've always been that way. But O'Brien, according to Eric, was badly in need of money, too, and Eric is softhearted."

"Oh, sure, he is!"

"I beg your pardon?"

"Callahan, what do you know about this O'Brien?"

"Nothing beyond what Eric told me. I never met him until that day he came to your office with Eric."

"If what I've learned is true, O'Brien is a killer, at least a wouldbe killer, since he tried to kill April at least once. There was also an attempt on her life in Ireland, which could be his work."

"Deke, Carlos O'Brien might be a killer, but Eric isn't capable of killing anyone!"

"How many times have I heard that? The nice man next door, who wouldn't hurt a fly, turns out to be a mass murderer. Now, you said yourself that you've only known Ransom a few months. How do you know *what* he's capable of?"

"Deke, if Eric calls, I'll tell him about your suspicions of his friend and warn him to be careful."

"No!" Deke said sharply. "You'll tell him nothing! Not about my suspicions, not about my learning he's your lover, nothing! Let him think I'm still totally in the dark. Do you understand?"

"I understand," she said in a dead voice. "I don't blame you. I'll clean out my desk and be gone at the end of the day."

"What the hell are you talking about?"

"You're telling me that I'm fired." A note of hope entered her voice. "Aren't you?"

He was silent for a few moments. He was tempted to say yes. He felt betrayed, he was absolutely furious with her—she had placed April in jeopardy. No, strike that. *He* had put April in jeopardy, by his own abysmal stupidity. And if either Ransom or O'Brien called his office and found Maggie Callahan gone, they would naturally assume that he knew about the setup.

"Callahan," he said, "I can't decide about your future right now. I won't deny that I'd like to crack you across the head, but I need you there. And I need some time to assess this situation more calmly. You just stay there, and we'll reach a decision when I get back to New York."

"Thank—thank you, Deke," she said in a choked voice.

"You just remember one thing," he said grimly. "When or if either of those two call, this conversation never took place! Have you got that?"

"Yes, Mr. Travers."

"All right. I'll keep in touch."

He hung up but remained at the desk, deep in thought.

One fact was very clear—either Ransom or O'Brien, or both together, posed a definite threat to April. Their motive was cloudy, but that was of minor importance. He had to find her before they did!

Sighing, he leaned back. For three days he and Gabe had tried every means at their disposal and still had not discovered where April had gone. With the help of the attorneys Deke knew in Frankfurt, they had canvassed hotel after hotel, beginning in Frankfurt and radiating outward, for word that a Lisa Starr had registered. No results. They had queried custom officials in numerous airports in various countries, as well as consulate offices, all without results.

It almost seemed that April had disappeared without a trace.

Gabe was clamoring for him to enlist the aid of the police, but Deke was still reluctant to involve the authorities. He knew, however, that he would soon have to capitulate if they didn't find her.

Well, there were still a large number of hotels and entry points to several countries that he had yet to query.

Each night he compiled a list of numbers to call, gave half the list to Gabe, and they spent the day on the telephone. Deke got the list out. Today's list was made up of Austria and Switzerland. He reached for the phone to call Gabe's room.

April had to be somewhere, and it was more urgent than ever, with what he had just learned from Maggie Callahan, that she be found soon.

Seventeen

———◆◆◆———

Walker Longley surprised April. From the little she knew of him, she would have thought he would be a reckless gambler, betting heavily when he had a run of the dice. Instead, he was a conservative bettor, and he played the don't come line, wagering only small sums when he had the dice.

They had dined well in the restaurant at the Café Winkler, with its magnificent view of the city, and it was after nine when they entered the casino. It was quieter, less crowded, and had a more subdued atmosphere than some of the casinos Roger had taken her to in London. Also, most of the people in the London casinos had glittered—the men were in tuxedos and the women in evening gowns, sparkling with expensive jewelry. Most of the patrons of the casino at Café Winkler were in everyday clothes.

When she commented on this fact to Walker, he said, "The folks here, honey, are mostly from back home. Tourists. The way I get it, it's early in the season. The Beautiful People, they don't come around until the winter season. Never could quite figure out that phrase." He grinned crookedly. "Beautiful People, hah! The shit kickers out there seem to think that having big bucks automatically makes folks beautiful. Most of the rich folks I've met are ugly as sin. My old daddy said that greed makes 'em that way. My opinion, it's the holding onto the bucks that makes a person ugly, that and trying to get more."

This bit of philosophy struck April as a touch strange, when she considered the fact that Walker himself had money, evidently a great deal of it. They had found a place at the dice table now, and Walker's whole attention was concentrated on the table play, which gave April an opportunity to ponder something that hadn't occurred to her since she had finally straightened out her identity.

Did she have money? She could recall reading articles about John Morgan, liberally sprinkled with references to his wealth; therefore, it should follow that she was also wealthy, since she must have inherited. She had always had everything she ever wanted and had traveled first-class. Still did, she thought ruefully. She thought of the money in the hotel safe—almost eight thousand dollars.

Where had the money come from? There were many murky areas yet in her memory. Mr. Midnight, for instance, a shadowy figure made menacing by the mere fact that she could not reconstruct a picture in her mind of what he looked like. All she could recall was that hypnotic voice on the phone.

She could remember, now, the numerous identities he had given her, the midnight telephone calls and the sometimes stern commands, yet she could not remember where or when or how the money had been given to her. There was a checking account in a New York bank in her name she remembered—or had been before she started on this strange odyssey—but the balance was only a few hundred dollars.

But whatever Mr. Midnight's purpose, he must have funds and resources at his disposal. In every city, and with each new identity; there had been clothes, expensive clothes, a supply of traveler's checks, and new papers—and she was always registered at the most expensive hotels. Whatever else he was, she reflected, Mr. Midnight was not stingy.

Her reverie was interrupted by a whoop from Walker, and she turned to the dice table. A woman down at the end of the table had the dice and was riding a streak of luck. Walker was betting with her, not heavily, and each time she won, he hedged, pulling half of his winnings, while the shooter let all hers ride.

"Way to go, little lady!" Walker boomed. "Hope you don't mind if I ride along, ma'am?"

The woman—a fiftyish, plump, housewife type, face bright pink with excitement—blew on the dice cupped in her hands and beamed at him. "Course not, mister. You're bringing me luck!"

She threw the dice and came up with a seven. Walker whooped again and scooped in half his winnings. April watched, bemused. Now, with his winnings stacked before him, Walker was in exuberant spirits. He fitted the image she had formed of him; he seemed larger than life, swept along on a tide of self-confidence. He seemed to have shed years and showed a boyish quality that was endearing.

He grinned at her, pulling her against him. He beckoned to a waitress. "A pony of brandy for my lady!"

April had had a cocktail before dinner, several glasses of wine during dinner, and she was already high. She had consumed more alcohol during the past two days than was her habit and had to wonder if she was drinking too much. But Walker's excellent spirits were infectious, and she accepted the pony of brandy.

By the time they left the casino two hours later, they both had consumed two more ponies of brandy, Walker Longley had won several hundred more schillings, and they were both in ebullient spirits.

When Walker had cashed in his chips, he had won the equivalent of two thousand dollars. On the way out he hugged April, burying his face in her hair. "Honey child, you're my good luck charm! Hellfire, I should have you with me all the time!"

She laughed suddenly, and he peered down at her. "What's so funny?"

"You are, Walk!" She hugged his arm close to her. "Here you've been telling me about all the big deals you've been involved in, and now you're happy as a kid because you won at the dice table!"

"Different thing, honey." He grinned sheepishly. "The fun in gambling comes from the fact that you *can* lose. There's no boot in winning if you can't lose as well."

"You told me that was the fun in your—uh, investments." They were alone in the high-speed elevator going down the mountain. "The risk involved."

"True, true. But the thing with the investment game is that the money's never on the table before you. The only things you ever eyeball are the papers, contracts, and such like."

She shook her head. "It all strikes me as a game, a power game."

"You're right, honey, but ain't it all a game? Life, the whole ball of wax?"

Remembering her own life of late, April thought that, if what Walker said was true, it was a game that she would just as soon not participate in.

"Now there you go again, clouding up on me." His face was very close, so close that his warm breath fanned the fall of hair around her ear.

Then she was in his arms, and he was kissing her. It was a surprisingly gentle kiss from such a bear of a man, yet there was passion in it, a rather desperate urgency that aroused a spark of response in her, and she gave way to it.

Neither noticed that the elevator had come to a gentle stop, the doors sighing open, until April heard giggles and pulled free of his embrace. There were two young couples waiting for the elevator, obviously amused at the tableau.

Walker, unabashed, swept April out of the elevator and beamed at the couples. "You wouldn't begrudge me a kiss from my lady, would you?"

But as they progressed toward the Goldener Hirsch, Walker's mood changed drastically. His high spirits seemed to desert him, and he was strangely silent. April thought of questioning him, but a quick glance at his scowl dissuaded her.

He was silent all the way up to the corridor outside her rooms. As she got her key out, Walker took it from her, inserted it into the lock, and opened the door.

"Good night, Walk. I had a great time." She turned her face toward his expectantly.

"Lisa." He took her hand tentatively. There was a hesitant, almost timid note in his voice. "I'd like to come in with you. I know it's a little soon but—may I, honey?"

April realized anew that she'd had too much to drink. Her wits were befuddled. She shook her head in an attempt to clear her thoughts. But any reservations she might have had were pushed from her mind as she remembered how lonely she had been since Roger's death. How nice it would be to be cradled in a man's arms again—to feel warm and protected and loved!

"Yes, Walk," she said softly. "You may come in."

It was awkward at first. Walker was bold and shy by turns, and the act of undressing proceeded by fits and starts. Walker was subdued until they were finally on the bed together, flesh against flesh.

April had left the lights off, but enough light filtered in through the window to allow him to see her. Propped up on one elbow, Walker gazed down the length of her body.

"Ah-h, Lisa, honey, you're lovely, the loveliest thing I've ever seen!"

His big hand stroked down her body, beginning with the swell of her breasts, across her belly, down to her Venus mound, and then down her flanks. His fingers had callus pads, and although he was very gentle, his touch rasped her skin.

It wasn't an unpleasant sensation, however, and April shivered, her eyes fluttering closed. She let all doubts go out of her mind, all thought, and gave herself up to pleasure. Walker's touch was still tentative, unsure. He was fully aroused, her blindly groping hand had found evidence of that. Her body responded to his caresses, yet she forced herself to lie passive—she did not wish to be aggressive in the least. Her body was greedy for him, but she made herself wait, to be content for the moment with his touch.

Finally a guttural moan came from Walker, and he moved over her, taking her with a roughness he had not heretofore shown.

But if he had calculated it that way, his timing was perfect. He brought her to quick spasms of ecstasy, followed an instant later by his own shuddering climax.

The room was quiet except for the creaking of the bed as Walker rolled away to lie beside her. Still caught up in the afterglow of pleasure, April remained still, her mind utterly empty of thought. It was a pleasing condition, the first time since London and the realization of what was happening to her. She was grateful to Walker Longley for that.

Beside her, he made a small movement. "Lisa, I—"

She turned her head lazily toward him. "Yes, Walk?"

He said huskily, "I—I'm not sure what I wanted to say. But I do want you to know, honey, that this has been the best evening that I can remember. And this"—his knuckles touched her hip—"this is—well, you're the greatest!"

"Walker," she said gently. "Don't talk. Don't talk it to death, okay?"

April woke the next morning to the ringing of the telephone. She raised her head dazedly. It was late, light was pouring into the room. A look at her watch told her that it was after nine. Memory flooded back, and her glance darted to the other side of the bed.

Walker Longley was gone.

The phone continued to ring, and now apprehension nibbled at the edges of her mind. She sat up in bed, cowering away from the ringing instrument. Not since London had she heard that sinister sound. It rang on. She thought of throwing on her clothes and taking flight.

She fought with herself and got her trembling under a semblance of control. She reached out tentatively for the receiver, recoiling at the cool feel of it.

Then she drew a shuddering breath, snatched up the receiver, and put it to her ear. "Hello?" There was a silence, but she could hear breathing on the other end. She said again, "Hello?"

"Yes, Miss Starr, I am sorry. This is Susan Longley. Have you seen my brother this morning?"

"Oh, hi, Susan." April laughed shakily. "No, not this morning." Her gaze went to the indentation left by Walker's big body, and she stopped herself just short of telling Susan that Walker had slept with her but left before she woke. Instead, she said, "We were out together until late last night, up at the casino up on the mountain."

"Yes, I know. Walker told me you two had a date."

"Isn't he in his room?"

"If he is, he doesn't answer the phone. I've called a number of times."

There was a dour note in the woman's voice. Jealousy? Sexual jealousy? April remembered the ancient taboos against incest and shuddered away from the thought. Naturally they were very close. Clearly Susan had little public life, in her condition, and her dependency on her brother must be very great.

As if the other woman had read her mind, Susan said, "I reckon I lean on Walk too much. Since the accident, I've been confined to that damned wheelchair, and I've come to depend on him for everything. I've wanted to hire a nurse, but he won't hear of it. Walk's just too softhearted for his own good."

"I think such devotion speaks well of him, Susan. Not many brothers would go to such lengths."

"Oh, don't I know it! And I do appreciate it. If I ever walk again, I'll make it up to him. Uh, do you like him, Lisa?"

April was silent for a moment, surprised at the audacity of the question.

Susan Longley rushed on. "I'm sorry, that's none of my business, now is it? I suppose you think"—she laughed nervously—"that I'm trying to keep him all to myself. That isn't the way of it. I would dearly love to see Walk married to some nice girl. He's a confirmed bachelor, you know. I don't know how many times I've told him it's past time he was finding a wife! I'm embarrassing you, aren't I? But he has told me how much he likes you."

"I've only known him for one day," April said stiffly. "And I certainly haven't given any consideration to marrying him!"

"I know, I know, and I do apologize." Susan laughed again. "Now you have to promise me that you won't go tattling to Walk about what I've just said!"

"I promise," April said. It was an easy promise to make, since she certainly had no intention of mentioning the subject of this conversation to Walker Longley. "I'm sure your brother is okay, Susan. He probably just took an early morning walk around the city. It's fascinating, and time passes before you know it."

"Sis told me that she called you this morning, honey, asking about me."

"That's right, she did," April said cautiously. So much for promises, she thought. They were having an early supper in the hotel dining room. Walker had told her earlier that he'd had enough gambling the night before to do him for a spell.

Now Walker looked away from her steady gaze and said self-consciously, "Sis gets upset sometimes when I'm not around."

"Did you ever think that you might be spoiling her, that she might become too dependent on you? What if the doctors fail, and she never walks again?"

"Don't say a thing like that! I mean," he amended quickly, "don't say it in her hearing. Yeah, I've thought that the docs might fail. But what can I do? She's the only relative I've got left. I reckon I feel a little guilty. You see, after I got big enough, daddy and me, we went traipsing off, leaving her with daddy's sister. My mother died when we were both just little kids. By the time daddy died, Susan and me, we were almost strangers. Now, with the accident and all, we're close again, and I have to do my best for her."

"But you do have your own life to lead, Walk. I think what you're doing is admirable, but you can't devote the rest of your life to taking care of her. Perhaps that sounds heartless but . . ."

"No, no, I understand what you're getting at." His big hand covered hers on the table. "But that's the thing, you see. I haven't given up my life for her. I neglected her, and now I figure I owe her."

April was remembering her own life before tragedy struck; how utterly dependent she had been on her father. If she had been more independent of him, she might be better equipped to deal with her own plight now.

Walker squeezed her hand gently. "It's only until sis is able to walk again, until she's better able to take care of herself."

"But what if she doesn't ever walk again?"

He frowned, nodding slowly. "I know. I'll have to face that when and if it happens. She's a strong old girl, she'll learn to cope, if she has to." His gaze was intent. "All I ask of you, honey, is that you wait, just be patient. It'll all work itself out."

Startled, she sat back, withdrawing her hand. "*I* should be patient? What does it have to do with me?"

He said gravely, "Everything has to do with you, little lady. Now that I've stumbled onto you, you think I'm going to let you walk out of my life? No, sir! No way am I going to just let you walk off into the sunset!"

"Walk, you're going a little fast for me. I haven't thought that far ahead."

"You can say that after last night? Maybe I'm being old-fashioned, but then I'm an old-fashioned fella."

April felt color rise to her face. "Walk—last night was—well, last night."

"Nope, not to me. You're it for me, the gal I've been looking for, and I've been looking a long time."

"I'm flattered, any girl would be, Walk, but this is all too sudden."

"Like I said, just be patient. That'll give you time to get used to the idea," he said cheerfully.

She seized on this with a feeling of relief. "Yes, we'll wait and see."

"Now—" Walker looked at his watch. "I hate to eat and run, but I promised sis that I'd help her do a couple of things tonight."

He smiled at her. "Honey, I still haven't seen much of the town. How's about we meet for lunch tomorrow, and then you be my guide for a walking tour? Reckon you can do that?"

"Yes, Walk. We'll do that."

Walker signed the check and left April idling over a cup of coffee. As her gaze followed him out of the room, she was considering the idea of leaving Salzburg—slipping away in the morning without a word to him.

●   ●   ●

And yet, the next day, with the late afternoon sunlight slanting into her bedroom, she was again with Walker Longley, making slow, languorous love on the king-size bed—for the second time within the half hour.

Afterward, April sank down onto the bed's softness, depleted and pleasantly weary. She had met Walker for lunch, and they had taken a long, leisurely stroll through the city of Salzburg, ending up on the heights above the city, where April showed him Castle Hohensalzburg.

It had been a delightful afternoon, made even more delightful by their lovemaking. April was glad now that she hadn't packed and taken flight.

Listening to Walker's even breathing beside her, she felt safe and loved. Certainly there was none of the sweep of excitement that Liam's love had brought into her life, nor the rollicking sense of fun that Roger had given her, yet Walker's great physical bulk beside her provided a feeling of comfort.

April did not love him, and she was uncertain where the relationship would lead, yet she decided that she would simply wait and see what the future brought.

She could always flee. She was getting good at that, she reflected bitterly. Perhaps with Walker between her and any danger she might face, she would not find it necessary to run again.

She dozed, and then, in that area between sleep and waking, she heard Walker say softly, "Look at this. Isn't it pretty?"

April opened her eyes slowly and stared into a colored prism held up to catch the rays of the slanting sun. She blinked sleepily.

"I want you to fix your eyes on the prism." Walker's voice was a rumbling whisper. "That's it. Relax now, and listen to my voice. You are growing very relaxed. Very, very relaxed. Take a deep breath and let it out slowly. Your eyes are growing tired. You cannot keep them open." His voice quickened. "Are you relaxed now?"

"—yes."

"I will now ask you some questions. You will answer me truthfully. What did you see on that cliff at Cape Cod?"

"I—"

"Answer me, April! What did you see?"

"I—"

April? She shook her head sharply and forced her eyes open, staring at Walker Longley in dawning horror. She shrank away from him. "How did you know my name? Who are you?"

Walker grimaced and said under his breath, "Damn! I blew it!" He tried to smile reassuringly. "April—Lisa, I mean you no harm. I swear! I love you, you know that by now." He reached out a hand toward her.

She inched farther away. "Don't touch me! Who are you, and how did you know my real name?"

"None of that matters, April. I want to help you, that's all. Just answer some questions and—"

"No! You—you're the one who has been following me all over Europe! You tried to kill me!"

"April, please don't be frightened. Just cooperate and you won't be harmed."

She had moved all the way across the bed now, and her back struck the lamp on the bedside table. Blindly she groped behind her to right it, and her hand encountered the telephone.

Walker was inching toward her, one hand outstretched, a smile fixed on his lips, lips that had kissed her in passion scant moments before.

The face that had struck her as kind and pleasant now seemed evil incarnate. Dear God, how could she have been so gullible! She had been a fool to trust him!

He moved closer. "April." His face was so close that she could smell his warm breath. It had a sour, unpleasant smell.

In an instinctive motion she picked up the telephone, swung it around before her, gripped it in both hands, and raised it high.

Walker gaped at her in astonishment. "April, what are you doing? Don't be an idiot!"

She brought the telephone down with all her strength, the heavy base striking him high on the temple. The blow broke the skin, and blood spurted. He raised his hands to protect himself as she brought the telephone down again and yet again. Fear had given her a maniacal strength, and she used the phone as a club, beating through his defenses and pounding at him until he collapsed and lay inert. His forehead was battered, and blood streamed down in tiny rivulets onto the bed.

April finally halted, her breath coming in heaving gasps, her heart thudding in her chest. She peered at Walker suspiciously, but there was no doubt that he was unconscious. On the face of it, it seemed illogical that she should have been able to render him senseless. But her terror, combined with the unexpectedness of her attack, had given her the needed edge.

She sank to her knees, letting the blood-covered phone drop to the bed. For several moments her mind was a blank, then a faint sound penetrated her daze.

A voice, a voice was speaking to her. She finally found the source—the receiver was off, and a voice was speaking on the other end. Hastily she hung up the receiver and replaced the telephone on the nightstand. She stared at the instrument and gave a short, involuntary laugh. It was ironic that an object that had held such terror for her for so long should be the instrument of her deliverance—at least for the moment.

The thought galvanized her into action. She

couldn't bring herself to check to see if the man on the bed was still alive.

She had to get away.

Quickly she climbed out of bed and began throwing on her clothes. She would, again, not have time to take anything with her. It seemed her fate to always have to leave anything she might have grown used to, or attached to, behind.

She locked the door of the suite behind her, dropped the key into her purse, and hung the Do Not Disturb sign on the doorknob. Maybe Walker would stay unconscious for a time. Maybe no one would find him until she was well away. Maybe he was dead!

Suppressing a shiver, she moved away from the door and over to the elevator. As the cage descended, she quickly looked in her wallet. Only a little over two hundred dollars—what her father would have called "walking around money."

She would have to stop at the desk and ask to open her safety deposit box. But when she reached the desk, she stopped, dismayed. There were people two deep around the desk, waiting to be helped, and the clerk was involved in a rather loud-voiced altercation with a stout guest who evidently spoke no German.

She would have to go on, forget the money. She did not dare wait around—Walker might come to any minute.

It took April some time before she found a hotel with a vacancy. It was a small hotel, and the plump woman at the desk was suspicious when April said she didn't have any baggage.

April lied about her passport and luggage, saying that everything had been misplaced by the airline but that a new passport had been promised to her shortly. She knew this would only gain her a day or two's grace at the most, yet she didn't dare use the Lisa

Starr passport. Walker Longley, if and when he recovered, would soon be prowling through Salzburg looking for her. She needed time to plan her next move.

Yet, once in the room, she seemed unable to think. What could she do now? Where could she go? She had the equivalent of a hundred and eighty dollars in her purse, hardly enough to pay for transportation anywhere. And where could she go without a new passport?

Pausing in her pacing of the small room, she found herself staring at the telephone.

Mr. Midnight, that compelling voice on the telephone. He had told her repeatedly that she was in danger, that someone was after her. Events had proven him correct. And a feeling crept over her that she would never have thought possible—a longing to hear that voice reassure her, to tell her that she would be all right, that everything would be taken care of.

Perhaps she was foolish; Mr. Midnight could be the person behind all the attacks on her. But what alternative did she have? If someone didn't help her, she was doomed.

She had unconsciously moved closer now, until she stood over the telephone. She caressed the cold plastic with her finger tips. Her longing to hear that voice was almost overwhelming, and the telephone lured her with a magnetic pull.

Besides, the number engraved in her memory was in the United States. If she did not like what he had to say, there was time to run again before he could reach her. Unless Walker Longley was doing his bidding!

Such thoughts would lead to madness. She had to trust *someone!*

It was not midnight, not even close to it. There was no help for that.

She picked up the receiver, gave the remembered

number to the operator, and waited for an interminable time before she heard the connection made on the other end and heard a voice.

To April's astonishment and consternation, a woman's voice answered the phone.

Eighteen

◆◆◆

April sat looking at the meal she had just ordered, not seeing it, but concentrating instead on the scene inside her mind.

The dinner menu at the small restaurant next to the hotel offered Wiener schnitzel, and she had ordered it, thinking of her father. It had been one of the few foreign dishes, other than Mexican food, that he had enjoyed, and it was a taste they shared.

Thinking of him, another piece of the past had suddenly slipped into place, and she was, again, opening the door to her darkroom, facing her father, hearing his words . . .

"... I ain't getting any younger, you know."

"You'll live forever!"

"I've always had it in mind to, but the Almighty may have a different idea."

"Is that all you meant, getting old?"

"Sure was. Now what else could I be thinking of? Now you listen to me and don't forget what I'm telling you. In Zurich, in Switzerland, there's a numbered account. Five numbers. The numbers match the letters in your name, in alphabetical order. Do not forget. If anything ever happens to me, go to the bank, identify yourself. All you'll need are the numbers and papers identifying you as April Morgan. There are also some documents for your eyes only—"

"Daddy, you're frightening me! Why are you telling me this?"

"Just in case, sugar, just in case. In this old world a man never knows. Now I want you to promise me

252

you won't forget. Shouldn't be too hard to remember, just go down the alphabet, matching the letters with corresponding numbers."

"I won't forget, Daddy."

But she had forgotten, perhaps because his sudden confidence had aroused a fear of his death in her, a fear that had been realized only an hour later.

A numbered account in Switzerland. Was that the reason she was being pursued? That hardly seemed reasonable. After all, whoever was following her had tried to kill her more than once. If she was dead, the account would certainly do *them* no good.

Of course, there was Walker. She winced. The thought of him still hurt. One moment in his arms, the next . . .

Keep your mind on the business at hand, she scolded herself. Walker Longley had tried to hypnotize her, evidently with some purpose in mind.

Could he have been after the number of the Swiss account? It seemed possible. But if he was after the money in the numbered account, what had Rudi Ernst been after, besides her life?

And that was another puzzle. Walker had used the same technique, or tried to use the same technique, that the psychiatrist had used to hypnotize her—the prism. Was this a coincidence, or could he and—what was the psychiatrist's name?—Dr. Kemble, yes. Could they be working together?

April shook her head angrily. She was becoming paranoid. Soon, she would think that the whole world was after her!

Suddenly she became aware of the scent of the food on the plate before her. She had better start eating, or the waiter would begin to wonder what was wrong with her.

The Wiener schnitzel was delicious, but April was so excited over the rediscovery of her father's last words that she had little attention for it.

She ate a few bites, pushed the rest of the food around on her plate so that it looked as if she had eaten more, and signaled for the check.

As she looked up at the waiter, her eyes met those of a tall, thin, good-looking man just coming in the door. His gaze had been scanning the room, as if looking for someone, and as their glances met, his eyes flared wide in what appeared to be surprise and acknowledgment.

Did she know him? He looked familiar, but April couldn't recall who he was or where she might have known him.

He took his gaze away from hers and continued to scan the room. Strange. He had looked at her as if he knew her and now seemed to have changed his mind. As if to throw her off guard, she thought.

Was she being paranoid again?

The elation that had filled her at remembering her father's exact words was rapidly fading, and a formless apprehension was taking its place.

There was something about this man. He was good-looking in an understated way, like a young Jimmy Stewart, which should have been reassuring, and yet something about him frightened her.

The waiter put the check on the table, and April quickly paid it and left the table. She wanted desperately to be in her room, behind the locked door, where she could think this thing through.

Almost running, she left the restaurant and hurried to the hotel. Her key suddenly seemed too large for the keyhole, and it was only after several seconds of fumbling that she managed to open the door. Once inside, she quickly bolted the door and stood trembling, her back against it.

Who was that man? What did he mean to her?

Still trembling, she walked over to the bed and dropped down upon it.

What was happening to her? What was going on? Her destiny seemed to be controlled by events she was unaware of and was unable to alter. It made her feel helpless, and that was a very terrifying thing.

Her heartbeat was just beginning to slow when she heard the knock upon her door. Three firm raps. Not loud, but authoritative. Who could it be? The police? Walker Longley?

If she was silent, perhaps whoever it was would give up and go away.

She stiffened as the door knob turned slowly, first left, then right, and the door rattled.

Then the knock came again. More insistent.

April sat frozen, her tongue cleaving to the roof of her mouth; and then the voice spoke, a voice that she knew.

"April! I know you're in there. You must open the door. April, this is Mr. Midnight. You must do as I say. Do you hear me?"

At the sound of the key phrase, April's apprehensions drained away.

"April! Open the door. You *will* open the door. I am here to help you."

Feeling strangely relaxed, April stood and walked slowly toward the door, unbolted it, and opened it wide.

Standing on the other side, facing her, was the man she had seen in the restaurant.

Quickly he entered the room and bolted the door behind him, then turned to her. "April! Thank God, you're all right! I've looked everywhere for you."

She stared at him placidly.

"Oh, hell! April, you will awaken now. When I count backward to one, you will be awake and relaxed. You will feel fine. You will not be frightened. Five, four, three, two, one. You are awake now."

April blinked and looked at the tall figure gazing down at her. He *did* look like Jimmy Stewart, and somehow he was no longer frightening. But what was he doing here?

"You're—" She paused. "I know you! You were Daddy's lawyer. I met you several times."

He nodded. "Yes, I'm Deke Travers."

She frowned. "Your voice, I know that voice." She began to feel agitated and was not quite certain why. "You—you're Mr. Midnight!" The words came out accusingly.

Deke winced. "Yes, April, I am. But I want you to know that whatever I have done, right or wrong, foolish or helpful, I've done for you."

April experienced a mixture of shock and anger and several less definable emotions. "I called you," she said, still accusingly. "I just called you in New York."

"You talked to my secretary. I was already in Salzburg, and she called me immediately. We've been looking for you everywhere."

April put her hand to her temple. There were so many questions she wanted to ask. "We?"

"Gabe and myself. You remember Dr. Gabe Kemble, the psychiatrist who visited you in the sanitarium?"

The familiar feeling of paranoia washed over her. "Yes, I remember Dr. Kemble." She looked at Deke sharply. "Why?" she demanded, almost shouting as anger surged up in her. "Why did you do all this to me? Why did you send me running from city to city, country to country? It's been hell!"

Deke's face paled, and even through her anger, April could see that he was hurting. "I'm sorry," he said softly, reaching out as if to touch her. "I didn't mean. . . . I did it for your good. To save your life. At the time it seemed the only way."

"What do you mean? To save my life? Someone has been trying to kill me, and almost succeeded several times. For all I know that could have been you, or Dr. Kemble. Why should I trust you?"

Deke let out a shuddering breath and shrugged his shoulders. "I can't answer that. I guess maybe you shouldn't trust me. But I really have tried, and I still think that if I hadn't sent you away, you would be dead by now. In fact, I'm sure of it."

"Why? Explain yourself. I'm going crazy not knowing what's going on! Tell me everything."

"All right, April, I'll try. After your father's death, you were, well, you were emotionally withdrawn and were sent to a sanitarium."

She nodded, tight-lipped. "Yes, I remember that now."

"Well, in the sanitarium, someone made an attempt on your life and came close to succeeding. It was clear that there was some mystery, something unusual about your father's death and your withdrawal. Since I didn't know who was involved, who wanted to kill you, I sent you away, thinking that if you were out of the country, with only me knowing where you were, you would be safe until I could find out what was going on. Unfortunately, I *didn't* find out.

"I used hypnosis because you were in no condition to cooperate with me and because it's a technique I know, since I use it on many of my clients to assure myself of their guilt or innocence. With their consent, of course."

April swallowed convulsively, and her shoulders slumped. Suddenly she felt very tired. Turning, she sank down upon the bed, bowing her head. "That's more than you had from me," she said softly. "You didn't have my consent for any of this."

Deke pulled the small chair away from the dressing table and sat on it, facing the back, his long legs incongruously sticking out to the sides. "You weren't in any condition to give it, April. I'm sorry, but I did what I thought was best. I used posthypnotic suggestion, hoping that with a new identity they would not be able to find you and also that having a new, untroubled identity might take the pressure off and might help your mental state."

A snort of laughter came from her. "Oh, it was just great for my mental state." She leaned forward determinedly. "I want to know how you did it. For my own peace of mind, I have to know."

"Like I said, I hypnotized you," he said wearily. "I admit that it was without your permission, but that was the only way I could figure out to get you away, to keep you safe."

"I know you hypnotized me. I'm not stupid. What I don't know is how it worked over such a long period of time and over such long distances."

He raised his hands, palms upward, in a gesture of acquiescence. "All right, April. I owe you at least an explanation."

"At least," she said coldly.

"You were in danger. I realized that after the attempt on your life. You were also in an almost cataleptic withdrawal from reality, and your doctor and Gabe Kemble both warned me that you couldn't take another shock. It seemed to me that the best and safest thing I could do for you was to get you away from New York, out of the country. Send you some place where you could forget what happened and get yourself together. Regular means of doing this were out, for several reasons. First, you would have had to have a nurse along with you, and, since it would be easy enough for anyone who was really interested to find out where you were gone, it would necessitate a couple of bodyguards as well.

"Then it came to me. I would change your identity, making it difficult for whoever was after you to find you. Make you into a new person, so to speak. Since I use hypnotism regularly in my work—"

April frowned. "In your work?"

"My practice is mostly in criminal cases, but I only defend clients who are innocent of the charges brought against them. To convince myself that they really *are* innocent, I ask them to submit to questioning while under hypnosis."

"I thought Dr. Kemble was the hypnotist. I had no idea you knew or used hypnosis."

"That was a natural assumption. I'm sorry about that, too. It seems there are a great many things I have to apologize for."

She nodded grimly. "That's the truth. Well, go on!"

"Gabe taught me most of what I know about hypnosis. I use his services occasionally, on the more difficult subjects. Which you, April, are not." He smiled. "I knew, from Gabe, that you were an exceptionally good subject for hypnosis, and so I tried it on you, to see if what I wanted to do was at all possible.

"You were, and are, an incredibly good subject. When I set you up with a mythical identity, history, and career, you went with it all the way, each time. I had you change your hair color and makeup, and I continually gave you posthypnotic suggestions, deeply implanted, to call me every seven days, as near to midnight as possible. I made the cue words 'Mr. Midnight' because it was something you would not be likely to overhear in everyday conversation. Each time you called, I reinforced the posthypnotic suggestion. Each time, you went under more deeply. And each time I had you move to a different place, under a new identity, with a different life history. I provided you a new passport, money, and identification, as well as different clothing. Originally I had thought it would only be necessary to have you leave the States for a short time, but as things began to grow more and more complicated"—Deke spread his hands—"it turned into a Frankenstein monster. It got away from me, grew in directions that I could not have foreseen."

April said slowly, "I thought Dr. Kemble told me that no one could hypnotize a person into doing something they did not want to do."

Deke nodded. "That's true. But I never asked you to do anything that went against your moral or ethical code. Think about it. And I was helped greatly by the fact that your unconscious mind *wanted* to escape. *Wanted* to be someone else, someone who did not have something terrible to remember."

April thought for a moment. Then she fluttered her hands and sighed. "I don't know. I just don't know. I suppose I must assume that you were acting for my best interests. But, Deke, why would anyone want to kill me? Why *does* someone want to kill me?"

"It could only be one thing." Deke's glance slid away. "That night on the cliff, the night your father died, you must have seen who killed your father and stepmother."

"But I didn't!" she said hotly.

"Evidently the killer thinks you did, which amounts to the same thing."

"It wasn't an accident?"

Deke shook his head slowly. "You know that it wasn't."

April swallowed convulsively, and her shoulders slumped. Suddenly she felt very tired. Turning, she sank down upon the bed, bowing her head. She nodded. "You're right. Daddy knew those cliffs like the back of his hand. He wouldn't have fallen. But who would have wanted to kill him?"

"And his wife?"

She brushed aside the mention of her stepmother. "Everyone liked my father."

"That's not quite true, April. Your father had some business enemies. Every successful man has. Your father was a good man, April, and you loved him, but he was capable of a certain ruthlessness in his business dealings. Many successful men are."

April shook her head, tears stinging her eyes.

"April." Deke leaned forward. "Have you remembered any more details of what happened that night?"

April hesitated, then said, "No."

Should she tell this man about the Swiss numbered account? She watched him as he got up and prowled restlessly about the tiny room. He had been her father's attorney, but after the things that had happened to her—much of which she could not help but blame him for—she wasn't sure that she could trust him. She could remember seeing him with her father, but John Morgan had never spoken to her of Deke Travers. Perhaps her father hadn't fully trusted Deke, or he would have confided in *him* about the secret account.

No, for the time being she would keep that knowledge to herself.

Deke stopped pacing and turned to face her. "If there was someone else on that cliff that night, April, you *must* have seen him." He ran a hand through his hair, ruffling it, a lock falling across his forehead.

"It was foggy, I was—disoriented," she said defensively, "and when I saw Daddy fall, everything else went out of my head."

"I can understand that, but why can't you remember more clearly, after all this time?" His gaze was probing. "You sure you haven't remembered and kept it from me?"

"Kept it from Mr. Midnight, you mean?" she said with an edge of sarcasm.

He winced. "Well, yes, if you must put it that way."

"How else should I put it? And, no, I haven't remembered any more than I've told you. I think I went a little crazy when I saw daddy—" She broke off, trembling, hands clenched in her lap. "I *must* have gone a little crazy, since I was placed under psychiatric care."

"That wasn't it, April. You had suffered some trauma, yes—"

"And in London? I wasn't crazy when you hauled me out of the hotel, or had me hauled out, and into a sanitarium? So you could fiddle around with my mind again, make me into someone I wasn't?"

"April, I thought I was doing it for your benefit, give me that much credit at least," he said miserably. "And that breakdown was understandable. You'd just

learned that the man you loved had been killed." He
stared into her eyes. "You did love this Liam
O'Laughlin, didn't you?"

"Yes! Yes, I loved Liam!" she said in a whisper.
"And I'll never forgive you for that. You turned me
into someone else again and took me away from him.
I didn't even have a chance to explain to him, and
because of me he was killed in that accident!"

"It might not have been an accident," he said quietly. "I talked to the police in Ireland. It's possible
that his brakes were tampered with."

"What?" She stared at him, confused. "Who would
do that?"

"The same people who have been trying to kill you.
Why, I don't know, unless they thought you may
have told him something they didn't want to be general knowledge."

"I didn't tell him a thing!"

"That may be, but whoever killed him had no way
of knowing that."

"Liam murdered? I don't believe you. I think you
made that up, hoping to expiate your own guilt!"

"I can't blame you for thinking that, and it may have
been an accident, not murder. The police aren't sure.
Yet the possibility exists."

She raised her head abruptly as a thought came to
her. "You know something? I've just realized—you
think *I* killed Daddy and Sheila!"

Deke's eyes flickered, and he looked away without
answering.

"You *do* think that!"

"It has crossed my mind. It would explain some
things, April. Like your not remembering, your
unconscious throwing up a mental block, so you
wouldn't have to face the horror of it. I don't think it
was deliberate, Christ, no!" he said harshly. "But it
could have happened by accident. Your father and
Sheila were quarreling, you didn't like her. Maybe

you intervened, and in the struggle they fell to their deaths."

"You told me you used hypnosis to learn if your clients are innocent or guilty. Why didn't you do that with me, since you were hypnotizing me, anyway?"

"I did."

"You did? Then why didn't you get the truth from me?"

"It doesn't always work. Gabe tried to question you under hypnosis, remember? Every time he got close to those moments on the cliff, you balked. So—" He shrugged.

"If you thought that I might be guilty, why didn't you tell the police?"

"I couldn't do that."

"I don't believe you. Rationalizations! You're rationalizing," she said bitingly. She was driven by a primal urge to strike out, to hurt him for what he had put her through. "I don't believe a word you're saying. Mr. Midnight, for example. How did you dream that up? It sounds juvenile, something out of a comic strip!"

"I know, I know," he said somewhat sheepishly. "But I told you. I needed a key phrase, one you wouldn't be likely to overhear inadvertently."

He stepped toward her. "April, I know how hard this has been on you. I think I can understand what you've been through, but at least you're *alive*. I really think that if I hadn't done this, hadn't sent you away like I did, you might not be."

She stood, staring at him. His face was furrowed with evident sincerity. She couldn't help but respond to the plea in his eyes. Was this wise or foolish? Was he really sincere and honest, or was he just a very good actor? Walker Longley had seemed sincere, too.

"April, I know what a shock this has been, me showing up here like this, but there are some things I need to know. Can we talk about that?"

She shook her head. "I don't know. I don't know anything right now, I'm too confused."

"It's nothing about the night your father died, or even about London or Frankfurt. I know pretty much what happened in Frankfurt, anyway. But why are you here, in this cheap hotel? You must have money. You certainly can't accuse me of being stingy, no matter what else I may have done."

April hesitated. Should she tell him? Why not? She couldn't see how the story of Walker Longley, with certain details deleted, could hurt her. She told him the story of what had occurred. As she came to the end of her tale, Deke's face tightened.

"Could you describe him for me, this Walker Longley?"

April did so to the best of her ability.

"It sounds very much like Eric Ransom. Different color eyes and hair, probably changed with colored contact lenses and dye. And with a phony Texas accent, but I'll bet it's him. I don't know who the woman is, some girlfriend he recruited to help him, no doubt." His voice was harsh. "You're lucky he didn't kill you, instead of just trying to hypnotize you." He got a puzzled look. "I wonder why he did that? What questions did he ask you?"

She shook her head. "He didn't get that far."

"Good for you!"

"Who is Eric Ransom?"

He took a deep breath. "When I sent you to Ireland, I employed two men. One of them is Eric Ransom. I told them that they were hired to find you, and dropped a hint about Ireland. Under the circumstances I couldn't very well tell them that I knew where you were."

She shook her head dazedly. "I don't understand. Why did you do that?"

"Since I couldn't be with you, I hoped they would be able to watch you when they found you. I warned them not to make contact with you without notifying me first. In that way, I hoped they would sniff out anyone who might be trying to kill you. On the face of it they seemed reliable enough. But I have just learned that my secretary, the one you talked to, contrived to get them the job. Eric Ransom was her lover. She met him after you supposedly disappeared. I now suspect that he contrived to meet her, in the hope that, through her, he could get a lead on you. And what did I do?" He grimaced disgustedly. "I provided them with the opportunity. If my guess is right, he's out to kill you and I pointed the way."

April frowned, trying to take it all in. "But if all this is true, how did he know the method that Dr. Kemble used to put me into a trance?"

"Gabe's file on you was stolen some time ago. I'm sure Ransom filched it, or had it done. You think this Longley is still alive?"

"He was when I left the room."

Deke paced for a moment in thought. April watched him in silence—this tall, rangy, loose-jointed man, with the shy manner. Yet for all his diffident appearance, she sensed the competency underneath and concluded that much of his manner was a guise, a manner he adopted to put people off-guard. Her outrage at discovering that he was Mr. Midnight had lessened slightly, especially when she remembered the times that his voice on the telephone had lulled her fears. At the same time she recognized that her dependency could become a drug that she could easily become addicted to. She had cut herself loose from that now and was able to stand alone. Since London, she had managed to survive through her own resources.

Deke faced her. "I'd better check and make sure. If he is dead, the police could be after you by now. God knows, we don't need that, on top of everything else."

April recoiled. "I hope I didn't kill him."

"Why worry about him? He'd been doing his damnedest to kill you!"

"I know, but still—"

"He probably survived. He seems to have a talent for that. And if he is alive, I'd like to get my hands on him." He frowned at her. "Now I won't be gone too long. I want you to stay in this room, behind locked doors, until I get back. Do you understand? Now that I've finally found you, I don't want to lose you again. When I get back, we'll decide what to do next."

She shuddered and said faintly, "I'm afraid to go out."

"Good! Hold that thought." He smiled, a forced smile, and held out his hand. "Give me your room key."

She picked her purse up from the bed and gave him the huge brass key.

Deke took it, bounced it once in his palm. He started to speak, then turned away to the door.

"Deke?"

He swung back. "Yes?"

"Do you have any of my papers with you? April Morgan's papers, I mean?"

"Why?"

"I'm tired of being someone I'm not," she retorted. "From now on, I'm April Morgan, but how could I prove it without identification? I'm entitled to that much."

"Yes, you're right. I have your old passport, still good, and a New York state driver's license."

From his inside jacket pocket, he took a long envelope and held it out.

April took it and gave a sigh of relief. "Thank you. Now, if you don't come back, at least I can prove who I am."

"I'll be back."

"I have only your word for that."

"April, you *must* trust me."

"Why should I?" she said. "Mr. Midnight kept saying that, and my trust almost got me killed!"

"You must trust me because—" He flushed. "Because I love you, damnit!"

He went out quickly then, closing the door softly after him.

April stared at the door for several moments, then dropped down onto the edge of the bed.

His abrupt declaration of love had touched something deep within her. Yet hadn't Walker Longley said much the same thing? Her feelings about Deke Travers were ambivalent. She wanted to believe him, wanted to trust him, but at the moment her ability to trust anyone was badly bruised.

It seemed that almost no one in her life of late was who he seemed. Every person had two or more identities, including Deke Travers, who was Mr. Midnight, a voice linked to her via a telephone cord, a voice sending her careening into danger.

How could she possibly trust him?

April was glad now that she had been cautious enough not to tell him of the numbered account in Switzerland. John Morgan had mentioned that the bank was also holding documents for her eyes only. Was it possible that those documents would throw some light on who had killed him or give a clue as to who wanted her dead?

She opened her purse and counted the money she had left. Certainly not enough for plane fare.

She reached for the telephone book and began leafing through it.

Deke breezed through the cramped lobby of the Goldener Hirsch with aplomb, his hand clenched around the key in his pocket. Since it was a relatively small hotel, he feared someone might realize that he wasn't a guest and question him, but no one spared him so much as a glance.

He rode the elevator up and catfooted down the corridor. There was a Do Not Disturb sign on the door. Deke eased the big key into the lock and pushed the door open. It was long after dark, and the rooms were dim, only a faint light from outside coming in through the windows. He went quietly down the length of the entry hall, peering around the doorjamb into the sitting room, which was empty, and then he crossed down to the bedroom.

His glance went immediately to the bed. It was empty. He flicked on the light and sucked in his breath sharply at the sight of the bloodstained sheets. At least it would seem that Walker Longley, or Eric Ransom, was still alive, if sorely damaged.

For the first time it occurred to him to wonder why the man had been in April's bedroom in the first place. The answer was obvious, of course.

He walled his thoughts off from any images of April and the man together on the bed and, instead, looked around the room more carefully. Now he noticed that everything had been tossed in a hurried search—drawers were standing open, and clothes were strewn across the floor. The other rooms showed the same signs of a hasty search.

Deke had to wonder what they were looking for, and if they found it. Maybe April would have some idea.

He left the suite quickly, locking the door after him. Since it was late, it likely would be tomorrow some time before the blood would be discovered. Hopefully he would have April out of the country by then.

Downstairs, he stopped at the desk. "I was just up to Walker Longley's room. There was no answer to my knock. Do you know where he might be?"

"Walker Longley and his sister have checked out, sir," the tall man said formally. "Herr Longley had an unfortunate accident. He fell in the bathroom and injured his head severely."

"Did he leave a forwarding address?"

"He did not, sir. Naturally, I offered to stand the expense of medical aid, but Herr Longley stated that he preferred the services of his own doctor. In Switzerland, I believe, but he did not say precisely where."

Deke nodded his thanks and left the hotel. The place where he and Gabe were staying was across the river, not too far from the hotel to which April had fled. Gabe was pacing restlessly about the lobby.

Seeing Deke enter, Gabe rushed over to him, wearing an angry scowl. "Where the hell have you been, Deke? Going off like that without a damned word to me!"

"I've found April, Gabe."

Gabe's mouth fell open, and it was a moment before he found words. "The hell you say! Where?" He peered past Deke. "Where is she?"

"In a hotel only a few blocks from here."

"But how? How on earth did you find her?"

Gabe, of course, did not know about Mr. Midnight, about what April called the "charade," and Deke had no intention that he ever should. He said merely, "It's too involved to go into right now. Suffice to say that I found her, safe and sound."

"But why did you leave her alone?"

"I had something to do, and she's safer in the hotel than she would have been with me. Come on, let's go to her."

Gabe almost skipped along by his side and kept peppering Deke with questions, most of which Deke managed to turn aside. He was relieved when they reached the hotel and went up to the second floor. He knocked softly on April's door. "April? It's me, Deke Travers."

There was no answer, no sound of movement inside, and a chill sped down his spine. He turned the knob and found the door unlocked. He threw it open and rushed inside. The room was empty.

Behind him Gabe said, "Where is she?"

There was a bathroom down the hall. Without answering, Deke hastened down to the bathroom, although he had little hope of finding her. His fears were realized—the door stood half-open, and the room was empty.

Gabe was waiting back inside April's room, hands on his hips. "Well? Where is she?"

Deke gave a helpless shrug and said tiredly, "I don't know."

"You don't know!" Gabe squinted at him. "Did you really find her?"

"I found her, Gabe. What reason would I have to lie?"

"Goddamnit, Deke Travers, you've screwed up all down the line!" Gabe said furiously. "Sometimes I think you've done it purposely. In fact, you could be behind all these attempts to kill her. You hired that pair! Did you pay them to take her off somewhere again?"

"Gabe, that's hardly called for."

"Hardly called for!" Gabe shouted. He raised his fist and advanced a step.

Deke stood his ground, too dispirited even to defend himself. "Go ahead, Gabe. Take your best shot."

"Aw-w, hell!" Gabe placed both hands flat against Deke's chest and shoved hard. Caught off balance, Deke was thrown back and onto the bed.

By the time he had raised up on his elbows, Gabe was storming out of the room. "Gabe, where are you going?"

Gabe Kemble was already out of hearing, and Deke let him go. His thoughts were already turning to April. Why had she disobeyed him and run again? The answer, of course, was fairly obvious. Why should she trust him, of all people?

Could Ransom have possibly found her in the brief time that he, Deke, had been gone? No, it was hardly likely that she would have opened the door to anyone but Deke, and the door hadn't been forced.

Deke sat up and glanced around the room. There was no sign that she had ever been here. Then his gaze settled on the telephone book on the table beside the instrument, instead of on the shelf underneath. Without a great deal of hope, he began leafing through it.

Not knowing what he expected to find, he kept doggedly at it. Suddenly, his pulse began to race. There was a penciled notation on the margin of one page. A time and the price of something had been written down, and the notation was right beside the telephone number of the railroad station.

Could the notation have been made by April?

He glanced at his watch. It was already past the time written on the margin. But it was worth exploring. He picked up the receiver and dialed the number of the railroad station.

Nineteen

❖

It didn't seem to April that she was in flight now. Perhaps it was the relatively leisurely pace of the train in contrast to the speed of the jets she'd flown on recently. Or it could be that she was moving toward some sort of conclusion in Zurich. Perhaps she was being overly optimistic in hoping that the documents held for her in the Zurich bank would resolve all her problems, yet it was the way she felt.

The train ride was relaxing. Being a night train, it wasn't too crowded, and she had a whole compartment to herself. She did wish that it was daytime. It was a cloudless night, with a full moon, and the parts of the landscape that she could see were breathtaking as the train crawled up into the Alps and sped across the meadows, but she could have seen it far better in the daylight.

At one of the numerous quick stops, she stood in the vestibule while the doors were open. The combination of the high altitude and the approach of winter made the air chill and crisp. The picturesque Alpine villages marking the train's passage had a powerful attraction, and she was strongly tempted just to step off the train at this one, and not return.

As the train began moving again, she sighed wistfully and returned to her compartment. Perhaps after her business was completed in Zurich, she could take the train back, pick a village at random, and get off.

There was one tense moment as the train crossed the Swiss border. A new conductor came through the car, checking passports. He took April's, opened it, looked from the photo to her face, then returned it to her, and continued on his way.

It was just daylight when the train arrived at the station in Zurich. The station was large, and even at that early hour, it was alive with people, departing and arriving.

April stood for a little, gazing around bewilderedly. She had no concept of the city itself and no idea as to where the bank she wanted was located. It was far too early, anyway; the bank wouldn't open for some time yet. What would she do during that time? She wasn't even hungry.

A middle-aged man, who had a round, beaming face and was wearing a dark suit like a uniform, approached her along the platform. He said something in German.

April shook her head. "I'm sorry, I don't speak German."

"Ah, ah! The lady is American." He struck a pose, one finger wagging at her. "I speak American, too. Very good, no?"

April smiled. "Your English is good, yes."

"American lady like taxi? Right outside the station."

April hesitated, mentally calculating how much money she had left.

"To hotel?" he pressed.

"No, not to a hotel. I have to be at a bank when it opens." She gave him the name of the bank.

The taxi driver bobbed his head. "Oh, yes! I know. You hire my taxi by hour until time to open? Much to see in Zurich."

"How much?"

He squinted at her, then looked skyward. "Ten dollars hour? American?"

She made a decision. What did it matter how much ready money she had on her person? There was money waiting for her at the bank, there must be! "All right. The lake, I've read that it's lovely. Can you drive me around the lake, at least partway?"

"The lake is fine drive." Beaming, he bowed and extended his arm.

April took the proffered arm, and he adroitly escorted her through the throng and to a line of taxicabs outside the train station. His taxi was several years old, a Mercedes, but it had been kept in good condition and was polished to a high gloss.

She sank back onto the seat and gave a relieved sigh. At least now she wouldn't have to worry about how to pass the time. As the driver put the car in gear, she leaned forward. "Don't forget now, I want to be in front of the bank when it opens."

"Will have lady back, I promise." He beamed his broad smile at her. "I am Hugo."

"I'm—" April hesitated, then thought, what difference does it make now? "I'm April Morgan." Using her real name after all this time gave her a feeling of great satisfaction.

"Nice name, lady. Nice month, April, in Zurich."

Hugo drove at a sedate pace through the city and before too long, the Mercedes was passing through the city limits and onto the highway following the shoreline of Lake Zurich. There was little traffic at this early hour, and the lake was visible intermittently through the trees and houses on the left as the taxi moved along. The lake was beautiful in the early morning light. Even at this hour a few sails dotted the water, like swift-moving clouds.

Occasionally Hugo spoke back over his shoulder, pointing out points of interest, but for the most part he was silent, as if respecting her exhaustion.

April *was* tired, having slept very little on the train, and the sound of the motor lulled her into short naps, from which she woke from time to time at the sound of Hugo's voice.

She was awakened from one such nap by an exclamation of anger from Hugo. "Bastard!"

April sat up, suddenly apprehensive. "What is it, Hugo?"

Even as she asked the question, April saw a large black car alongside the taxi. The windows were tinted, and she could see little of the interior, only the vague bulk of a figure behind the wheel.

To her horror she saw the big car swerve toward the taxi. Swearing, Hugo wrenched the wheel to the right just in time to avoid a collision.

April said again, "What is it, Hugo?"

Hugo merely grunted, all his attention on his driving. The large black car now pulled ahead slightly, until the rear bumper was even with the front of the taxi.

April said in relief, "It's going on ahead. Why did they do that—?"

Before the words were out of her mouth, the big car angled sharply right, cutting in front of the taxi. The taxi shuddered, and there was the sound of metal hitting metal. Hugo slammed on his brakes, throwing April forward against the front seat.

Again, the black car swerved into the taxi. This time Hugo lost control, and the taxi plunged off the road and plowed nose-first into the low embankment. The impact threw April to the side, and her head struck the side of the car, dazing her. Dimly she realized her danger, and she knew she should open the door and run. Her hand reached out for the door handle, but she was still partially stunned, and she couldn't summon up the necessary strength.

She heard Hugo groaning, and her glance went to the front seat. The driver was shaking his head dazedly. Then, just beyond him, April saw a figure blocking the driver's window. She glimpsed the glint of sunlight on metal. An arm poked through the window, and a gun barrel was laid alongside Hugo's head. He yelped in pain and slumped across the wheel. A gloved hand snaked in and switched off the ignition.

April still hadn't seen a face, but the clubbing of Hugo fully alerted her to her own peril. She had to get away; she couldn't allow herself to be trapped in the taxi. Pressing down on the door handle, she tumbled out of the taxi onto her knees. There wasn't another car in sight; the area was deserted. Suddenly she heard footsteps pounding around the front of the taxi. Using the taxi door, she pulled herself up and started to run—away from the footsteps.

She had managed only a few stumbling steps before she was seized from behind. A long, powerful arm whipped around her waist, and she was pulled hard against a muscular figure.

She began to struggle, twisting her head up just enough to glimpse a white bandage wrapped like a turban around her attacker's forehead.

Then she felt the icy prick of a needle in her arm. She strained against the pinioning arm around her waist. The man's grip tightened cruelly. The strength drained out of her like water, and she slumped in his grasp. Her gaze dropped, and the last thing she saw before darkness swooped down was the pointed tip of a cowboy boot.

The Aztec Deke had chartered in Salzburg landed at Zurich shortly before sunrise. Unable to get a seat on a scheduled airline, it had taken him several frustrating hours to locate a charter plane and pilot. Consequently, the train carrying April arrived in Zurich ahead of him. He tried not to think about what might have awaited her. He had learned at the Salzburg Airport that a man and a woman had left in another private plane an hour prior to Deke's own departure, and the woman had been in a wheelchair. It had to be the pair passing themselves off as the Longleys, brother and sister.

He fretted his way through customs and fidgeted in the taxi all the way to the train station in downtown Zurich. The train on which April had traveled had already left the station for its next destination, thus depriving him of any chance of questioning the crew about April. He queried the drivers in the taxi rank outside the station. Not a single one admitted to seeing anyone vaguely resembling April Morgan.

His heart heavy, Deke finally decided to give in to the inevitable—he would have to seek official help. Given time, he might be able to find her on his own, but if Eric Ransom had been here before April arrived, the conclusion was inescapable—he had April, if he hadn't already disposed of her.

So now he would have to do what Gabe Kemble had urged all along, go to the police. Before leaving Salzburg he had called the hotel. Gabe hadn't answered the ring, and Deke had left word of his destination. Gabe would undoubtedly fly to Zurich the minute he learned where Deke was.

He was lucky in one respect—he knew a man on the Zurich police force. He had gone to law school with Tony Renaldi. Renaldi, although Italian, had been born and raised in Switzerland. He had wanted to become an attorney and had gone to Harvard Law School, in Deke's class. They had become good friends and corresponded irregularly over the years since. On his return to Zurich, Renaldi had opted for something more secure than a private law practice and had joined the police. In the years since, he had risen up through the ranks and was now what would correspond to a commander on the New York force.

Deke had a ten-minute wait before Renaldi showed up at his office. Renaldi was a short, dark man, tending to plumpness. His limpid eyes had a shrewd twinkle, and Deke knew that the Italian could be ruthless when the occasion warranted.

At the sight of Deke, his round face bloomed with a smile, and he embraced him in front of his receptionist, much to Deke's embarrassment.

"My good friend!" Renaldi exclaimed. "Why didn't you let me know you were coming?"

"Hello, Tony." Deke smiled tightly. "I didn't have time to let you know. I have a problem, and after I drop it on you, you may not be all that happy to see me."

Renaldi sobered, his expression hardening. "If it has anything to do with a criminal client involved with a numbered account, forget it, Deke."

"Now why would you jump to that conclusion?" Deke asked in surprise.

Renaldi said, "Because most of the people from the States who come to me asking for assistance want me to help them get information from one bank or another here in Zurich about a numbered account. Even if I wanted to help, I couldn't. The bank security is very tight about that."

Deke shook his head. "No, it's nothing like that. Could we go into your office?"

"Sure thing, paisano. Come along." Renaldi led the way into a spartan office, furnished with a small desk, walls of filing cabinets, and one chair for visitors. Renaldi gave Deke a wry smile. "In my job these days, I don't get many visitors, Deke. Sit, and lay it on me."

Renaldi sat down behind his desk and lit a foul-smelling cigar. Deke was quiet for a moment, getting his thoughts in order. "Tony," he began, "there's a woman here in Zurich, and I have reason to believe that she's in grave danger. I have to find her as fast as possible."

Renaldi's gaze was steady, probing. "A client?"

"Well, yes. Her father was a client, anyway, and now that he's dead, I'm the trustee of his estate."

"I need to know the whole story, Deke, but since you say it's urgent, I'll put out word to be on the lookout for her. Give me a name and description."

"Her name is April Morgan, but she may be going under the name of Lisa Starr." Deke described her.

Renaldi nodded and picked up one of the phones on his desk and spoke into it at length. When he finally hung up the phone, he ground out the cigar in an overflowing ashtray and immediately lit another.

He leaned back with a curt nod. "Now, old buddy, tell me what this is all about."

Deke told him, choosing his words carefully.

When he was finished, Renaldi studied him thoughtfully. "You say it appears that these two goons are trying to kill her. Why? What's their stake in this?"

A flicker of amusement played across Deke's mind at Renaldi's use of out-of-date American slang. "I'm afraid I can't answer that, Tony. I just don't know."

Renaldi stared. "You hired them, and you don't know?"

"I hired them, but I also fired them." Deke stirred. "For Christ's sake, Tony, you think I'd hire them to kill April Morgan?"

Renaldi rolled the soggy cigar back and forth between his lips. "I haven't seen you in ten years, Deke. A man can change in that length of time. After all, you are the trustee of the Morgan estate. Maybe you want the girl dead. Maybe you've looted the estate and stand to go to the slammer if she noses into it."

"Now, goddamnit—!" Deke started to his feet.

Renaldi waved him back down, grinning suddenly. "I'm not saying I believe that, but someone else might. It wouldn't be the first time such a shenanigan took place."

Deke sank back into his chair, anger evaporating. "I can't blame you too much for that. It could be that I *am* responsible, in a way. What I did, in effect, is sic a pair of bounty hunters onto April—"

A telephone buzzed on Renaldi's desk. He scooped it up and talked into it in a low voice. Then he banged up the receiver and bounced to his feet. Energy seemed to explode from him, and his blunt nostrils actually seemed to quiver.

"We've got something, chum! A taxidriver picked your girl up at the train station about an hour ago and took her for a drive around the lake. Halfway around, he was forced off the road, conked on the noggin, and the girl was snatched. Let's move it!"

There were a number of police cars parked around the ancient Mercedes taxi on the lake drive, and a crowd of curious citizens had collected. One uniformed officer was interrogating the groggy taxidriver when Deke and Tony Renaldi arrived. Renaldi pushed his way through the crowd, Deke on his heels.

Renaldi spoke in rapid Italian to the interrogating officer, his gaze on the driver slumped against the side of his taxi. The driver's forehead was bloody, and a knot the size of a walnut showed just above his left eye.

Renaldi switched to English. "Do you understand English, driver?"

"Yes, sir." The driver straightened up.

"Then we will speak that language for the benefit of Mr. Travers here, who has an interest in April Morgan. According to my information, your name is Hugo, and you had the woman, April Morgan, as a fare?"

Hugo blinked. "That is name she gave me, sir. She engaged my taxi for drive around lake, to pass time until a bank opened."

Deke's interest sharpened. A bank? She had come to Zurich to visit a bank? Why hadn't she confided in him?

Renaldi was saying, "So you were driving along the lake and—?"

"This big bastard black car pulled up alongside my taxi. He began swerving toward me." Hugo lapsed into German briefly, the sound of profanity unmistakable. Then he went back to English. "Driver went ahead and cut right in front of me, forcing taxi off road or be wrecked. Taxi ran into embankment, and my head struck roof. Then bastard driver came up to my side and clubbed me with barrel of pistol!"

Hugo's fingers felt the lump on his forehead, and he winced, closing his eyes.

Renaldi said, "Can you describe this man?"

Still with his eyes closed, Hugo replied, "He was big, big man!"

"You can do better than that. You said he came up to your window."

"But he knock me unconscious—wait! A bandage, he had a bandage around his head."

Deke said, "That's the man April knew as Walker Longley, it must be. In the fight she had with him, Tony, she clubbed him with the telephone. Whacked him pretty good. And I'm almost positive that Walker Longley is Eric Ransom."

Renaldi said, "Hugo, is there anything else you can tell us about this man?"

Hugo frowned, then shook his head slowly. "After he ran my taxi off road, I was dazed. I had only one look at him when he struck me."

"You must have had a good look at the automobile he was driving. How about the license number?"

Hugo shook his head again. "He was beside me when I first saw him, and after that—" He shrugged. "It was a big black auto and"—his face brightened— "auto windows were tinted. You could not see inside auto. Everything was blurred."

"Well, that's something. Not all that many cars around like that." Renaldi had taken a fresh cigar from his pocket and was engaged in lighting it.

Deke said urgently, "Then do something about it, Tony!"

Renaldi got the cigar going, then gave him a hard look. "Keep your pants on, amico."

Renaldi motioned one of his officers over and spoke to him in an undertone, then waved him away. The officer hurried to a patrol car, and Deke saw him talking on the radio.

"I'm getting out a bulletin on the car," Renaldi said. "Satisfied?"

"No, goddamnit! We have to find her, she could be dead by now!"

"I'm open to suggestions," Renaldi said dryly. "You have any to throw around? At the moment I can't think of any, not until we have more to go on—" At the sound of loud voices nearby, he broke off, frowning in annoyance.

Deke looked in the direction of the voices and saw an argument taking place. A portly man in a business suit was arguing heatedly with one of Renaldi's officers.

Renaldi raised his voice, speaking German. The officer faced around, still restraining the civilian, and answered quickly. Renaldi waved him silent and beckoned the fat man over.

He said to Deke, "This civilian says he overheard the officer radioing info about the black car with the smoky windows. He claims to have seen it along the lake, farther up."

When the civilian reached them, Renaldi questioned him. With mounting impatience Deke listened to the rapid exchange in German.

Finally Renaldi broke off the conversation and motioned imperiously to Deke. "Come."

"But what—?"

"In the car. I'll explain on the way."

Renaldi hustled both Deke and the civilian into his car and headed the car onto the highway. One of the police cars trailed them as Renaldi accelerated his own, the siren wailing.

Driving expertly if at a dangerous speed, Renaldi said, "The guy in the back seat said he noticed this heap with the tinted windows about twenty minutes ago, turning off toward the lake. He was struck by it because it reminded him of a hearse. He couldn't see inside it. Then he was attracted by all the cars back there, pulled in to find out what was going on, and overheard the officer radioing an alert for a black car with tinted windows."

Deke winced at the mention of a hearse. He hoped that it was not, in fact, a hearse carrying April's body.

Ten minutes up the road, the man in the back seat leaned forward, speaking to Renaldi, pointing to their left. Renaldi wheeled the car across the highway, narrowly missing an oncoming truck, and into a parking lot. The lot was empty except for the long black car parked at the end of the jetty, which jutted out into the lake. There were no boats tied up at the jetty.

Renaldi braked the car hard and was out of it, all in one fluid motion. Deke had to struggle with the door for a moment. By the time he was out and around the car, Renaldi was already reaching for the door handle of the black automobile, a pistol in his other hand.

He jerked the door open just as Deke reached him. Renaldi grunted. "Empty, naturally. But then I didn't expect anything else."

The man who had led them here remained in Renaldi's car, peering apprehensively out the window, watching as Renaldi made a quick search of the black car. Deke stood back out of the way, staring disconsolately out at the lake. The surface was choppy in a strong breeze, and within the range of his vision, he could see more boats than he could count. A feeling of hopelessness swept over him.

Renaldi ranged alongside him, lighting a cigar. "Zilch, Deke. There's nothing in the car to indicate who was in it and no sign of your April Morgan. I'll have it gone over for fingerprints."

"What good will that do?" Deke said dully. "By that time it'll be far too late. They've taken her out there, haven't they?" He swept his hand around the lake. "On a boat?"

"That seems a good bet."

"And there must be hundreds of boats out there on that lake. Not a hope in hell of picking out the right one."

The Italian sighed, blowing smoke. "It would help if we could find out who owns the boat that was tied up here and get a description."

A spark of hope flared in Deke. "How much time would that take?"

Renaldi's answer plunged him into despair again. "Too much, my friend."

April woke slowly. Her head throbbed, and her right arm pained when she moved it. Her first awareness of her surroundings was of a rocking motion, then the sound of a powerful motor. She opened her eyes.

She was lying on wet planking, and she felt a mist of water in her face. She was on a boat. Just on the edge of her vision, she saw a big man at the wheel, a white bandage around his head. Walker Longley.

She remembered then. Hugo's taxi had been forced off the road. She had stumbled out of the taxi and had been seized from behind, and she had felt a needle prick in her arm. The last thing she saw was the sharp toe of a Western boot.

She moved involuntarily and groaned as pain shot through her head.

"Well, I do believe our friend is with us again."

April sat up, her glance seeking the owner of the voice. She saw Susan Longley in a deck chair on the other side of Walker. April climbed awkwardly to her feet, holding onto the railing around the cabin window for support. Her gaze never left the woman in the chair.

Although April couldn't quite put her finger on it, there was something subtly different about Susan Longley. Her face seemed paler and had harsher lines. She was smiling, but the smile had a cruel, mocking edge. And her eyes. Before, her eyes had been dark, now they were an icy green!

The woman stood up abruptly and took a limping step toward April. With one hand she whipped off the dark, white-streaked hair, revealing blond hair, cropped close to her skull.

Giving a gasp of recognition, April stepped back.

Sneering, the woman said, "Welcome back, stepdaughter!"

Twenty

April felt as if she had been plunged into a nightmare. Her throat was constricted, and she felt as if she could not get enough air. The woman standing before her was dead. She had seen her die!

"Sheila!" she whispered.

The other woman nodded as a self-satisfied smile twisted her lips, turning her precise features into an ugly mask. "You seem surprised to see me, stepdaughter. Why is that?"

April swallowed. She felt faint and disoriented, and her head began to ache. She put her hand to her head, feeling herself sway. Sheila's smile widened, and she laughed as April shook her head, trying to close her mind against the memory that was intruding there, the memory that she had successfully blocked out for so long:

Two figures struggling on the cliff, outlined against the sky; herself, running toward them, crying out in alarm as she recognized the taller figure as that of her father and the smaller as her stepmother, Sheila. She recalled the fear, the terrible fear she had felt as she had watched them sway there, locked in deadly combat, trembling on the brink of death; then the knowledge that she could not reach them in time; and then relief, as the taller figure, her father, broke away, standing poised for a moment apart from the other; and then the terror again, as Sheila had lunged, straight at her father, striking him chest high with her outstretched arms.

April heard herself again, crying out, "Daddy! Oh, God! Oh, God!" She saw herself stopping, frozen, unable to move as her father staggered, waved his arms, and tried to regain his balance; she saw herself stand there as her father began to fall backwards, arms flailing while the other figure, her stepmother, stood there, watching. And then his groping hand had struck her stepmother's arm, clutching, and in an instant so abrupt that it seemed not to have happened, they were both gone, and Sheila's terror-stricken scream had ripped the night.

"If I had kept running, I might have reached him in time," April said dully, her throat thickening with tears. "You killed him! You pushed him off that cliff? I remember now. Oh, God, I wish I didn't! And he pulled you after him. Why are you alive?"

Sheila's cruel smile faded. "No thanks to your father, Cinderella. But for once, I was lucky. I landed on top of him, so I guess the old bastard *saved* my life in a way. I did get this, though." She slapped her leg. "I'll limp for the rest of my life. But it won't matter too much. People ignore things like a little limp if you have money, and I will, soon, have money, thanks to you, Cinderella."

"Why?" whispered April. "*Why* did you kill him?"

Sheila shot a glance at the man at the wheel. "See, Eric? Didn't I tell you the girl was simple?" And then to April: "For money, sweetcakes, something you've always had, and never had to yearn for. As John Morgan's weeping widow, I would have inherited most of his fortune and property, except what he had set aside for you. But then you spoiled that when you saw us on the cliff. I heard you call out as you came toward us, and unfortunately, with a witness, I didn't stand a chance of collecting. So you can understand my interest in disposing of you."

The man at the wheel looked back over his shoulder. "But she didn't remember, Sheila. She had it blocked out. I told you that was the way it was."

"Shut up, Eric! Just shut the hell up! Even if you are right, it wouldn't matter. There was always the possibility that she *would* remember." Giving April a speculative glance, Sheila reached for a small purse hanging on the arm of the chair and removed a small, lethal-looking automatic. "Just in case you show a little spirit, stepdaughter."

She motioned with the gun. "Sit down. Over there."

April glanced behind her and saw a built-in bench along the side of the cabin. She felt too shaken to argue. Also, she instinctively knew that she needed time to pull herself together.

Sheila sat down in the chair across from April and placed the automatic in her lap. "Do you know what we're going to do, Cinderella? Aren't you even curious?"

"For God's sake, Sheila!" the man at the wheel snapped. "Do you have to enjoy this so much? Can't you leave the girl alone?"

"You're awfully concerned," Sheila said tightly. "Taken with her, are you?"

"For God's sake, Sheila!"

"You're repeating yourself, luv."

She raised her eyebrows at April. "It's a bad habit of his, you know."

April kept her face expressionless. Her mind was finally beginning to clear, and she was terribly afraid. This woman was mad, quite mad, and completely ruthless. The man, Walker, or Eric, or whoever he was, was less hardened, but he was controlled by her, by Sheila.

April cleared her throat. "Even if I'm dead, Sheila, you won't be able to collect daddy's money. They think you're dead, too."

Sheila laughed. "That's where you're wrong, Cinderella. After you're out of the picture, I'll come back to life. I'll claim that the fall from the cliff caused me to lose my memory. Amnesia is common in accident victims. I'm a good actress, I'm sure you'll grant me that. Wasn't I convincing as Susan Longley? And how about Rudi Ernst, the friendly German tourist guide?

I was *very* good there, now you'll have to admit that."

April gasped, and Sheila laughed again. "You didn't know that, did you? Hey, Eric, how about that? Do I get an Academy Award?"

Eric retorted, "Not so damned good. You failed, didn't you? You didn't kill her!"

Sheila said acidly, "How about Old Sarum? If you hadn't blown that, Lorelei would never have been necessary!"

He hunched his shoulders. "I left them both for dead. And don't forget the truck stunt in Ireland was your show, and *that* didn't come off too well."

April listened in mounting horror and anger. "How about Liam?" she whispered. "Did you kill him, too?"

Both of her captors stared at her. Sheila said coolly, "Well, that was one thing Eric *did* do right. I suppose I'll have to give him credit for that."

"But why?" April cried. "Why Liam?"

"We had no way of knowing how much you'd told him," Sheila said casually. "Women in love are usually great talkers."

"But I didn't tell him anything! I didn't even *remember* anything to tell him. It was all for nothing!"

Sheila shrugged. "Couldn't take that chance. You don't even know the ground rules for survival, Cinderella. You know, we're really doing you a favor, putting you out of your misery. I don't think you could make it alone in the real world."

April stared at her, trying to mask the hatred and rage that were roiling inside her. It would do no good to rail at Sheila—or Eric. She had to keep her mind clear. She must think. Her mind was the only tool she had, the only weapon of defense.

"Well, *you* certainly know the rules," April said, mimicking Sheila's conversational manner. "You are easily the most cold-blooded pair I have ever met, or heard of. What about Eric-Walker? Is he your brother? Your lover? Your husband?"

"My lover, *and* my husband, as soon as I get John Morgan's money," Sheila said. "Eric Ransom, meet April Morgan. I knew dear Eric long before I married your daddy, Cinderella. We'd been planning to take your old man for a long time." Then her lips thinned. "But sometimes I do wonder why I got mixed up with such a damned bungler!"

Eric Ransom hunched his big shoulders, not looking around. "Watch your tongue. Like I told you, I thought they both had been killed in that pit."

"How about yesterday in Salzburg? Wouldn't you call that bungling? You were supposed to take care of her, not try to hypnotize her! Of all the stupid—! God! Whatever gave you such an idea?"

"I thought it would be a good idea to first find out what she knew," he said defensively. "What good did it do me to steal that shrink's files? The information was all there, why not use it?"

Sheila shook her head. "It never dawned on you that you might spook her? If I hadn't had a brainstorm and guessed that she'd try to get out of town by train, we'd be hunting all over hell and gone for her again! And broke as we are, we'd have to hold up a bank to keep it up." She glared at April. "You've cost us a bundle, stepdaughter. Chasing all over Europe after you. If Eric hadn't gotten lucky at the casino the other night, we wouldn't even have had the money to pay our hotel bill in Salzburg, much less charter a plane to get us here before you."

April was only half-listening as they bickered back and forth. Her mind was busy calculating what chance she had, if any. At the same time she was astounded at her sudden lack of fear. For the first time in a long while, she was not afraid. Perhaps it was knowing that the next few minutes would resolve her life, one way or another; perhaps it was the fact that the cobwebs were finally swept out of her mind—she knew now who had killed her father and why.

For whatever reason, fear had left her, and she was

capable of thinking clearly and calmly. There was no doubt that if anything was to be done about saving her life, she had to do it herself.

She tuned in on the pair again, and at the sound of their querulous voices, an idea formed in her mind.

Eric Ransom slammed his hand down onto the control panel in exasperation. "Look, Sheila, this isn't getting us anywhere, lobbing blame back and forth like a tennis ball. It'll soon be over."

"You're right about that," Sheila said. "How soon will we be there?"

"Another ten minutes or so. It's a small, isolated bay along the shoreline. No houses overlooking it, and the water's very deep. We weigh her down, she'll sink like a rock and may never be found."

April suppressed a shudder. They were discussing her death and the disposal of her body. "You've changed your mind then, have you, Walker?" she said. "Oh—I'm sorry. Eric."

"What do you mean by that?" Sheila demanded, her eyes narrowing.

April shrugged slightly. "Eric knows."

"Eric, what the hell is she going on about?"

Eric turned his head, shooting a worried glance at April. "Beats me."

April said, "In my hotel room yesterday, after you made love to me, you said—"

Sheila's face tightened. "So you *had* to do it!"

"No, babe, that's not true."

April said softly, "Eric, how can you say that, after the things we said to each other?"

"Sheila, I don't know what the hell she's—"

"Shut up!" Sheila gestured violently, her glittering gaze never leaving April's face. "Go on, Cinderella. I want to hear this. What things?"

"Why, Eric said that he loved me, that if I'd marry him, he wouldn't need his sister any longer," April said guilelessly. "He asked me to leave with him right away. When I said I needed some time to think, that's when he hypnotized me. He was trying to hypnotize me into running away with him."

"She's lying," Eric Ransom said nervously. "Surely you can see that! She's just trying to divide us, it's plain as hell!"

"What's plain to me, you sonofabitch, is that you screwed her!" Sheila said, her face contorted in fury. "Did you like it? Screwing a little milque toast like that?"

"You know me better than that. I wouldn't—"

"*Did* you screw her?" Sheila took a step forward, ramming the pistol at him. "You'd better tell me the truth!"

"All right, damnit! But it was just so she'd let her guard down." Ransom's voice turned cajoling. "Babe, you know there's no one but you for me."

"Sheila, those are the very same words he used to me," April said calmly.

"Who needs you, you bastard?" Sheila raised the gun, her face a glacial mask. "With the pair of you dead, I can claim the money, and then it'll all be mine. With the Morgan money I can buy all the men I want."

"You wouldn't shoot me." Ransom had recovered his composure and stared at Sheila without fear. "Not after all we've meant to each other, not after all we've been through . . ."

A silence fell, and April became aware that she had been hearing the sound of a throbbing motor overhead for several minutes, growing louder and then receding. Sheila and Eric were apparently too engrossed in their personal recriminations to notice, and April didn't dare draw their attention to it by looking out of the cabin.

Ransom took his hands from the wheel and turned toward Sheila, his hand held out, a confident smile on his face. "Now be nice, babe. Give me the gun, and we'll just forget this ever took place."

The automatic spat—once, twice, the sounds loud in the small cabin.

A stunned expression transfixed Ransom's features. A spot like a scarlet flower bloomed on his shirt over his heart. In a musing voice he said, "You're crazy, you know that, Sheila? Out of your tree. Now you've—"

He fell, striking the wheel on his way down and falling to the deck with a thump that shook the boat. The wheel started to spin, and the boat, with no one at the helm, began to veer wildly back and forth across the surface of the lake.

Deke and Tony Renaldi sat together in the glass bubble of the helicopter, which was tracing a zigzag pattern across the lake, flying about fifty feet above the water.

Both men had binoculars and were scanning the lake. So far they had seen nothing resembling the vague description of the boat they had gotten from the lake police. Any faint hope Deke had had was dwindling moment by moment. More than enough time had elapsed for Ransom to have killed April and dumped her body into the lake.

Renaldi had contacted the lake patrol to get the vague description of the missing boat. The owner was not available, and the only description they had been given had come from a member of the lake police, who had seen it tied up at the wharf while he had cruised past. It would have taken too much time to trace down the registration for a more detailed description.

All they knew was that the boat was approximately thirty-six feet in length, was diesel powered, and was blue and white in color. During the few minutes they had been in the air, Deke had seen at least a dozen boats of the right size, and several with the colors blue and white.

Renaldi had borrowed a helicopter belonging to the

lake police for the sweep of the lake, and the patrol boats on the lake were all on the alert.

But Deke had the sinking feeling that their efforts were too little and too late. To search all the suspect boats would take hours.

Suddenly he held the binoculars steady. He shouted above the clatter of the rotors, "Tony, look down there!"

Renaldi leaned across him to follow Deke's pointing finger, to where a blue and white boat was behaving erratically, weaving back and forth at high speed.

"That must be the one!" Deke said excitedly.

Renaldi was already on the radio, contacting the lake police.

As he finished, Deke said, "Something's happening down there, Tony. If we wait until a patrol boat can reach them, it'll be far too late!"

Renaldi shrugged fatalistically. "Nothing we can do, Deke. I told you that all we could do is help spot the boat. It's in the hands of the patrol now. Besides, we don't *know* that your lady is on that particular boat."

"Then why is it acting like that?"

"I don't know." Renaldi grimaced. "I hate boats and water. Never been on one and don't intend to."

"Well, we have to check it out and now."

"Just how do we go about doing that?" Renaldi asked matter-of-factly. "We're up here, and the boat's down there."

Deke twisted around to look behind him. "There's a rope ladder back here—"

"Oh, no! I'm not dangling in midair from a rope ladder! Besides, I'm city police. I have no jurisdiction out here."

Deke was already unwinding the rope ladder. "Well, *I* have jurisdiction, Tony. It's my damned fault April is in this predicament, and I can't stay up here while she needs help."

Renaldi said incredulously, "You're going down

there on a rope ladder? You're out of your gourd, man! Have you ever climbed down one of those things?"

"Nope," Deke said, his voice tight. "But there's a first time for everything. Tell the pilot to get us as close as he can."

"I won't allow it! Anything happens to you, it'd be on my head."

"You'll have to tie me up to stop me," Deke said grimly. "Look, Tony, I have to do it, don't you see? Now, pass the word to the pilot like a good guy, okay?"

He was already opening the door. It took all his strength to shove it open against the backwash. Fifty feet below the blue and white boat was still weaving wildly. He pushed the ladder out the door and watched it fall.

Renaldi sighed and said, "Okay, my friend. It's your neck. I hope to hell you can swim."

He leaned over to speak to the pilot. The pilot argued heatedly, waving his arms. Renaldi spoke more forcibly, and after a moment the chopper began to lower.

Deke fervently hoped that the pilot was good, good enough to weave a zigzag pattern to match that of the veering boat. He took a deep breath, motioned for Renaldi to hold the door open, and he backed out of the bubble, feet fumbling for the first rung.

He didn't dare look down, but felt for the rungs blindly with his feet. In a moment he was clear of the cabin. He looked up once and saw Renaldi's concerned face peering down at him. An unlit cigar bobbed in the Italian's mouth.

Doubts assailed Deke almost at once. The moment he was clear of the aircraft the ladder began to swing violently, buffeted by the rush of air from the whirling blades and the strong wind over the lake.

Doggedly he continued, rung by rung. Then his foot missed a rung, and he realized that he had reached the bottom. Now, one foot dangled out into space, and he was drenched in sweat, despite the cold wind. His hands were as slippery as though they'd been greased.

As the helicopter traced a holding pattern, Deke risked a glance down. The boat was still performing its weird gyrations, and he could appreciate how difficult it must be for the pilot to hover above the deck long enough for Deke to drop.

The distance wasn't great—Deke judged that his feet were approximately ten feet above the deck level. Now the chopper lined up with the deck again, and Deke readied himself to let go and drop.

Then the boat swerved once more, sharply to the right; he would have landed in the water if he'd let go.

Once again, the pilot tried to line up. Deke never once took his gaze from the boat. He realized that he had to make a judgment as to which way the boat would swerve as he dropped.

He would only have the one shot at it. If he missed and landed in the water, the boat, traveling at the speed it was, would be long gone. He couldn't possibly swim fast enough—if he didn't drown first.

As the wildly swinging rope ladder arched over the boat, Deke let go, trying to throw himself to the left. For a long moment he thought he had misjudged—there was nothing but water beneath him. Then the boat swung to the left as he'd hoped, and he cleared the railing by the narrowest of margins.

The impact drove him to his knees, then full-length to the deck, knocking the breath from his body. Slightly stunned, he remained still for a moment. Then the boat cut sharply to the right. Caught unaware, he was thrown hard against the rail.

He started to pull himself upright and then froze as the bark of a gunshot came from the cabin.

For a long moment both April and Sheila had stood

motionless, staring down at Eric Ransom's body on the deck, oblivious to the noise of the helicopter above them. Then the roll of the unpiloted boat threw April against the bulkhead, and Sheila started for the wheel.

Knowing the other woman's inattention would be brief, April pushed herself away from the side of the cabin, using the wild gyrations of the craft to propell her into Sheila.

She struck Sheila just as she reached for the wheel and wrapped both arms around the woman. The boat swerved again, and both women were thrown to the deck. The automatic flew out of Sheila's hand, skittering all the way across the cabin.

April had landed on top of the other woman. Sheila lay without moving, and April thought that the fall had knocked her out. She relaxed her vigilance for a second, and Sheila erupted like the uncoiling of a steel spring. She came up off the deck, knocking April aside, and scrambled across the deck toward the automatic.

April managed to twist herself around just enough to seize Sheila's ankle and jerk. Sheila fell headlong to the deck, and April rolled toward her.

Then they were locked together, rolling over and over across the deck until they struck the cabin wall. April was astounded at the woman's strength. Her slender body was wiry and as muscular as a man's. She was like a spitting cat—long nails scratching, knees pummeling, teeth biting. Her eyes were wild, and she spewed unintelligible obscenities.

Within moments April was bleeding from the scratches and was bruised and aching all over, her clothes torn. But she was grimly determined that this woman who had killed her father would not get the better of her. All the hostility toward her stepmother came back to her in a rush. Yet she knew that Sheila was much the stronger, and she herself could not hold out much longer.

She tried to tangle her fingers in Sheila's hair, but it was so short that her grip kept loosening. In desperation she locked both hands tightly around Sheila's head and raised it enough to pound it down onto the deck with all the force she could muster.

Then Sheila fastened her teeth in April's wrist and bit down hard. The pain was excruciating, yet April refused to let go her grip. Once more, she raised the other woman's head and brought it smashing down onto the deck, harder this time.

Sheila yowled with pain, her teeth released April's wrist, and she slumped, her muscles going slack.

April risked a glance around, just as the boat executed another one of its sharp rights. Something thumped against her leg. Glancing down, she saw that it was Sheila's automatic. April quickly scooped it up, backing away.

She was just in time, for Sheila began to stir. April gripped the automatic tightly, aiming it at the supine woman. She had never fired a gun, had never even held one before.

Sheila's eyes were open in a malevolent stare. Slowly she got up, then got to her feet by using the cabin wall. Her gaze never left April.

The boat lurched, and April lurched with it but managed to remain on her feet. Sheila started for her, taking two steps away from the bulkhead.

April held the automatic out the full length of her arm. In a shaking voice she said, "One step more and I'll shoot!"

Sheila laughed harshly. "You don't have the guts, Cinderella. You won't shoot me."

"At any other time, maybe not." Her voice steadied. "But you killed daddy and Liam. For that I'd gladly kill you."

Sheila took another sliding step, and April fired, the bullet splintering the deck beside Sheila's right foot. Face going pale, Sheila stopped. Keeping the automatic aimed at the other woman, April edged toward the wildly spinning wheel, just as the cabin door crashed open.

April jumped at the sound and shot a glance in that direction. Deke Travers was coming toward her.

Relief washed over her. "Deke—I never thought I'd say this, but I was never so glad to see anyone in my life!"

"Likewise, I'm sure," he said in a dry voice. "And thank Christ you're okay! I was—"

The boat swerved, and Deke careened against the bulkhead. April had been prepared for it and had never taken her gaze from Sheila.

Deke said, "Let's see if I can get this thing under control. It's damned lucky you haven't rammed into another boat out here." He made his way quickly to the wheel.

April said, "How did you get here?"

He jerked his thumb skyward. "A whirlybird, then down a rope ladder."

In a minute he had the boat throttled down to a crawling speed and the wheel under control. Then he looked down at Eric Ransom's body and up at April. "You?"

"No, she killed him."

Deke looked at Sheila in dawning recognition. He grunted. "What the hell! Carlos O'Brien, I do believe. A woman! Lady, you sure made a fool out of me, didn't you?"

Sheila simply glared her hatred at him.

"Carlos O'Brien?" April asked in confusion.

He gestured. "It's all a part of the mess I started, April. I'll explain later."

"But don't you know who she really is?"

He squinted at Sheila again. "I'm afraid not."

"It's Sheila. My stepmother!"

Deke looked at her in astonishment.

"She killed my father, pushed him off the cliff. She wanted his money."

Deke looked at Sheila Morgan carefully. "Then, she didn't die?"

Sheila sneered defiantly. "A brilliant observation, counselor."

"I never met her, you know, April, except as Carlos O'Brien," he said musingly.

"She didn't die, Deke, and she knew that I saw her kill daddy."

"And of course in her twisted logic, that meant that she had to kill you."

April nodded. "They were behind all the attempts on my life, her and him." She gestured to Ransom's body on the deck. "After I was dead, Sheila intended to come back, claiming temporary amnesia, and claim Daddy's estate. And they almost succeeded."

"My God!" Deke began to laugh. "What a farce! The irony of it!"

April looked at him curiously. "I don't understand."

"The estate, April. Your father's money." He looked at Sheila. "All of it would have been for nothing, Sheila. All of the killing and the plotting and the scheming. There *is* no estate, no money. Sometime during the last few months before he died, John Morgan sold off all of his assets and withdrew all of the funds from his accounts. He died broke!"

Twenty-One

◆━◆━◆

April woke to the shrill ringing of the telephone. She opened her eyes slowly, unsure of where she was.

Then Deke's voice answering the phone brought her fully awake. The sensual memory of last night sent warm waves of pleasure along her nerve ends. She turned her head and looked across the bed at him.

"Yes, Gabe. April is fine. It's all over, finished . . ."

Yesterday had been crammed with excitement. It had been late afternoon before she and Deke were finished at the police station. Both had to make lengthy statements, and Deke's policeman friend, Renaldi, had questioned them exhaustively.

They had enough evidence to convict Sheila for the murder of Eric Ransom, but Renaldi had assured them that he would not stand in the way if the authorities in New York desired to extradite Sheila to stand trial for killing John Morgan. Now that it was all over, April didn't really care *where* Sheila was tried, just so long as she paid for what she had done; and Deke had told her that Switzerland meted out swifter and more severe punishment than was the practice in the States.

All in all, yesterday had been a full day, and it was too late to visit the bank after Renaldi was finished with them, so Deke and April had checked into separate rooms at a hotel. Then they had gone to a late supper and ended up in Deke's room. To April, it had seemed the most natural thing in the world.

Now that it was over, all the questions answered, she was no longer angry at Deke. Even if his scheme had misfired, his intentions had been of the best, and after a night spent in his arms, April knew that something good was beginning between them.

She still didn't wish to explore her feelings too closely; her emotions were yet too raw from continued buffeting. But there was no rush—they had all the time in the world.

Deke was saying, "Here, Gabe, if you don't believe me, I'll let you talk to April." His face grave, he held the receiver out to her.

Taken unaware, April automatically put the receiver to her ear. "Hello? Dr. Kemble?"

There was a long silence on the other end. Then he said in a gruff voice, "April? Is that you?"

"Yes, Dr. Kemble. And I'm just fine, thanks to you and Deke. I'll always be grateful to both of you for all you've done for me."

"Uh, yes—well, you'd better give me back to Deke."

April returned the receiver to Deke. "Satisfied now, Gabe? She's okay, believe me." He listened for a moment, his face falling into melancholy lines. "I'm sorry you feel that way, my friend. But it just—well, happened. I love her, Gabe, and I intend to marry her, if she'll have me." He listened again, face turned away from April. "You're flying back today? Wouldn't you like to have dinner with—? Okay, Gabe, okay! We'll see you back in New York, then."

Deke hung up the phone, his expression regretful.

April said, "What was that all about?"

He sighed. "I suppose that was the wrong way to handle it, a little rough on him. On the other hand, maybe it's best this way, short and sweet."

"What *are* you talking about?"

"I think Gabe's in love with you." He took her hand. "I think he has been from the beginning, but then so am I, damnit!"

She snatched her hand away. "I don't know as I like this conversation much!"

"Why? Because I said I love you?"

"No, not that." She softened, allowing him to take her hand again. "Deke, I'm confused about something you said on the boat yesterday. You said daddy was broke. How could that be? Who's been financing me? First-class all the way."

"I have, April. I—well, I felt responsible for you." His glance dropped away diffidently. "Now there's something I want to ask *you*. According to the taxi driver, you came to Zurich to go to a bank. Why?"

"Because—" She hesitated, then smiled secretively. "Daddy gave me the number of an account here, in my name."

Deke's eyes widened. "Why didn't you tell me?"

"Because that's one of the things I didn't remember until the day before yesterday in Salzburg, right after I called the Mr. Midnight number."

"But you knew when I saw you. Why didn't you—? No, never mind." He gestured wearily. "You didn't trust me."

"I do now," she said, and gave him the number. "Deke, what do you suppose it means?"

He ran his fingers through his hair. "I don't know. I suppose there's some money there for you. But I wouldn't get my hopes too high, baby. There can't be too much."

"Daddy also said the bank was holding some documents for me. 'For your eyes only,' he said."

He glanced at his wristwatch on the bedside table. "Well, the bank will be open soon, we'll find out."

"I'd better get dressed."

She started to scramble out of bed, but he caught her hand, pulling her back. He smiled suggestively. "What's the hurry? You've waited all this long."

As she settled back against him, a stray thought entered her mind. "There's something that's been puzzling me. In Ireland, with Liam, I didn't know if I was a virgin. Now isn't that strange?"

Her eyes danced with mischief as she gazed at him. Deke turned a bright red and looked away.

"Now, you indoctrinated me well about the other aspects of Angela Williams's past life, but you didn't give her a sex life. Why is that?" she asked innocently.

Face turned away, he mumbled something.

"What was that, Deke? You'll have to speak up!"

"Goddamnit, that's not something you talk about to a woman you hardly know!" he growled. "It would have been embarrassing, like being a voyeur."

"You think it wasn't embarrassing for me?"

"All right, I'm sorry! Okay?" Suddenly he grinned. "Think how much fun it's going to be to build a sex life for you, starting from scratch."

She began to laugh and was still laughing when his lips silenced her.

Two hours later, they were closeted in a small cubicle in the bank. On the table before them was a bank statement and a sealed envelope with April's name written on it.

"Jesus H. Christ!" Deke whispered in awe as he looked at the bank statement. "I don't believe this! At a quick estimate you're worth five million dollars!"

April wasn't really listening. She weighed the envelope in her hands for a moment and then quickly opened it, her heart thumping.

Deke was saying, "John must have been busy as hell the last month of his life. He liquidated everything he owned, everything except the New York apartment and the house at Cape Cod, and he converted it into cash! Now why would he do that, for God's sake?"

"Maybe there's an answer in here," April said in a barely audible voice. The envelope contained two thin sheets of paper, covered with her father's sprawling handwriting. She noted that it was dated two weeks after he had married Sheila. She read the first few lines hurriedly, then looked up at Deke and began to read aloud:

Sugar,

If you read this, it will mean I'm dead and gone. Weep no tears for me, because it will be my own damned fault.

No fool like an old fool.

Since your mother died, I've been lonely. Not that I didn't have you, but that's not the same thing. Knowing how you felt about your mother, I never made any lasting relationships. But now you're a woman, grown and about to go out on her own, and that's as it should be. And now that you are, well, I've found myself a woman I want to marry.

The trouble is, when a man my age starts thinking of a woman, he wants a young one. And old fool that I am, that's what I'm marrying. The second trouble is, when a man my age and with my money gets hitched, how can he tell if the woman loves him, or his money?

That's why I've sold off almost every damned thing I own and deposited it here for you. No matter what happens to me, it belongs to you, not the woman I marry. If I live, she'll get a good chunk eventually.

It seems like the making of money has lost all its taste for me. I've made it about every way possible, I suppose. There's no boot to it any more. That's why I'm liquidating everything.

It's yours to do with as you please. You're free, white, and twenty-one. Invest it wisely. Spend every dime. Live off the interest. It's up to you.

As for Sheila, I know you don't like her. I'm not even sure that I do. But hell's fire, she sure knows how to make a man feel young again.

Old fool I may be, but I'm hedging my bets. If things work out okay, you'll never see this letter. If I'm dead, well, unless it's my old ticker giving out, I'd advise you to be mighty suspicious of the new Mrs. Morgan.

But what the hell! It's been a blast, and I don't feel sorry for myself. And don't you be neither, you hear, sugar? Don't be sorry for your old daddy. I've had a full life.

April was crying long before she finished reading the letter. It was almost as if John Morgan was there with them, his booming laughter filling the room.

Deke squeezed her hand. "Fool he may call himself, but he wasn't, not really. And the final irony is, even if Sheila had succeeded in her scheme, that letter would have been her undoing."

Deke took his hand away and hunched over the financial statements again, his face serious. With one hand he idly rolled a pen back and forth across the table.

April, her emotions under control now, sensed his withdrawal. "Deke?"

He glanced up with a start. "Yes?"

"What is it? What's wrong?"

"What could be wrong?" He waved a hand at the balance sheet and gave a not very enthusiastic laugh. "Hell, you're a rich woman. Like your daddy says in the letter, you can spend it, live off it, do any goddamned thing you like!"

"You don't sound particularly pleased."

He shrugged. "Of course I'm pleased. I'm very happy for you."

She gazed at him in dawning comprehension. "I'm beginning to understand! Before, when you thought there was no money and you could take care of me, you wanted to marry me! But now that you've learned that I am wealthy after all. . . . Tell me, Deke, if you had just discovered that all this money was yours, would you still happily marry me?"

He squirmed in the hard chair, refusing to meet her eyes. "That would be different, April."

"Oh? This morning in bed you proposed to me, in a rather oblique way. Does that proposal still stand?"

"I just think that maybe you should think about it, in view of what's happened."

"*I* should think about it? It seems to me that *you* want to think about it." She leaned back, amusement in her voice now. "I have no need to think about it. The answer is yes, I'll marry you. Now it's in your court, Deke Travers!"

He fidgeted, then got to his feet. "I'll leave you to go over the financial statements, April." He started for the door.

"Deke?"

He looked back. "Yes?"

"Would it make you feel any better if I gave away all the money? I could, daddy said that I could do whatever I liked."

He looked shocked. "Of course I don't want you to do that! That's idiotic, April!"

"I didn't intend to, anyway." She smiled. "I just wanted to hear what you'd say. Where are you going, Deke?"

He shuffled his feet. "Back to the hotel."

"Will you be there when I return?"

He hesitated, then said slowly, "Yes, baby, I'll be there."

He went on out, without looking at her again.

April sat on, a musing smile on her lips. Would he really be there when she returned? She loved this man, she was sure of that now. Perhaps not in the same way she had loved Liam O'Laughlin, yet she sensed that love between her and Liam would have blazed brilliantly for a time and then have burned itself out. Liam had been a wild man, unpredictable, and, she strongly suspected, totally incapable of remaining faithful to any one woman. On the other hand, Deke was steady, one of those rarities—a one-woman man, and she was sure that he loved her.

Yet, she thought, if he was gone when she got back to the hotel, she could live with that. She was her own woman now, forged in the adversity of the past few months.

As she pulled the bank statement toward her,

April's smile became tender, softening with antici-
pated love.

Deke would be waiting for her, she was confident
of that.

A few years ago PATRICIA MATTHEWS was just another housewife and working mother. An office manager, she lived in a middle class home with her husband and two children. Like thousands of other women around the country she was writing in her spare time. However, unlike many other writers Patricia Matthews' own true life story has proven to have a Cinderella ending. Today she is "America's leading lady of historical romance" with ten consecutive bestselling novels to her credit and millions of fans all over the world.

For CLAYTON MATTHEWS, author of more than 100 books, 50 short stories and innumerable magazine articles, writing is not only his profession but his hobby. Born in Waurika, Oklahoma in 1918, Matt (as he is known to his friends) worked as a surveyor, overland truck driver, gandy dancer, and taxi driver. In 1960 he became a full-time author with the publication of *Rage of Desire*. More recent books by Clayton Matthews include his highly successful book *The Power Seekers* (winner of the WEST COAST REVIEW OF BOOKS Bronze Medal for Best Novel in 1978), *The Harvesters* and *The Birthright*, the first book of a trilogy. Books two and three, *The Disinherited* and *The Redeemers*, are slated for future publication.

The Matthews, who say they have a "paperback perfect" marriage, live in Los Angeles.

Dear Friends and Readers:

Because both of us have received so many wonderful letters from so many of you, we feel as if you are friends, and because we feel this way, we would like to share with you our enthusiasm for our up-coming books.

Patricia's next book, Embers of Dawn, *coming from Bantam in May, 1982, will be set in Durham, North Carolina. The story begins just after the Civil War, when the South is on its knees. The heroine, Charlotte King, is trying to keep the family farm from complete destruction. Her father has been killed in the war, her mother is dying, and her only brother, Jefferson, has returned from the war a beaten and perhaps permanently broken man, useless to her, and to her dream of re-establishing the family fortunes by going into the tobacco business.*

Charlotte's life is both enriched and complicated by three men: handsome Ben Ascher, a Jewish Peddler, who becomes her friend, lover, and partner in the fledgling cigarette industry; Clint Devlin, a soldier of fortune and man of parts, who also becomes her lover and a partner in her newly-formed King Tobacco Company; and finally, Sload Lutcher, a cold, woman-hating, greedy man who becomes Charlotte's sworn enemy, threatening all she has managed to build.

The story is played out against the colorful background of the growing tobacco industry, and concerns Charlotte's struggles to establish a business and make her way in the male-oriented business world while being torn between her feelings for two men and her desire to be loved as a woman.

Matt's book, The Disinherited—*the second book in the* Moraghan Saga Trilogy—*focuses in on Debra*

Moraghan, Sean Moraghan's granddaughter, and takes place during the late 1800s.

The Disinherited picks up with Debra as a young girl who hates the barren wastes of her father's farm and the stifling life of the Rio Grande Valley. She yearns for the excitement of the life she is certain is waiting for her if she can only get away from her family.

Feeling bitter and disgraced after being attacked by the son of the man her grandfather killed, the worthless and evil Tod Danker, she flees to Corpus Christi. There she sets up a brothel, and considers herself forever cut off from her family, and from Stony Lieberman, the handsome lawyer she has admired and loved since childhood.

Harrassed by the city fathers, threatened by Tod Danker and his blood hate for her family, accused and tried for a murder she did not commit, Debra struggles to keep her body and spirit alive.

Both of us hope that you have enjoyed Midnight Whispers, and that you will look for and read both Embers of Dawn and The Disinherited when they are released. We will also be doing other books together, romantic suspense novels on the order of Midnight Whispers.

Thank you,
and may all good things come to you.

Patricia Matthews and
Clayton Matthews